The Mission . . .

It was van Horne who broke the silence.. "All right, so you could be Lord High executioner if you wanted to be. You've made your point. What's it all about? What's the game?"

"A good word for it," Bonilla said. "Rather apt, but it's really quite simple. I want you, Señor van Horne, to play the priest again, something you seem to have a talent for."

Van Horne stared at him in amazement. "What did you say?"

"And Señor Janos will make an excellent business-man. He has the build for it. He looks substantial, therefore people will believe he is in other ways."

"I am complimented, sir," Janos told him with con-siderable irony.

Bonilla ignored him. "And you, Señor Keogh. Your task is the simplest of all. It might have been created especially for a man of your peculiarly dark talents."

He smiled gravely. "All you have to do is kill some-one for me."

Berkley books by Jack Higgins

A GAME FOR HEROES
THE KHUFRA RUN
THE WRATH OF GOD

JACK HIGGINS

WRITING AS

JAMES GRAHAM

THE WRATH OF GOD

BERKLEY BOOKS, NEW YORK

This Berkley book contains the complete
text of the original hardcover edition.
It has been completely reset in a typeface
designed for easy reading, and was printed
from new film.

THE WRATH OF GOD

A Berkley Book / published by arrangement with
Doubleday & Co., Inc.

PRINTING HISTORY
Doubleday edition published 1971
Berkley edition / June 1985
Second printing / July 1985

ISBN: 0-425-07748-9

A BERKLEY BOOK ® TM 757,375
Berkley Books are published by The Berkley Publishing Group,
200 Madison Avenue, New York, New York 10016.
The name "BERKLEY" and the stylized "B" with design
are trademarks belonging to Berkley Publishing Corporation.
PRINTED IN THE UNITED STATES OF AMERICA

For David Godfrey with thanks

Mexico
1922

ONE

THE CHIEF OF POLICE usually managed to execute somebody round about noon on most days of the week, just to encourage the rest of the population, which gives a fair idea of how things were in that part of Mexico at the time.

The sound of the first ragged volley sent my hand down inside my coat in a kind of reflex action when I was half-way up the hill from the railway station. For most of the way I had managed to stay in the shade, but when I emerged into the Plaza Cívica, the sun caught me by the throat and squeezed hard, bringing sweat from every pore.

The executions were taking place in the courtyard of the police barracks and the gates stood wide open to give an uninterrupted view to anyone interested enough to watch, which on that occasion meant a couple of dozen Indians and mestizos. Not a bad audience considering the noonday heat and the frequency with which the performance was repeated.

At the rear of the small crowd, an automobile was parked, a Mercedes roadster with the hood down, the entire vehicle coated with a layer of fine white dust from the dirt roads. An exotic item to find in a town like Bonito at that time. More surprising was the driver who was getting out just as I arrived, for he was a priest, although like no other priest I'd seen outside of Ireland—a great ox of a man in a shovel hat and faded cassock.

He ignored the rest of the audience, most of whom were surprised to see him there, produced a cigarillo from a fat leather case and searched for a match. I found one before he did, struck it and held it out for him.

He turned and looked at me sharply, giving me a sight of his face for the first time. A tangled greying beard, vivid blue eyes and the unmistakable furrow of an old bullet wound along the side of his skull just above the left eye. One of the lucky ones to survive the Revolution.

He took the light without a word and we stood side-by-side and watched as they marched three Indians across the courtyard from the jail and stood them against the wall. There were already half-a-dozen bodies on the ground and the wall was pitted with scars. The three men stood there impassively as a sergeant tied their hands behind their backs.

The priest said, "Does this happen often?"

He had spoken in Spanish, but with an accent that indicated that he was anything but Mexican.

I replied in English, "The Chief of Police says it's the only way he can keep down the numbers in the jail."

He glanced at me with a slight frown. "Irish?"

"As ever was, Father."

"A long way from home."

New England American, or somewhere near unless I missed my guess.

"I thought the Revolution was supposed to be over?" he said, and looked back towards the scene in the courtyard. "What a bloody country."

Which was a reasonably unpriestlike remark although understandable in the circumstances. I said, "The discontented are always with us, Father, even after revolutions. Why, there are some in these parts who think it's still open season on priests."

"We're in God's hands," he said harshly. "All of us."

Which was arguable, but I was prevented from taking the question up with him for one of the condemned against the wall inside the courtyard cried out sharply and pointed to us as the sergeant was about to tie his hands.

There was some kind of disturbance and then a young officer strolled in the direction of the gate and beckoned to the priest, who left me without a word and went towards him.

"Believe it or not, Father, but one of these pigs wants to confess," I heard the officer say.

The priest said nothing; simply took a breviary from his pocket, spat out his cigarillo and started through the gate. By the time he reached the wall, all three were on their knees waiting for him.

I didn't stop to watch for I had seen men die before or at least that's what I told myself as I turned and went across the square to the Hotel Blanco on the far side. It was a tall slender building, which had been used as a strong-point by the government forces during the war, and the crumbling façade was pitted with bullet holes.

In the patio a fountain splashed water across scarlet tiles and the cool darkness of the terrace looked very inviting. The owner of the place lounged in a wicker chair by the screen door, fanning himself with a palm fan. His name was Janos and he was Hungarian as far as I could make out, although his English was excellent. The most noticeable thing about him was his great size. He must have been seventeen or eighteen stone at least, with a great pendulous belly, and sweated constantly.

"Ah, Mr. Keogh. A hot day. You will join me in a beer?"

There were several stone bottles of lager in a bucket of water at his side. I helped myself to one and pulled the cork. As I did so, another volley sounded in the courtyard opposite. I sat on the rail beside him as the crowd began to disperse.

"A nasty business," Janos said, managing to sound as if he didn't give a damn.

"Yes, too bad," I answered automatically, for I was watching for the priest.

He emerged from the gateway with the officer, who walked to the Mercedes with him. They stood talking for a while, then the officer saluted and the priest got into the car and drove away.

"A strange sight, that," Janos commented. "Not only a priest, but a priest in an automobile."

"I suppose so." I emptied the beer bottle and stood up.

"But not to you, Mr. Keogh. Here, have another beer." He lifted one, dripping wet from the bucket and held it out to me. "In your Ireland you will have been familiar with many such vehicles. Here, they are still a rarity. You can drive yourself, I understand?"

Which was leading to something. I said, "It's not very difficult."

"For an intelligent man, perhaps not, but these peasants." He shrugged. "They are incapable of learning anything beyond the simplest tasks. I myself have a truck. The only one in Bonito. Most important to my business. I imported a driver mechanic specially from Tampico, but the wretched man had to go and involve himself in politics.''

"A dangerous thing to do in this country."

He wiped a fresh layer of sweat from his fat face. "He was in the first batch they shot this morning. Most unfortunate."

He obviously meant for himself personally. I said, "That's life, Mr. Janos. He shouldn't have joined."

A pretty hard way of looking at it, but then most of the more human feelings had been burned out of me a long time ago, particularly where that kind of situation was concerned. It was none of my affair and I was tired of the conversation which for some reason had a strange air of unreality to it. I was hot and I was tired and wanted nothing so much as a bath and perhaps a couple of hours on my bed before the train left.

I stood up and Janos said, "I have a rather important consignment to go to Huila. You know the place, perhaps?"

I saw then what he wanted, but there was no reason why I should make it easy for him. "No, I can't say I do."

"Two hundred miles north of here toward the American border. Dirt roads, but not too bad in the dry season."

But by then, I'd had enough. I said, "I'm catching the two-thirty train for Tampico."

"You could be back by tomorrow night. Catch the train the following day."

"But miss the boat to Havana tomorrow evening," I said. "And there's no refund on the ticket."

"How much was it? Forty-two American dollars?"

He shrugged. "I will pay you five hundred, Mr. Keogh. Five hundred good American dollars and very easily earned, you must admit."

Which brought me up rather sharply because after paying for my tickets I'd no more than twenty or thirty dollars left.

"That's a great deal of money for running a few supplies up country," I said carefully.

So he decided to be honest with me, the great shining face creasing into a jovial man-to-man smile. "I will be frank with you, Mr. Keogh. The crates in my truck contain good scotch whisky. A commodity in short supply in Mexico, God alone knows, but over the border they have what is known as Prohibition. There it will be worth considerably more."

"Including a five-year prison sentence if you're caught running the stuff," I pointed out.

"A risk someone else assumes," he said. "The man who takes over the consignment in Huila. You, my friend, will be breaking no law known to me. Not while you are in Mexico. To trade in alcohol here is perfectly legitimate."

Which was true enough and the prospect was tempting for even if I forfeited that boat ticket I'd still be considerably better off.

He thought he had me and gave it another push. "I'll tell you what I'll do, Mr. Keogh. Five hundred and another boat ticket. Now can I say fairer, sir? Answer me that."

He was being jovial again, which didn't become him, but his eyes, those sad, grey, Hungarian eyes were still and watchful and I think it was that which really decided me, combined with the fact that I wasn't at all sure that I liked him.

"No thanks," I said. "The price is too high."

The smile was wiped clean, the eyes became totally blank. "I don't understand you. I know your financial situation. What you say doesn't make sense."

"It wouldn't," I said. "I wasn't talking about money, Mr. Janos. I was talking about Mexico. I've had all I can take. Six months of heat, flies and squalor. And I haven't known a day when they haven't been shooting somebody. You'll have to find someone else."

"I don't think you understand," he said carefully. "There is no one else."

"Which is your problem, not mine."

The palm fan had stopped moving and he sat there staring at me and yet not at me, sweat pouring down his face, those grey eyes fixed on a point somewhere beyond me. The fan started to move again, rapidly, and he wiped the sweat away with his enormous silk handkerchief.

And suddenly that jovial smile was back in place. "Why then, I can only wish you luck, sir, and shake you by the hand."

He held it out and I took it for it would have seemed churlish not to, but it was the wrong kind of grip for a fat man who did nothing but sit and sweat. Firm and strong—very strong, which made me feel distinctly uneasy as I walked away for he had given in too easily.

Before the Revolution the Hotel Blanco must have been rather spectacular, but now there were cracks on the marble stairs, great slabs of plaster flaking away from the walls. It was as if the place were disintegrating slowly. There was no lock on my door, which always stood open a little, and inside the room was like an oven for the electric fan in the ceiling hadn't turned for five years, which was when they'd dynamited the power plant.

I managed to get the shutters open, breaking a couple of slats in the process, and let in a little warm air. I was soaked in sweat and the revolver in the leather shoulder holster under my right arm had rubbed painfully. I took off my jacket, unstrapped the holster, with some relief, and put it down on the bed.

Once this room had been something quite special for it still had its own bathroom through the far door, but now it had that derelict air common to cheap rooms the world over. It was as if no one had ever really lived here. For no accountable reason I ached for some soft Kerry rain on my face again. Wanted to stand with my eyes turned up to it, to let it run into my mouth, but that was not to be. That was foolishness of the worst kind.

The bathroom had the same air of tarnished magnificence as the rest of the hotel. The floor and the walls were covered with imported Italian tiles, all sporting little naked cherubs offering bunches of grapes to each other. The bath itself was cracked in a hundred places, but big enough to swim in and, although most of the brass fittings had been stolen at one time or another, tepid brown water still gushed from a gilded lion's mouth when you turned the handle.

I returned to the bedroom, took off the rest of my clothes and pulled on my old robe. Then I went back into the bathroom, taking the shoulder holster with me for old habits die hard.

The water was by now so brown that I was unable to see the bottom of the bath, but I lowered myself in without a qualm and lay back and stared up at the cracked ceiling.

How easily things become what we want them to. The cracks on that ceiling became a map, line by line flowering into shape before me. The railway snaking down through Monterrey to Tampico. Then the route across the Gulf north of the Yucatán Peninsula to Cuba and Havana town.

And what would I do there? I had an address, no more than that. A man who might be able to give me work or might not. And afterwards? But there was no answer to that one and each day would have to bring what it chose.

There was a sudden muffled crash from the bedroom that had me out of the bath and reaching for my revolver all in the same moment. I flattened myself against the wall beside the door, out of the line of fire if anyone intended to shoot their way in.

I got my robe on one-handed and not without difficulty and listened. There was no sound, so I did what seemed the obvious thing, flung open the door and dropped to one knee.

The man who stood by the bed searching my jacket was straight out of the market place, a mestizo in ragged trousers and shirt and palm leaf sombrero. He had just taken the wallet from the inner pocket. Everything I had in the world.

"Not today, *compadre*," I said. "Put it on the bed and quickly."

At first it looked as if he was going to do as he was told. His shoulders sagged. He said brokenly, "Señor, my wife, my children. For pity's sake."

Which didn't particularly impress me for any painter specializing in theological subjects would have found him a fair likeness for Judas Iscariot. It worked to a certain degree for when he turned to fling the jacket in my face and ran, he definitely caught me off balance.

When I reached the door, he was almost at the head of the stairs, which didn't give me a great deal of choice as he was still clutching my wallet in his right hand, so I brought him down with a snap shot in the right leg.

He went over the edge of the stairs without a cry and I heard him crash against the ironwork banisters twice. When I reached the head of the stairs he was lying face-down on the next landing. He glanced back over his shoulder, his face twisted with rage and to my complete astonishment, started to slither down the rest of the broad marble stairs leaving a snail's trail of blood behind him.

Several things happened at about the same time then. Janos came stumping out of the shadows leaning on his black ivory walking stick, a couple of retainers from the kitchen at his back. "By God, sir, what's going on here?"

"My wallet," I said. "He stole my wallet."

The thief slid the rest of the way down to the hall and collapsed at the fat man's feet. Janos leaned over him and poked around in the shadows. When he straightened, his face was grave and baleful.

"Wallet, sir? I see no wallet here."

Which was when my heart really started to sink as it suddenly occurred to me that there was just a faint possibility that there was more to this than met the eye.

The police arrived on the run, armed to the teeth as usual, ready to spray everything in sight as they came through the door, although the sergeant in charge was exquisitely polite and listened to my story with the utmost patience.

The wretch on the floor, whom no one seemed to be particularly concerned about, clutched his leg, blood oozing between his fingers and cursed all gringos and their seed to the tenth generation. He was wholly innocent and employed by Señor Janos as a general porter. The sergeant booted him casually in the ribs, left his men to search for the wallet and took me up to my room to get dressed.

"Do not worry, señor," he comforted me. "The man is a known thief. Señor Janos gave him honest work out of the largeness of his heart and this is how he serves him. We will find this wallet. Fear not, your name will be cleared."

But when he returned to the foot of the stairs and he discovered his men's lack of success, a fact to which I had already become resigned, his face assumed a more melancholy expression.

"This is a grave matter, señor, you realise my position? To shoot this man for stealing your wallet is one thing . . ."

"But to shoot him, full stop, is quite another."

"Exactly, señor, I am afraid you must accompany me to headquarters. The *jefe* himself will wish to question you."

His hand on my arm was no longer gentle and as we moved forward, Janos said passionately, his jowls shaking, "By God, sir, I'll stand by you. Trust in me, Mr. Keogh."

Hardly the most comforting of thoughts on which to be led away.

Above the town the Sierras floated in a blue haze, marching north towards the border. It was all I could see when I hauled myself up by the iron bars on the narrow window and peered out.

I was in what was known as the general reception cell, a room about forty feet square with rough stone walls that looked as if they might very well pre-date Cortez. There were about thirty of us which meant it was pretty crowded and the smell seemed compounded of urine, excrement and human sweat in equal proportions.

An hour of this was an hour too much. An *indio* got up and relieved himself into an overflowing bucket and

I moved out of the way hurriedly, took a packet of Artistas out of my pocket and lit one.

Most of the others were *indios* with flat, impassive brown faces, simple men from the back country who'd come to town looking for work and now found themselves in prison and probably for no good reason known to man.

They watched me out of interest and curiosity because I was the only European there, which was a very strange thing. One of them stood up from the bench on which he sat, removing his straw sombrero and offered me his seat with a grave peasant courtesy that meant I couldn't possibly refuse.

I sat down, took out the packet of Artistas and offered them around and hesitantly, politely, those closest to me took one and soon we were all smoking amicably, the lighted cigarettes passing from mouth to mouth.

The bolt rattled in the door which opened to reveal the sergeant. "Señor Keogh, please to come this way."

So we were being polite again? I followed him out and along the whitewashed corridor as the door clanged behind me. We went up the steps into a sweeter, cleaner world and crossed towards the administration block of the police barracks.

I had been here once before about four months previously to obtain a work permit and had been required to pay through the nose for it, which meant that the *jefe* in Bonito was about as honest as the usual run of police chiefs.

The sergeant left me on a bench in a whitewashed corridor under the eye of two very military-looking guards who stood on either side of the *jefe's* door clutching Mannlicher rifles of the type used by the Germans in the war. They ignored me completely and after a while the door opened and the sergeant beckoned.

The room was sparsely furnished, desk, filing cabinet
and not much else, except for a couple of chairs, one of
which was occupied by my fat friend from the Hotel
Blanco, the other by the *jefe*.

Janos lurched to his feet and swayed there, propped
up by his ivory stick, sweat shining on his troubled face.
"A dreadful business, Mr. Keogh, but I'm with you, sir,
all the way."

He subsided again. The *jefe* said, "I am José Ortiz,
Chief of Police in Bonito, Señor Keogh. Let me first
apologise for your treatment so far. A regrettable error
on the part of my sergeant here who will naturally
answer for it."

The sergeant didn't seem to be worrying too much
about that and the *jefe* opened a file before him and
studied it. He was a small, olive-skinned man in his
fifties with a carefully trimmed moustache and most of
his teeth had been capped with gold.

He looked up at me gravely. "A most puzzling affair,
Señor Keogh. You say this man was stealing your
wallet?"

"That's right."

"Then what has he done with it, señor? We have
searched the stairs and the foyer of the hotel
thoroughly."

"Perhaps he had an accomplice," I suggested.
"There were several people milling around there."

"By God, he could be right," Janos cut in. "It could
explain the whole thing."

The *jefe* nodded. "Yes, that is certainly a possibility
and on the whole, I am inclined to believe your story,
señor, for the man is a known thief."

"That is very kind of you," I said gravely.

"There was much in the wallet of importance?"

"Twenty or thirty dollars, some rail and steamer tickets and my passport."

He raised his eyebrows. "So? Now that is serious. More so than I had realised." He looked in the file again. "I see from your papers that you were registered as a British citizen. This is correct?"

I said calmly, "That's right."

"Strange. I thought you Irish had your Free State now since the successful termination of your revolution."

"Some people might question that fact," I told him.

He seemed puzzled, then nodded brightly. "Ah, but of course, now you have your civil war. The Irish who fought the English together now kill each other. Here in Mexico we have had the same trouble." He glanced at the file again. "So you would be able to obtain a fresh passport from the British Consul in Tampico."

"I suppose so."

He nodded. "But that will take some weeks, señor, and what are we to do with you in the meantime. I understand you are not at present employed."

"No, I worked for the Hermosa Mining Company for six months."

"Who have now, alas, suspended operations. I foresee a difficulty here."

"Oh, I don't know," I said. "I'm sure Mr. Janos can suggest something."

"By God, I can, sir," he said, stamping his stick on the floor. "I've offered Mr. Keogh lucrative employment—highly lucrative. For as long as he likes."

Ortiz looked relieved. It was really a quite excellent performance. "Then everything is solved, Señor Keogh. If Señor Janos makes himself personally responsible for you, if I have this guarantee that you will be in secure employment, then I can release you."

"Was there ever any question of it?" I asked politely.

He smiled, closed the file, got to his feet and held out his hand. "At your service, Señor Keogh."

"At yours, señor," I replied punctiliously, turned and went out.

I heard a quiet, murmured exchange between them and then Janos stumped after me. "All's well that ends well, eh, Mr. Keogh? And I'll stick to my bargain, sir. I shan't take advantage of your situation. Five hundred dollars and your steamer ticket. That's what I said and that's what I'll pay."

"A gentleman," I said. "Anyone can see that."

His great body shook with laughter. "By God, sir, we'll deal famously together. Famously."

A matter of opinion, but then all things were possible in that worst of all possible worlds.

TWO

WHEN WE GOT back to the hotel, Janos took me round to the stables in the rear courtyard. A couple of stalls had been knocked out at one end and the truck stood in there.

It was a Ford and looked as if it had spent a hard war at the Western Front. There was a canvas tilt at the back and it was loaded to the roof with medium-sized packing cases. I checked the wheels and discovered that the tires were new, which was something, then I lifted the bonnet and had a look at the engine. It was in better shape than I could have reasonably hoped.

"You find everything in order?" he demanded.

"You lost a good mechanic this morning."

"Yes, an inconvenience, but much of life generally is."

"When do you want me to go?"

"If you left now, you could make the half-way point by dark. There is an inn at Huerta. A poor place, but adequate. It was a way-station in the old stage coach days. You could spend the night there. Be at Huila before noon tomorrow. This suits you?"

Amazing how polite he was being about it all. "Absolutely," I said, but the irony in my voice seemed to elude him.

"Good," he nodded in satisfaction. "Let's go in and I'll give you the final details."

His office was just off the patio at the front of the building, a small cluttered room with a polished oak desk and a surprising number of books. My shoulder holster and the Enfield were lying on the desk and he tapped them with the end of his stick.

"You'll be wanting that, I've no doubt. Rough country out there these days."

I took off my jacket and buckled on the holster. He said, "You look uncommonly used to that contrivance, sir, for a man of your obvious education and background."

"I am," I told him shortly and pulled on my jacket. "Anything else?"

He opened a drawer, took out two envelopes and pushed them across. "One of those is a letter to Gomez, the man to whom you'll deliver the goods in Huila. He has a supply of petrol by the way, so you'll be all right for the return trip. The other contains an authorisation to make the journey signed by Captain Ortiz, in case you are stopped by *rurales*."

I put them both in my breast pocket and buttoned my jacket. He selected a long black cigar from a sandalwood box, lit it, then pushed the box across to me. "You'll have a drink with me, sir, for the road?"

"We have a saying where I come from," I told him. "Drink with the devil and smile."

He laughed till the tears squeezed from his eyes, the flesh trembling on the gross body. "By God, sir, but you're a man after my own heart, I can see that."

He shuffled across to a side cabinet, opened it and produced a bottle and a couple of tumblers. It was brandy and good brandy at that.

He leaned one elbow on the cabinet and eyed me gravely. "If I might be permitted the observation, sir, you don't seem to care very much about anything. About anything at all. Am I right?"

That strange, rather pedantic English of his had a curious effect. It made one want to respond in kind. I said, "Why, it has been my experience that there is little in life worth caring about, sir."

I could have sworn that for a moment there was genuine concern in his eyes although I considered it unlikely he could ever have afforded such an emotion.

"If I may say so," he observed heavily, "I find such sentiments disturbing in one so young."

But now, the conversation had gone too far and we were into entirely the wrong territory. I emptied my glass and placed it carefully down on top of the cabinet. "I'd better be on my way."

"Of course, but you'll need a little eating money." He produced a wallet and counted out a hundred pesos in ten peso notes. "You should be back here by tomorrow evening if everything goes smoothly."

By now he was looking quite pleased with himself again, which simply wouldn't do. I stuffed the money carelessly into my jacket pocket and said, "Life has taught me one thing above all others, Mr. Janos, which is that anything can happen and usually does."

His face sagged in genuine and immediate dismay for as I discovered later, there was a strongly superstitious streak in him, his one great weakness. I laughed out loud, turned and walked out. A small victory, perhaps, but something.

I was eighteen years of age when I first saw men die. Easter, 1916, and a sizable section of Dublin town going up in flames as a handful of volunteers decided to have a crack at the British Army.

And I was one of them, Emmet Keogh, hot from my books at the College of Surgeons, still young enough to believe a cause—any cause—could be worth the dying. A Martini carbine gripped tightly in my hands, I sweated in ill-fitting green uniform and crouched at the window of an office in Jacobs' Biscuit Factory, a romantic place to die in, waiting for the Tommies from the Portobello Barracks to find us, which they did soon enough.

During a slight lull in the proceedings, a Mills bomb came through the window and rolled to a halt in the very centre of that busy office.

There were six of us in there who should have died, but for some reason it didn't go off until I'd thrown it back out of the window at the troops who had chosen that precise moment to make a rush across the yard.

Life, then, or death, was an accident one way or the other. Time and chance and no more than that. Let it be so. Certainly from that day on it conditioned not only my actions, but my thinking. Janos had been closer to the truth about me than he knew.

For the first few miles out of Bonito the road wasn't too bad, in fact had obviously been metalled at some time in the past, but not for long. Soon it changed into a typical back-country dirt road with a surface so appalling that it was impossible to drive at more than twenty-five miles an hour in any kind of safety.

In the distance, the Sierras undulated in the intense heat of late afternoon and as I drove towards them but slightly to the north-west, a great cloud of white dust rising from the loose surface coated everything including me.

A flat brown plain stretched on either hand as far as the eye could see, dotted with thorn bushes and mesquite and acacias. I was alone on a road that led to nowhere through a land squeezed dry by the sun, barren since the beginning of time.

God, but there were times when I ached for my own country, for the sea and the mountains of Kerry, green grass, soft rain and the fuchsia growing on dusty hedges. The Tears of God we called it.

I passed nothing that lived for the first hour, then a dot in the far distance grew into a herd of goats, an old man and two young boys in charge, barefooted, ragged, so wretchedly poor that even their straw sombreros were falling to pieces. They stood watching me, faces blank, making no sign at all, the sullen despair of those truly without hope.

I stopped a mile or two further on to get rid of my jacket, being well soaked with sweat by then and drank and sluiced my head and shoulders with lukewarm water from a four-gallon stone jug someone had thoughtfully roped into place in front of the passenger seat.

From there on things became so bad that I had to drive very cautiously indeed, sometimes at not more than ten or fifteen miles an hour and the heat and the dust were unbelievable. I had been on the road for three and a half hours, had seen no one except the goatherds, was beginning to believe I was the only living thing in this sterile world when I found the priest.

The Mercedes was a little way off the road and had ploughed its way through a clump of organ cactus. The priest stood at the side of the road, his cassock and broadbrimmed hat coated with dust and waved me down. I braked to a halt and got out.

He recognised me at once and smiled. "Ah, my Irish friend."

His front near-side tire had burst, which explained his sudden departure from the road, but he had come to rest with his rear axle jammed across a sizeable rock and had spent a futile hour trying to push the car free.

The solution was ludicrously simple. I said, "If we raise her off the rock with the jack and give her a good push she should roll clear soon enough."

"Why damn my eyes," he said. "Why didn't I think of that?"

He would have gone down well on the Dublin Docks, but I didn't say so. Simply opened his boot, which was full of five-gallon cans of petrol, got out the jack and started to work.

"No reason why I shouldn't do that, it seems to me," but he didn't try too hard to dissuade me, lit one of those long, black cigarillos he favoured and stood watching. I was sweating hard and the shoulder holster was something of a nuisance so I unstrapped it and put it on the rear seat of the Mercedes. Chancing to glance up a moment later, I saw that he was holding the Enfield in his right hand.

"Careful, Father," I warned. "What's known in the trade as a hair trigger. She'll go off at a breath."

"Wouldn't it be better to have the pin fall on an empty chamber for the first pull," he suggested. "In case of accidents?"

Which was reasonably knowledgeable for a man of the cloth. "Fine, if you have the time to waste."

"Presumably you don't."

"Not very often."

He stood there, still holding the Enfield in one hand, the holster in the other. "You were out in the Troubles," he said. "Against the English, I mean?"

It was the kind of language American newspapers had been fond of at the time. I nodded. "You could say that."

"This Civil War back there is a bad business." He shook his head. "From what I read in the papers the Irish are killing each other off more savagely these days than the English ever did. Why, didn't Republican gunmen kill Michael Collins himself only three or four months ago, and I always understood he did more to beat the English than any man."

"Then settled for half-a-loaf," I said. "Not good enough."

"A die-hard Republican, I see." He hefted the Enfield in his hand and said, "Not that I know about such things, but it doesn't feel very comfortable."

"It wouldn't," I told him. "I'm left-handed. The grip has been altered to fit."

He examined the gun further, obviously intrigued by the absence of a sight at the end of the blue-black barrel, the way most of the trigger guard had been cut away. I concentrated on the jack lever and as the axle started to clear, he dropped the shoulder holster inside the Mercedes, hitched up his cassock and got to his knees beside me.

"What do you think?"

"Put your shoulder to the boot and we'll find out."

It took the two of us, and some considerable effort. There was a moment when I thought it wasn't going to go and then the jack tilted forward and the Mercedes rolled free, scraping the rear bumper on the rock in the process. He lost his balance and fell on his hands and knees and I ran around and got the handbrake on before the Mercedes got clear away from us. When I turned, he was getting to his feet, rubbing dust from his beard and grinning like a schoolboy.

"A hell of a way to spend an afternoon."

"I could think of pleasanter things to do," I admitted. "In more comfortable places." I stretched my aching back and looked out across the wilderness. "The last place God made."

He was about to light another of his cigarillos and paused, the match flaring in his right hand, his face grave and somehow expectant. "At least you give him some credence, even for this."

"In a place like this it's difficult to say God doesn't exist, Father." I shrugged. "Try, and he'll more than likely remind you of his presence rather forcibly."

"Something of an Old Testament view of things, I would have thought," he said. "A God of wrath, not of love."

"A view of the Almighty my own experience would tend to support," I said flatly.

He nodded, his face grave. "Yes, life can be very hard. It's difficult to live each day as an act of faith. I know, I've been trying for forty-nine years, but it's the only way."

I picked up the jack, went round to the front of the Mercedes and set to work. He was carrying two spare wheels, a wise precaution in such country and the changeover took me no more than five minutes. He didn't offer to help, didn't try to carry our conversation any further, but walked some little distance away to a slight rise where he stood looking out at the mountains.

When I called, he didn't seem to hear me and I went towards him, cleaning my hands on an old rag. As I got closer, he turned and said harshly, "Yes, my friend, you're right. In a place like this it must be difficult to believe in anything."

But I was no longer interested in that kind of conversation. "I think everything's all right now," I said. "Drive her back to the road and we'll see."

The Mercedes had a self-starter and the engine turned with no trouble at all, a change from most of the vehicles I'd had experience with. I jumped on the running-board and he took her round in a wide circle, joining the road a few yards behind the Ford.

I got my shoulder holster and the Enfield from the

rear seat and buckled them on. "You see, Father, everything comes out in the wash if only you live right."

He laughed, switched off the engine and held out his hand. "Young man, I like you, damn me if I don't. My name is van Horne. Father Oliver van Horne of Altoona, Vermont."

"Keogh," I said. "Emmet Keogh. Catholic priests who've been shot in the head must be rather thin on the ground in Vermont."

His hand went to the scar on his temple instinctively. "True enough, but then I was the only one to my knowledge, who served as chaplain to an infantry brigade on the Western Front."

"Aren't you rather far from home?"

"I'm on a general fact-finding trip on behalf of my diocesan authorities. We understood that in the back country in Mexico the Church has been in great difficulties since the Revolution. I'm here to see what help is needed."

"Look, Father," I said. "I wasn't joking this morning in Bonito when I told you there were people in these parts who thought it was still open season on priests. I know places where they haven't seen one in years and don't want to. Last month in Hermosa a young French priest tried to re-open the church after eight years. They hung him from the verandah of the local hotel. I saw him swinging."

"And did nothing?"

"I've seen priests who stood by and did nothing in my own country," I said. "It's easy to take the last walk with a prayer book in your hand when someone else is going to do the dying. Damned hard to stand up and fight for what you believe in against odds."

For some reason I was angry, which was illogical in the circumstances and I think I knew it. In any event, I

went round to the front of the Ford and turned the starting handle. As the engine jumped into life, van Horne
joined me.

"I seem to have annoyed you," he said. "And for
that I'm sorry. A shocking tendency to preach on each
and every occasion is my besetting sin. I'm hoping to
make my way through the Sierras to a place called
Guayamas on the west coast. What about you?"

"Delivering a load of bootleg whisky to a man in
Huila," I said. "You'll find petrol there if you're
short."

"Do you hope to get there tonight?"

I shook my head. "There's a little place called Huerta
about twenty miles further on. Old stage line way-
station."

"Perhaps I'll see you there."

I smiled and climbed into the cab of the Ford. "If you
do, for God's sake keep religion out of it, Father."

"Almost impossible," he said. "But I'll do what I
can. God bless you."

But sentiments like those had long since ceased to
have any effect on me and I drove away quickly.

Suddenly, it seemed to be late evening, the sun dropping
behind the Sierras taking the heat of the day with it, the
great peaks black against gold as the fire died. There
was no sign of the Mercedes coming up behind and I
wondered what he was doing. A strange one certainly,
although priests, like anyone else, were entitled to their
idiosyncrasies.

I came over the brow of a small hill just before dark
and saw the way-station at Huerta lying below me,
lights winking palely at the windows. It was a small,
flat-roofed building, which must have been a hundred
and fifty years old at least, and was enclosed by an

adobe wall, most of which had crumbled away where the place faced the road.

The sky beyond was like molten gold, the great black fingers of the organ cactuslike cut-outs pasted in place against a stage set as I coasted down the hill. When I turned in across the courtyard and switched off the engine, I heard laughter and singing and there were half-a-dozen horses tied to the hitching post. The door opened as I got out and a man appeared, bare-headed, a couple of bandoleers criss-crossing his ornate jacket, a rifle in his hands.

"Stand and declare yourself," he called and his speech was slurred with the drink.

I could have shot him, been back behind the wheel of the Ford and away before his friends inside knew what was happening, but there was no need, for I had already noticed the large silver badge so conspicuously displayed on his right breast, worn only by the *rurales,* the country police, as fine a body of men who ever cut a throat or raped a woman and got away with it.

"I'm taking supplies to Gomez in Huila," I said. "I have a permit from Captain Ortiz, the *jefe* in Bonito."

"Inside," he said, "where we can see you."

The place was lit by a single oil lamp hanging from one of the beams in the low ceiling. There were four of them sitting at a long wooden table, two holding pistols at the ready as I went in. They wore the same ornate braided jackets and crossed bandoleers as the man behind me and, if it had not been for the silver badges of office, one might well have been pardoned for confusing them with those on the wrong side of the law.

There was a strange uniformity in their general appearance. Heavy moustaches, unshaven chins, brooding suspicious eyes. The only one not wearing his sombrero seemed to be in charge. "What have we here?"

"I'm delivering supplies by truck to Gomez of Huila." I produced the *jefe's* travel permit and offered it to him. "My papers."

He examined it, then passed it back. "Luis Delgado, at your orders, señor."

"At yours," I gave him politely.

"You intend to stay here tonight?"

"If it can be arranged."

"No difficulty, eh, Tacho?" He looked over his shoulder at the old, white-haired man standing behind the small bar. "The señor desires accommodation. You will see to it?"

The old man, who was looking distinctly worried, nodded eagerly and Delgado chuckled. "They jump, these back-country pigs, when I crack the whip. You will drink with me, señor?"

It seemed a reasonably politic thing to do. I downed the glass of tequila he offered, gave him his health and moved to the bar. The old man, Tacho, was frightened —really frightened. There was a mute appeal in his eyes that I was unable to answer because I didn't know what it was all about, not realising then that these visits by Delgado and his men were an old story.

Delgado slapped his hand hard down on the table. "The food, you miserable worm. You turd. What about our food?"

Tacho moved to the other end of the bar and the door opened and a young woman came out of the kitchen. As I later discovered, she was barely past her seventeenth birthday, but looked a little older as women of mixed blood tend to do. She wore the usual ankle-length skirt, an Indian-work blouse and black hair hung down her back in a single braid.

She was small for I would say I had at least three inches on her and I can barely touch five and a half feet. Dark, dark eyes, high cheekbones, a wide mouth and a skin of palest olive that reminded me of my own mother, God rest her soul. She was not beautiful, yet after turning away I felt a compulsion to look at her again. Now why should that be?

Her face showed no emotion of any kind. She put the tray down on the table, turned to go and Delgado caught her wrist. "Heh, not so fast, little flower. An appetiser before the main course is the sensible man's way of eating."

He grabbed at the neck of the loose blouse, pulled it down and was put out to discover she was wearing a bodice underneath.

He roared with laughter. "Playing the lady, eh? We'll soon fix that."

She put her nails down his cheek, drawing blood and he slapped her solidly across the face as he might have slapped a man, forced her back across his knee as he put a hand up her skirt.

His friends were roaring with delight and, when old Tacho ran round the end of the bar and tried to intervene, someone sent him staggering back against the wall so forcibly that he fell to the ground.

The girl struggled desperately and two of the others got a wrist each and pinned her back across the table. She didn't scream, didn't show any fear at all, simply fought with all her strength, would struggle for her soul's sake to the final, bitter end, expecting nothing, not even from me, for when our eyes met, she looked through me as if I did not exist.

It was happening all over the country seven days a week, but that didn't make it any easier to swallow. No business of mine, so I pulled out the Enfield and blew the tequila bottle on the table into several score pieces.

The effect was considerable and I have seldom seen a group of men scatter so rapidly. Delgado was the only one who didn't move. He glanced back at me, still clutching the girl, his eyes wary, watchful, no fear there at all.

"Be easy, señor," he said softly. "Your turn will come."

"The next one is through the back of the skull," I told him. "Now move to the bar, hands high, all of you."

They obeyed reluctantly, warily, going backwards slowly, waiting their opportunity. The girl's reaction was interesting. She moved to my side and stood very close, holding on to my jacket tightly like a child recognising a loved one in a crowd after being lost.

Tacho had picked himself up from the floor and stood staring at me, shaken and dazed. I said, "Get their guns, old man, one-by-one. No need to fear. If anyone moves I'll shoot Delgado through the belly."

He didn't seem to hear me. Simply stood there swaying from side-to-side. I spoke to the girl without looking at her. "What's your name?"

There was no reply, but her grip tightened on my jacket. Delgado laughed harshly. "No help there, my friend. Little flower hasn't had a word to say for herself in years."

I reached down for the hand that clutched at my jacket and brought her round to the front where I could see her face which was calm and watchful.

"You understand me?" She nodded. "Right, get their guns and don't be afraid. I will kill any man who tries to harm you."

Something stirred deep down in those dark eyes, something happened to her face, although it was difficult to say what exactly. In any event, she turned and moved towards the men at the bar.

A spur jangled in the stillness behind me. I started to turn, remembering too late that there had been six horses at the hitching rail, which meant another *rurale* not present in the room, and was struck a heavy blow somewhere behind the right ear which put me down on my hands and knees before I knew where I was.

The Enfield fired when it hit the floor, for as I have said elsewhere, all that delicate trigger mechanism needed was a touch. There was noise, confusion, a dull pain in the chest where a boot landed. I didn't really lose consciousness and finally surfaced to find myself on my knees, hands tied behind my back.

Delgado was busy fashioning a noose at the end of a length of saddle rope. He patted my face gently, then slipped the noose over my head and tossed the other end across a beam.

Two of his men held the struggling girl, the other three got on the rope behind me. Delgado smiled. "At first we hang you only a trifle. Then we have some fun with little flower. You should enjoy that. Afterwards— we'll see. I'll try to think of something special. A fine gentleman like you deserves it."

The rope tightened under my chin, jerking back my head, pulling me upright to sway on tip-toes before him. Old Tacho crouched in a chair by the wall, a hand to his mouth, eyes round, even the girl stopped struggling and her captors slackened their grip, watching me. Waiting.

The door opened and Father van Horne stepped into the room, lowering his head to get through. "Good evening," he said harshly.

He was holding a Gladstone bag in his right hand and presented a strangely menacing picture in his shabby, dust-covered cassock, the shovel hat shading the great, bearded face, another of those cigarillos jutting from his teeth.

"You would appear to have got yourself into a little trouble, Mr. Keogh," he observed.

The men holding the other end of the rope had slackened their grip in astonishment and I managed to breathe again.

"Let's say I got bored with standing by doing nothing, Father," I told him.

Delgado had his pistol out in a second, reached for the girl and pulled her out of the way.

"Who are you?" he demanded. "We weren't expecting any priest in these parts. I would have known."

"So I observe," van Horne said. "Would there be any point in asking you to release this man?"

Delgado smiled nastily. "You could always try, but that might make me angry. I might remember that I haven't hung a priest lately and the temptation to string you up beside this other gringo might well prove irresistible."

"That would be most unfortunate," van Horne said.

"For you, not for me. Now let's see your papers and quick about it."

"Happy to accommodate you, señor." Van Horne put the Gladstone bag down on the table and produced a key. "Humiliation, Mr. Keogh, is a specific for many ailments. It does a man good to get down on his belly occasionally and repent, if you follow me."

I didn't. Not until he opened the Gladstone bag, took out a Thompson sub-machine gun and blew the top of Delgado's head off.

THREE

IT WAS ALL over very quickly. The men who had been waiting to haul me over the beam let go the rope and reached for their pistols. They were too late. As I flung myself forward, my shoulder catching the girl behind the knees, bringing her down with me, van Horne took care of all three, the stream of heavy bullets knocking them back against the wall.

He certainly knew his business. There was a round drum magazine on the Thompson and he kept firing, swinging in a wide arc which shattered the mirror behind the bar and ripped up the floor behind the two remaining *rurales* who were running for the kitchen door.

The first one made it, mainly because his companion acted as a shield, the bullets driving him headfirst through the door, shredding the brocade jacket across his back, the material bursting into flames.

The rear door banged as the lone survivor ran into the darkness and van Horne went after him.

The girl rolled over and sat up. I got to my knees with

some difficulty because of my bound hands. "Are you all right?" I asked her.

She nodded, turned Delgado over, pulled a knife from his belt and sliced through my bonds. When I got the noose from around my neck the skin was raw and broken on one side. The girl examined it, her face still quite expressionless, then got to her feet and ran into the kitchen.

Outside, a horse broke into a sudden gallop, there was a wild cry followed by the sound of another burst from the Tommy gun. I got to my feet and looked around me. There was blood everywhere, the stench of cordite and burning flesh, a butcher's shop in hell. Tacho was behind the bar pouring tequila into a tumbler, his hand shaking.

I reached for the bottle and a glass and helped myself. It was the nearest thing to pure alcohol I have ever drunk, but it pulled the pieces together again, which was what I needed.

"Not so good is it?" I said.

Tacho's face had sagged into complete despair. "To kill the police, even the *rurales,* is a very bad thing and there's a lot of federal cavalry out between here and Huila. There has been much trouble in this area lately."

The girl appeared with a stone jar containing some kind of grease. She rubbed a little into the raw places on my neck, frowning slightly in concentration, her fingers delicate and birdlike, then tore a strip of muslin off her petticoat and wound it round my neck a couple of times.

I patted her face. "That's a lot better. I'm very grateful."

She smiled for the first time, glanced uncertainly at Tacho, then went back into the kitchen. "Your daughter?"

He shook his head. "Her name is Balbuena, señor.

Victoria Balbuena. Her father owned a hacienda near here. I used to work for him. Five years ago it was burned to the ground during the fighting and the *patrón* and his wife perished. Victoria saw it all. She was twelve at the time, only a child. Something happened to her, something most strange.''

"What do you mean?"

"Oh, up here in the head, señor." He tapped his skull. "She has been unable to speak from that day to this."

There was a step in the doorway and van Horne moved inside, the cigarillo still clamped between his teeth, the machine gun under his arm.

"What happened?" I demanded.

"He got away, that's what damn well happened."

It was as if a cloak had slipped away revealing another kind of man entirely underneath. Everything had changed, the way he moved and walked and his voice had become harsher, the speech clipped, incisive. There was a powerful, elemental force to the man which he had kept hidden before for obvious reasons.

He slammed the machine gun down on the bar and snapped his fingers at Tacho. "Give me a bottle quick. Anything. I've got to think this out."

My Enfield was stuck in Delgado's belt. I pulled it free, checked the loading mechanically and shoved it into its holster. I stirred Delgado's body with my toe. "Something else you picked up on the Western Front, Father?"

"Son," he said solemnly, placing a hand on my shoulder. "I've got a confession to make. All is not what it seems."

"It very seldom is."

He laughed, that strange, harsh laugh of his. "Explanations can wait till a more suitable time. Right now,

I've got other fish to fry. This is a mess. How long before the guy who got away reaches friends?"

"Tacho says there are *federales* all over the place between here and Huila. There's been a lot of trouble in the area lately. Did you mean it when you said you were hoping to get through the Sierras to Guayamas?"

"Yes, a friend of mine tells me they get trading schooners in there all the time from the Pacific islands with cargoes of copra. It seemed to me like a nice quiet way to leave."

"And you need that kind of passage out?"

"I think you could say that. I'll go and get a map."

He went out to the Mercedes and while he was gone, the girl, Victoria, came in from the kitchen with a pot of coffee on a tray and several cups. When she filled them, she served me first which was, for some reason, curiously disturbing. She stood at the end of the bar watching me gravely, not even responding when I smiled at her, like some good dog waiting for its master's command. Van Horne came in briskly with a large-scale map of northern Mexico which he spread out across the bar counter.

"North, south or east seem out of the question to me," he said. "They'll be telegraphing ahead of us within a few hours."

"Which only leaves the Sierras." I ran my finger along the road to Huila. "That way would be by far the best. The road through the mountains branches off about forty miles this side of Huila."

"We'd never get that far, not without running into trouble."

"You're including me in this business?"

"Have you any choice? You'll swing anyway if they ever lay hands on you, and two could make out better than one if things get a little rough."

In other words he needed me. The true reason for his suggestion as I realised a moment later when he slammed a hand down hard on the map.

"God, what a mess. Why the hell couldn't I mind my own business?"

Which had already occurred to me, but I said nothing. It was Tacho who spoke then, leaning over the map, squinting at it short-sightedly. "There is another way through the mountains by way of the Nonava Pass. A very bad road and seldom used, but during the Revolution some Yankee gringos brought arms through from the coast that way in two trucks. It has never been done since to my knowledge."

"He could be on to something," van Horne said. "They'd never look for us going through that way if what he says is true."

"What about petrol?"

"There's still about twenty-five gallons in the tank including the reserve and I'm carrying another fifty in the boot in five-gallon cans. Enough to get us all the way to the coast."

I looked at the map again. We had to stay with the road to Huila for about fifteen miles, indeed had no choice in the matter. Then we cut off across the foothills through rough country, following what was obviously going to be little more than an old pack trail.

"We could run into trouble out there in the dark," I said. "Lights or no lights."

"So what do we do? Sit on our backsides till sunrise and the *federales* get here? Be your age, Keogh. Sure, we might end up nose down in a hole or even drive straight over the edge of some *arroyo,* but we don't exactly have a choice, do we, so let's get moving."

He folded his map, grabbed an unopened bottle of tequila and went out. I said to Tacho, "He's got a point.

No sense in hanging about.''

The girl caught me by the arm as I turned away. Her eyes tried to speak for her, the mouth opened and shut, the whole face working.

''What is it?'' I demanded.

''I think she wishes to go with you, señor,'' Tacho said.

She nodded eagerly as I turned to her and I took her by the shoulders and gave her a shake. ''Don't be a damn fool. What could I do with you? Where would you go? I'm running for my life.''

She gripped my hands convulsively, the eyes still pleading and I shook my head. ''No, it just isn't on.''

Something went out of her, I don't know quite what. Hope perhaps, or something even more important to her. Some vital essence that is in all of us. She turned away, her shoulders sagging.

Tacho said, ''In a way, she is running too, señor. For such a young one, she has known much sadness, many bad things. The Balbuenas were a name in these parts, and her father was a great aristocrat, but he committed the unforgivable sin for one of the high blood. He married an Indian. More than that—a Yaqui. A woman from the Wind River country. His family never forgave him.''

''So the girl has no one?''

''Not here, señor, but on the other side of the mountains where her mother was born it would be a different story.''

''All right,'' I said to the girl, bowing to the inevitable. ''I'll give you two minutes to get your things together.''

She gave me one startled glance over her shoulder, then disappeared into the kitchen. ''Sometimes God looks down through the clouds, señor,'' Tacho said.

"Not very often in my experience. What about you? How will the *federales* treat you?"

"An innocent bystander and roughly treated, señor." He shrugged. "Besides, where would I go, an old man like me?"

The Mercedes horn sounded impatiently and a moment later, Victoria came in from the kitchen, clutching a small bundle, a heavy woollen shawl about her shoulders.

"You will look after her, señor," Tacho called as I pushed her towards the door. "She is in your care from now on."

A disturbing thought to know that one had some sort of responsibility towards another human being again, but too late to draw back now.

As we approached the Mercedes I took the girl's bundle and threw it into the back. Van Horne said, "What in the hell do you think you're playing at?"

"The girl goes with us," I said. "No arguments."

"Over my dead body."

"That could be arranged," I told him flatly.

I didn't know what would happen next, already had a hand to the butt of the Enfield in the darkness, when surprisingly he capitulated.

"Oh, get her inside for God's sake and let's get out of here. I can always crack your skull later."

I put her into the rear seat, climbed in next to him and he drove away.

The fifteen miles for which we stayed with the Huila road were no problem and took us about thirty minutes to cover, a remarkable performance considering the darkness and the state of the road.

It was when we reached the place where we were to turn off that we ran into difficulties. For one thing it took a good half-hour to find the start of the trail, so faintly was it marked. When we turned onto it, I knew we were in trouble.

It was almost impossible to see, even with the head-lamps full on and we seemed to be threading our way through a ghostly maze of thorn bushes and organ cactus. We kept this up for a while, crawling at five or ten miles an hour for most of the time and on two occasions it was only van Horne's quick reflexes that prevented us from plunging into a dry arroyo.

In the end he braked to a halt, and switched off the engine and lights. "So you were right and I was wrong. I don't even know if we're on the trail any more. We'll move on at first light."

I turned and looked back at the girl. "Are you all right?"

She reached for my hand, pressed it gently. Van Horne said, "Now may I ask why in the hell you had to bring her along? Can't you do without it or some-thing?"

"The *federales* would have passed her from hand-to-hand."

"If it doesn't happen to her here, it happens some-where else," he said. "So what's the point?"

"Her mother's people live on the other side of the mountains. They'll take her in. Look after her properly. Yaquis have a strong kinship system. They wouldn't turn her away."

He was in the act of lighting one of his cigarillos and turned to look at me in surprise, the match flaring in his cupped hands. "Are you saying she's Yaqui?"

"Her mother was. Her father was straight out of the top drawer. One of the big land-owning families."

"Son, that doesn't mean a damn thing. She's branded clean to the bone. Why the Yaqui are worse than the

Apache and that's going some, believe me. First night she doesn't like you in bed, she'll take a knife to your privates."

"My affair, not yours."

"It touches both of us while we're together. You get rid of her the moment we break through to the other side, understand?"

"We'll see about that."

"We certainly will." And then, with one of those puzzling about-turns that I was to find so typical of the man, added, "It's going to get a damn sight colder than this before morning. If she cares to lift up the back seat she'll find some car rugs."

He turned, as if suddenly exasperated and repeated the information in Spanish. The girl stood up and fumbled about in the darkness. After a while, she passed a heavy car rug over to me.

"No, for you," I said.

Van Horne laughed uneasily. "She's going to hang onto you like a leech, Keogh. You mark my words." He grabbed an end of the rug, unfolded it and spread it across our knees. "She should be snug enough back there. There are two more. On the other hand I don't mind if you want to get under the covers with her."

I think he was deliberately trying to bait me. I refused to be drawn, but turned and said to the girl, "Wrap up well and go to sleep. We'll move on at first light."

Van Horne switched on the dashboard light, found the bottle of tequila he had taken from the bar and uncorked it.

He took a long pull and sighed. "Heaven alone knows what this stuff does to the liver, but it's all that's going to get me through this night. You'd better have some."

I took a mouthful, fought for breath as it burned its

way down and handed the bottle back hurriedly. "I think old Tacho must have made that himself in the back room."

"I can believe that all right. I can believe anything of this damned country." He shivered. "God, if I had my time over again."

"Would anything be any different?"

The neck of the bottle chinked on his teeth, there was a gurgle, a long gurgle and then he sighed. "No, it's a long, dark night at the mouth of nowhere, Keogh, and we're both far from home, so the truth for once."

"Which is . . . ?"

"The old, old question." He laughed shortly. "Would you believe me, Keogh, if I told you I spent four years in a seminary? That I actually trained for the priesthood?"

"You certainly made a convincing enough job of it at Huerta this morning when they were executing those men."

It was as if I had touched an open wound and he turned on me sharply. "They were dying, Keogh, they'd only minutes to live. They went easier thinking they'd had a priest. Whether they did or not doesn't matter a damn where they are now."

"So you think they've gone to a happier place, do you?"

It was a stupid and ill-judged remark in the circumstances and received the reply it merited. "Don't get clever with me, boy."

"All right, I'm sorry." He took another pull at the bottle and passed it to me. "What do you do when you're not wearing a cassock?"

"You might say I'm in the banking business." He laughed loudly and without the slightest sign of having taken drink in spite of the quantity he'd already put away. "Yes, I like that. You know I was once in a little town in Arkansas where the local police insisted on a permit if you owned a hand gun and you had to state your reason for needing one."

"What did you put?"

"I told them I often carried large sums of money. I didn't say it was usually other people's."

"I see—so you're a thief."

"I rob banks, if that's what you mean and believe me you've got to be good to get away with it."

"Which is why you're running round Mexico playing the earnest priest?"

"That's it exactly. I knocked over the National Bank at a little place called Brownsville in Texas two days ago all on my own. It's a funny thing, but priests and nuns —everybody trusts them. I knocked on that door a half-hour before time and the guard opened it without a qualm."

"How many dead men did you leave behind you?"

"Dead men." He seemed surprised. "I told you it was a nice, clean job. Four guys lying on their faces with their hands tied and an empty vault was all I left behind that day." He leaned forward as if trying to see my face. "Anyway, how many men have you killed, Keogh, that's the question."

He was right, but if I'd told him, I'd have given him the shock of his life. "One too many."

"It always is, even when you think you've got an excuse for it like you with your politics. We're a lot alike you and me, Keogh, in our different ways and I'll tell you why. We've both got death in the soul, it's as simple as that."

Which was probably the most terrible thing anyone

had ever said to me, mainly because it was the kind of
remark that brings out into the open a truth one has
always attempted to avoid.

"What was it you called it?" van Horne said. "The
last place God made. That about sums it up. My old
lady would say I'd ended up with what I deserved. She
and my father were Pennsylvania Dutch. Moved to Vermont when he opened a little printing shop in Altoona.
Her religion was everything to her. Believe me, boy,
nobody takes it more seriously than Dutch Catholics.
When I walked out of that seminary on account of a
stupid, little bitch who left me six months later, my
mother laid it straight on the line. The Wrath of God
and the Day of Judgement rolled into one. That's what
I'm going to get and any time now the way things are
going."

He rambled on in this way for quite some time, not
drunk and yet it was the drink talking. Finally, it started
to rain in great, heavy cold drops that hurt where they
made contact. We got out quickly and put the top up
and only just in time for the rain soon increased into a
persistent downpour.

"My God, this is all we needed," van Horne said.

I wondered if he appreciated the seriousness of this
new turn of events. That by morning, half the ground
we had to traverse would be quagmire and a hundred
dry arroyos, rushing torrents and quite impassable.

There seemed little point in going into that now and it
certainly wouldn't change anything so I pulled an end of
the car rug around my legs against the cold and turned
up my collar.

How many men have you killed, Keogh? It was a hell
of a thought to go to sleep on.

The morning dawned grey and bleak, heavy rain still

falling. We had stopped close to the edge of what had once been a dry stream bed. Water was rushing through it now in full spate like a moorland burn on a November morning back home. The mountains were closer than I had expected and we got out the map and finally managed to place ourselves.

We had about ten or twelve miles of open country to traverse before reaching the trail we were seeking, the one which would take us up through the Nonava Pass. It was marked quite clearly on the map between two mountains, one a sugar-loaf and the other with three distinctively jagged peaks. We could see them both in the distance quite clearly in spite of the rain.

That magnificent engine fired without difficulty when van Horne pressed the self-starter and he took the Mercedes away slowly, working out his route as he went, for any remaining trace of the track we had been following had been washed out by the heavy rain.

It was still bitterly cold and the girl, Victoria, stayed muffled in the two car rugs she had used during the night and peered out into the morning, her face as serious and grave as ever. I asked her if she was all right and she nodded and actually smiled, which was something.

Van Horne said, "How come you speak Spanish as well as you do?"

"My mother was born in Seville."

"Is that so? Your old man must have got around. I picked mine up in Juárez one year, working as manager in a small casino there. I had to stay out of circulation for a while on account of the fact that I'd broken out of Leavenworth—that's the Texas State Penitentiary."

"What were you in there for?"

"Shooting a guy who was trying to shoot me, only he had friends at court and I didn't."

Strange, the change in him. The brash, confident

manner, the excessive toughness in the voice as if he was
trying to prove something, though whether to me or
himself was debatable. I was thinking about that for
want of something better to do when we went over a
slight rise a couple of minutes later and saw federal
cavalry in the hollow below.

They were saddled up and grouped in a rough circle as
if waiting to receive their orders after breaking camp.
The surprise was mutual and the whisper of the engine
at the slow speed at which we were moving combined
with the heavy rain, explained why they had not heard
our approach.

There was a single, excited cry as we were seen and as
van Horne swung the wheel and slammed his foot hard
down, a couple of shots whistled through the air. We
went down the slope in a great sliding loop that took us
through a patch of water a foot deep and out into the
final stretch of open plain rising into the mountains.

By now, the hunt was up with a vengeance and the
result by no means a foregone conclusion for the
federales, as usual, were superbly mounted and try as he
could, there were stretches where van Horne had no option but to slow down considerably.

We were perhaps two hundred yards in the lead when
he cursed and braked sharply as we went over a small
ridge and found the way blocked by a flooded arroyo.
By the time we had extricated ourselves, the gap had
narrowed to no more than fifty yards. We started to
climb steeply, cutting across a broad shoulder at the
foot of the sugar-loaf mountain, the wheels spinning in
the loose shale.

"Once over the top there we're certain to hit that
trail," he shouted. "They don't stand a cat in hell's
chance of keeping up with us. The Thompson's under
your feet. Give them a little discouragement."

I pulled out the celebrated Gladstone bag and found the sub-machine gun inside resting on top of dozens of packets of crisp bank notes. An interesting discovery, but I had more important things on my mind. I leaned out and loosed off a long, rolling burst well above the heads of our pursuers. It certainly started them reining in, but when I attempted to repeat the performance, the drum magazine jammed, a common fault with them at that time.

The *federales* urged their mounts up the slope, but a moment later, we were over the shoulder of the hill and saw the trail quite plainly no more than fifty yards below us. It was in much better condition than I had expected and the moment we reached it and the Mercedes started to climb, I knew we were home and dry.

Van Horne turned and grinned savagely at me, dropping a gear as the trail lifted along the side of the ravine and then, as he looked back, he gave a sudden exclamation and jammed on the brakes. A whole slice of mountain seemed to have broken away in a great wave of earth and rock, probably a result of the heavy rain during the night, wiping the trail off the map for all time.

He slammed the gear stick into reverse, and started to turn the Mercedes, but he was already too late as a dozen or so *federales* came over the rise and boiled around us like an angry sea.

The Enfield was ready in my hand and there was little doubt that I could have dropped a couple of them, but no more than that, which seemed rather futile in the circumstances. I put it down on the seat and raised my hands as ostentatiously as I could.

FOUR

THE NEXT FEW minutes could well have been my last and probably almost were. I got a boot between the shoulder blades as I stepped out of the Mercedes that put me down on my hands and knees. No place to be with a dozen horses doing their best to trample me into the ground. I was kicked twice, the second time with such force that I thought a rib had gone and then a grip of iron fastened on my collar and brought me to my feet.

Van Horne steadied me with one hand and swung a fist into the rump of the nearest horse with such force that it reared up, almost unseating its rider. Someone struck at him with a plaited leather riding whip. He allowed it to curl around his arm, then pulled the owner from the saddle with no apparent effort, the first hint I'd been given of the man's enormous strength.

There was considerable confusion for a moment or two after that as the soldiers frantically hauled their mounts out of the way to avoid trampling their unfortunate companion. One or two of them drew sabres and for a moment things looked decidedly nasty and then a single pistol shot sounded and a young officer burst through the outer ring and reined in sharply.

He had a thin, sallow face, a dark smudge of moustache and wore the silver bars of a lieutenant. Unlike most of his men, he was not wearing a rubber poncho and his tailored uniform was soaked with rain.

He smiled coldly, leaned down from the saddle and touched van Horne between the eyes with the barrel of the pistol. "Large or small, strong or weak, señor, one bullet is all it takes."

"Just call the dogs off, that's all," van Horne told him. "We'll come quietly."

"You will indeed. My orders were to apprehend you alive if possible, but I would be happy for you to give me an excuse to act otherwise. I find you an affront to all decency. Take off that cassock."

Van Horne glared at him, hands on his hips. "And what if I tell you to go and do the other thing, you pip-squeak."

The lieutenant dismounted, tossed the reins of his horse to one of his men and faced van Horne squarely, raising his revolver to belt level. He thumbed back the hammer very deliberately.

"Señor, for reasons of my own, which are none of your business, I do not like you or anything about you. I assure you now, on my mother's grave, that if you do not do exactly as I say, I will give you what you so richly deserve."

He was no longer smiling and if one looked closely, the gun was shaking a little. Van Horne raised a hand as if to placate him. "All right, soldier boy, anything for a quiet life."

He unbuttoned his cassock at the neck, pulled it over his head and tossed it into the Mercedes. He was wearing a pair of very clerical-looking trousers in black worsted and a white shirt.

The lieutenant said, "The collar also, if you please."

Van Horne removed it and threw it into the Mercedes after the cassock. "Satisfied?" he demanded.

"Only when I see you hang, señor," the lieutenant said. "You will now drive this automobile back down the trail under my instructions. The slightest attempt to escape and I shoot. You understand me?"

"You've got a big mouth with that in your hand, that's all I understand, sonny." Van Horne turned and moved back to the Mercedes.

"You can walk," the lieutenant told me and started after van Horne.

"What about her?" I nodded towards the girl who was being held quite unnecessarily by two of his men. "Can't you take her with you?"

He looked towards her and frowned. "She's the one from old Tacho's place, isn't she? The one who can't speak."

"That's right. Have you spoken to him? Did he tell you what happened last night?"

"No, but I've had a reasonably full account from the sole survivor of the *rurales* you butchered."

"Very interesting," I said. "Did he tell you what they were trying to do with the girl? Did he mention they were about to hang me for trying to intervene? Would have finished me off if my friend there hadn't arrived when he did?"

He believed me, which was the only important thing, his face turning paler than ever and the expression in his eyes was terrible to see.

"A dirty word, Lieutenant," I said softly. "And that kid couldn't even raise a scream to save herself."

He turned away without a word, grabbed Victoria by the arm and shoved her into the back seat of the Mercedes, then climbed in beside van Horne and told him to get moving. It took van Horne quite a bit of manoeuvring to get the Mercedes pointing the right way but he managed it after a while and we all got out of the way to let him drive past.

We started down the trail, the rest of us, the troopers riding, but the sergeant in charge, a small dark-haired man with a heavy moustache, dismounted and walked beside me, a pistol in his hand.

I produced a packet of Artistas. "All right if I smoke?"

"Sure, I'll have one with you." I gave him a light and he blew out the first lungful of smoke expertly. "Had yourselves a ball last night at old Tacho's, you and your pal, didn't you? How many *rurales* was it you saw off—five?"

"What's happening now?" I asked.

"Oh, the colonel's waiting to see you down there. Colonel Bonilla. He's the military governor in this region. He joined us for a routine patrol yesterday morning, just to see how things were going for himself. He's like that. We were bivouacked for the night at an old *ranchería* near the main road when this *rurale* rode up. The one you let slip through your fingers at Tacho's." There was sincere admiration in his voice when he added, "You and your pal must be hell on wheels."

"What made you come straight out here instead of going to Tacho's?"

"That was the colonel." He put a finger to his nose. "He's really got it upstairs, that one. He figured you'd make a break for it so he only sent half-a-dozen guys to Tacho's with a sergeant in charge, then he had a look at

the map with the lieutenant. He said if it was him, he'd
make a break for it through the Nonava Pass because it
didn't look possible.''

"He certainly hit the nail right on the head.''

"He usually does. He pushed us hard last night. Only
stopped when it really started to rain, but he was right
again. If we hadn't been where we were, you'd have got
through, wouldn't you?''

Quite a man, this Colonel Bonilla. We reached the
place where the trail finally merged with the desert to
find the Mercedes standing in the entrance to a narrow
ravine. Someone had already started a fire in spite of the
rain, no great feat with so many thorn bushes around
and the smoke curled lazily on the damp air.

Van Horne was standing beside the Mercedes and I
realised that someone, presumably Bonilla, was sitting
in the rear seat, the door open. He was a tall, handsome
man with sideburns which were prematurely white for I
judged him to be no more than forty years of age. He
made a rather gallant figure in his caped cavalry greatcoat and he had an intelligent, cynical air to him, the
face of a man who has seen it all, everything possible in
life and simply doesn't believe in anything any more.

The sergeant handed me over to the lieutenant who
took me the rest of the way. Bonilla looked me over
calmly.

"Your name, señor,'' he asked politely.

"Emmet Keogh. I'm a British citizen.''

"Keogh?'' He frowned slightly. "An unusual name,
señor, and I have heard it before. You are the one who
was in charge of security at the silver mines at Hermosa.''

"That's right. You seem surprised.''

"You are not what I would have looked for, señor. I
had expected a different kind of man.''

"In what way? Two horns and a tail?"

"Possibly even that. Your papers."

I took out the travel permit signed by the *jefe* in Bonito. "That's all I've got with me."

He examined it gravely. "So, you are supposed to be delivering a truck-load of supplies to this man Gomez in Huila."

"That's right. For Señor Janos, the owner of the Hotel Blanco in Bonito."

"To know Señor Janos is not much of a recommendation, believe me. This man has just given me his personal version of what happened at the way-station last night. Now I will hear yours." He nodded to the young lieutenant. "Take him away."

The lieutenant gave van Horne a shove to get started and none too gently. Bonilla chuckled. "I'm afraid Lieutenant Cordona doesn't care for your friend overmuch. You see he is a very correct young man. When he was a boy his parents intended him for the priesthood and he was educated to that end. You will readily understand that to someone like him, a man like your friend who represents himself to be a priest when he is not . . ."

He produced a silver cigarette case, selected one, lit it and blew smoke into the rain. "So, we will now hear what you have to say."

I told him the exact truth. When I had finished, he nodded slowly. "Remarkable—truly remarkable." He reached behind him and produced the Gladstone bag. "There are fifty-three thousand dollars in here, did you know that?"

"I saw van Horne for the first time yesterday morning in Bonito when he administered the last rites to three men who were publicly executed at the police barracks. He looked like a priest. He acted like a priest and that's what everyone took him to be, including me. When he walked in on what was happening at Tacho's last night, he saved me from getting my neck stretched. Saved the girl from God knows what . . . That should count for something, whatever else he may do.''

"Whatever the circumstances, five at one blow, my friend, is a little hard to take, but we will speak again later when I've heard from my other patrol.''

He snapped a finger and the sergeant moved in fast. "Put him with his friend and then get me some breakfast.''

I joined van Horne who squatted against a rock. His shirt was plastered to his body and he was shivering slightly. "Well, what did you tell him?'' he demanded.

"The truth—what else?''

"Fair enough.'' He smiled faintly. "Not that it will make any kind of difference. Only one way out of this, Keogh.''

"Perhaps.'' I looked around me. "What happened to the girl?''

"They've put her to work.''

She was wearing one of the cavalrymen's rubber ponchos and a military cap, which was why I hadn't noticed her at first, and she crouched beside the fire cooking *frijoles* in a frying pan.

She saw me looking, poured coffee into a mug and started toward us. Cordona beat her to it, knocked the mug from her hand and sent her back to her place at the fire with a shove.

"Now there's a guy I could really learn to hate," van Horne commented.

"The feeling's mutual. It seems he has a thing about people who pretend to be priests.''

"I'm breaking my heart," van Horne said and faintly in the distance, a cavalry trumpet sounded.

Half-a-dozen soldiers, a sergeant in the lead, rode out of the rain. "These will be the boys he sent on to Tacho's last night," I told van Horne.

We watched the sergeant go forward to make his report. Bonilla glanced towards us a couple of times, then appeared to question the man closely. Finally he called to Cordona to bring us to him.

"Tell me, Señor Keogh," he said. "What were you carrying in that truck of yours?"

"Whisky," I said. "For delivery to a man called Gomez in Huila. I've already told you."

"But forgot to mention the rifles."

"Rifles?" I stared at him stupidly. "I don't know what you mean."

"Martini-Henry carbines. Those packing cases in the back of your truck are full of them, or so my sergeant here informs me and he's usually reliable."

"Nice friends you've got, Keogh," van Horne said bitterly. "I'd say that just about puts the lid on things."

"Why in the hell should it," I demanded angrily. "It's Janos who owns that truck, not me. He only hired me to drive the damned thing." I turned to Bonilla. "You've seen that permit for yourself. It's Janos you want. Janos and the *jefe* in Bonito, Captain Ortiz."

"All will be taken care of, Mr. Keogh, in God's good time." He ran a hand over the back of the Mercedes' driving seat. "This is really a very handsome vehicle." He turned to Cordona. "Did you know that I could drive an automobile, Lieutenant? A minor accomplishment, but rewarding when presented with a machine like this. In fact I have decided to give myself the pleasure of driving back to Huila in it. Detail two men to accompany me. I should like to get started as soon as possible."

"And the prisoners, Colonel?"

"Oh, they can walk, I think. The exercise will prove both salutary and beneficial. You should arrive tomorrow afternoon. Report to me when you do."

He turned away, dismissing us completely and Cordona ordered us back to our original position. We watched the preparation for Bonilla's departure. Two soldiers clutching their carbines got in the rear seat and when Bonilla pressed the self-starter, the Mercedes rumbled into life for him as easily as it had for van Horne.

We watched him drive away into the rain and I said to van Horne, "Well, what do you think?"

"Think? What in the hell am I supposed to think." He glared angrily at me. "Be your age, Keogh. You've reached the end of the road and you'd better get used to the idea."

When we broke camp and moved out, the girl was put up on the back of one of the pack mules, Cordona's orders, but van Horne and I walked each at the end of thirty feet of rope, wrists lashed together.

I say walked, but in fact this meant keeping up with the horses come what may. When they trotted, we trotted too and when they cantered, we ran.

It was a hell of a morning for even after the rain stopped, the going was very rough and, on occasion, both of us fell to be dragged impatiently several yards.

We stopped at noon and again, a small fire was lit so that coffee could be heated. Van Horne and I crouched wearily on the ground beside the horses and watched. Everyone had coffee except us. The girl was particularly distressed by this. She glanced towards us constantly and once, filled a mug with coffee and pulled at Cordona's sleeve, but he shook his head impatiently.

"That creep has decided to make us suffer, do you

know that?'' van Horne said.

''I'm beginning to think it the general idea. If only you'd played at being a Methodist. Maybe he wouldn't have minded so much.''

For some reason that struck him as being really funny and he laughed out loud, which didn't please Cordona. He glared across angrily, then ordered his men to strike camp.

The afternoon was a repetition of the morning, which is to say it was another long agony that seemed as if it would never end. Towards evening, it started to rain heavily again and I stumbled along at the rear of the column, cold, wet and utterly wretched, my legs so tired that it was a small miracle each time I took another step.

When we finally made camp in the ruins of an old *ranchería* in the late evening, I collapsed on the ground and crawled into the shelter of a broken adobe wall the moment the trooper who had been leading me released the rope.

We had covered something like thirty miles and there were another twenty to go. I opened my eyes wearily and found van Horne beside me.

''I'm getting old, Keogh, that's what it is.'' His face looked grey and drawn and yet he still managed to smile. ''You want to know something? I've decided I don't like our friend one little bit.''

Three separate fires were lit, the men scavenging for wood in a nearby thicket and soon I could smell coffee and bacon on the damp air.

After a while, the girl appeared holding a tin mug of coffee in one hand, a pan containing a couple of frijoles in the other. Cordona arrived on the run and kicked the mug from her hand, catching her wrist and really hurting her.

''I said no food for these two, damn you,'' he said

and then hesitated, obviously considerably put out at the sight of the pain in her face.

"Does that make you feel better, sonny?" van Horne asked him.

Cordona turned, a fist raised, restraining himself only with the greatest difficulty, then grabbed the girl by the arm and pushed her back towards the fire.

The rain increased and so did our misery as darkness fell. Several of the troopers glanced towards us as we crouched there in the heavy rain. Cordona ignored us. Simply sat at his own small fire chain-smoking and drinking cup after cup of coffee.

Finally the girl, Victoria, got up very deliberately, picked up two horse blankets and came towards us. She gave one to van Horne, then crouched beside me and spread the other one around both of us. Men glanced furtively at Cordona, then at each other. I could hear the whispering and yet he made no sign, staring straight ahead of him, too proud to provoke an incident.

I was shaking like a leaf, my teeth chattering, but already I was beginning to warm up, the girl's body pressed against me. When the shaking continued, she pulled my face down into her shoulders and drew the blanket over my head, rocking gently to and fro. I forgot her age then, forgot her background as my eyes started to close in sleep. She was just a woman doing the right thing at the right time and all women, after all, are born old and knowing most things.

It stopped raining during the night and the following day dawned to a sky of cloudless blue, the sun starting his climb early. By mid-morning it was so hot that all moisture had been sucked out of that barren land again and dust rose in a great cloud stirred by the horses' hooves.

Van Horne and I marched in the thick of it, which didn't make breathing any easier and the heat was unbearable. By the time we were ready for the noonday halt, I was at the end of my tether and beyond. I had fallen so many times that the column had to be halted constantly and even Cordona had raised no objection when I was given water.

I'd existed in my own small world of suffering and had been unaware of how van Horne was managing. When I finally opened my eyes and found him lying beside me at the noonday camp, he seemed in no better case than I was myself.

"I've decided to live, just to spite this guy," he croaked faintly. "A small victory, but mine own."

I rolled over on my back, my whole body on fire, and found Victoria kneeling over me with a canteen of water. She looked frightened and yet angry at the same time. I tried a smile, but my lips were cracking and it hurt.

She poured a little water into my mouth, then bathed my face. Cordona walked across from the fire, a mug of coffee in one hand and stood looking down at us.

"Satisfied?" van Horne croaked. "Or were we supposed to die?"

Cordona turned away and went back to the fire. Yet he still wouldn't give in. When we resumed the journey, I was carried to one of the mules and my wrists looped over the high wooden pommel of a pack saddle. It meant that I couldn't fall down any more, which was something, but I still had to walk.

Van Horne was undergoing the same treatment a few yards in front of me and this was the manner in which we covered the final miles into Huila, although in my case it was simply a matter of hanging on, for my toes seemed to be trailing most of the time.

I have no clear memory of entering Huila itself, only of surfacing to a bucket of water in the face and finding myself on my back, Cordona leaning over me.

"All right, Keogh, pull yourself together," he said. "You're here."

A couple of soldiers dragged me to my feet and we started across the courtyard. Van Horne was ahead of me, also supported by two soldiers and we went through a large oaken door to a smell that said I was back in prison again.

The cell was no better than a sewer which was, I suppose, the intention. Even that wasn't enough for Cordona and he had them place us in leg irons before leaving. I was past caring and as the door clanged shut, plunged into blissful, easeful dark.

I must have slept for sixteen or seventeen hours after that. I can remember waking a couple of times to relieve myself and finding van Horne snoring in the corner and on each occasion, plunged into a deep sleep again by the simple expedient of closing my eyes.

When I finally awakened, it was late afternoon of the following day and van Horne was standing by the small, barred window of the cell looking out.

He turned with a smile. "How do you feel?"

"Terrible." I put a hand to my belly, which felt as if there was a hole in it. "Is there anything to eat around here?"

"You'll find a pan of slops in the corner with so many maggots in it I lost count. I'm waiting for your girl friend."

"Victoria." I got up and groaned involuntarily at the stiffness in my limbs. "What are you talking about?"

"She was here at the window earlier so I slipped her a fifty peso note I had in my shoe to go and get us a few things." He grunted suddenly. "Here she comes now."

I peered through the bars into a small courtyard with a fountain in the centre. There didn't seem to be anyone about and the gate to the street outside stood open.

Victoria looked up at me, her face grave and anxious. I said softly, "You shouldn't be doing this."

She smiled and started to pass things through the bars one-by-one. A bottle of wine, bread, olives, a couple of long sausages and two packets of Artistas and matches.

"Good appetite, my friends." Colonel Bonilla stepped out of the shadows of an archway to the right of us.

"Don't take it out on the girl, Bonilla," I said as he approached. "She was only trying to help."

She looked up at him anxiously. He patted her on the head and said, "On your way, child, and stay out of trouble."

To my amazement, she smiled for him, fleetingly and yet it was there, and smiled again for me before hurrying away.

Bonilla said, "Yes, my friends, it is always wise to eat well when you can, for in this life, one can never be certain if one will ever be able to eat again."

On which pleasant note he left us to eat and disappeared into the shadows of the archway.

FIVE

My FATHER, a dedicated Fenian till the day he died of tuberculosis in an English prison, left me to the care of my grandfather, Mickeen Bawn Keogh of Stradballa in the county of Kerry.

Now it must be understood that Mickeen Bawn means small white Michael, a description that never made much sense to me, for although his hair had been snow white since boyhood, he was six and a half feet tall. A gentle giant of a man except with the drink taken. In that state, I have seen half-a-dozen hard men of their hands run from him, for in his youth he had been, amongst other things, a prizefighter.

So, I was raised on a Kerry farm along with the best horses in Ireland, which is to say the world, and nothing else life has to offer could ever match up to those days. Back country so quiet you could hear a dog barking in the next county. Sweet-smelling mornings and sunsets to thank God for. No beginning, no end, time a circle until the day my grandfather decided I had brains and sent me to the Jesuits at Knockbree to be made into a scholar and perhaps even a gentleman.

When I was accepted by the College of Surgeons, went up to the university, there was no prouder man and yet each of us is what he is from the day he is born and no escaping. I went to Dublin town to learn something of the art of healing and met a man called Michael Collins who found another use for me.

After the Easter Rising, I went back to the university on his orders and bided my time. Stayed there during the years that followed. A medical student by day, which was as good a front as you could find, and a member of the Squad in my spare time. Emmet Oge Keogh—little Edmund Keogh. His strong left hand, he used to call me and God knows, I killed for him often enough in those days or for Ireland, whichever way you care to look at it.

Some of these things I spoke of to van Horne during the first three days after our capture. The fact is I found that I rather liked the man because he reminded me pleasantly of my grandfather. In any case, there was little else to do except talk for we were given no work, no exercise of any description during those first few days.

We were even reduced to eating the slops provided once a day in an old enamel bucket at noon because there were no more visits from Victoria with supplies from the town. After that first evening when Bonilla had appeared, there was a guard posted outside the window.

Three days we had of it and that was three days too much with tempers starting to fray. I remember van Horne standing at the window, just before dark, trying to get a little air, suddenly turning in a kind of irritation, looking for somone to kick at.

"They tell me you never had more than ten thousand men under arms against the English at any one time.

What was wrong with the rest of the country?''

He was trying to bait me for some reason of his own, I knew that, but I would not be drawn. "We didn't have the arms for more."

"Come off it, Keogh." He laughed harshly and wiped the sweat from his face with an old rag. "I think guys like you, the ones who turned out, did it because you got a bang out of killing people. You enjoyed it, the whole thing. A game for schoolboys playing with real guns."

"You could be right there," I said cheerfully, taking the last cigarette from my crumpled packet of Artistas.

He was annoyed and said sourly, "Didn't I read somewhere that there was so much shooting in the back going on they had to introduce a law making it compulsory for any man passing a policeman on the street to raise his hands in the air?"

"I believe that was so in some areas."

"I just bet it was." By now, he was thoroughly irritated. "How many did you see off then, Keogh, for the sake of your bloody cause?"

"Why, as many as was needed, Mr. van Horne," I told him evenly.

He stood there staring at me, really angry like some great sullen bull getting ready to charge. What would have happened next is debatable, but the course of action was chosen for us as a key rattled in the lock.

Lieutenant Cordona entered, spic and span in a freshly pressed khaki drill uniform, highly polished boots glistening in the dim light.

"Well, damn me if it isn't the soldier," van Horne said. "Don't tell me we're going to get some service at last."

"You will get more than that, I assure you," Cordona replied and motioned us outside.

He took us out through the courtyard between half-a-
dozen soldiers, leg irons rattling on the cobbles. We
went through an archway into a cloistered patio and
finally entered a small, enclosed garden. There was a
fountain, a flame tree vivid with blossom and Bonilla
taking his ease in a wicker chair on the terrace.

Like Cordona, he wore a well-tailored uniform and
highly polished boots and looked very correct, very military. He told Cordona to bring us inside, got to his feet
and led the way in through open french windows.

The room was sparsely furnished and was obviously
used as his office. There was a desk and chair, various
large-scale maps of the area on the wall, a narrow iron
cot in one corner and not much else.

He sat down behind the desk and put a cigar in his
mouth, which Cordona lit for him. He leaned back in
his chair, looked at us both for a reasonably lengthy in-
terval and then spoke.

"Yes, in many ways you couldn't be more comple-
mentary to each other. It is really quite remarkable.
Two rogues together."

"Oh, I wouldn't say that," van Horne said.

"Wouldn't you, Father? You don't mind if I still call
you that, do you?"

"You can call me what you damn well please," van
Horne told him cheerfully.

"Which gives me something of a choice. Murderer?
Yes, many times over. Thief?" Bonilla turned to me.
"Would you believe me, Señor Keogh, if I told you he
would cut the fingers off a dead man to get at his rings?
Totally without scruple or pity. In at least two states in
the U.S.A. he faces the death sentence."

"Peck's Bad Boy, that's me," van Horne said. "So
what?"

"And in excellent company, Father, I assure you. I

have here a most interesting communication from Mexico City from the representative of the Irish Free State. This Emmet Keogh is a very dangerous man. An Irish gunman, he was for several years a member of what was known as the Squad. An organisation used by the Irish patriotic leader, Michael Collins, as chief weapon in the campaign of deliberate terrorism he waged against the English. Señor Keogh has killed so many men he has lost count.''

"For what it's worth, I was a soldier of the Irish Republican Army," I said.

"How noble. Were you fighting for Ireland when you were trouble-shooter for the Hermosa Mining Company, señor? How many men did you kill in the disturbances up there? Four or was it five?''

"They'd hung a priest as you damn well know," I told him. "I was doing what I was paid for.''

He ignored me completely. "Yes, a dangerous man, Señor Keogh, a fanatic. Not content with getting rid of the English, he and his friends turned on their own leaders, plunged their country into civil war of the worst kind. As a matter of interest, the Irish Government is anxious to have you back, but only to face a firing squad. The statement I have received from them particularly refers to an affair in the town of Drumdoon four months ago when you ambushed a vehicle in which four high-ranking Free State officers were travelling and killed them all.''

The heart seemed to stop inside of me, the throat dry as what I had tried to keep down all this long while forced its way to the surface.

"One of them was your elder brother, I understand. Colonel Sean Keogh.''

I was aware of van Horne's startled glance, swayed forward and grabbed at the edge of the desk as the walls undulated. "You go to hell, you bastard," I told Bonilla.

"Your own destination, my friend. You and the good father here were both sentenced to death by a military court this afternoon. You will be shot in the morning."

He stood up and walked out without a word and I stayed, leaning heavily on the edge of the desk, fighting for air.

There was a hand under my elbow. Van Horne said quietly, "Are you all right? Can you make it?"

"No sympathy," I said.

"That word doesn't figure in my vocabulary." As I turned to look at him, the craggy, used-up face broke into a smile that was like no smile I'd seen on top of earth. Courage and strength. Genuine strength and infinite compassion.

"We will go now, señores," I heard Cordona say, polite for the first time and only because we were dead men walking.

Van Horne said softly, "You will walk out of here on your own two feet and smile. Do you understand me, boy?"

My grandfather all over again, but he was right and let it be so. I would not disgrace my name this night or any other. I took a deep breath to steady myself and went through the french windows ahead of them all.

It was cold in the cell, bitterly cold and the stench of the place seemed worse than even after our brief visit to the outside world. I stood at the window, staring into the night. After a while, the key rattled in the lock again, the door opened and Cordona reappeared with a couple of packets of Artistas and a straw-covered bottle of tequila. He put them down on the floor and went out without a word.

Van Horne said, "Well, I'll be damned, even that bastard has a heart. Here, take a pull at this."

He passed me the tequila bottle. As I have said, I never did care for the stuff, but it was warming if nothing else. I took a couple of swallows and gave it back to him.

He said, "Do you want to talk about it?"

Now here is a strange thing. I had known him play-acting the priest, I had seen him as another kind of man entirely after the shooting at Tacho's, but this calm, worldly-wise, compassionate man was someone else again. Even the manner of speech had altered.

"How many different people are you, for God's sake?" I demanded.

"Oh, it amuses me to confuse people, but that isn't answering my question."

"All right," I said. "But it's soon told. My brother was six years older than me. He joined the Dublin Fusiliers in 1914, and went to fight England's wars for her, a habit Irishmen find hard to break. He was com-missioned in the field, invalided out as a captain at the beginning of 1918."

"Were his politics the same colour as yours?"

"I think you could say that. He rose to command a Flying Column in spite of his bad right leg. We parted company over the treaty, with the English. He was one of those, like Collins, who thought we'd suffered enough. That half-a-loaf was better than nothing."

"And you were a die-hard Republican."

I couldn't see his face, so dark had it become, which was perhaps a good thing. I said, "I didn't know he was in the car that day in Drumdoon. We were expecting the divisional commander."

"These things happen in war."

"I killed him," I said. "Killed all four of them neatly

and expeditiously with a Thompson gun from the upstairs window of Cohan's Select Bar. It was raining hard
at the time and not a soul on the streets. They knew better. The purpose of terrorism is to terrorise, that's what
Mick Collins used to say and I believed him. In the end,
it was too late to change. Even after Drumdoon. All I
could do was run for the hills."

"It's never too late for anything in this life."

"Now you're playing priest again."

He changed, just like that. "Damn me, but you're
right, Keogh, and that won't do at all. Seems to me a
man ought to stand by what he's been, even at the final
end of things, or his whole life's been nothing."

"That's me," I said. "A perfect description."

"Oh, I don't know. What about that Indian kid. You
saved her bacon back there at Tacho's, didn't you?
That ought to count for something."

There was a kind of comfort in that and I thought of
her for a moment, the dark, calm eyes, the olive skin,
the warmth of her body when she had held me close on
that night of torrential rain.

"I'd say she owes as much to you as she does to me,"
I said. "If you hadn't taken a hand in the game when
you did . . ."

"Don't make the mistake of assigning a motive to my
conduct that didn't exist, Keogh." His voice was harsh
again, his old cynical self. "I didn't intend anything
when I stepped into the bar at Tacho's that night. What
took place just happened to be the way things worked
out. There was no method intended in my madness.
And now, I've talked enough. I'm going to sleep."

He relieved himself into the bucket in the corner, then
lay on his straw mattress, his irons chinking as he arranged his legs.

I stayed there at the window, clutching the bars and

staring up into the cold night sky at stars older than time itself, that would be still here tomorrow night when little Emmet Keogh was long gone. God help me, but looking back on it all, this rag of a life of mine, it seemed such a pitiful waste.

The sergeant of the guard brought us coffee at seven o'clock, but no food, which was reasonable enough under the circumstances.

After that, we were left alone for a good two hours. Van Horne had nothing to say. In the cold morning light he looked older than his years and his beard was tangled, the face dirty. I can have been in no better case and was feeling understandably depressed. The sounds of activity in the courtyard outside didn't help.

There was the tramp of marching feet, a shouted order or two and van Horne got to his feet and went to the window. There was a certain amount of confused shouting and then a high-pitched scream.

"What's going on?" I demanded.

"They're getting ready to shoot some poor bastard and he isn't taking it too well."

I joined him at the window and peered through the bars. There was a wooden post in front of the wall on the other side of the courtyard and the prisoner they were tying to it was struggling so hard that it was taking four soldiers to control him. As they moved away leaving him upright against the post, I got a look at his face and could not avoid a short, ironic laugh.

"As old Tacho said, sometimes God looks down through the clouds."

"You know him?"

I nodded. "Captain José Ortiz. Chief of Police in Bonito."

"Well, I'll be damned," van Horne said. "Bonilla

certainly doesn't let the grass grow under his feet.''

Ortiz was unable to disgrace himself further for they had gagged him with an old bandanna and blindfolded him. Cordona was in charge of the execution and I stayed to watch for some perverse reason of my own, but then I had seen a great many men die this way in my time and there was no reality to it at all. A single sharp command, a ragged volley and the pitiful creature strapped to the pose ceased to exist. No satisfaction to be had there and in any event, as I turned away they came for us.

We were taken by the sergeant and half-a-dozen men through the cell block into a cool, white-walled corridor with windows so high that one could not see out into the courtyard. The sergeant produced a key and removed our leg irons, and we waited.

After a while, the door opened behind us and I could tell by the rattle of leg irons on the floor that another prisoner was being brought up. I looked over my shoulder casually and got the shock of my life. Janos was standing there between two guards, his linen suit filthy beyond description, sweat oozing from that great fat face.

His eyes widened and without the slightest hint of embarrassment he said, "Why, Mr. Keogh, sir. We meet again."

The effrontery of the man was such that I was unable to contain my laughter. "Meet my good friend Mr. Janos from Bonito," I said to van Horne.

"The character who confuses whisky with guns?" Van Horne gave him a hard smile. "At least you'll present them with a sizable target, my friend."

Janos ignored him. They had still left him his stick and he stumped forward as the leg irons were removed. "Mr. Keogh. I feel this whole sorry business very deeply. My fault, sir. If I could make amends I would, believe me. If it is any satisfaction, we are to suffer the same fate.''

"No satisfaction at all," I told him.

The door opened and Lieutenant Cordona entered, a sheaf of papers in his right hand. He nodded to the sergeant who took Janos by the arm and led him forward.

"Paul Janos," Cordona said, reading from the first sheet. "Age fifty-nine, otherwise Count Rakossy, sometime Colonel of the Austrian Imperial Guards."

"Must we really rake up all that sort of thing?" Janos said wearily.

"You have been tried by a military tribunal on the charge of treason against the state and have been found guilty as charged. The sentence of the court is that you be shot to death."

"Then I would suggest that we get it over with as quickly as possible."

Cordona saluted formally and opened the door. Janos turned and said gravely, "I am sorry I got you into this mess, Mr. Keogh, and that's the truth of it, sir. Good luck."

The impudence of the man was breathtaking and when he went out through the door it was as if he were taking them and not the other way round.

It was over very quickly. A shouted command, the fusillade, a single revolver shot and no more than a couple of minutes after that the door opened and Cordona and his men returned.

They took van Horne, the sergeant and half-a-dozen men closing in on him before we knew what was happening as if they anticipated trouble.

As they pushed him through the door, he turned and called over his shoulder. "No regrets, Keogh."

Which put a lump in my throat the size of my fist. I closed my eyes and waited, the coldness seeping through me. The inevitability of death is something few men ever consciously consider for to do so would make life itself unbearable, but now, in a real and frightening way, I knew that I was going to die. That I had only a few more minutes to live.

The rifles crashed outside and I stayed there, eyes closed, listening to the marching feet as they approached the door. When I opened them again, Cordona was before me, the final scrap of paper in his hand.

"Emmet Keogh, age twenty-four, British citizen . . ."

His voice droned on and I looked beyond him out into the terrace at his side of the courtyard, the hard black shadows of the pillars falling across the flagstones like iron bars in the morning sun. And then we were moving out through the door and across the courtyard to the wooden post, blood fresh on the cobbles at its base.

I stood quietly while they strapped my ankles, waist and chest. Cordona said gravely, "I regret the absence of a priest, señor. You must make your peace with God in your own way."

Then they fastened a bandanna about my eyes and walked away. My mind seemed frozen. It was as if this was happening to someone else, not me. I didn't even feel fear any more, could think of no prayer worth the saying.

He gave the order to load and it was as if I could hear each bolt click home separately for they were not particularly well trained or perhaps they had no stomach for the work.

His voice brought them to the ready. There was a single breathtaking moment in which I begged my brother to forgive me and then an ear-shattering roll as they fired.

I was still alive, that much was obvious, had not even been hit, which made no kind of sense at all. There was silence for a moment and then steps approached. The bandanna was untied and I blinked in the sudden glare of the sun.

Cordona was pale, but calm. "You will come with me now, señor," he said impassively.

The sergeant was busy with my straps and I moistened my lips and croaked, "What in the name of God are you playing at, Lieutenant?"

He turned without a word and led off across the courtyard and the sergeant applied the butt of his rifle gently in the small of my back and sent me after him. We went through the archway into that small enclosed garden again. There was no sign of Bonilla but Oliver van Horne and Janos stood against the wall, guarded by three soldiers.

I paused, staring at them in astonishment and Janos called, "You are familiar with Alice in Wonderland, sir? Curiouser and curiouser was the phrase she used as I recall."

Van Horne said nothing, his face grim like any predatory animal sensing danger and we were given no opportunity for further conversation for Cordona went straight in through the french windows and the sergeant brought the three of us after him.

Colonel Bonilla was sitting behind his desk enjoying a late breakfast. He glanced up, wiping his mouth with a napkin and nodded to Cordona who ordered the sergeant and his men outside and took up position by the window.

"An unpleasant start to the day, gentlemen," Bonilla

observed. "But one which I trust makes the point that I hold you all in the hollow of my hand."

It was van Horne who broke the silence. "All right, so you could be Lord High executioner if you wanted to be. You've made your point. What's it all about? What's the game?"

"A good word for it," Bonilla said. "Rather apt, but it's really quite simple. I want you, Señor van Horne, to play the priest again, something you seem to have a talent for."

Van Horne stared at him in amazement. "What did you say?"

"And Señor Janos will make an excellent business-man. He has the build for it. He looks substantial therefore people will believe he is in other ways."

"I am complimented, sir," Janos told him with con-siderable irony.

Bonilla ignored him. "And you, Señor Keogh. Your task is the simplest of all. It might have been created especially for a man of your peculiarly dark talents."

He smiled gravely. "All you have to do is kill some-one for me."

SIX

"IN THE YEAR since the Revolution there has been much unrest, much violence in many parts of Mexico, but nowhere more so than in this area. Worst of all is Mojada in the northern foothills of the Sierra Madre."

Bonilla indicated the right spot on the map with the end of his riding crop and I took a close look. It was perhaps thirty or forty miles from Huila, the sort of place that had sprung up a couple of centuries earlier at the side of the old pack trails across the mountains.

"All right, so what's the story?" van Horne demanded.

"It is soon told, señor. I am military governor for this entire area based on Huila and yet a bare thirty miles away, there is not only no law and order, but a state of complete anarchy that none of my predecessors succeeded in doing anything about."

I said, "I thought that's what you had troops for?"

"I have two hundred men to police the whole of my command area. An army would not be enough to handle the situation in Mojada and the few I have been able to spare in the past have never succeeded in achieving anything. You see, gentlemen, the key to the whole affair is to be found in the personality of one remarkable man, Tomás de la Plata, once a major under my own command until he turned his back on honour.''

He said the last bit as if it really meant something to him and continued, ''Once, the De la Platas were great landowners in these parts. Now, all that is left is a decaying hacienda outside Mojada and a few acres of land plus an old silver mine that hasn't been worked in ten or twelve years.''

''Does anyone still live there?'' I asked.

''His father, Don Angel de la Plata and his sister, Chela.''

''And Tomás? What about him?''

''God alone knows where he is from one moment to the next. Last month he and his men robbed the night express to Madera. Not content with that, he shot the driver and left the train to free-wheel down a gradient. It ran off the track after five miles. Over thirty people were killed, many injured.''

''And he can still find people to follow him after that?'' van Horne said.

''Death and suffering has been the story of my country for years now, señor. It has become something of a way of life to us. Three million dead in the Revolution alone. What are thirty more compared to that?''

''Fair enough,'' I said. ''But I still can't get a clear picture of the man in my own mind. What is he? Dissatisfied revolutionary or plain bandit?''

''God alone knows and Tomás himself.'' Bonilla carefully fitted a cigarette into a black, ivory holder. ''When I first knew him he was just out of university. The complete idealist. Everything was wrong, therefore everything had to be changed."

"Which can hardly have made him popular with people of his own class, surely," Janos put in.

"No, he lost a great deal by aligning himself with the people and their cause so completely. Even his own father publicly disowned him."

"But he didn't mind," I said. "All for the cause. He sounds familiar."

Bonilla smiled rather sadly. "It has been my experience that idealists of this type tend to be complete fanatics who cannot tolerate less than perfection either in the cause they fight for, or in the conduct of their associates."

"Perfection is hard to come by in this world," van Horne said.

"Life, on the whole, is something of a compromise between what we would like and what we can have. Tomás was never capable of making that kind of accommodation."

"So what exactly went wrong in the end?" I asked.

"A great mystery. On the successful conclusion of the Revolution, Tomás was transferred to Huila because of his special knowledge of the area and made second-in-command to the then military governor, a Colonel Varga. It seems they didn't get on very well."

"Any particular reason?"

"Varga was a great ox of a man, a peon who had risen through the ranks. A good soldier in his own rough way, but still inclined to eat with his fingers, if you follow me. He was found in bed one morning with his throat cut from ear to ear. He had also been deprived of his manhood, a macabre touch if you like."

"And Tomás de la Plata?"

"Gone, señor, vanished from the face of the earth, to

re-appear a month later at the head of twenty or thirty rogues who attacked and robbed a military supply column on its way here. The first of many such acts of lawlessness.''

"And where does he get the men from?'' van Horne asked.

"There are always those dissatisfied after every revolution, as Señor Keogh knows better than anyone from his own country.'' Which was hitting pretty low. "Just as there are always those who will reject any kind of authority if they can. In the area of Mojada, the people enjoy complete freedom from state control. Taxes are not collected for no tax collector can operate. There is no law, no justice because no police officer can live there. They have even rejected the church. Three priests during the past eighteen months. Two murdered and one found wandering in the desert, stripped of his clothes, beaten half to death. Quite out of his mind.''

To my surprise, van Horne made no comment to that one and it was Janos who said, "Are you saying that De la Plata actually uses Mojada as his headquarters with the active support of the people?''

"Let us say he is to be found in that general area most of the time and occasionally in Mojada itself although it is no secret that there are always a few of his followers on view, just to keep the general population in line.''

"So most people up there don't particularly care for him?'' I said.

"They fear him, señor. I have visited the place on three occasions myself. I have quartered troops there for a month at a time and all we meet is a wall of silence.''

"All right, Colonel," van Horne said. "Let's get down to cases. What's all this leading up to?''

"Ten years of war, gentlemen, three million dead, the economy ruined. My country has suffered enough. Now we need stability and quiet, an end to killing. There is no room for men like Tomás de la Plata. The longer he survives the more the disaffected will seek to join him in the mountains and that won't do at all. I want his head."

"And you expect us to get it for you?" van Horne said.

"If you do, señor, you can have your freedom and the contents of a certain Gladstone bag. Señor Janos may have his hotel back, which would have otherwise been confiscated by the state."

"And me?" I said. "What about me?"

He eyed me speculatively and then sighed. "Why you will be free to go to hell in your own way, Señor Keogh."

A thought I hardly found pleasant. Janos made the obvious point. "And what is to prevent us from simply clearing off into the blue, sir, once we leave here? Why go to Mojada at all?"

"Because you have nowhere to go, señores. Not one of you. How far would you get? One hundred miles? Two? And next time there would be no choice. I have not only taken you out of the jaws of death, I have given you a chance of surviving with something in hand. I had thought you all intelligent men, whatever else you are."

Van Horne turned to look at me enquiringly, then Janos. He said, "All right, Colonel, we're in. What's the plan?"

Bonilla showed no emotion at all for, as it soon became clear, the fact that we might refuse had never entered his calculations.

"I told you there was a silver mine on the De la Plata land. For some time now the old man has been trying to interest one mining company after the other in the idea of working the mine again on a partnership basis. He is very short of money.''

''Doesn't Tomás help out?''

''He and his father have never been reconciled although he visits the hacienda frequently to see his sister, Chela. They have always been very close.''

''So what about this mining thing?'' van Horne demanded.

''No one will play because of the unsettled nature of the country. I know this because as all mail for the area passes through Huila, I have been privileged to read the various letters. I decided to take a hand in the game myself the day before yesterday and forwarded a letter to old De la Plata in your name, Señor Janos.''

''Did you, by God,'' Janos exclaimed.

''You will be interested to know that you represent the Herrara Mining Company of Mexico City and will be arriving at Mojada to inspect the property within the next few days, together with your assistant. Your previous experience should prove useful, Mr. Keogh.''

''You think of everything,'' I said.

''I need to, my friend. I have been a soldier a long time. Survival has become something of a habit.''

Van Horne leaned across the desk, helped himself to a cigar from the box at Bonilla's elbow. ''You've left me to the last, Colonel, so it must be good.''

Cordona took a quick, impatient step forward, but Bonilla waved him back, struck a match and gave van Horne a light. ''They need a priest in Mojada very badly, Father. I think you would suit them admirably.''

Van Horne's face was extraordinarily calm. ''Two priests dead and one mad, isn't that the record up there?''

''True, but it does give you an excellent reason for

being there which is highly important. Strangers are usually taken to be government spies and treated accordingly. A priest and two mining experts visiting Don Angel at his own request stand some chance of survival, especially when all three are gringos. As some sort of support in case of need, I am sending Lieutenant Cordona with twenty men to Huanca which is some fifteen miles from Mojada in the foothills of the mountains. We frequently use the abandoned *rancheria* there as a base for patrol activity in the area so his presence will excite no particular comment.

I said, "What about Tomás? When is he supposed to show up?"

"He will know you are in the area within a matter of hours just as he will know the nature of your business with his father. I think we may take it for granted that he will put in an appearance at the hacienda without too much delay to find out for himself what exactly is going on. After all, the possibility of the mine being put to work again is certain to be of more than passing interest to him."

"Why not just send us back out to the stake and have done with it, Colonel," I said. "Mojada is just as certain."

"Hell it is," van Horne cut in. "This way depends on us and no one else. Jesus, boy, didn't you take on the whole bloody British army and beat them at their own game? Well, no bunch of greasy peons with their backsides hanging out is going to put me under the sod. I'll go to Mojada for you, Colonel. I'll even play priest for you again, but anyone who tries to blow my head off will get the hardest sermon of his life. Understand?"

"Perfectly." Bonilla stood up. "I would prefer Tomás de la Plata alive, but will accept him dead as long as you provide me with his corpse. A necessary encour-

agement for the local population." He turned to Janos.
"You may use the Mercedes. It should go well with your
new role and a lift to an impoverished priest with the
same destination would be an act of kindness no one
could quarrel with."

"A real nice thought, Colonel," van Horne said with
some irony. "Anyone can see your heart is in the right
place."

"Lieutenant Cordona will conduct you to more comfortable quarters elsewhere. He will also take care of all
your requirements. I wish you luck, gentlemen." Which
was a reasonably polite way of dismissing us and as he
also sat down and busied himself with some papers, he
made his point pretty thoroughly.

Cordona led the way out through the french windows
into the garden. He dismissed the sergeant and his men,
then carried on without even checking to see whether we
were following him.

On the far side of the garden, a door opened into a
small, quieter courtyard with a covered terrace on three
sides and another fountain splashing across blue and
white tiles in the centre. It was cool and pleasant and
remote and the sounds of life from the town beyond the
wall might have been from another world, which may
have been something of an exaggeration, but the con-
trast between this and what I had been exposed to for
the past few days could not have been greater.

As I discovered later, the rooms which surrounded
the little courtyard were officers' quarters and Cordona
didn't approve. In fact I would say it was all he could do
to contain his rage, especially where van Horne was concerned.

He and I had to share and Janos was in the next room
on his own. They were both identical. Two beds in each
together with the bare essentials of bedroom furniture,

whitewashed walls, the complete absence of any kind of religious images, an indication of the anti-clerical line events were taking at that time.

"There is a bath at the end of the row," Cordona said. "With an orderly in charge. When you are ready, he will see that hot water is brought, also anything else you may require."

"Well now, I'd like a woman myself," van Horne told him. "Not too young. Around thirty, black hair, someone who knows what it's all about."

A deliberate attempt to upset Cordona and nothing more, for in all the time I knew van Horne, one noticeable thing about him was his lack of interest in the opposite sex. It almost worked. Cordona's face went very, very white and his hand dropped to the butt of his revolver and for some stray, perverse reason that made no sense to me, I felt sorry for him.

The moment passed. He took a deep breath. "Clothing and various personal belongings that you may need have been provided and for you, señor," he said to van Horne, "something extra."

The cassock which van Horne had been wearing until our capture lay on the bed, washed and ironed from the look of it, the shovel hat on top. The Gladstone bag was there, too, although it contained, as it turned out, only the Thompson gun and its spare ammunition clips, the money being elsewhere. On the floor was a black steamer trunk which Cordona nudged with his toe.

"We haven't had a priest here for several months. The last one died of blackwater fever. This trunk contains his belongings, particularly the vestments and other things you will need to sustain your role."

"Of which you don't approve, I take it?"

"Señor," Cordona said calmly. "If I had my way, I would see you burn in hell before I even allowed you to open this trunk which belonged to a good and kind man. A man of God who died serving his people."

He turned and walked out abruptly and van Horne stayed exactly where he was, staring out of the door, a strange, set expression on his face and then he laughed and slapped his thigh.

"You know, I expected to be dead by now. Isn't life the strangest damn game you ever did play, Keogh?"

A thought, certainly, and I moved to my bed and discovered not only the Enfield in its shoulder holster, but the two suitcases I had last seen in my room at the Hotel Blanca in Bonita.

Janos said, "Only one thing interests me at the moment, gentlemen. The bath and the copious quantities of hot water mentioned."

"Don't you think we should discuss things first?" I said.

"What in the hell is there to discuss?" van Horne put in. "Anything could happen and probably will when we get to Mojada. They might even shoot us on sight. This kind of game is a lot like poker, Keogh. You play it according to the way the cards fall."

"I couldn't agree more," Janos said. "I should have thought this morning an admirable object lesson on the follies of thinking on the possibilities of tomorrow. But the pleasures of the bath call, gentlemen. I shall see you later."

"You could certainly do with it, fat man," van Horne observed.

The Hungarian produced two feet of steel from inside the black ivory walking stick and had the point nudging van Horne under the chin before he knew what was happening.

"You were jesting, of course, sir." Janos smiled good-humouredly.

Van Horne raised a hand. "That's all I wanted to know, Count whatever-your-name-is."

Janos rammed the sword back into place and chuckled. "By God, sir, but you're a character. I can see we're going to get along."

Someone else he was going to deal famously with. He left, his great frame shaking and van Horne said, "Now there's a man I very definitely would prefer to have for me rather than against me."

He got down on his knees and opened the steamer trunk. The first thing he took out was a cope in faded green that looked as if it had seen many years of service. That was for ordinary use, of course. There was also one in tarnished gold for important feast days and a third in regulation sombre black for requiem mass.

There was a silver chalice carefully wrapped in a piece of old blanket. A ciborium containing the Host, a silver pyx on a chain, holy oils in small silver vials, a thurible, incense. Finally, he discovered a religious image of some sort, very carefully wrapped in several layers of woollen cloth. It was perhaps two feet high and was obviously very old, being carved from wood and hand-painted. It was a remarkable piece of work by any standard and van Horne looked at it for quite some time in silence.

"Who is it?" I said.

"At a guess, I'd say St. Martin de Porres, mainly because he's the only coloured saint I can think of right now. He was illegitimate. The son of an Indian woman and a conquistador. If ever there was a saint for the poor and the downtrodden, I'd say it was he."

Strange how it all came back to me, my boyhood at Knockbree and the scarlet cassock and white cotta of the acolyte that I had hated so much to wear, the horror I felt as my turn approached to serve week-day mass. I was never particularly religious by persuasion and had not been helped by the fact that my grandfather in his old age, and to the great scandal of the country, had forsworn his religion and joined the Plymouth Brethren which made life, as he constantly told me, considerably more comfortable.

But I had long since ceased to believe in any kind of a God of comfort. The only God I had ever known was a God of wrath who brought violence and anger, rage in heaven, not love, and I could manage very well without him.

Van Horne replaced the statue in the trunk, closed the lid slowly and looked up. "It looks as if I'm in business, doesn't it, Keogh?" he said, but he was not smiling.

I had half-an-hour in the tub after Janos, wallowing in the water so hot that it almost took the skin off me, then I made way for van Horne, returned to our room with a towel round my waist and dressed in clean clothes, thanks to the suitcases Bonilla had thoughtfully provided.

I found Janos seated at a large, round table on the shaded terrace on the other side of the courtyard. An Indian orderly danced attendance and the table was loaded with good things. Tortillas, frijoles, a great plate of anchovies, green olives—never a favourite of mine—and sweetcorn cooked in butter. There was also fresh fruit and several bottles of red wine.

Janos ate surprisingly little but drank a great deal and seemed disposed to talk. I had little doubt about my ability to pose as a mining surveyor or engineer and told him so, which appeared to satisfy him. We decided between us that his own role would be that of the non-specialist financier interested merely in the economics of the thing. In other words, a good, solid businessman.

By this time, he was into his second bottle of wine and

had grown considerably more loquacious. "A dangerous enterprise, sir. A dangerous enterprise, but we shall
come through, never fear. Your friend, van Horne, is
obviously a man of parts and you, sir . . . why you remind me of myself when young. Quicksilver."

God knows how I kept myself from laughing out loud
for he leaned across, as serious as you please and said,
"Glands, sir. Glands. Nature's curse since I was thirty-
one years of age. Until then I was as normal as the next
man, a cavalry officer of distinction, bearer of an ancient name and now—all gone. All gone." He snorted
like an old bull and to my amazement there were tears in
his eyes and then his chin dropped to his chest and he
started to snore.

I left him to it, lit a cigarette and went for a walk. The
garden outside Bonilla's quarters was deserted and so
was the main courtyard where the morning executions,
fake or otherwise, had taken place.

I wandered across to the stake to which I had been
strapped, examined the bullet-scarred wall behind and
wondered, and not for the first time, what life was all
about. Certainly an affair over which few human beings
had any kind of control.

I turned and sauntered towards the main gates which
were great, iron-barred affairs, now closed, through
which I could see into the street beyond. It was only as I
got close that I realised a soldier leaned negligently on
his rifle in the sentry post which had been hollowed out
of the thickness of the wall in the archway. He opened
half-closed eyes, blinked as I approached and straightened warily. I nodded, bade him good evening and
peered out through the bars casually.

The street was deserted except for two Indians sitting
against the wall of an adobe house opposite. The man
wore rawhide leggings and a red flannel shirt, his shoul-

der-length hair bound with a band of the same material.
He cradled an old Winchester repeating rifle in his lap.

The woman had hair as black as any raven's wing, a
dark curtain to her shoulders, a scarlet band around her
head. Her shirt, heavily embroidered with Indian-work,
was also of scarlet and the belt at her waist was of hand-
beaten silver. A black skirt fell to just below her knee
and as she stood up, I saw that she wore boots of un-
tanned leather underneath.

She ran across the street, reached in through the bars
and grabbed for my hands. It took me several seconds
to realise that this proud, barbaric little beauty was Victoria Balbuena.

I held on tight, aware of emotions I couldn't explain
even to myself as I looked down into her face, the eyes
that tried to speak for the voice that could not.

"It's all right," I said. "I'm fine. There's nothing to
worry about."

The sentry had me out of the way with a quick unexpected shove and drove the butt of his rifle at those
small, brown hands in a blow of such savagery that any
kind of contact would have crippled her.

She got her hands out through the bars just in time
and, as the rifle butt rang against the iron, I had him by
the throat and started to squeeze, a black rage in me so
strong I was close to ending him.

There was a certain amount of confused shouting. I
was aware of the Indian with the white hair at her
shoulder, the lever of the Winchester clicking as he put a
round into the breech and then van Horne was somehow
between me and the sentry forcing us apart.

The sentry ended up back against the wall on one
knee and started to raise his rifle and Cordona arrived
on the run to kick it from his grasp. The unfortunate

sentry tried to stand and went down again, the lieutenant's fist in his mouth.

I helped the poor devil to his feet, propping him against the wall, but when I turned, Victoria and her companion had disappeared.

"Where did she go?" I grabbed at the bars. "Did you see who it was?"

Van Horne nodded. "I told you about Yaquis, boy. She's reverted to type. Gone back to her own kind."

Cordona nodded. "The man she was with, Nachita, he is an elder of the Wind River Yaqui, her mother's tribe. Twice a year he comes to Huila, leading a pack train over the mountain. Only the Yaqui dare do such work these days."

"But what was she doing with him? Why was she dressed like that?"

"He noticed her sitting outside the gate here the other day, recognised the Yaqui blood and questioned her. To these people, family ties are all important and he and the girl are of the same blood. Her mother was his cousin. I questioned him closely on this yesterday."

So, she had found her own people after all in spite of events. I said slowly, "Will she be all right?"

"To these people, descent is through the mother so the girl is considered wholly Yaqui and her mother's father was clan chief, which makes her a person of much status. Very important in every way. They will be honoured to have her back amongst them. Believe me I know these people. This man, Nachita, and his men would have the eyes of any man who even looked at her in the wrong way."

"Like I told you, Keogh," van Horne said. "Yaqui are worse than Apache."

But I turned and walked quickly away, aware of the strange, illogical hurt in me. It made no kind of sense—

none at all. When I stretched out on my bed and closed my eyes, her face rose to haunt me. Not beautiful, yet more beautiful than any I had known in my life before.

I slept for three or four hours, waking just before ten o'clock according to an old tin alarm clock at the side of the bed.

There was no sign of van Horne, but when I opened the door and looked out into the courtyard, I saw that he and Janos were sitting at the table on the other side playing cards in the diffused lemon glow of an oil lamp.

I felt restless and slightly depressed and certainly not at all in the mood for company, so I skirted the edge of the courtyard, keeping to the shadows and went into the garden.

There was no sign of Bonilla and his quarters were in darkness so I had the place to myself. The air was fresh after the heat of the day, a slight wind blowing the fountain in a silver spray and a nearly-full moon was hooked into a cypress tree, black against a curtain of stars.

It was very peaceful and beyond the wall in the town, a guitar played and someone sang softly. Picture-book Mexico, just the stuff for the tourists. The breeze ruffled the cypress trees again and something moved with it, a dark wraith that had an arm round my throat like magic, a knife blade gleaming dully before my eyes.

The voice was like dry leaves whispering through a forest in the evening. "You will be sensible now, señor, for there is nothing to fear."

Victoria Balbuena stepped out of the shadows. The arm was removed from my throat and she put out her hands to grasp mine. She smiled and it was a smile to turn the night over.

She started to pull me into the shadows and I restrained her. "Hold hard, there, where are we going?"

The eyes were eloquent, but it was Nachita who spoke for her. "We will go now, señor, leave Huila tonight. By dawn we will already be into the mountains and in that country, no *federale* known to man can catch a Yaqui. In four days you will be safe in the Wind River country."

"Buy why?" I said.

"Because my lady wishes it."

It was the nearest he could come to expressing her status in Spanish and certainly seemed to indicate that Cordona had known what he was talking about.

I held Victoria's hands very lightly and shook my head. "It isn't possible."

Nachita said, "This morning you faced death at the stake, señor, tonight you live. This is an interesting turn of events."

He had a remarkable face and I think it was then that I really noticed him for the first time, directly confronting him as it were. Straight-nosed, thin-lipped with pale brown skin. Full of strength, intelligence and calm pride. I was even more impressed when I discovered later that he was seventy-two years of age.

I said, "Three lives for one. Colonel Bonilla gave me and my two comrades ours in exchange for that of a man named Tomás de la Plata."

He said calmly, "But De Plata still lives, señor, all men know this."

"We're going to Mojada tomorrow to try to remedy that."

"Then you go to a bad end," he said simply.

Victoria had me in a grip like iron. I leaned close and said deliberately, "There is honour in this. Van Horne saved us both at Tacho's, you as well as me. Should I desert him now?"

God alone knows why I came up with that one, but

she took it seriously and nodded, her hands going slack in mine. I reached out to touch her cheek, she turned her face sideways and kissed the palm of my hand. About her neck she was wearing a round silver amulet of Indian workmanship on the end of a plaited leather thong. With a sudden, quick gesture, she took it off, pulled it over my head and down around my neck, then reached up, kissed me in a thoroughly European way, turned and disappeared into the darkness.

Nachita said, "I know Mojada, señor, it is an unfilled grave. Think again."

"It is another step along the way, my friend," I told him. "I never go back to anything. Look after her."

He vanished, melted in the shadows as if he had never been and I stood there, fingering the silver amulet, quite unaware of its significance, a great sadness on me as if now, at last, I was at the final bitter end of things and had nothing.

SEVEN

WE LEFT AT six o'clock on as grey and dreary a morning as you could wish for. A bad omen or perhaps that was just the Celt in me. Van Horne, who had been busy with the cards and wine until the small hours, looked about a hundred years old, although Janos seemed much the same.

Cordona was there to see us off, the boots and uniform absolute perfection, every inch the soldier, even at that time in the morning. He told us he would be leaving with his patrol for the *ranchería* at Huanca later in the day and wished us luck in his usual tight, reserved way. It was obvious that he never expected to see us alive again, which was a cheerful thought on which to depart.

I drove and van Horne sat beside me leaving the rear seat to Janos, who took up space for two men anyway. The streets were quite deserted as we drove through Huila and beyond, the road, if road you could call it, vanished into the gray morning in the general direction of the Sierra Madre.

There was a heavy ground mist that made it difficult to see for more than a few yards in any direction although it varied greatly in intensity. About five miles out of Huila, it cleared a little and I caught a glimpse of something moving up ahead, a flash of scarlet.

As we approached, I saw that it was a pack train of a dozen or more heavily laden mules. The Yaqui, Nachita, guarding the rear, the old Winchester in his right hand, the butt against his thigh. There were three other Indians strung out along the train, hard, danger-ous-looking men in head bands and red flannel shirts like a uniform, armed to the teeth and ready to take on the world.

Victoria Balbuena rode at the head of the procession, dressed exactly as when I had last seen her in the garden with the addition of a cloak of some kind of animal fur which hung from around her shoulders against the cold.

I drove past very slowly and Nachita raised the Win-chester a foot or so as if in greeting, but Victoria stared straight ahead into the morning, giving no sign, a fierce little queen ignoring the commoners.

At least it brought van Horne to life. "Well, I'll be damned," he said. "I said she'd reverted to type, but this is ridiculous."

About fifty yards further on I pulled into the side of the road and switched off the engine. "Now what are you playing at?" he demanded.

I ignored him, jumped out and ran back into the mist. There was an ornamental bell around the neck of her horse. I heard that first and then she seemed to float into view.

She showed no surprise, no emotion at all to find me standing there. The man closest to her urged his mount forward and Nachita called to him sharply in his own language. Victoria kept on moving, staring straight ahead and I took hold of her stirrup leather and walked beside her. When we reached the Mercedes, I released my grip and she kept on going, still without a glance.

The pack train, Nachita bringing up the rear, vanished into the mist. Janos said, "What was that all about?"

I climbed back behind the wheel. As I leaned forward, the silver amulet she had given me swung free and van Horne reached out to examine it.

"She gave you that?"

"And what if she did?"

He laughed harshly. "Let me tell you about the Yaqui, boy. Some of their clans put the womenfolk first. Why it's even the woman who chooses the man. Each girl-child at birth is given the symbol of her sex and power by her mother in the form of a silver amulet. When a girl wants a husband, she simply puts her amulet on him. When she wants a divorce, she takes it back."

For some reason, the whole thing seemed to strike him as extremely humourous. "Damn me, Keogh, but you've just been to the altar and didn't know it."

He laughed so hard I thought it likely he might do himself an injury and Janos joined in. Strange, but I saw nothing funny about the business at all.

"So what?" I said. "I'll likely be dead meat in a day or two. We all will."

Which wiped the smile from both faces very effectively, and I drove away.

Within another hour, the grey skies had lifted, the mist dispersed and the sun was climbing high into the heavens. The semi-desert plain we drove through was a dun-coloured haze rising into the mountains, the canyons dark with shadow.

If ever there was country not intended for the automobile it was this and, although the Mercedes was

built like a tank and could obviously stand a great deal
of punishment, there seemed no point in asking for
trouble, so I drove with extreme caution for most of the
way. Indeed there were occasions, especially as we
started to climb into the mountains, when it was necessary to get out and clear particularly large rocks out of
the way.

Naturally, Janos was of no help at all in this kind of
situation and he sat in the rear seat, smoking a cigar and
commiserating with us loudly. Amazingly, van Horne
took this quite well. In fact he grew progressively more
cheerful as the morning drew on.

About ten miles out of Mojada, we stopped and had
what amounted to a picnic for food had been provided
in a basket carrier. Cold meat, anchovies, olives and
fresh bread and a couple of bottles of red wine.

It was all rather gay and Janos toasted the general
direction of Mojada, glass raised. "We who are about
to die, salute thee."

"Fine sentiments, but not for me," van Horne said.
"What about you, Keogh?"

"It comes as God wills," I shrugged. "Isn't that what
the bull fighters say just before they go into the plaza?"

It touched something deep inside him, I realise that
now looking back on it all, for I think the change was
already working in him although it is difficult to say in
life where anything begins or ends. Certainly the good
humour left him and there was a strange, bleak look on
his face as he stood and looked up into the mountains.

"It's a thought, Keogh, a hell of a thought." He
shivered quite distinctly and forced a smile. "Strange
how cold the wind can be, even in the sun."

And there was no wind blowing.

There were horsemen in the hills as we moved closer to

Mojada. Janos drew my attention to them, but they were far, far above us and it was impossible to see who they were. They kept pace and only dropped out of sight completely when we came over the final rise in the trail and looked down at Mojada in the hollow below.

It was little more than a village, surrounded by a crumbling adobe wall perhaps fifteen feet high, a relic of the days when there had been a constant threat from Indians. Access was gained through an arched gateway and inside, there were thirty or forty adobe *casas*, a small crumbling church with a bell tower that looked as if it had once been whitewashed and what looked like the hotel Cordona had mentioned, if hotel one could call it in such a place.

I negotiated a flock of sheep on the way down, the three old men in charge staring at us in amazement and moved in through the gateway in the wall. Once inside, we were besieged by a dozen or so ragged and barefoot children who ran at the tail of the car. Janos threw a little loose change to scatter them as I pulled up outside the hotel. It was a poor sort of place, the façade crumbling, eroding a little bit more day-by-day in the heat and no one doing anything about it. A board sign over the door said CASA MOJADA.

I got out and opened the rear door for Janos. The children stood in a silent half-circle at a respectable distance, only moving away with considerable reluctance at the urging of four or five women who had appeared from nearby houses.

There were three or four men squatting in the shade of the hotel porch, backs against the wall. Typical peons, poorly clothed and with the weary, lined faces of the prematurely old. Men who had worked like dogs since childhood to keep body and soul together. They had started with nothing and would end the same way.

Inside it was cool and dark. The floor was stone-flagged, there were two or three tables and chairs and a bar counter with a neatly scrubbed top, bottles ranged behind it. There wasn't a customer in sight and no one to serve either. Janos hammered on the counter with his stick, then slumped into a chair, the sweat already pouring from his face again.

There was a sudden, startled gasp. I swung round and found a woman standing in an open doorway to the left of the bar. She was perhaps forty years of age and looked frightened out of her wits at the sight of us. The most significant thing about her was that she was pregnant and at that stage when she could expect the child at any time or I had wasted four years medical training.

A man appeared behind her pulling on a jacket, tall and thin, middle-aged, hair iron-grey as was the large moustache he wore. He muttered something to the woman, pushed her back through the door and came forward.

"At your orders, señores."

"And who might you be?" Janos demanded.

"Rafael Moreno, señor, I run the hotel. I am also mayor of Mojada."

"Is that so." Janos wiped sweat from his face. "My names is Janos and this is my associate, Señor Keogh. We are here at Don Angel de la Plata's invitation to inspect his mine." Moreno didn't seem to be able to think of anything to say and Janos added sharply, "We shall require accommodation, man, don't you understand? Two rooms."

At that moment van Horne came in through the door and the look of shock and amazement on Moreno's face had to be seen to be believed. He took an involuntary step backwards and crossed himself briefly.

"This good man, Father von Horne, begged a lift of

me when he heard my destination in Huila," Janos told him. "You will perhaps be good enough to direct him to the priest's house."

"The priest's house?" Moreno looked at him in stupefaction. "But there is no priest's house, señor. We do not have a priest in Mojada."

"But you do now, my son," van Horne said with surprising gentleness. "You have a church. Now you have a priest again."

A look of genuine horror appeared on Moreno's face. "We have no priest, Father, it is not permitted." He flung out his arms wildly. "There are no rooms available. The hotel is full, do you understand? You must go away, all of you. And you, Father," he said to van Horne, "you most of all." Then he quite simply walked out, closing the door behind him.

There was a reasonably heavy silence. I went behind the bar, found three glasses and filled them with beer from a stone jug cooling in a bucket of water.

"I should have thought he'd have been warned we were coming," I said.

"Or should have been." Van Horne drank a little of his beer and nodded. "That's more like it. There's a game of sorts being played here."

"Then what, may I ask, is our next move?" Janos said.

"The obvious one under the circumstances. We all play our parts. You two deliver me to the church with my belongings, the courteous thing to do, then you drive out to the hacienda and see Don Angel with your tale of woe. He'll probably offer to put you up."

"Which leaves you on your own," I said.

He smiled gravely and raised his left hand and I saw that he was holding the Gladstone bag. "Not as long as I've got this," he said. "Now let's get moving."

• • •

When we went into the porch at the front of the church the smell of dirt and decay was immediately apparent. The door stood open for the simple reason that the lock had been smashed. Van Horne pushed it back with his boot and led the way in.

The place was a shambles. Wooden benches over-turned and smashed, obscene words scrawled in charcoal on the whitewashed walls. There were piles of excrement everywhere and not only the canine variety. Humans had been here also. Even the altar, a plain block of grey stone that looked very ancient had not been missed. As obscene a version of the sexual act as I have ever seen had been chalked on the front.

Van Horne stood looking at it for quite some time, then put out a hand and touched the top of the altar gently. "The poor ignorant fools," he said. "I wonder if they knew what they were doing? The whole place will have to be re-consecrated after this."

He opened a door to one side and led the way into what was obviously the vestry. There was a desk and an old wardrobe, even a narrow iron cot in the corner, although the mattress looked as if it could give one just about every disease known to man.

Van Horne said, "This will do me. Help me in with my trunk, then get started on your end of things."

We brought it in between us and put it down in a corner of the room. I said, "Do you know what you're doing?"

"I usually do. I'll use the blankets from the car and beg a mattress and a lamp from Moreno. He'll hardly refuse me that much."

He seemed abstracted, his eyes moving restlessly about the tiny church, the great hands clenching and unclenching nervously. I glanced enquiringly at Janos who shrugged and we left him to it and went outside.

"He is taking his part seriously, our friend," Janos observed as he climbed into the rear of the Mercedes.

"You think so?" I shrugged. "Oh, I don't know. It's bad enough, what's been done to the place, in all conscience. I wasn't exactly laughing out loud myself."

But I didn't really believe that, not for one moment for I had seen the look on van Horne's face at the desecration of the altar. A kind of agony had showed there for a moment, and his voice had changed again, perhaps the most significant thing of all.

The hacienda was three miles on the other side of Mojada according to the map, and yet we came to the beginning of the land area within a mile, a great archway across a side road with a coat of arms and the name De la Plata carved into the stone.

I drove on through a rolling plain of tawny grassland with here and there, cows bunched together in small groups, usually in the shade of a thicket of cottonwoods.

A mile beyond the archway a shot sounded on the warm air and three horsemen galloped out of a fold in the ground parallel to the dirt road we were following. I kept right on going and the leader levelled a rifle across his left arm and fired again, raising dust no more than a couple of yards in front of us. I did the sensible thing and braked to a halt.

"If you are interested, I obtained a revolver from Cordona before leaving and my ability to shoot straight is one thing my glands haven't altered in the slightest," Janos said calmly as they approached.

"We'll see," I said. "Try laying down the law first."

They were all dressed as working vaqueros in straw sombreros and rawhide leggings, but the one who ap-

peared to be in charge, the man with the rifle, was cast
in his own mould. He was about the size of van Horne
with a hard, brutal face and the largest hands I have
ever seen on any man.

"What do you think you're playing at?" Janos
roared.

"This is private land," the other told him in a voice
roughened by a great many years of disease and liquor.

"I am here at the express invitation of the owner of
this property, Don Angel de la Plata," Janos said
crisply.

"You are a bad liar, señor, for I am Raúl Jurado,
foreman to Don Angel and would be the first to be informed of such a visit."

He raised his left arm bringing the muzzle of his rifle
up. My fingers were already touching the butt of the Enfield, but there was no need. Janos said, "You will notice that my hand is inside my coat pocket, my friend,
where it holds a loaded revolver. You are a large man
and at this range I would have considerable difficulty in
missing you."

The barrel of the rifle didn't even flicker and Jurado's
face might have been carved from stone. I don't know
how it would have gone, but the situation was solved for
us by a new arrival.

A voice called, "Jurado, you fool, what are you
doing?"

A young woman cantered over the rise and came
towards us. She was booted and spurred like a man,
wore Spanish riding breeches in black leather, a white
silk shirt open at the neck and a Cordoban hat tilted forward to shade the pale, oval face from the sun.

"What's going on here?" she demanded and struck at
the barrel of Jurado's rifle, knocking it askew.

"Strangers," he said gruffly. "Trespassers."

"Señora, allow me to introduce myself and my companion." Janos stood up and managed a slight bow. He had style, whatever else you could say about him. "My name is Paul Janos representing the Herrara Mining Company and this is Señor Emmet Keogh, a mining engineer. I am here at the express invitation of Don Angel de la Plata and yet for some obscure reason, this man chose to fire on us."

The girl's face was suddenly contorted with rage, her arm swept up and the leather thong at the end of her riding whip slashed across Jurado's face.

"Animal!" she cried. "What are you trying to do?"

He got an arm up to defend himself. "I had my orders, señorita."

"Orders?" she spat the word out as if she didn't like the taste. "I give the orders here, not my brother. Now get out of my sight and take my horse with you."

She swung to the ground and flung the reins at him in a single swift movement. For a moment, I thought he would argue and then his hand went to the brim of his sombrero and he turned and cantered away, taking her horse with him, his companions following behind.

The girl removed her hat and I realised at once that she was older than she had at first appeared. At least thirty, with a skin so pale that it was almost translucent and great, dark eyes that seemed to contain all the tragedy in the world.

"Chela de la Plata at your orders, señores," she said. "If you will permit me to ride with you, I will guide you to my father's house."

There was a whole complex of stabling and outbuildings of one sort or another, most of which looked to be in a general state of decay. The hacienda itself lay beyond them, a line of cypress trees behind it. It was built in the old colonial style in weathered brown stone, single storeyed and collonaded at the front.

When I stopped the Mercedes at the foot of the broad flight of stone steps, the first thing I noticed were the bullet scars in the pillars and the wall beyond. There had been hard fighting here at one time, so much was evident.

We followed Chela de la Plata up the steps and entered a cool, dark entrance hall with the heads of several bulls mounted on the walls. The great oaken door she opened on the left could also boast a bullet scar or two, but the room was truly delightful. Heavy, eighteenth-century Spanish furniture in black oak, a floor of polished pine with here and there a bright splash of colour from an Indian rug and a great stone fireplace which at the moment contained no fire.

"I will bring my father to you, señores. Please wait here," she said and went out.

"They must have lived in style at one time," Janos said and he sank into a tapestry-covered armchair and looked about him admiringly.

I went to the great window at the far end and looked out. Beyond, there was a garden surrounded by stone walls. Once it must have been quite spectacular, but now it was greatly decayed. One of the saddest things in the world, a garden in decline.

The door clicked open and Chela entered pushing a wheel chair. The occupant was a frail, sick-looking man with grey hair so long that it almost reached his shoulders. The face bore no resemblance to hers at all for it was long and rather bony with moist brown eyes that seemed to look out at the world in wonder and dismay. He had a rug around his legs and looked, not to put too fine a point on it, not long for this world.

"My father, Don Angel de la Plata, señores."

He extended a limp hand to Janos. "Señor Janos? I cannot tell you how delighted I was to receive your letter. Delighted. Everything is ready for you. I have had men working at the mine for some weeks now. Some weeks. I am certain you will find things more than satisfactory."

He rambled on in this fashion pausing barely long enough to allow Janos to introduce me and repeated himself constantly, delivering all this in a sharp, querulous old woman's voice that didn't sound healthy at all.

She managed to stop him long enough to make the point that a meal was about to be served in another room. I pushed the wheel chair for her and she led the way out into the hall and through to the rear of the building where a table had been set on a terrace overlooking the overgrown garden.

We were served by two Indian women with dark sullen faces who never said a word, but appeared and disappeared as required.

There was claret in what I can only describe as quantity, tumblers of the stuff, not wineglasses. Each time mine was empty, one of the Indian women filled it again. The food was plain and wholesome and in immense quantities. Typical back country ranch fare. Frijoles with plenty of chile. Fried steaks that were as big as the plate and the finest goat's cheese I have ever tasted. The old man plucked at his food and ate nothing. In fact he even managed to stop speaking, leaving the girl to carry the conversation alone.

"You had a reasonable trip from Huila?" she enquired.

"Quite excellent," Janos told her. "Of course, the automobile makes a great difference. The priest was most impressed, was he not, Keogh?"

"Priest?" she said blankly.

"We found him in Huila trying to arrange transport
to Mojada. A Father van Horne, an American. He has
been assigned to this parish, I understand. We left him
at the church which was, I must say, in a remarkable
state."

"Yes, it would be." She was frowning deeply.
"Señor, I would like very much to accompany you back
to Mojada to speak with this man. Do you mind?"

"Our pleasure, señorita." He coughed. "There is,
however, just one slight snag. We were told at the hotel
that it would be impossible to accommodate us."

She said calmly, "I will speak to Moreno, the proprietor, there will be no difficulty."

"And when do we get to see the mine, señorita?" I
asked.

"I think perhaps in the morning if that would suit
you. It is about three miles from here. I would think it
impossible for your automobile to negotiate the track,
but if you would not mind a buckboard, señor?" she
said to Janos.

He bowed slightly. "At your service, señorita. There
is just one thing."

"And that is?"

He cleared his throat awkwardly, giving what I had to
admit was a most excellent performance. "To be frank
with you, señorita, I was approached by the military
governor for the area in Huila, a Colonel Bonilla, and
advised against coming. He seemed to think my associate and I would be in danger of our lives."

"There is no such danger," she said tonelessly.
"Colonel Bonilla is not in full possession of the facts."

"Señorita," he said patiently. "You must excuse me
for pressing the point, but it was suggested to me that

your brother, who is, I understand, unfortunately at odds with the authorities, might interfere in our business."

"I am in charge here, señor, in my father's name." She stood up. "My brother holds no sway here. I will return directly and we can then leave if this is convenient to you."

She went out and I glanced enquiringly at Janos. He shook his head slightly and proceeded to light a cigar.

The old man, who had been sitting in silence for so long, glanced up suddenly, glared malevolently at both of us and shrieked, "Who are you? What are you doing here?"

We both stood up slowly and, behind us, the door opened and Chela de la Plata returned. The old man started to swear monotonously and with considerable obscenity. She held the door wide for us and we walked out.

We left her to it and went out to the Mercedes. As I handed Janos into the rear seat, he said out of the side of his mouth, a fixed smile on his face, "And why didn't Bonilla mention that little item?"

Exactly what I had been thinking myself, but we were prevented from continuing the conversation by the arrival of Chela, still dressed for riding.

She got into the front passenger seat and smiled brightly. "When you are ready, señor."

Just like that without even an attempt at an explanation but as I drove away it was Bonilla I was thinking about and his obviously deliberated omission of the important point that Don Angel de la Plata was as mad as a hatter. Now why was that?

EIGHT

SMOKE DRIFTED INTO the late afternoon air in a dense cloud as we approached the village.

"Something seems to be burning," Janos said calmly. "I hope it isn't the church."

Chela de la Plata said in a low, desperate voice, "Hurry, señor, I implore you."

But the church was still standing as we went over the rise and got a clear look at the village below and the smoke seemed to be coming from the other side of the bell tower.

Thirty or forty people were standing in a wide semi-circle, silently watching as we drew up. There was a splintering crash from inside the church and van Horne emerged from the porch. He was stripped to the waist and carried a couple of planks on his shoulder.

"Spring cleaning, Father?" I called as we approached.

He grinned. "Something like that."

I followed him round to the rear of the building and discovered a sizable fire. He hurled the planks into the centre of it and turned.

"I've salvaged what I could. Some of the benches are still intact. What the place will need after this is a damn good scrub and a coat of whitewash."

"You look as if you're enjoying yourself." He ignored the remark and I added quickly, "I'll give you the story on De la Plata later. We've got his daughter with us."

He looked beyond my shoulder and smiled. "Good afternoon, señorita."

When I turned she was standing a short distance away watching. Janos shuffled forward, leaning heavily on his walking stick. "Hot work, Father. Allow me to introduce Señorita de la Plata. Señorita, this is Father van Horne, whom we brought from Huila with us."

Chela de la Plata came forward with a rush, ignoring me completely, directly confronting van Horne. Her face was very white now, the eyes like great dark holes. "You cannot stay here, Father, you must not. They must surely have warned you."

"Of a great many things, señorita." He smiled gently. "My place is here, now, it can be no other way. You must surely realise that."

"They murder priests here, Father," she cried violently. "They will see no reason to treat you differently and I am in this thing. I am involved without wishing to be, have no choice in the matter. And I am tired, Father, tired of the burden of it."

Van Horne responded to the undoubted agony in her voice in a quite astonishing way. He took one of her hands gently in his and smoothed the hair back from her brow with the other. His face was grave, his voice firm and kind.

"This is not on you, child, this business. Not any of it. Do you understand me?"

She gazed up at him in wonderment and then tightened her grip on his hand so much that her knuckles whitened. She closed her eyes momentarily and a great, shuddering sigh slipped from her mouth.

When she opened her eyes again, much of the strain seemed to have left her face. "They will not help you, Father, they have much fear."

"I know."

"Of my brother," she said flatly. "Who hates all things that live."

He smiled and gently disengaged her hand. "Go with God now, señorita. I have work to do. Perhaps when things are more in order here you will come and see me again?"

She walked away back towards the car. I looked at van Horne with a frown, but he ignored me, picked up a plank and put it on the fire. By now he had completely lost me and I turned and went back to the Mercedes. Chela de la Plata ran past me, back to van Horne and I helped Janos into the rear seat of the car and put a foot on the running board.

"What do you think?" I asked him.

"A remarkable performance. I think he almost believed it himself."

"But what if he did, or at least, began to?"

Janos chuckled hoarsely. "By God, sir, that would be ironic."

Something of an understatement, but I was unable to take it further for Chela returned at that precise moment, van Horne at her side.

"I have asked Father van Horne to visit the hacienda tomorrow," she said. "I should like him to meet my father. Perhaps you gentlemen would be good enough to bring him with you?"

"A pleasure to serve you, señorita," Janos said. "This must have been a pleasant little church once."

"Over two hundred years old," she said. "Dedicated originally to the Blessed Martin de Porres. He was always greatly reverenced in these parts. He had an Indian mother, you know."

"So I believe," I said. "Father van Horne was telling us about him only yesterday. In fact he has a rather interesting image of the saint in his possession."

Van Horne was frowning, for some reason that at the time I did not fully comprehend, although I realise now that he must have seen more than coincidence in the turn events had taken. "This church is dedicated to St. Martin de Porres?"

"But surely you must have known that, Father?" She appeared to hesitate. "This image you have with you. Could I see it?"

"But of course." He glanced at us, taking her by the arm. "If you gentlemen wouldn't mind waiting?"

They went inside and Janos said, "Now what do you make of that?"

"I know one thing," I told him. "She's well and truly hooked."

"Precisely, which cannot but be to our advantage. He has a way with him, our friend."

"He'll have her confessing to him next."

He paused in the act of slicing the end off a cigar with a small silver penknife. "And this offends you?"

"Shouldn't it?"

"He came here to play a part. You now appear to be jibing at the fact that he's playing it so well."

Which was fair enough and yet the strange, illogical coldness that I felt in the pit of my stomach would not go away, for I had a feeling that events were already

taking a completely different course from any considered by us at the beginning of things.

When they emerged into the sunlight again, van
Horne looked serious and grave and Chela de la Plata,
very pale. He put a hand on her shoulder and blessed
her, then went back inside.

"You found the image pleasing, señorita?" Janos enquired as we drove away.

But she didn't answer him, had not even heard as far
as I could judge, and stared straight ahead of her into
space, seeing only that which was locked fast in the
secret mind of her.

When we reached the hotel, she seemed to have re-
covered herself and went up the steps briskly, her spurs
jangling. Moreno was behind the bar cleaning glasses
and came round to greet her rather uncertainly, drying
his hands on a cloth.

"At your orders, señorita."

"These gentlemen are here on my father's business,
Rafael. Two days, perhaps three. Your best rooms will
be sufficient."

There was the same look of horror on his face as
when he had first seen van Horne. "But señorita," he
whispered, "how can I do this thing. It is not permitted."

"Tell me, my friend," she said coldly. "Who owns
this place?"

"Why, your father, señorita."

"Then your choice is simple. Either you do as I say or
I will have you on the street, bag and baggage. You
would like this?"

He fluttered helplessly, a fly in the web. "My wife, as
the señorita knows, is in no condition . . ."

"Exactly." There was a ruthless streak in this one a mile wide. "My decision, not yours, Rafael. No harm will come to you."

He collapsed completely. "Very well, señorita, on your head be it."

She turned, a slight, pale smile of triumph on her face. I think that was the first time that it occurred to me that she and her brother must be alike in a great many ways.

We left our baggage for Moreno to take up to the rooms, but didn't bother to inspect them for there was Chela de la Plata to be taken back to the hacienda.

For most of the way, she said absolutely nothing and then, with about half a mile to go, she said suddenly, "You may find the mine rather primitive by your standards, Señor Keogh. It is many years since it was properly worked. I trust you will make allowances."

"As long as there is silver there in economic quantities, señorita, that is the only important thing. Equipment is something we can always bring in."

"Of course." She leaned back in the seat and said, with an abrupt change of course, "Father van Horne is a remarkable man, don't you agree?"

"I'm afraid I don't know him well enough to make that kind of judgement. But he looks the kind of man who could survive most things."

"As do you, señor." She touched the silver amulet around my neck briefly. "A strange thing for a man like you to wear. May I ask where you acquired it?"

"A gift," I said. "From a good friend."

Her eyebrows went up, she seemed to withdraw from me if I can put it so, but in this they were all the same, pure blood or mestizo, they despised the Indian. In

some way, I suppose, she looked upon me as contaminated.

"Did I detect a sudden frost?" Janos enquired as I
took the Mercedes back along the track.

I turned, touching the amulet briefly. "My impression is that I've let the side down."

"I'm afraid so," he said. "In Texas or Arizona they
would call you squaw man and ride you out of town on
a rail, one of the more civilized contributions that great
nation has made to Western culture. Would you enjoy
living in the Wind River country, Keogh?"

"I can't say, never having been there."

"I have visited the fringes only when I first came to
this country. It is not like your Ireland, I assure you. A
savage, sterile place. A nightmare landscape of mesas
and buttes, lava beds and twisted forests of stone. Life
there would be a struggle most days of the week."

"It sounds interesting," I said, humouring him.

"The Apache are known as the enemy of all men," he
said. "Yet they fear the Yaqui. For over four hundred
years, since Spain first claimed these lands, they have
fought the invader and with considerable success, I
might add. For many years the government, in despair,
attempted a policy of extermination. A cruel and barbaric people, Keogh. They mutilate the bodies of their
enemies."

"I've seen men maimed just as effectively with a Mills
bomb." I rammed my foot hard down on the brake as a
horseman cantered over a rise to the left and reined in
his mount in the middle of the road.

I knew who he was instantly for there was no one else
it could be. He sat there, slim and erect in the saddle,
black jacket and tight-fitting black trousers, not a silver
button in sight to relieve his sombre appearance. The

face beneath the black sombrero was the face of a
ravaged saint, an Anthony burned through to the bone
by the heat of the wilderness. The pale blue eyes were
quite empty. No love, no cruelty either. Nothing.

He said calmly, "Tomás de la Plata at your orders,
gentlemen."

"At yours, señor," Janos gave him back. "My name
is . . ."

"I know who you are, just as I know why you are
here. This dream of my father's, an old man's foolishness, is this not so?"

On first sight he was not armed, but as he leaned forward slightly, I saw that he carried a revolver in a strap
under his left arm.

I said, "How can we know this until we've had a
chance of inspecting the mine?"

He nodded slowly and sat there silently staring into
space, his face calm as if waiting for something. On the
face of it, I would never have a better chance of killing
him. He was mine for the taking. Above us on the hill,
birds lifted in alarm from the shelter of the cottonwoods.

It had happened once before, just like this, outside a
village in County Clare, just after the start of the Civil
War. A damned rogue of a tinker leading us in and he
playing both sides against the middle. The rooks calling
angrily as they drifted up out of the beech trees at the
side of the road should have warned me, but by then it
was too late and a heavy machine gun cut down every
man in the first Crossley tender.

We learn by our mistakes. I said politely, "Your sister
has invited us to inspect the mine in the morning,
señor."

He said abruptly, "Two days, no more, then you go

and I see your report before she does. Do you understand?"

He raised his hand and half-a-dozen riders emerged from the cottonwoods, each man carrying a rifle. They milled around the Mercedes, an unsavoury looking group, mostly dressed like working vaqueros, but all heavily armed.

"This priest you brought with you," Tomás de la Plata said. "He goes back with you when you leave and only because I am in a good humour. Tell him this from me and in the meantime, he approaches the people of Mojada at his peril. No services, no religious propaganda of any kind. I will not have it here."

Janos cleared his throat. "We are not his keepers, señor."

"You would perhaps prefer to be his mourners?" He smiled gently. "There is no choice for this man, señores. There never was. If he stays, he dies."

He put spurs to his horse and galloped away followed by his men. Janos sighed heavily. "For a while there I thought you might try to take him. If you had, we would both have been meat for the crows by now. You knew they were there?"

"They shouldn't have disturbed the birds," I said.

He chuckled. "By God, sir, but you know your business, I can see that."

As I drove away, I could feel the sweat soaking through my shirt and jacket and my hands were trembling.

I left Janos at the Casa Mojada to settle in and strolled through the streets, smoking a cigarette and greeting whoever I saw, although not one single person gave me as much as a good evening in reply.

These were poor people, leading lives as wretched as any lived before the Revolution and their condition made its ideals laughable. Truly, nothing in this life ever did change. What was virtually an open sewer ran down the centre of one street, little children playing listlessly in an atmosphere where the stench of urine and human dirt touched everything.

It ran into a small plaza with a well standing in the centre. An old woman, so old that it seemed a miracle she lived at all, struggled with a stone pitcher of water.

I took it from her, in spite of her protestations and followed her when she turned and fled to one of the hovels opposite. I stooped to enter the door, which gives some indication of its size, considering my modest height, and almost choked on that fetid air. When my eyes grew accustomed to the half-light, I saw that there were no windows and that the only furniture, if you could call it that, was a heap of Indian blankets for bedding in the corner. The old woman crouched fearfully by a smouldering fire. I put the pitcher of water down, pressed a five-peso piece into her hand and left hurriedly.

When I emerged, I saw van Horne standing outside the porch of the church looking down towards me. He was wearing his cassock and clerical collar again.

"Good evening, Father," I called loudly as I got near.

"Mr. Keogh," he turned and led the way into the church. "What have you been doing? Visiting the poor?"

"I wouldn't put a hound-dog I thought anything of into that place," I said. "God knows, I've seen poverty in my time, but the worst slum in Dublin would seem a palace to these people."

"A hard country," he said. "I told you that. Now,

what happened at the hacienda?''

I told him everything from the first incident with Jurado to the final confrontation with Tomás de la Plata. When I had finished, he sat on the edge of the vestry table staring into space, a frown on his face.

"Two days," he said at last. "That doesn't give us very long."

"Why do you think Bonilla kept quiet about the old man being crazy? He must have known. Damn, he knows everything else about the family."

He looked at me, frowning slightly. "I get the impression you have your own answer to that one?"

"All right," I said. "If you must know, I think you are more important to this business than Bonilla made clear. I think he intended you to be a stalking horse."

"To draw him in from the mountains where you could get a crack at him?" He shrugged. "That's all right by me, boy. I will kill him myself on the first opportunity, I promise you."

"Then you will disregard the message he sent?"

"I did not come here to take his orders, Keogh. I came to see him under the ground and from what I hear, I'd be performing a public service."

"And what about the woman. What kind of game are you playing there?"

"What game would you have me play?" He was genuinely puzzled. "I'm priest here, boy, and priest I must be. Does that offend you in some way? I had got the impression that religious belief was hardly a strong point with you."

"It isn't," I said. "You seemed to be someone else again, that's all."

"You'll have to take that further. I don't follow you."

"For God's sake, man. I accepted you for a priest

myself watching you with her. The way you spoke and acted. Don't take yourself too seriously, that's all.''

I walked out of the vestry into the church, my knees shaking for some reason and he followed me, catching me by the arm, turning me easily with that enormous strength of his.

"I'm a murderer, Keogh, and a thief many times over. God doesn't exist for a man like me. He can't.''

"If that's true," I said, "if he doesn't exist, then why do the things you've done bother you so much?''

It was the one and only time I got through to the heart of him. His face, or the mask that was his face, melted away and underneath was a man in torment if ever I have seen one. He reached out and grabbed for the front of my coat. I have never known such pure, elemental strength. He had me off the ground like a rubber ball and I thought my final hour had come. And then, abruptly, he seemed to be shaken with some kind of spasm and released me.

"And what about you?" he said. "A man who lives for nothing, believes in nothing, not even himself any more. No emotion left in you. Neither love, nor hate. A dead man walking, Keogh.''

He turned, went into the vestry and closed the door and I stood there, filled with a kind of horror, for in describing me, he had duplicated, almost word for word, my own impression of Tomás de la Plata.

I started to turn away and paused, the breath catching in my throat. The obscene chalk drawing on the front of the altar had been washed away and on top stood a small wooden crucifix, another of the items from the trunk. The figure of Christ was in silver and a final dying ray of the evening sun reached in through the narrow window to touch it brightly.

I turned and fled as if all the hounds in heaven were snapping at my heels.

The rooms at the hotel were as Spartan as I had expected with the whitewashed walls, old brass beds and furniture that looked as if it had been made locally and not by an expert.

I found Janos sitting by the side of his bed at the open window. He had a cloth spread across his knees and was engaged in cleaning his revolver, a Smith & Wesson .38.

"Did you see van Horne?" he asked me.

I nodded. "Yes, I saw him."

"And quarrelled from the sound of you."

"Something like that, but it isn't important. I looked in the mirror for a moment and didn't care for what was there."

"A pointless exercise, my friend, as I discovered long ago. Let's see if we can get some food out of our reluctant host and perhaps a drink or two. You'll feel better for it."

Reluctant Moreno certainly was although he certainly saw that we were fed in a private room at the back and served by his wife who was obviously having trouble in hauling herself around with that great swollen belly of hers. I felt like telling him so forcibly, but then it was hardly my affair and this was a land where women, at least in the back country, were beasts of burden from the day they were born.

I watched her drag herself out at the end of the meal and Janos said, "She doesn't look too healthy."

"An understatement," I said. "If she carries on like that, she'll be in real trouble."

"But of course," he said. "I was forgetting. You had medical training. But never qualified?"

"A year to go."

"Which seems a pity. Have you ever considered going back to complete the course?"

"To Dublin?" I laughed shortly. "I'd get short shrift there, believe me. Let's try the bar and see what he's got to offer."

Which was as good a way of cutting off the conversation as any as I think he knew. A wise old bird, there was no doubt about that.

Moreno was not in the bar when we went in, which was fortunate in a way for when I went behind to help myself, I discovered a stock of scotch whisky of excellent quality. I could guess who it was kept for, but helped myself to a bottle anyway and two glasses. Moreno came in at that moment and seemed about to protest but thought better of it.

"Is there anything else you require, señores?"

"A pack of cards, I think, or perhaps even two." Janos looked at me hopefully. "You don't play bezique, by any chance?"

"No, but I once spent two months with my leg up in a Connemara farmhouse with an English general we were holding hostage who taught me a diabolical little game called piquet."

An expression of complete and utter delight suffused his face. "My God, sir, but I never thought to see the day again when I could play a gentleman's game."

He gave me a cigar and while we were lighting them, Moreno returned with the cards. He put them on the table and said diffidently, "Perhaps the señores would be more comfortable in a private room. It gets a little crowded in here later on."

"We're perfectly happy where we are, man," Janos snapped, his hands already busy with the pack, discarding all the cards below seven. "Now leave us in peace."

I should have known how good he would be, but even being rubiconed by Janos was an enjoyable experience. It took my mind off things admirably to such an extent that when we paused after the first hour, I was surprised to find a dozen or fifteen other customers in the place.

We were intruders, so much was obvious and mostly they sat in silence, watching us sullenly while they drank or muttered together in low voices. They were all local men, simple peons from their dress and certainly nothing to worry about.

We started on a fresh game and I was on the third deal of the *partie* when the door opened and Raul Jurado entered, spurs jingling. There were two other men with him, dressed like him as vaqueros, pistols at their belts and one of them had been with Tomás de la Plata when last I saw him.

Jurado scowled heavily and stood glaring at us for a moment, a leather quirt dangling from his left wrist. He would have dearly loved to throw us out or worse, but that course of action was denied him now on the word of the man who was obviously his true master.

He moved to the bar and ordered tequila for himself and his friends from Moreno who looked absolutely terrified. A moment later the door opened again and Oliver van Horne stepped inside.

There was complete and utter silence of a quite remarkable kind and the astonishment on the faces of everyone there was something to see.

Van Horne said pleasantly, "Good evening."

"And a good evening to you, Father." I was the only one to speak.

He was wearing his cassock and shovel hat and carried a bundle under his arm wrapped in a woollen blanket. He went over to the bar and addressed Moreno.

"Señor, I'm sorry to bother you but I'm in urgent need of one or two items and thought you might be able to assist."

Moreno stared at him, petrified, and Jurado turned to watch, an ugly glint in his eye.

"A mattress for my bed," van Horne continued in the same calm voice. "An oil lamp and as much whitewash as you can spare and the brushes to apply it."

"There is nothing for you here," Jurado said. "Go away."

Van Horne said mildly, "I am a poor man and unable to pay in cash until my funds come through, but it occurred to me that you might be willing to hold this as security."

He unwrapped the blanket and set the image of St. Martin de Porres on the bar counter. There was a startled gasp, more than one, a chair went over with a crash as someone rose involuntarily. Two men went down on their knees and most there crossed themselves.

"Merciful heaven," Moreno said and there was awe on his face. "But where did you find him, Father?"

"You recognise it?"

"Ah, yes." Moreno crossed himself with as much devotion as any man could. "He belongs here, Father, here in our own church where he stood in the side chapel from the day the church was built. For two hundred years. He is ours, Father, he belongs to the people of this place. When he was taken during the Revolution, he took our luck with him."

"He will be yours again, my friend," van Horne told him. "Back in his place in the chapel once the church has been cleaned and re-consecrated."

"I will get you the things you need now, Father,"

Moreno said, "if you will come this way."

Jurado's quirt lashed down across the bar counter. "And I say no!"

Van Horne faced him. "By what authority?"

"Will this do, señor priest?"

Jurado pulled out his pistol, extended his arm and shoved the muzzle into van Horne's belly.

I had my hand inside my coat ready to draw, but there was no need. Van Horne calmly pushed the barrel of the pistol to one side. "Hardly a contest, señor, when I am not armed. I had thought you a man of honour."

Jurado was stupid enough to fall for it. He glared at van Horne, looked around the room as if to assert his authority and holstered his pistol. "You are proposing some kind of contest?"

"Why not?" van Horne said. "A little harmless amusement and no harm done. A trial of strength. If I win, you allow Moreno to give me what I need."

"And if you lose?"

Van Horne shrugged. "That will be up to you, señor."

Jurado laughed, and struck his nearest companion in the chest sending him half across the room. "Trial of strength—with me? That's funny, isn't it? That's the funniest thing I ever heard." He turned back to van Horne. "What do you propose?"

"Indian wrestling," van Horne said.

Jurado's mouth gaped. "Indian wrestling? A game for children."

He looked angry, suspecting he was being played with. Van Horne said, "I have a variation which adds a little interest. Let me show you."

There were several candles burning in holders on the top shelf behind the bar. He asked Moreno for two of them, took them to the nearest table and positioned them carefully. I saw the purpose of this at once as did most others watching. In Indian wrestling the antagonists sit opposite each other, right hands clasped, elbows on the table and the object is to force the opponent's hand down on to the table. Van Horne's variation meant a nasty burn for the loser into the bargain.

Jurado laughed and grabbed a chair. "Heh, I like this. I like this very much indeed, though I warn you, señor, I may forget to let go."

Van Horne sat opposite him, they placed their elbows on the table and clasped hands. Jurado was grinning, teeth bared, but I could not see van Horne's face for his back was towards me.

A muscle ridged in Jurado's face, his smile was a little tighter now as he realised he had taken on more than he had bargained for. Van Horne's arm started to go, slowly, but surely, down towards the candle flame.

The triumph on Jurado's face was there for all to see. He laughed out loud and then his smile slipped completely as his hand was forced upwards again, straight over the top and down to the other candle in a single smooth motion that told us all that van Horne had been playing with him.

He held the hand against the flame and Jurado's face twisted in agony, sweat standing out on his forehead in great drops and yet he would not cry out, teeth clenched and in the end, van Horne released him and stood up.

"A great French king once said, let any man who says he has not known fear try snuffing out a candle flame between his finger and thumb. Of course it all depends on how you do it."

He licked his finger and thumb and nipped both candles quickly. Jurado stood staring at him, pain on his face, nursing his injured hand, then turned and stamped out, followed by his two friends.

Van Horne picked up the image of St. Martin de Porres, wrapped it carefully during the silence that followed and went out through the door which Moreno held open for him.

Conversation burst through to the surface with a vengeance after that. I leaned forward and said to Janos, "What in the hell was he up to?"

"God alone knows, but he'll need a gun next time." He gathered up the cards. "Enough excitement for one night. I'm for bed."

I watched him go, then got to my feet and moved out to the porch. There were two or three men sitting there who fell silent at my approach. As I moved to the edge of the step, there was the rattle of wheels over the cobbles and a handcart came round from the rear of the building pushed by Moreno. Van Horne walked at his side.

I went down the steps and called to him. He paused, then told Moreno to continue. "What do you want?"

I said, "What were you supposed to be playing at in there?"

"Establishing my authority, that's all. When the woman recognised the image this morning and told me its history, I knew at once that I was on to a good thing, but it had to be exploited. I think I've managed that very satisfactorily, don't you? I'll see you in the morning."

He walked away into the darkness after the handcart and I stood there listening to him go, wondering again which one of him was the real Oliver van Horne, but that was a puzzle to which I might never get an answer.

I felt restless and ill-at-ease, certainly in no mood for sleep. I went down through the main street, such as it was, aware of the foul stench of the open drain and moved quickly to the main gate in the wall. Outside, the air was fresh and sweet, stars strung away to the horizon, snow on the high peaks glittering in the moonlight.

Higher up the slopes in the cottonwoods by the stream, a fire glimmered in the night in the centre of a small encampment and horses and mules grazed peacefully, hobbled for the night. I heard the faint tinkle of an ornamental bell round one animal's neck, gentle on the night breeze and the heart in me seemed to stop beating.

I passed one guard and then another and neither challenged me. One man slept beside the fire rolled in a blanket. Nachita sat cross-legged on the other side smoking a pipe, his Winchester across his knees.

His face seemed ageless in the flickering firelight as he looked across at me, but not as timeless as hers when she raised the tent flap and stood watching me calmly. As old as time, every woman who had ever lived rolled into one and in that moment I could understand those people in other days who had worshipped a goddess instead of a god.

She smiled and that smile was for me alone and I went past her into the tent. A storm lamp hung from the ridge pole and she pulled down the flap, closing out the world and dropped to her knees.

I squatted in front of her, watching as she unbraided her hair expertly until it hung in a dark curtain below her shoulders. Then she did a thing which surprised me. She opened a flat wooden box, took out a pad of writing paper and a pencil and wrote something quickly.

It was in Spanish, of course, and in excellent handwriting. It said quite simply: "Did you think I could ever leave you?"

A difficult thing to answer, but there was no need for she stood up and blew out the light.

NINE

FOR YEARS I had lived a life in which everything had, of necessity, to be sacrificed to the Cause. There had been no room for honour, friendship, love or any kind of human response that might be considered a weakness.

I was not used to involvement and the responsibilities that came with it. I was a solitary, lonely man and content to be so and mainly because of the fact that for so many years I had not expected to live beyond the day after tomorrow.

But now there was Victoria, had been from that first moment at Tacho's when she had run to my side, clutching at my jacket like a lost child recognising a loved one in a crowd.

She is in your care now, señor. Tacho's words came back to haunt me, but I was beginning to wonder if it wasn't the other way round. She had changed considerably since choosing sides. Had become all Yaqui. Van Horne had once said that she would take a knife to me in bed the first time I displeased her. Most likely on last night's performance, that she would take a knife to anyone who harmed me.

So, she was wholly in my mind as I drove the Mercedes out through the gate on the following morning, van Horne beside me and Janos in the rear as usual and when I saw the encampment still there by the stream, smoke rising from the fire, I was filled with a feeling of real and conscious pleasure.

She was standing by the fire, leaning over a cooking pot. Nachita spoke to her and she glanced up, shading her eyes from the morning sun. Then she did a strange thing. She ran across to the nearest horse, swung up on its bare back and urged it into a gallop.

There was only the rope halter to hang on to, but she was a marvellous rider and was beside us in a moment, her face turned towards me. She was laughing, perhaps at the very joy of living on such a morning although I like to think it was because of me. I waved and as we drew away, she pulled her mount round and went back towards the camp.

Van Horne said, "I told you she wouldn't let go, Keogh."

"Did I ever say I wanted her to?"

He seemed surprised, but said simply, "You go to hell in your own way, boy."

"Exactly," Janos said patiently. "Could we now discuss the day's plan of campaign?"

"Simplicity itself," van Horne said. "I came here to get De la Plata one way or the other as Bonilla suggested, not to commit suicide."

"I could have taken him yesterday," I said. "And been dead meat after, his men would have seen to that."

"Exactly, so we have to draw him into some kind of direct confrontation, either alone or with the kind of backing we can take care of."

"And how do we manage that?"

"We play it by ear and hope. I suggest you make your

inspection of the mine this morning, then tell the girl
and the old man you'll consider all the relevant facts,
compile a report on the situation this afternoon. She'll
ask you back for a meeting to discuss things this evening, nothing is more certain."

"And you think Tomás will put in an appearance?"
Janos asked.

"There or at the hotel. He'll want to know what's in
that report. Wouldn't you agree, Keogh?"

I nodded slowly. "I'd be surprised if he didn't. The
thing is, will he turn up on his own?"

"We'll just have to wait and see, won't we?"

He lit a cigarillo, leaned back cheerfully, took a book
from his pocket and started to read. It was a copy of St.
Augustine's *City of God* in Latin, but I had ceased to be
surprised at anything now where van Horne was concerned.

As we drove into the courtyard and came to a halt at the
bottom of the steps, Chela de la Plata appeared in the
doorway. She was dressed for riding as she had been
the previous day in leathern breeches and boots, the
Cordoban hat tilted over her eyes. The riding whip in
her left hand tapped nervously against her leg and she
seemed tired and drawn, the pale skin stretched tightly
over the cheekbones.

She came down to meet us, a manilla folder in one
hand bound with red tape which she handed to me.
"You will find assay reports in there for the last five
years the mine was fully operating and other information which I presume you will need."

Janos removed his hat. "May I enquire how your
father is this morning?"

"Not well, I'm afraid. He is confined to his bed."
She hesitated, then turned to van Horne. "He is in no

condition to see visitors, Father. I am sorry to have wasted your time in this manner."

"I understand perfectly," he told her, and for a moment, there was that strange quality of intimacy between them that I had noticed during their first meeting at the church.

She brightened suddenly. "Perhaps you would care to accompany us to the mine? Many of the village men are working there at the moment. You might find it of interest."

"I'd like nothing better."

"You ride, Father?"

"I've been known to."

She smiled in a way she hadn't smiled in a long, long time unless I was mistaken. Strange, but they had talked together as if Janos and I had ceased to exist.

The trail was difficult, mainly because of the kind of terrain it had to cross, but it had also deteriorated due to neglect over the years. It was obviously the first matter that would require attention if the mine was ever to become fully operational again.

Van Horne and I followed Chela in single file, allowing our mounts to pick their own way and Janos toiled along behind in a buckboard hauled by two horses, one of the hacienda's peons at the reins.

We ascended into a country of broken hills and narrow, twisting water courses. The slopes were covered with mesquite and greasewood and as we climbed higher, a few *piñones* rooted in the scant soil, pushing their pointed heads into the morning.

We went over a rise to a small plateau and found half-a-dozen men ranged across the path, each with his reins in his left hand, his rifle in the right. All very military, but as I remembered, Tomás de la Plata had been an army officer.

He appeared from the *piñones* above us, a sombre, rather clerical-looking figure in his black clothes. Chela was angry and frightened at the same time.

"What is it?" she called. "What do you want? You gave me your word. You promised two days."

One of his men urged his horse in close, reached inside my coat and plucked the Enfield from my shoulder holster, had obviously been told beforehand exactly where to look.

"Tomás!" Chela cried, a kind of agony in her voice.

"I gave my word," he said. "Now carry on to the mine. Your friends will follow when I have finished with them."

She knew him, I suppose, well enough to know the futility of arguing, but her face was white and angry as she hauled her mount round viciously and rode away.

The buckboard was still some considerable way down the trail behind us and Janos was well out of things. Tomás pushed his hat back to hang round his neck and stood looking down at us for a while. He had pale flaxen hair, strange for a Mexican, blue eyes and the aesthetic face was calm, empty. Yes, empty was an excellent word to describe it.

"Come up here, Señor Keogh," he said, "and bring the priest with you."

We did as we were told, not that we had any option in the matter, dismounted and scrambled up the bank to find him leaning against a tree smoking a cigarette.

He behaved at first as if van Horne didn't exist. "When will you be ready with an opinion on the mine?"

"I'm not sure," I said. "I'll have to look at the place this morning, go through the figures your sister has given me this afternoon, then prepare a report."

"You have arranged to see her and my father this evening?"

"No, I understand he's not too well. He's confined to his bed."

"I wish to see this report when it is finished, you understand me?"

"I would have thought that your sister's business under present circumstances, not yours," van Horne told him quietly.

Tomás de la Plata said in a voice of dreadful calm, "I was not aware that I had given you permission to speak, but now I have started, let me make one thing clear. I allow you to survive at my sister's urging for two days only and in that time, no preaching, no approaches to the people, no priest's tricks. Two days, then you go. If you break my conditions in the meantime, I shall kill you."

"And that would give you some kind of pleasure?" van Horne said.

"No more than to put my foot on a beetle." He turned and looked at me speculatively. "You saw Colonel Bonilla in Huila. He warned you against coming here?"

"That's right."

"And what did he tell you about me?"

"He said that the people had had their Revolution. That what they and the country need now is stability and order, which means there can be no room for men like you."

Why I had said it and in quite that way, I do not know, but the words were out and impossible to retrieve. It didn't seem to matter for only one aspect of what I had said registered with him.

He turned to look at me and his eyes seemed to have

changed colour, glittering like pieces of ice in the pale face. "The people," he said. "You speak to me of the people? Shall I tell you what they are? Dung on the face of the land. I went to prison for them, spent three years in a penal colony for political offenders in the jungles of Yucatán. Suffered every conceivable degradation. I gave my life to a struggle whose one ideal was to win them their freedom and freedom they took. To murder, to rape and burn and turn this land into a charnel house."

"They were under the boot for a considerable time," I reminded him. "A reaction that might have been expected."

"You think so?" He shivered as if suddenly cold and stared out over the mountainside and it was as if he was speaking to himself. "Not by me, señor. I came home after ten years of fighting the people's war to find my father a broken old man more out of his wits than in them, a sister who cried out in terror if a man even brushed her sleeve in passing."

There was a stillness, only the slightest of breezes through the *piñones* and for a moment, it was so quiet that I could hear the wheels of the buckboard on the hillside below.

"They came to my home one night in the last months of the war, soldiers of the ranks of the Revolution and their commanding officer, an animal named Varga, military governor in the area. My father, they beat half to death, left him for dead after defecating on his body as he lay there. As for my sister, Varga took her for himself, abused and degraded her in every possible way, then gave her to the men."

The story was such a commonplace one, that was the dreadful thing, for I could have capped it with accounts of a score such incidents known to me, the details of which were even more horrifying.

It was van Horne who spoke then, his voice harsh and angry. "And no one did anything to prevent this? No one stood by them?"

"The people of Mojada stayed home like whipped dogs and the priest of that time, their spiritual adviser, had room in his life for only two things each day. At least one full bottle of tequila and the stinking bed of the widow who kept house for him. A father to his people as you can see."

"And for this you became the enemy of all the world?"

"Once I believed in reason and the intellect, señor, but I learned better. I learned the true worth of men. I cut Varga's throat with my own hand, hung the priest and the one who came after him and as for the people? They would eat their own dirt if I ordered it."

"And this makes you a happy man?" van Horne asked.

Tomás de la Plata glared at him and the eyes seemed to enlarge, grew darker. When he extended two fingers of his left hand, that hand was shaking. "Two days, priest. Two days." He turned and in the same breath added, "And you, señor, will be hearing from me at the appropriate time. Now go."

As we scrambled down the bank his men urged their horses up to join him. There was a brief flurry and they were away through the *piñones*. The Enfield was lying on top of a boulder. I picked it up carefully, checked the loading and pushed it into the shoulder holster.

Van Horne's face was grey. He said, "I don't know about you, but he scared the hell out of me. He's over the edge, that one."

"And beyond," I said.

The buckboard came over the rise below us and rolled

to a halt. Janos called, "I thought you'd be there by now. What happened? Did you run into trouble?"

"Oh, I think you could say that," I told him and van Horne started to laugh, but it was flat, cold stuff, no mirth in it at all.

Our final destination proved to be a small plateau against the great rocky face of the mountain. Chela de la Plata had ridden down to meet us, reining in her horse beside van Horne who led the way.

I didn't hear what she said, but he reached out to take her hand and smiled confidently. "Everything is fine, I promise. He has no intention of breaking his word."

The relief in her face was there for all to see and she pulled ahead to lead the way up on to the plateau, reined in and dismounted. It was a drift mine, the entrance, a large irregular hole in the cliff face and nearby an old steam engine, obviously the major source of power, puffed smoke into the still air.

Water had been channelled down the face of the mountain in several places, running finally into a wooden conduit that emptied into a large dilapidated shed, open at both ends and used to process the ore.

It was a scene of great activity. Periodically, a truck laden with ore emerged from the mouth of the mine pushed by a couple of sweating peons stripped to the waist. The rusting rails took this down a short incline into the ore shed where the processing took place.

Inside the shed, the only piece of machinery was a steam operated crusher and the heat from its furnace made working conditions almost unbearable. The water ran into a tank lined with clay against leakage, and there were the usual cradles and puddling troughs. Perhaps half-a-dozen men worked in there, all stripped to the waist and a young boy spent his time dousing them with buckets of water when called upon to do so.

"As you can see," Chela said, "our methods are primitive by the standards you gentlemen are used to."

"Which can be remedied easily enough," Janos told her. "As long as the prospect exists for the right kind of return, then the introduction of modern machinery and methods will be our first priority."

"Since starting again, what particular problems have you had?" I asked her.

"So many rockfalls that I have lost count."

"Then your timbering must be at fault," Janos said. "Only to be expected after so many years of idleness and decay. Have you any kind of expert assistance available?"

"Many of the villagers worked here before when the mine was fully operational. Rafael Moreno from the hotel was shift foreman as a young man and also an expert shot-firer. He is supervising the work at the rock face for us and Jurado organises the actual labour force."

On her brother's insistence, presumably, but Janos let it go and smiled brightly. "Señorita, I have a confession to make. I have had a hatred of confined places since childhood. Surprising, I know, in one with my business interests. That is why I employ professionals such as Mr. Keogh to give me the benefit of their expert advice."

"Which means you'll sit out here enjoying a cigar while I do the necessary tour of inspection," I said.

"Correct." He smiled rather complacently and perfectly in character. "The privilege not only of age, but of position, Mr. Keogh. I shall sit on a boulder in the sun contemplating this extraordinary view and think of you down there in the darkness—often."

Chela de la Plata smiled. "Then if I may be your guide, Señor Keogh and yours, Father?"

And so the three of us left him in the sunlight and ventured into the darkness.

At the Hermosa Mine there had been a considerable criminal element provided by the local state prison and the rest of the labour force had consisted of men newly released from the ranks of the army of the Revolution. A pot constantly on the boil.

The company had operated according to the age-old formula of working them until they dropped, but one essential requirement always faced up to was the need for adequate ventilation for underground, you either breathed or died. A step inside the tunnel and the heat seized me by the throat, which gave me an opportunity to play mining engineer.

"What's wrong with the ventilation?"

"The main airshaft was blocked by a rockfall a week or two back. Moreno says it would take quite an operation to clear it so we decided to carry on for the time being."

"Surely he told you how dangerous that could be?"

"We are short of everything, señor, time as well as money and we needed as much ore out as possible to be in a position to raise more capital. A vicious circle."

We turned a corner and the light faded, leaving us in a corridor of shadows, patches of light illuminated by guttering candles in niches in the rock, marching into the darkness at spaced intervals. We stood to one side as a truck rattled over the rails pushed by a couple of weary, dust-covered men who seemed at the end of their tether.

"As you can see, the work takes a great deal out of

them. They can only manage an hour or two at a time in the heat and are then compelled to return to the surface."

"Which would all be effectively remedied by a reasonable ventilating system, I presume, as Mr. Keogh indicates," van Horne said helpfully.

We reached a fork and Chela paused. "There are two main faces. Have you any preference?"

"I think I'd like a chance to speak to Moreno," I said.

"Then we must try what we call Old Woman. He is usually there."

There was a lamp on a hook in the wall. She took it down and led the way, stooping as the tunnel closed in. There was a strange, humming vibration in the rock, sure sign that picks were at work not too far away, a light in the distance, and we emerged into a low-roofed cavern illuminated by a couple of pressure lamps.

A dozen or fifteen men worked at the rock face, jabbing away with short-handled picks. Three or four more gathered ore into baskets which they then emptied into another truck. It was almost impossible to breathe because of the heat and the dust. One of the men at the face got up and came to meet us and in spite of the sweatband around his forehead, the patina of dust, I recognised Moreno.

"Señorita." He nodded his head awkwardly.

"You will answer any questions Señor Keogh puts to you," she told him.

He turned to me, obviously uncertain. There was a sudden shower of soil and pebbles in the corner and one of the men got out of the path fast.

"The timbering could be better," I said.

He took out a knife, sprung the blade and jabbed at the nearest prop, breaking away a large, brittle flake.

"As you can see, the wood is old, dried-out to the point of desiccation. The whole mountain waits to come down on us. Each time a man coughs another rock falls."

"Which is why you aren't using machinery down here?"

"The vibration might be all that is needed."

I asked him one or two more reasonably intelligent questions about ore samples and so on, then we left and went back along the tunnel until we reached the place where it forked.

"Would you like to see the other face?" she asked me. "The one we call Crazy Man?"

It was necessary, I suppose, to make things look as authentic as possible although the sooner I was out of the place, the happier I would be.

I said, "A brief visit only, señorita, I promise you."

She turned to van Horne. "The tunnel to Crazy Man drops to four feet in places. An uncomfortable journey for you particularly and not necessary."

"Then I'll wait for you here," he told her.

I didn't blame him for his enormous size was ill-suited to the conditions we had found and he had scraped his head on roof trusses more than once on our way to the other face.

We left him there and started along the tunnel, which was in many ways a replica of the first except for the fact that the roof came down to meet us rather sooner than I had expected, in spite of her warning. I was aware of the same vibration in the rock, the tapping of picks. We got out of the way of another truck which scraped past us, its top almost touching the roof. When it had gone, we moved on towards the dim light at the far end.

There was a considerable amount of angry shouting, disagreeably loud in that confined space and when we finally emerged into the cavern which contained the working face, I quickly discovered the cause—Jurado, his face a mask of dust and sweat, a rawhide whip in one hand.

He cracked it at the heels of the men who loaded the baskets with ore. "Come on you lazy scum. Faster!"

Like van Horne, the man had not been built for such work and his enormous bulk obviously made his existence in such a place extremely uncomfortable. The anger and frustration showed clearly in the eyes, the twitching whip and his face and chest were thick with dust.

He nodded to Chela, ignoring me completely. She said, "Is there anything you wish to know, Señor Keogh?"

"I don't think so," I replied. "Conditions here seem much the same as at Old Woman."

She turned to Jurado. "Everything is in order?"

"It would be if these miserable swine would put their backs into it."

"Surely the fault of their working conditions?" I said. "I would have thought the whip possessed only a limited application."

"You don't know these people as I do. It is all they understand."

One of the men collecting ore hoisted his basket to the edge of the truck, paused to take breath and lost his grip, tipping the contents over the floor. Jurado sprang forward and started to belabour him with the weighted handle of the whip.

Chela de la Plata grabbed his arm and cried, "Leave him, Jurado, I order you."

His control had gone to such a degree that he lashed out, catching her across the side of the face with his clenched fist, sending her back into my arms. In the same moment, the unfortunate peon who had been the cause of things tried to make a run for it. Jurado lunged at him, lost his footing and fell against one of the timber roof supports, his great weight knocking it from position.

A waterfall of shale and pebbles erupted from the darkness above. The men who had been working at the face were on their feet with cries of alarm, already moving towards the tunnel and already too late.

There was a distinct cracking sound as a twenty-foot roof truss split in the centre and the mountain rushed in on us.

The air had changed into layers of thick whirling dust that was impossible to breathe. I found myself on my back. The most frightening discovery of all was to find that my legs were trapped and yet, at the first frantic kick, they pulled free of what turned out to be nothing more than a great mound of earth and shale.

I groped forward blindly through the curtain of dust towards a dim glow on the floor and found the pressure lamp half buried. I pumped it up quickly to increase the brightness and held it above my head.

Chela crouched on her hands and knees, dazed and frightened, a streak of blood on her cheek staining the dust and on a first quick check, most of the miners seemed to be in one piece.

Jurado was standing against the rock face, a look of complete incomprehension on his face. It was as if he could not believe that this was happening to him. As I held up the lamp, illuminating the working and its furthest corners, he gave an angry growl and scrambled up the sloping ramp of rubble which now blocked the entrance to the tunnel.

He started to tear at the top of the mound with his bare hands and several of the miners joined him, coughing spasmodically as they choked on the thick dust. Chela got to her feet and stood there, swaying a little as if uncertain of her balance. I put out a hand to steady her and she pulled away from me violently. So, even in circumstances like this she could not help but react on being touched by a man as her brother had described, but before I could do or say anything, there was a hoarse cry from Jurado.

When I scrambled up beside him with the lamp, I saw that there was now a distinct gap between the heap of rubble and the roof of the tunnel and there was a steady current of air moving through. It was all that was needed. The men started working like beavers and I went back to Chela and took her firmly by the arm.

She started to react in the same violent manner, trying to pull free of me. I slapped her face and shook her hard. "Will you damn well listen to me? It's going to be all right. We're going to get out."

She stopped struggling, staring at me rather vacantly as if unable to comprehend, and the mountain chose that moment to deposit another couple of tons of rubble in the far corner. She came into my arms and held on tight.

Not too long after that, Jurado called to me again. I sat her down against the rock face, climbed up the sloping pile of rubble to join the others. There was a gap a good foot wide now, light streaming through from the other side, voices.

It was with no particular surprise that I saw Oliver van Horne peering through at me.

It took perhaps an hour of hard work from both sides to create a gap on top of the rockfall about ten feet long and two high, just right for a cautious passage out, and not before time for the mountain groaned above our heads and the roof trusses moved uneasily as if in protest at having to continue to carry all that weight.

Chela was second out and only because Jurado went through the instant the passage was clear in what can only be described as indecent haste. I brought up the rear and found Moreno waiting on the other side with two or three men to help me through.

"Father van Horne has gone on ahead with the señorita," he told me. "She seemed much disturbed."

A remark which certainly ranked as the understatement of the day, but I was concerned with only one thing at that moment, which was getting to some fresh air. When I finally stumbled out into the sunlight, everyone was there, not only the workers, but also Tomás de la Plata and his men.

He had Chela on the ground against his knee, one arm about her shoulders as he gently wiped the filth from her face with a damp cloth provided by one of his men who stood holding a bucket of water. As I discovered later, he had been attracted by the sound of the alarm bell which hung in a tripod by the ore shed and was always rung in time of disaster.

Van Horne watched, stripped to the waist, exhibiting the kind of muscular development that would not have disgraced a heavyweight wrestler. Jurado, the cause of it all, stood hesitantly by, wild-eyed.

Tomás de la Plata looked up as I appeared, his face white and angry. "So, now you know how things stand here, Señor Keogh, and no need of any official reports. I will hear no more of this nonsense which has almost cost me my sister's life."

Interesting that the emphasis should be upon his own loss and not hers. If there was a time to throw Jurado to the wolves it was then, but to my surprise, Chela opened her eyes and said simply, "Take me home, Tomás."

He murmured something softly that was for no one but her, kissed her on the brow, then picked her up in his arms. When he went, he took her on the saddle before him, his men following behind and all watched them go in silence.

It was Janos who spoke first and the remark was typical. "By God, sir, Mr. Keogh, but you have a remarkable facility for survival in all things."

"It can't come any closer than that. The roof was still coming down as we got out." I managed a weary grin for van Horne. "A beautiful sight, that face of yours peering through."

I walked to a nearby water trough, sluiced my head and shoulders, then slumped down on the ground, my face turned to the sun. It was too good to last, of course, for Moreno, who had been moving amongst the men making a tally, came and stood before me, his face grave.

"We are missing one man, señor."

I got up wearily and van Horne, who was washing himself at the trough, turned at once.

"Are you certain?"

"Oh yes, señor, José Jardona, the shot-firer on that face. There can be no question."

Jurado, who had been sitting sullenly on the ground, his back against one wall of the ore shed, got to his feet and came forward. "He will be dead by now."

"We can't be certain," I said. "We'll have to go and see."

"Don't be a fool," he said. "How long were we in there before getting out? An hour at least. Did anyone hear a sound?" He turned in appeal to the miners who stood listening in a semi-circle. No one answered and he turned back to me. "He must have been killed instantly under that first fall."

I said to Moreno, "You'll come with me?"

There was fear on his face, real fear and he was, after all, no longer young. He took a deep breath and gave me a queer little bow. "At your orders, señor, but no one else, not under the circumstances."

Hardly a pleasant thought, but it made sense. He started towards the mine and Jurado caught me by the shoulder. "Don't be a fool, the mountain still moves."

But he was more afraid for himself than me and I pulled away and went after Moreno. When I joined him, he already had two pressure lamps burning, gave me one and we started in.

Van Horne caught up with us just as we reached the fork in the tunnel.

Crawling back across the rockfall, the roof of the tunnel close enough to occasionally scrape my back, was not the most rewarding of experiences, especially as the rattle of falling stones and soil could be heard monotonously in the darkness ahead.

When I went back inside the working, it was to find a scene of even greater chaos. There had obviously been a bad fall quite recently and the mountain, squeezing in, had reduced the size of things by half, roof trusses and props smashed like matchsticks and pointing every which-way.

Just to move amongst them was a hazard and yet it was not to be avoided for a low, continuous moaning, as of someone in great pain, led us to the corner where the full force of the first fall had been felt.

Jardona was under a ton or so of rock, his head and shoulders and one arm only clear, the dust-covered face glistening with sweat. I can only presume that he had lost his senses at the first shock and had lain unconscious in the darkness of the corner during the time we had been clearing our way out.

Moreno started to dig carefully with his hands, feeling his way gingerly. After a while he looked at me and shook his head slightly. Not that it mattered for José Jardona was a dying man, had only clung to life this long by a miracle.

He opened his eyes and stared blankly at us and then something clicked, a kind of wonder. His lips moved and he said quite distinctly, "Father, is it you?"

I found van Horne at my shoulder. He was stripped to the waist again, the face a mask of dust. He ran the back of a hand across his eyes as if to clear them and edged forward.

"I saw you at the church," Jardona said. "There was a fire." He closed his eyes again, shuddering in pain, then opened them and said weakly, "I am going to die, Father, and I've done so many terrible things. I didn't think it would matter, but it does."

There was a sudden rumble like distant thunder above us and I ducked, arms raised to cover my head as shale and rubble cascaded across us.

There was blood on Jardona's mouth. He spat it out and said weakly, "Don't leave me, Father."

Van Horne took his hand and a roof truss cracked and sagged in the far corner. He glanced over his shoulder and said, "No sense in you two staying."

Moreno, poor devil, looked as if he expected to meet his Maker at any moment and yet some stubborn streak would not allow him to betray his manhood. "José is my cousin, señor." He smiled apologetically. "A matter of family, you understand me?"

I held up the lamp and said, "A little light against the dark, Father. I suggest you get on with it."

Van Horne did not waste further time in argument. He leaned close and said in a calm strong voice, "I want you to make an act of contribution. Say after me: O, my God, who art infinitely good in Thyself . . ."

Jardona, choking in his own blood, followed him, painfully, brokenly, each word a personal Calvary. Step-by-step van Horne moved through the final rites, his voice never faltering and for a while, even the mountain seemed to stop moving and there was silence.

There was a final effusion of blood from Jardona's mouth and his eyes closed. Moreno crossed himself and started to slide out backwards. "Go with God, José," he called softly.

I touched van Horne on the shoulder. He ignored me, leaning over the body, listening, and in the silence I heard slight irregular breathing, Jardona still clinging fast to life. Soil, the merest trickle dribbled out of the shadows, and van Horne, leaning forward to protect the body, started to recite the prayers for the dying.

"Go, Christian soul, from this world, in the Name of God the Father Almighty Who created thee; in the Name of Jesus Christ, the Son of the Living God, Who suffered for thee; in the Name of the Holy Ghost . . ."

With a mighty rush that was like no sound I had heard before, the mountain shook itself and poured in on us.

Moreno cried out urgently from the tunnel entrance. I grabbed van Horne by the hair and pulled him backwards with all my strength. José Jardona disappeared from sight forever and I scrambled for the way out as fast as any terrified animal seeking a bolt hole.

A flying stone shattered my lamp and I dropped it and crawled into the darkness over rough stones and then Moreno was there, his lamp above his head, a hand outstretched to help me.

I fell to my knees, but got up frantically and turned and when his head and shoulders appeared above me, could not believe it. There was no time for anything but survival now. Moreno and I got an arm apiece and pulled van Horne through, then we ran for our lives as the mountain shook itself above us.

I don't suppose any of those waiting expected to see us emerge from the great cloud of dust that billowed from the entrance, but when we did, there was an incredulous roar and everyone crowded round.

I pushed my way through the press, fell on my hands and knees beside the trough and plunged my head into the cool water. Then I rolled over on my back. I closed my eyes, breathing deeply. When I opened them again, Janos was standing over me.

"By God, sir, but this is really too much," he said. "I was beginning to imagine myself alone in a strange land."

"Van Horne's the man you should talk to," I told him. "He seems to have some sort of death wish, if you ask me. Either that or he's tired of living."

He asked me what had happened and I told him briefly. There was a frown on his face when I had finished, unusual for him. "So, he is taking the part seriously again?"

"When the mood's on him."

"And you?" I frowned in bewilderment. "You stayed also, Mr. Keogh. You could have died, sir, and for what?"

Which was certainly a point. I got up and saw van Horne coming towards us, men easing out of his way, yet staying close, many crossing themselves.

He sluiced water over his head and shoulders and smiled. "We have our moments, Keogh."

But the smile was fleeting and beneath it, there was a new seriousness. He reached for his shirt and Moreno approached, the rest of the men crowding behind. I noticed Jurado lurking on the outskirts of things, obviously waiting to see what was going to happen. I ignored him for the moment, for I was too interested myself.

Moreno said, "What you did in there, Father, for my poor cousin, to ease his going in such terrible circumstances . . . this was a remarkable thing. We are in your debt, all of us. If there is anything we can do . . ."

Van Horne stood looking at them, shirt dangling from one hand, water beading his head and shoulders. I could not see his face, but there was a peculiar quality of stillness to him.

He said clearly, "To mourn the death of one man would be to fly in the face of God's mercy when so many have been saved. I shall hold a service of thanksgiving in the church at two-thirty this afternoon. All who are truly grateful will be there."

There was consternation even on Janos's face. As for Moreno and his friends, I have seldom seen men more dismayed.

Jurado was already galloping away to bear the glad tidings to his master.

TEN

HE GAVE US no chance to discuss things with him, but announced that he had decided to ride back to Mojada and went off with fifteen or twenty of the miners, including Moreno, who had their own horses or mules. The rest were conveyed in a large wagon pulled by four mules.

Janos and I followed in the buckboard and he was anything but happy about the way things were going. "Did he get knocked on the head down there, by any chance?"

"Several times."

"I thought so. His brain has turned. It can be the only explanation for such madness. De la Plata can't allow a challenge to his power to go unpunished. It would be the beginning of the end for him."

"I suppose that's what van Horne wants. A direct confrontation."

"Which would only have purpose if De la Plata appeared alone and he certainly won't in this instance. If he turns up at the church during the service, he'll have at least a dozen men with him."

"Van Horne must have something up his sleeve," I said. "He certainly isn't doing it just to give De la Plata an excuse to hang him."

"There is another possibility," Janos pointed out. "As I said before, what if he simply can't resist playing the priest?"

An uncomfortable thought and I tried to push it away. "That wouldn't make sense."

"Then explain this morning if you can. He went into the mine with you and Moreno, stayed with that poor devil trapped in the rockfall. Shrived him as well as any priest could from what you tell me and sent him on his way happy. Now why would he do that? Why put his life in jeopardy for no good reason?"

I suddenly realised in a moment of illumination that down there in the dark, I had accepted van Horne for a priest myself, must have done for a while at least, however insane that sounded.

I said lamely, "Oh, I don't know. I went down myself, didn't I?"

"No answer." He smiled. "You see, sir, you are an Irishman and whoever heard of one of that breed ever doing the logical and expected thing in any circumstance?"

Which ended the conversation for the time being for we had reached the hacienda where we were refused admittance to the house by a couple of De la Plata's men standing guard in the courtyard, but allowed to go on our way in the Mercedes.

Janos dozed in the rear seat and I drove glumly down to Mojada trying to make sense out of Oliver van Horne, murderer and thief, who had deliberately walked into that situation at Tacho's to save my neck. Must have done, I saw that now. Who had made me walk proud in the face of imminent death and who

could crawl into darkness and extreme danger to hold a
dying man's hand and ease his going with prayers which
had no validity anyway, although I suppose that was a
matter of opinion.

The plain truth was that there was no sense to be
found in any of it.

Back at the hotel, I found a sudden and very definite im-
provement in the service. When we went into the bar,
Moreno was already behind the counter. He must have
had a bath because there was no sign of the mine about
him and he was wearing a clean white shirt and black
tie.

He produced a bottle of that special scotch and three
glasses and said diffidently, "If you gentlemen will
drink with me, I would deem it an honour."

"Very civil of you," Janos said, and we joined him.

Moreno filled the glasses, raised his own in a half-
salute. "Señor Keogh, for what you did for my cousin I
thank you. In my family's name, I thank you."

I murmured something suitably modest, remembering
that family was all important to these people. Moreno
said carefully, "Father van Horne, señor—do you think
he will do this thing?"

"Tomás de la Plata warned him against holding any
kind of service," I said. "That's all I know."

"Hardly our affair," Janos put in.

"You think there will be trouble?" I asked Moreno.

"Don Tomás will kill him if he holds that service,
señor, nothing is more certain. He will kill anyone who
takes part. I tried to tell Father van Horne this when we
rode in from the mine together, but he refused to discuss
the matter."

"With you perhaps, but not with us." Janos emptied
his glass and glanced at me. "Dammit, Mr. Keogh, but

we can't let the fellow hang himself for no sensible reason known to man, now can we?''

"I suppose not," I said, playing his game.

"Don't worry, Moreno," he said cheerfully. "We'll talk some sense into him."

Moreno was pathetically grateful and escorted us outside, opening the rear door of the Mercedes and handing Janos in. I suppose that as mayor of Mojada he simply didn't want any unnecessary trouble. On the other hand, van Horne had made his mark, there was no doubt about that.

I drove up through the village towards the church. There was no sign of van Horne, but as I braked to a halt, hooves clattered over the stony ground and I turned to see Victoria pulling in her mount, Nachita behind her. She ran forward, concern on her face, reached out to touch me in a dozen different places as if to assure herself no bones were broken.

I said to Nachita, "You heard about what happened at the mine?"

"I was in to buy supplies at the store, señor, they talk of little else."

I took her hands in mine. "I have business now with the priest. I'll come down to the camp later." She frowned as if uncertain or distrusting me, so I kissed her on the mouth in spite of the company. "Now go or I'll tie you across your horse."

She smiled delightfully, vaulted into the saddle, wheeled her horse in a tight circle and galloped away so fast that she caught Nachita off-balance. He was actually a couple of yards in the rear as he went after her.

"At least she does what you tell her," Janos observed.

"Only sometimes."

I helped him out and when we turned to the church,

van Horne was standing in the porch dressed in a cassock and clerical collar and wearing a black birreta, something else which must have come from the trunk.

"I wondered how long it would be."

He moved to the Mercedes, got in the back and raised the seat. There was a large piece of felt underneath which he removed, revealing bare metal. It proved to be a false bottom for he got his fingers into some special place and lifted, disclosing a tin box painted khaki with United States Army Ordnance painted on the cover in black.

He picked it up in both hands. "You'd better come inside, and don't forget the cigar," he added to Janos.

The Hungarian sighed and tossed the cigar away reluctantly. "Don't you think you are taking this all a little too far?"

Van Horne ignored the remark and led the way in. The worst of the charcoal obscenities had been scraped from the walls although he hadn't got round to giving them a coat of whitewash yet. The smell of dirt and decay I had noticed only yesterday was almost gone. Down at the altar, the crucifix glinted, a candle on either side and it was peaceful. It was a church again.

Van Horne put the box down on a bench and opened it. Janos said, "Keogh and I would like to know what the game is. You are not on your own in this and time you realised that."

Van Horne looked enquiringly at me. I said, "No one will come. They don't dare."

"Tomás de la Plata will come," he said. "And that is all that matters. He'll come to gloat at my failure and very possibly to kill me."

"But not on his own, man," Janos insisted urgently. "Why should he?"

Van Horne said, "Two days, that's all he gave us.

After this morning's fiasco at the mine, why should he indulge us further. The showdown must be now and on our terms.''

"He never goes anywhere without at least a dozen men at his back," I pointed out.

Van Horne walked to the other end of the church and mounted into the pulpit. He stood facing us, hands on either side of a small wooden lectern on which I noticed he had placed a Bible.

"When he and his friends walk in, this is where they will find me and they'll never know what hit them."

His hands dipped out of sight, re-appeared clutching the machine gun. God save us all, but he looked like the Angel of Death himself up there and it would work—I could see that. See Tomás de la Plata and his men walk into the empty church, could hear the jingle of the spurs, the jeers. I had seen van Horne in action, remember. Knew only too well how devastating a weapon a Thompson gun became in his hands. Tomás de la Plata and those with him would be dead before they knew it.

There was one snag that I could see and Janos voiced it. "What if he leaves some of his men outside, sir, what then?"

"That's where you and Keogh come in. You'll be on the first floor of the bell tower, twenty feet up, with a clear field of fire."

"With what?" I demanded.

"Look in the box."

I did and found a dozen Mills bombs, a sawn-off, double-barrelled shotgun, a Winchester repeater, at least a thousand rounds of ammunition and a Thompson gun that was twin to his own.

I drove Janos back to the hotel, dropped him there and left the village on foot for I wanted time to think.

Van Horne's plan was well enough, a dangerous, bloody ambush that had every chance of working, just as he had indicated. With the two machine guns and a grenade or two lobbed down from the tower, it was more than likely that we could kill or cripple every last one of them within seconds.

In the final analysis it all depended on Tomás de la Plata behaving as expected, which was hardly the most cheerful of thoughts. In the past, I had waited in ambush too many times for those who did not come or came another way and the change from hunter to quarry was easily made.

The pack horses and mules had gone, that was the first thing I noted as I approached the Yaqui encampment, but the tent was still there beside the fire, four horses grazing nearby.

There was a leather-bound book on a blanket by the fire. I picked it up and opened it. It was a copy of *Don Quixote* in Spanish. There was no greater sound than a breeze might make through grass and when I glanced up, Nachita was watching.

"A fine book, señor."

"Yours?" I said.

"As a youth I spent some time with the Fathers at Nacozari. For a while they talked of making me a priest, but my own voices spoke to me of different things and I returned to my people. A man has but one life to live."

I dropped the book back on the blanket. "Where are the others?"

"Gone, señor, across the mountains with the pack animals."

"But you stay?"

He smiled, or at least his face moved in what for him was the nearest equivalent to such a thing. "She is waiting by the pool on the other side of the cottonwoods, señor."

He dropped to the ground with a kind of easy grace, picked up *Don Quixote* and opened it, so I left him to the delights of great literature and went in search of different pleasures.

It was a pretty place. A waterfall dropping twenty or thirty feet into a small pool surrounded by great tilted slabs of stone. She sat on an old horse blanket, knees drawn up to her chin and stared into space, caught in some private place of her own, yet she knew it was me and was on her feet at the first footfall.

She stood looking at me warily as if expecting some visible sign of something, although of what, I had no idea. I said quietly, "It is good to see you. Good to be alone with you."

She smiled gravely and yet there was a slight frown on her face, a wariness, as if faced with something she did not fully understand. Above us clouds spilled out from the mountains, obscuring the sun for a little while and it was quiet there by the water at the edge of the trees, more quiet than I had thought it possible to be and cold. I found myself shaking violently and something even colder thrust like a sword into the deepest part of me.

It was a thing I had known on more than one occasion, the Celt in me again, and always before bad things happened. And she, God bless her, knew, understood in some strange way of her own, reached out and pulled my hands hard against her breasts.

"I know," I said. "I'm afraid. It happens to the best of us. Even to little Emmet Keogh, Emmet of the good left hand."

She was frowning now and I pulled her down on the blanket and kissed her lips. "Edmundo—Edmundo

Keogh. Would you like to hear about him?''

She nodded, half-smiling, still wary. "I've a grand-father back home who would bless the day he met you," I told her. "He always did say God's greatest gift to Man was a beautiful woman who could keep a still tongue in her head.''

She liked that, her smile said as much. Probably even liked the sound of him and it was as good a place to start as any. So I began to talk, a monologue to end all monologues, the personal testament of little Emmet Keogh. A story that took in most things and I shirked none of it. They all received an honourable mention. Big Mick Collins, the men I had killed for good reason or bad, my own brother included. By the time I had finished she knew all there was to know about our bargain with Bonilla, as much about van Horne and Janos as I knew myself.

All this I told her because out of some strange foreknowledge, I knew van Horne's plan was not going to work. Knew it for no logical reason possible to man, but could not prove it.

I lay with my head in her lap quietly, at peace at last, all talk ended and gazed into a sky of limitless blue and her fingers gently stroked my forehead, easing me into sleep. Her deliberate intention, I am certain, and she would have left me so, but I came awake with a start at the first note of the church bell, the bell which van Horne had said he would ring half-an-hour before the service.

She did not try to stop me and I did not kiss her in parting, the thing was too deep for that now. I simply looked at her for a long and final moment, then turned and walked away through the trees towards whatever waited for me in the heat of the afternoon.

• • •

Janos was on the verandah at the front of the hotel and came to meet me cheerfully, suggesting a walk, the remark obviously being intended for Moreno who sat in a cane chair looking thoroughly worried.

"He doesn't seem too happy," I commented.

Janos smiled. "His wife is, I understand, in labour, though whether at this precise moment in time he is worrying more about her than van Horne is a matter of doubt." He blew out a cloud of cigar smoke with a sigh of content. "Really a most excellent afternoon. Good to be alive."

I could never decide to what extent he said things for effect and yet on the whole, I am inclined to feel that his nonchalance was not studied, but real. The plain truth is that he was one of those odd people who really did live in the here and now and for whom the future and its prospects held few terrors for it simply did not exist.

We strolled casually through the village by the east wall, coming in the end, to the rear of the church where we were admitted by van Horne at the back door which led directly into the vestry.

He wore a white linen alb over his cassock and now, he put on a green stole, crossing it under his girdle to represent Christ's Passion and Death, as I remembered. The green chasuble came next and he was ready.

"I must say you look the part, sir," Janos told him.

"I damn well better do," van Horne replied grimly. "About fifteen minutes to go, so the sooner you two get up that tower, the better."

He took us out through the church and opened a small wooden door at the rear of the pulpit, which I had never noticed before, disclosing a stone spiral staircase.

"You'll find everything you need up there," he said. "Just remember one thing. You fire when I do. No private parties, no matter how it looks to you from up there. We want this thing to turn out just one way.''

The door slammed and I went up through the half-darkness behind Janos who was making such heavy weather of the steep and narrow stairs that I had to put both hands to his back and push.

We made it and found ourselves in a room perhaps ten feet square with long narrow windows on three sides reaching almost to the floor. Everything was ready for us as van Horne had promised, laid out neatly on a blanket. The shotgun with ammunition, the Winchester, several Mills bombs and the Thompson gun, half-a-dozen drum magazines in a neat pile beside it.

Janos collapsed on a wooden bench struggling for breath, sweat pouring from him. He took a flask from one of his pockets, unscrewed the top and had a long swallow as I examined our situation.

There was one snag. The position of the windows in the wall on the side which counted made it impossible to see down into the village itself unless one leaned out, although it gave a clear view of the immediate area around the porch twenty feet below and a little to one side.

I showed Janos, who seemed himself again, how things stood and he nodded soberly. ''That means we won't be able to see him coming so we had better be ready.''

I moved a bench, positioning it against the wall by the window so that Janos could sit in comfort, out of sight and yet with a clear view of the area around the porch. I gave him the Thompson gun and he nursed it on his knees, a cigar between his teeth. My intention was to support him with two or three judiciously placed Mills bombs and, if necessary, the Enfield or the Winchester. The shot-gun, because of the shortness of its barrels, didn't seem much of a proposition.

There was a single narrow slit, some nine inches wide, in the wall with no windows. When I peered through I found myself looking down into the pulpit, the church beyond. There was no sign of van Horne and then the vestry door opened and he came out holding the Thompson gun. He turned towards the pulpit, which meant that he now faced the altar and, as I watched, he genuflected smoothly, automatically crossing himself, then mounted into the pulpit, his face impassive.

"And what, my dear sir, would you make of that?" Janos breathed in my ear.

Van Horne placed the Thompson carefully on a small shelf where it would come to hand, sat down on a stool and opened the Bible. I straightened and shook my head. "God knows," I said and meant it. "I no longer try to understand him. I just accept."

It was very quiet and far too hot. Janos wiped sweat from his face and sighed. "I'm not built for this kind of thing any more."

"But you were once." It was a statement, not a question. As much for the sake of conversation as anything else.

"When I first came to Mexico I served as cavalry adviser to a federal force that was trying to exterminate the Yaqui in the mountains north of here and finding it hard work, in spite of the fact that the going rate for a Yaqui warrior's ears was one hundred pesos."

"They must have wanted rid of them pretty badly."

"The government wanted their land, it was as simple as that, which explains why the survivors now live in areas like the Wind River country where no one else could. This all took place in the bad old days under Diaz."

"And afterwards?"

"In the early days of the Revolution I served with Francisco Madero at the taking of Ciudad Juárez. There were many like myself. What he called his foreign legion. Men like the great Garibaldi's nephew, Giuseppe. A fine soldier."

"You must have had some interesting experiences."

"Indeed, but then they murdered Madero, or that at least is my own interpretation of what happened. Too good to live, poor man. If he'd been harder on the rogues that needed it. Dark days, sir. One never quite knew who to follow next."

Hooves rattled on the cobbles of the street out of sight to the right of us, laughter drifted up on the warm air, the jingle of harness. When they rode into view, I saw that we had all miscalculated woefully for there were at least two dozen of them, each man an arsenal in himself.

Tomás de la Plata was in the centre, as dark and sombre a figure as usual and greatest shock of all, his sister rode at his right hand.

ELEVEN

HE HAD BROUGHT her to witness van Horne's humiliation and for no other reason that I could see. She looked white and strained and came off her horse with considerable unwillingness when he reached up for her. He took her by the arm and went into the porch, seven or eight of his men following.

"Now what happens?" Janos whispered.

I moved to the slit in the wall and peered into the church. Van Horne was still seated only now the Thompson gun was ready across his knees. There was the rattle of spurs, a burst of laughter and De la Plata walked in, his arm around Chela's shoulders.

"Business is not so good today, Father?" he called.

Van Horne put the Thompson gun back on the shelf very carefully and stood up. "It would appear so. Does that give you satisfaction?"

"To discover that pigs behave predictably? Not particularly." De la Plata looked down at his sister whom he still held tightly. "Does it give you any satisfaction, my love?"

There was something unpleasant here, something

under the surface that should not be. She tried to pull free of him, but he held her tight. "You must forgive her, Father. Strange under the circumstances, but she was not anxious to come here. She only did so under my persuasion."

Behind him, his men ranged in a line, rifles cradled carelessly, a perfect target, yet van Horne would not try now, not with the woman there and if I disobeyed his orders and tried to pick off De la Plata himself, the return fire of his men must be met and Chela in the middle of it.

I could not see van Horne's face, but his voice was quite calm when he said, "What do you want with me, señor? My death?"

"Not necessary." Tomás de la Plata shook his head. "You will go, priest. Tomorrow you will leave the way you came with those who brought you. I would hang you with pleasure, but unfortunately I gave my sister my word and if she keeps hers, I will keep mine."

He turned and swept out, his arm still tight around her shoulders and his men trooped after him, the last one spitting on the floor. Van Horne went down the steps of the pulpit and hurried after him.

I got to the window just as Tomás de la Plata swung into the saddle beside his sister. As his men moved in around them, the whole group started to turn away.

Van Horne appeared from the porch and shouted, "Señor de la Plata. A word with you."

Don Tomás reined in his horse and the others followed suit. "What do you want?"

Van Horne spoke clearly so that all might hear. "I have in my possession the image of the Blessed St. Martin de Porres taken from this church during the Revolution. In these circumstances, before replacing such a relic in its rightful place, it is usual to carry it in procession through the town."

Only the nervous stamping of a horse broke the stillness as all waited for what was to follow.

"I intend to make that procession at nine-thirty tomorrow morning starting from the church."

Chela gave a short, anguished cry, stilled by her brother in an instant. "There is not a soul in this village who would take that walk with you."

"Then I walk alone."

Tomás de la Plata drew the pistol from under his jacket very fast and I snatched the Thompson from Janos in the same instant, ready to fire if needs be, Chela or no Chela, although even van Horne was too close for comfort now.

Chela cried out, a hand on her brother's arm and I think for a moment, things hung in the balance. He pushed the gun back into its shoulder holster.

"I keep my words, priest," he said. "You have until tomorrow at noon to go and live. As for this walk of yours. Try to take that and I kill you myself."

"Alone or with your men at your back?"

Tomás de la Plata's eyes glittered. His face was pale as white fire, but he said not another word, gave the signal and the whole group moved away.

I took a chance, leaning out of the window to watch them go, caught a glimpse of people standing in a ragged line fifteen or twenty yards away and drew back quickly.

"It seems he had an audience."

"By God, sir, I can believe anything," Janos replied.

I went down the spiral staircase, Janos following more slowly, and hurried along to the main entrance, pausing in the porch to peer cautiously through the side window which was minus its glass.

The crowd was fading away and beyond them, De la Plata and his men were already passing through the gate. Van Horne walked in through the porch rapidly, brushing past me as if I wasn't there. He pulled his chasuble over his head and threw it down on the nearest bench, then started to take off his alb.

"Quite a performance," I said, as Janos approached.

Van Horne turned on me, anger and frustration bursting out of him. "And what would you have had me do, Keogh? Kill the woman?"

"Never mind that," I said, evading an answer. "What about this other nonsense? This procession with that damned image. De la Plata was right. There isn't a man, woman or child in this village who dares to take that walk with you."

"Then I'll take it alone."

"And hope you'll shame De la Plata into barring your way on his own? He doesn't play those sort of games."

He did not reply and yet a muscle worked in his cheek, the great hands clenching and unclenching and there was something between us, something which could not be put into words. I knew and I think he did also.

I moved close and said in a low urgent voice, "Why, van Horne? Why?"

"Damn you, Keogh, I don't even know the answer to that one myself." He flung the alb to one side, turned and walked down to the vestry.

There was really nothing to say after that. Janos and I left him and went down to the hotel. There was no sign of Moreno in the bar so I went behind and served us both with a whisky.

"Now what?" Janos demanded.

"Don't ask me, ask him."

He sighed morosely. "You know something, my friend? It doesn't look good. It doesn't look good at all."

He reached for the bottle and helped himself to another drink and I left him there, went round to the rear courtyard where I had parked the Mercedes and drove back up the hill towards the church.

I had remembered the arms left in the bell tower. In his present mood van Horne would probably forget them and they were better in a safe place. I suppose the real truth was that I wanted to have another crack at him. I was wasting my time for as I reached the top of the hill, I passed him on his way down with Moreno.

I brought the arms down from the tower anyway, repacked them in the box, took it out to the Mercedes and put it back in its hiding place under the seat.

I returned to the church, sat on a bench and looked down towards the altar. All right, so I could manage without God these days, but it was peaceful in there in the half-light with the candles winking at the altar.

Victoria Balbuena appeared in the doorway. She paused, looking at me searchingly, automatically covering her head with a square of cotton and tying it under her chin.

I took her hands, smiling as I pulled her down beside me. "See, I survive all things."

We could take it no further. There was a shout outside, running feet and van Horne appeared in the doorway. The Enfield was already in my hand.

He said, "You won't need that. It's Moreno's wife. She's in a bad way. The baby won't come and the old woman who's midwife round here doesn't seem to know what to do."

I sat there, staring at him. He got me by the front of

the jacket and had me on my feet in an instant. "Good God, boy, did you spend four years training to be a doctor or didn't you?"

When I drove up to the hotel, there was a crowd of thirty or forty people outside for bad news travels fast. I told Victoria to come with me and we followed van Horne, who pushed his way through ruthlessly.

The scene in the bedroom was unbelievable. At least a dozen people, all close relatives, the women already mourning their loudest, Moreno with tears in his eyes and unable to control any of it.

The wretched woman on the bed was covered with a sheet and obviously terrified out of her life, crying hysterically. The old crone who leaned over her, presumably the midwife, was without a doubt the dirtiest-looking creature I'd seen in many a long day.

"Get them out," I told van Horne. "All of them. The midwife can stay as long as she washes her hands. Tell them I want hot water from the kitchen instantly and soap."

They went, protesting, although Moreno already counted her dead and I heard him say so brokenly as he went backwards through the door.

"Then pray for her," van Horne said calmly. "Pray that the Blessed St. Martin de Porres might intercede for her."

He closed the door, then went swiftly to the windows which stood open to the terrace, for the crowd was beginning to get noisy. I couldn't hear what he said to them, presumably something similar, but it certainly shut them up and he came in and closed the windows.

There was a tap at the door, Victoria opened it and returned with a pan of water and a block of cheap, carbolic soap. I started to wash my hands and told the old woman to do the same. Her only reply was to throw up her hands and run out of the room.

I pulled the sheet back over the woman's belly, pushed up her knees and made my examination, discovering immediately the reason for the old midwife's dismay.

"Can you still remember how?" van Horne asked.

We spoke in English for the mother's sake. I said, "A baby's normally delivered head-first. This is what's known as a breech. That means it's presenting its backside which is one hell of a complication."

"But can you handle it?" he said urgently.

"Let's say I've studied the theory."

The woman started to yell, I moved to her side and tried to calm her. It didn't do much good and van Horne went round to the other side and took her hand. "There is nothing to worry about, I promise you," he said. "Soon it will be all over and you will have your son."

There was that quality in his voice again. Compassion, love, call it what you will and complete authority. The woman's crying subsided into little broken sobs, but she would not let go of his hand, gazing up at him with complete trust.

I took Victoria into the corner, explained to her very rapidly in a low voice what I was going to try to do and her part in it and then I got to work.

I needed the woman as close to the edge of the bed as possible to facilitate the work, so to speak. We moved her between us which started her off again until van Horne quietened her.

In my time under training, I had delivered half-a-dozen children, all perfectly straightforward cases. I had only once seen the type of delivery I was going to attempt now, and that in hospital, but had naturally

studied the theory of the thing as I had informed van
Horne. I took the deepest of breaths and tried to remember, stage-by-stage as I might if confronted by the
examiners.

The first problem was to deliver the legs and success
in that area depends upon them being flexed. I probed
gently and found, as might have been expected, that the
legs were extended. Which meant more patient probing
until I could get a finger up against the back of one of
the child's knees and prod. The leg flexed instantly and
so did the other when I repeated the performance.

Señora Moreno gave a startled cry, her body shook
convulsively. I told her to start pushing. A moment
later, the legs delivered themselves.

Victoria had torn a linen sheet into several pieces and
was standing by. I held out my hands and she wiped
them clean and dried them quickly. I turned to begin the
next stage.

I grasped the legs, fingers beneath the thighs and
thumbs on the sacrum and pulled down until the shoulders were in sight. Now the arms were extended, but I
remembered how to handle that one too. I twisted the
child gently to the left. The shoulder flexed, I hooked a
finger into the left elbow and delivered the arm. Then I
rotated in the opposite direction and carried out the
same manoeuvre for the other arm.

I paused to take breath and van Horne said in English, "How is it going?"

"Fine so far, but I'm just coming into the most dangerous stage. Delivery of the head. Tricky even with instruments. There is a very real chance of brain damage
unless it's done just right."

The secret was to bring out the head slowly and
steadily and I remembered the procedure exactly. I put
my right arm beneath the child and got my forefinger

into its mouth which meant I was now supporting it on my forearm.

Next, I placed the forefinger of my left hand on the head to flex it and the index and ring fingers on the right and left shoulders respectively and started to exert traction. Slowly, very slowly, it began to move and yet the strength I had to exert was so considerable that sweat stood on my forehead in great drops.

And then it was clear and safe in my hands although it became obvious at once that it was not breathing. The whole body was a rather unpleasant deep purple as if everything was locked up and waiting to move.

I tried slapping it with no immediate result, so took a small piece of cotton Victoria passed me, cleared the mouth and nostrils of mucus and liquor. The heartbeat was strong, so there was nothing wrong there.

Very gently, I blew into the tiny mouth. Quite suddenly the child took a convulsive breath, then, most beautiful sound in all the world, it started to cry.

For some reason Victoria was crying too, although she took the child from me competently enough and held him while I saw to the placenta and checked the woman's own state, now that it was all over.

"A boy," I announced. "If anyone is interested."

Van Horne took the child, which Victoria had wrapped carefully in a linen sheet, and moved to the bedside. I didn't hear what he said to Señora Moreno, but I know she started to cry again and said brokenly, "Just as you promised, Father. Just as you promised."

He put the baby down beside her, opened the windows and went out on the terrace. All very dramatic and there was a satisfying outcry from the crowd in the street.

I seemed rather unnecessary, which was fair enough, because that is exactly what I was. I got up, went to the door and opened it just as Moreno appeared with the womenfolk behind him. They pressed past me into the room, making the kind of sounds one would have expected and I left them to it and went along the corridor to my own room.

God, but I was tired, more than I had been in years and yet strangely happy. For once I had given life instead of taking it, I suppose, although I was no longer able to think straight.

I lay on the bed, staring up at the ceiling and the door opened and Victoria came in. She sat beside me and gently smoothed my brow, untying the knots one-by-one and very gradually, I drifted into sleep.

TWELVE

I AWAKENED TO darkness, the pulsating beat of music. Guitars and maracas from the sound of it and someone was singing. I was alone, for there was no sign of Victoria, even when I swung my feet to the floor, found a match and lit the lamp. My boots were at the end of the bed. I pulled them on, went to the washstand in the corner, leaned over the bowl and emptied the earthenware jug of water over my head.

Which made me feel a lot better. I found a towel, opened a window and went out on the terrace and stood there, breathing in the cool night air and drying myself at the same time. The light from the hotel windows spilled out across the street and showed me Victoria and Nachita sitting on the edge of the boardwalk opposite.

"Victoria," I called softly and she looked up. "Why did you leave me? Come on up."

Her face was a pale blur indicating nothing. Nachita answered for her. "It is not permitted, señor."

"What in the hell are you talking about?" I demanded. "Wait for me there. I'll be right down."

I found a clean shirt, pulled it over my head and went

downstairs. I didn't bother going into the bar, but went straight out through the front door and plunged across the street without looking so that a couple of horsemen had to rein-in to avoid hitting me.

Victoria and Nachita rose to meet me and I took her by the arms. "What's all this about?"

Nachita said, "She was asked to leave the hotel, señor."

"That's nonsense," I told him.

"In Mojada it is not so bad." He shrugged. "I know places where an Indian, especially a Yaqui, would not be allowed in town limits."

And inside, the bastards were celebrating. The two horsemen had dismounted and were staring across at us. I recognised Jurado, but the other was a stranger to me. Jurado made some comment or other and laughed and then turned and went inside, closing the door behind him.

It was very quiet, the music muted and far away and I was no longer tired, only angry in a sad sort of way and sorry for humanity, if you understand me.

I raised her hands to my lips and said, "Wait for me here. I'll get a jacket and walk back to the camp with you."

The door to the bar was open as I went through the hall and as I passed, I heard van Horne bellow, "Keogh, in here."

I paused in the doorway. I should think just about every man in the village was in there and most of them with drink taken. Four musicians were banging away briskly in the corner.

Van Horne and Janos were at a table, jammed up tight against the bar and the Hungarian raised his glass. "To the hero of the hour. Join us, sir, I insist."

I stood at the bar beside them, Jurado and his friend

behind me, which was important in view of what happened. Moreno was dispensing free drinks, himself half-drunk. Van Horne glanced up at me. "You don't look pleased, Keogh, what's wrong?"

"I understand they threw Victoria out when I was asleep."

He shrugged. "A custom of the country. She's chosen her side, Keogh, and the plain fact is that the average Mexican can't stand Indians."

"Especially Yaqui," Janos put in. "Incredibly cruel people, Keogh. When I served with that federal punitive expedition we had a colonel called Cubero who'd bought himself a harem of five Yaqui women. Women, I say. As I remember, the eldest was only fifteen. A hundred pesos each."

"And you call the Yaqui cruel?" I said.

"They ambushed him with a patrol in the mountains one day." Janos was as drunk as I had seen him and spoke rather slowly as a consequence. "God knows what they'd done to him before they finished him off, but when we found him, he had an eyeball in the palm of each hand and his private parts had been stuffed between his teeth."

"What do you expect me to do, vomit?" I demanded. "I'd say he got what he deserved at a hundred pesos each for little girls."

Moreno leaned across the bar, grinning foolishly. "Heh, Señor Keogh, we have decided to name the boy for Father van Horne. A good idea, you agree?"

"I think it's bloody marvellous." I turned to van Horne. "Another van Horne miracle, is that how it turned out?"

His smile died, something close to pain in his eyes and Moreno touched my arm. "You will drink with me, señor?"

"No thanks," I said. "I've made other arrangements."

He seemed genuinely bewildered. "But I don't understand, señor."

I had not buttoned my shirt and the silver amulet Victoria had given me swung free. Jurado reached across and took it in his fingers. "It is very simple, Moreno. Señor Keogh prefers other company to ours. Darker meat." He laughed coarsely. "Is it true what they say about Yaqui women?" He followed this with probably the most obscene suggestion I had heard in my life.

I think I knew then that he was there to make trouble. Not particularly with me, but I had come easily to hand, so to speak. Van Horne started to get up and I shoved him back into his chair.

"I'd be very happy to drink with you," I said to Moreno. "In a moment."

As I turned and walked out, Jurado laughed. "Ah, the little one runs to avoid messing his pants." One or two of the drunks laughed dutifully.

Victoria and Nachita crossed the street to meet me. I said, "I've been invited to have a drink before I go."

She knew what was in my mind, I saw it in her eyes and so did Nachita. He said, "There is nothing to be gained from this, señor, they would spit on us."

A strange thing happened then. I went very cold, very calm, fire in my belly and when I spoke, the voice came from somewhere outside me and the sound of it would have frightened Finn Cuchulain himself.

"You will listen to me now," I said. "I am Emmet Keogh of Stradballa and afraid of no man on this earth. We will go now and God will go with us. I will see justice done and if I must break a head or two in the process, then well enough."

The blackness was in me then as it had been in my father, so they tell me. The violence there had been no escaping, that had sent my mother to an early grave. I turned without another word and they followed and when I reached the door, I kicked it open and went in like a strong wind. The silence had to be heard to be believed when they saw what stood behind me.

I walked to the bar, put my hands on the edge and confronted poor foolish Moreno, mouth agape. "I'll have that drink now."

I half-turned, leaning against the bar, back to van Horne and Janos, facing Jurado and his friend. Victoria stood a yard or two away and smiled when I looked at her. I raised my fingers to my lips and kissed them. There was a gasp from someone in the crowd. I saw Nachita's fingers ready in the lever of his old Winchester.

Moreno put a bottle on the bar, his good whisky, and one glass. I said, "You are forgetting my friends."

There was a look of agony on his face. Poor devil, he didn't know what to do next. Jurado solved the situation for him. His great hand wrapped itself round the neck of the bottle. "No," he said.

That close, the smell of him, his gross body, was quite overpowering. I said, "Did anyone ever tell you that you stink, my friend?"

There was genuine amazement in his eyes, shock that someone dare insult him so before everyone there. Especially a man so much smaller than himself.

He released the bottle in a kind of reflex gesture and I picked it up and smashed it across the side of his head. As he cried out, staggering back, I wrenched the pistol from his holster and tossed it to van Horne.

Jurado started to turn, blood on his face and I

grabbed the nearest chair and smashed it across the great head and shoulders. Once, twice and then again, breaking it apart.

He fell on his knees and stayed there for a while, then got up and stood looking at me, one hand wiping blood away mechanically.

"All right then, you bastard," I said, dropping into a fighting crouch. "Let's be having you."

My grandfather, they tell me, might have been a contender for the heavyweight crown had he so chosen and in his youth, had gone the distance with the great Bob Fitzsimmons himself.

From my earliest years at school, my small size earned me more kicks than halfpence. For some time this went undetected for I have always been considered close by nature, and then an ambush by a couple of tinker's boys one fine evening sent me home with a face like raw meat.

Mickeen Bawn Keogh examined that face, his grey eyes cold and rather frightening in spite of the smile on his face. "Two of them, did you say, *avic?*" He nodded. "Then it is time I took you in hand and long overdue."

Whereupon he took off his jacket, led me out into the yard and gave me my first lesson in the noble art and no holds barred.

So I was only five and a half feet and weighed barely ten stone, but I could punch every pound of it as Raul Jurado found to his cost that night.

He came in with a roar, I feinted with my left and smashed my right fist into his mouth, splitting the lips so that blood spurted. I followed it with a left below the breast that sounded like the crack of a whip when bone met bone.

Footwork, timing and hitting, that was the secret and in that first couple of minutes I gave him neither quarter nor peace, circling around, evading his ponderous blows with ease, feinting and jabbing, in and away again.

The crowd scattered, most of them scrambling for the door and there was a press of faces at the windows outside. Janos still sat at the table, hands folded on the knob of his stick, face shining with sweat, but van Horne was standing now, Jurado's pistol in his right hand.

I suppose I got careless, forgetting the rawhide quirt dangling from Jurado's wrist. I danced in to belt him again and he slashed out blindly, the rawhide curling around my face, drawing an involuntary cry of agony from me.

Worst of all, when he pulled, I had no choice but to lurch towards him and he delivered a stunning blow to my forehead that sent me back towards the bar. His friend stuck out a foot putting me flat on my back.

I rolled away as Jurado came in fast, boot raised to crush my face. I grabbed for that foot, twisted and he fell heavily across me. We rolled here and there between the tables trying to have each other's eyes out and when we stopped, I was on top.

He got his knee into me before I could do any damage and threw me backwards with a powerful kick. As I scrambled up, he rose to meet me, his face a mask of blood and I was not afraid. As I circled, I saw Victoria by the door, teeth bared like any she-cat, Nachita holding her arm.

Jurado was going to kill me now, it was in his face. His hands came up, hooked into claws and he charged like a bull. I threw a chair into his path that put him on his knees and kicked him in the side of the head.

He stayed there on his hands and knees for the second time that night and his friend at the bar, thinking, I suppose, that I would finish him off, pulled out his pistol. He was fast, but not fast enough. Two foot of steel flashed from the Hungarian's stick, blurred in motion. Jurado's friend dropped his pistol with a cry, blood spurting as he grabbed his wrist.

Even then, Jurado surprised me by the sheer bull-strength of him. He came in low, his shoulder sending me back against the wall. His foot slipped or I think he might have had me. As I straightened, he lurched forward again. I ducked under his arm, twisted a shoulder inwards and sent him over my hip through the window in a savage cross-buttock.

The crowd scattered in a snowstorm of flying glass and I scrambled over the sill and arrived on the terrace in time to put my boot in his face as he tried to get up, sending him back into the street.

He lay there on his back and I suddenly found it necessary to hang on to one of the verandah posts. I turned, leaning against it, and found Victoria on the edge of the crowd four or five yards away.

Her face seemed very pale, the eyes enormous. I smiled, or thought I did, though my face must have looked a sight and then, dear God above us, a miracle happened.

Her eyes filled with horror, her face shattered like a mirror breaking, the mouth opened wide in what should have been a soundless scream. Instead, she cried my name.

"Emm-et!" Broken in the centre, yet quite unmistakable.

I turned and swung to one side as Jurado lunged in, a knife in one hand. In the same moment, Nachita appeared from the darkness behind him and flung his own knife underhand so that it thudded into the boardwalk at my feet.

By God, but the power was in me then. Such release as I had never known to hear my name spoken by the one person who mattered most. She told me much later, that when I went down into the street to meet him, knife in hand, the look on my face was terrible to see.

Jurado must have agreed for he threw his own knife away from him and staggered into the darkness.

I swung round, challenging that sea of faces, yellow in the lamplight, fear on most of them and then van Horne stepped down and put a hand to my chest as if to stop me falling. His voice seemed to come from under the earth itself, remote, far away, but in any case, there was only one person I wished to see at that moment.

For some reason she was crying. Now why would that be? And then I remembered. I said gently, "My name? What's my name?"

But there was nothing to fear for the spell was broken. "Emm-et," she said. "Emm-et."

"We will go now," I said. "Before I fall down and disgrace us all in the face of the world."

She took one arm, Nachita the other and we left them there and went to our own place.

They got me to the camp and into the tent and I lay there in the cool darkness and let the night wash over me. After a while, Victoria came back with a bowl of water and a cloth. She started to gently wipe my face.

I was tired, my head adrift from my shoulders, but I was still conscious enough to need reassuring and took her by the wrists. "Speak to me—anything. Just let me hear your voice."

There was a hesitation I could almost feel and then slowly, hesitantly, each word separate, the voice rather remote and more than a little hoarse, she said, "What do you want me to say?"

"Not another word," I answered and started to laugh weakly and then the darkness really did close in on me.

I awakened to firelight flickering on the canvas walls of the tent and to voices. It took me a moment or so, not only to think back to reality, but to realise that one of them was van Horne.

I crawled out through the entrance, so stiff and sore that it was past belief and found the three of them sitting by the fire drinking coffee. Nachita saw me first and van Horne and Victoria turned in the same moment.

She was beside me in a flash, helping me stand. "You should be resting."

There was still that faintly unreal flavour to her speech. Van Horne said, "How do you feel?"

"Like a very old hound-dog."

"That was quite a performance. You can use yourself." My Enfield in its holster was lying beside him and he picked it up. "I noticed you'd left this in your room. Thought you might be needing it." There was more to it than that, of course. Had to be.

"Where's Janos?"

"Oh, he decided to have an early night."

My head still felt swollen and somehow disembodied and I was having difficulty in thinking straight and that would not do at all.

"I need to clear my head," I said. "And there's only

one way I'm going to do that in a hurry. I won't be long."

The moon was full, the cottonwoods a maze of light and shadow and beyond, the waterfall was silver in the moonlight as it cascaded over rocks.

I stripped and stood there for a moment, the night wind cold on my flesh, feeling for the bruises gingerly and any sign of real damage. My ribs and the rest of me seemed intact enough and I moved out across a patch of shingle and waded into the water.

It was cold enough to freeze the marrow in the bones or so it seemed. I swallowed a howl and swam to the other side and back again. The effects were remarkably bracing and I stood under the waterfall for a moment or so, for the pool was nowhere more than four feet deep as far as I could judge.

Ten seconds of that icy deluge was all I could stand and when I waded out to the shingle strand, van Horne was standing watching me, the Enfield in his hand.

"You forgot this again." He shook his head. "That's what women do to a man, Keogh. The beginning of the end."

"True enough," I said, catching the blanket he tossed me. "But what an end."

He smiled. "So your brains are unscrambled again? That's a blessing. Do you try to commit suicide often?"

I shrugged as I rubbed myself down. "You know how it is."

He paused in the act of lighting one of his cigarillos, the match flaring in his hand. "I'm not sure that I do."

"I don't like to be leaned on," I said. "To be shoved against the wall. Brings out the worst in me and men like Jurado do, certainly. Probably something to do with my size."

"I had noticed," he replied, a touch of irony in his voice.

I pulled on my shirt and found a crumpled packet of Artistas in my trouser pocket. "What did you want to see me about?"

He seemed surprised. "Why, tomorrow, of course. What else?"

"You still intend to go through with it, this walk nonsense?"

"I'll be outside the church at nine-thirty just like I said, ready to go and De la Plata will be there to stop me."

"With at least a couple of dozen men to back him up."

"And riding straight into ambush. Here, let me show you."

He found a stick and drew a crude plan in a patch of damp sand. "I'll be outside the porch waiting to go, with the image on a handcart I've borrowed from Moreno. I'll have the Thompson and two or three Mills bombs handy."

Strange what tricks the mind plays on us. For a moment, this might have been one of a hundred similar jobs I had planned and undertaken over the long dark years.

"What about Janos?"

"In the bell tower, same as yesterday, with the other Thompson. You'll be on the other side of the square." He indicated the spot on his plan. "There is a broken-down stable there, no longer used by anyone. I've been up there tonight and left you the Winchester and three Mills bombs under an old sack in the right-hand corner by the loft door."

"What kind of a field of fire?"

"Couldn't be better. Forty yards from the stable to the church. I paced it out. You can't miss from the loft door at that range. They'll ride straight into the cross-fire."

I thought about it for a while, but could find no real flaws beyond the usual one that you could never depend on anything in this life, which meant that something unexpected was almost certain to happen.

"One thing," I said. "I'll be firing in your general direction. I hope you realise that."

"Son, I'll be inside that porch so fast you'll wonder if I was ever there in the first place."

A fine, light-hearted attitude. I said, "It's funny, but you had Janos and me worried back there at the church when you threw down the gauntlet to De la Plata. We thought you might be taking your role a little too seriously."

He seemed genuinely astonished, then laughed harshly. "Sure I take it seriously, Keogh. Fifty-three thousand dollars' worth."

I could have taken him up on that, because in a way, he was protesting too much, but I had no choice for Nachita appeared from the cottonwoods like some grey ghost. Even allowing for his usual impassivity, I sensed there was something.

"What is it?"

"We have a visitor, señor. For you, Father," he added, turning to van Horne. "The Señorita de la Plata."

A night for surprises.

She stood holding the bridle of her horse just beyond the firelight. One could not see much of her face, but she seemed calm enough at first when she spoke. "Forgive me, Father, but I had to speak with you. I saw Señor Janos at the hotel who thought you might be here.''

Van Horne took the reins from her and handed them to Nachita. "What can I do for you?"

Her voice was still calm when she said, "Father, I know my brother and I can tell you this. He and his men will be at the church in the morning at the time you have indicated. If he finds you there he will kill you. Nothing is more certain.''

Van Horne took her hands and was obviously about to reply when she cracked wide open and stumbled against him as if for support.

"Help me, Father. In pity's name, help me. I can no longer carry this dreadful burden alone."

He glanced over his shoulder at the three of us, hesitated fractionally, then led her to the tent and they went inside.

For quite some time there was bitter, agonised weeping, which finally subsided, to be followed by the low murmur of voices. It was strangely embarrassing, as if one were eavesdropping on something essentially private. We squatted by the fire without talking and drank the bitter coffee Victoria provided.

It must have been at least half-an-hour before the tent flap was thrown back and they emerged, Chela de la Plata first. She avoided my eye rather obviously and hurried to where Nachita had tethered her horse to a tree.

Van Horne went after her and she turned and asked for a blessing. He responded without the slightest hesitation, the words clear on the night air as his fingers traced the sign of the cross.

"Benedicat te Omnipotens Deus, Pater, et Filius, et Spiritus Sanctus."

She mounted and galloped away and he stayed there looking after her. I moved to his side, but before I could speak, he said, "I expect you and Janos to be in position by nine in the morning, just in case. No need to meet again before then."

He actually started to walk away and I grabbed his sleeve. "Just a minute, what was it all supposed to be about?"

"You heard, she came to warn me."

"Not that, I mean the other business."

"She had a lot on her mind. She hadn't spoken to a priest in a long time, that's all."

I said, "Are you trying to tell me you confessed her?"

He turned on me, eyes starting from his head and grabbed me by the lapel. "Does the thought amuse you, Keogh? What was I supposed to do? Say no?"

If ever I have looked at a soul in torment it was then. He pushed me away and snarled, "Anyway, what's the odds. We could all be dead by nine-thirty-five in the morning."

I watched him walk away, clear in the moonlight. For some reason I was filled with the most terrible feeling of desolation I have ever known. But no, that isn't quite true. I had known it once and once only. A century or more before. The square at Drumdoon in the rain, my brother dead before me.

I went and lay on the blankets in the tent, staring into the dark and after a while, Victoria brought me a warm drink which obviously contained a sleeping draught of some description, for within minutes of taking it, I was asleep.

THIRTEEN

I SURFACED TO the patter of rain against the canvas, the dim grey light of the old tent and lay there for a while, staring up at the ridge pole, relaxed and comfortable until I tried to stretch my arms and found that I could not.

For a moment, it was as if I was still asleep and dreaming, but I was very much awake as I realised when I kicked out frantically and discovered that I was bound hand and foot. I tried shouting, but after a while, the tent flap was pulled aside and Nachita ducked in. He crouched over me, his face grave.

"Where is she?" I demanded.

"Gathering wood by the stream, señor." I tried to sit up and he shook his head. "You will not go to Mojada this morning. She will not have it."

I tried to stay calm. "What time is it?"

"A little before nine, señor."

"For God's sake, Nachita, you must release me."

There was no sense in pleading for he simply got up and went out again. There wasn't much left to do after that except pull the blankets away, which was easily enough done, for my hands were tied at the front, presumably because she had wanted to hurt me as little as possible.

I barged through the tent flap head-down, falling on my face. They had rigged up an old tarpaulin from the tent to a couple of poles, the fire underneath and rain ran off the edge in a steady stream. Beyond, a heavy mist rolled down from the peaks reducing visibility considerably.

I tried to sit up and Nachita turned from the fire and gave me a hand under my elbow, putting my back against the saddle. At the same moment Victoria appeared from the trees, a bundle of branches in her arms. She wore an old blanket coat and a straw sombrero against the rain.

"What in the hell are you trying to prove?" I demanded.

She dropped the branches on the ground, knelt down and started to feed the fire without replying.

"You found your tongue again last night, or had you forgotten?" I leaned forward. "Answer me, you bitch."

Nachita's hand caught me across the mouth. She moved as quickly, getting between us and pushing him away. Her speech was slow and careful, the voice a little remote. "Your friend dies this morning, this is certain."

"But not me, is that it?"

Nachita was on his feet, rifle ready. He was too late. Horses splashed through the stream, riders pouring out of the trees to surround the camp, at least thirty of them. I recognised two or three faces although Jurado was conspicuous by his absence and then the line parted and Tomás de la Plata rode through.

He was dressed as usual with the addition of a cavalry officer's caped greatcoat open down the front, presumably so that he could get to his gun if needs be.

He stared down at me for a moment, a frown on his face, and then dismounted and squatted on his heels before me. "So, a reluctant suitor, Señor Keogh? This is not what I was told."

"She thinks I'll stand by the priest and get my head blown off if she doesn't keep me here," I told him.

"Indeed." He glanced at Victoria, then Nachita and returned to me. "She could have a point. Gringos stick together, an undeniable fact of life."

"All right, so I don't want to see the man die. He's an American citizen, remember? Kill him and there could well be a lot of political pressure to have something done about it."

"His own choice, not mine."

"Then set me free and I'll persuade him otherwise."

"But I do not want you to." He seemed surprised. "Why should I? If he wishes to martyr himself, I'll be happy to accommodate him."

I still had to play my part, to react as he might reasonably expect the person I was supposed to be to react. "But why? What can there possibly be in it for you?"

He waved a hand in a gesture that sent everyone back a few yards, then leaned towards me. "Have you ever considered that when Christ rode into Jerusalem, the authorities were compelled to act as they did? Had no choice? You see, it was impossible for them to exist side-by-side. A contradiction in terms."

All this, he delivered in tones of the utmost seriousness and with a perfectly grave face. I had felt from the first there was a streak of madness in the man. Now I was certain of it.

"An interesting parallel," I said.

"Remarkably exact. How could a man like me exist in Father van Horne's world or he in mine? I would have no reality and that would be impossible, for I truly do exist as all men know, which means this priest of yours should already be dead."

I did not need that twisted logic to confirm me in the impression of a man who had definitely gone over the edge of things, for I saw nothing but madness in his eyes as he stood up.

He produced a gold hunter from inside his coat and flicked it open. "You will excuse me now, but in exactly twelve minutes I have an appointment and I like to be on time." He swung into the saddle and pulled in his horse which trampled through the fire, upsetting the coffeepot. "I am sorry to leave you like this, my friend. Someone should have warned you that you were playing with fire. Let us hope this little barbarian here keeps her knife in her belt."

He cantered away into the mist, his men following him and I turned to Victoria and said desperately, "Release me now, I beg you, while there is still time."

She started to turn away so I did the only thing left to me, which was to drop forward on my knees and thrust my bound wrists into the scattered embers of the fire. The pain was unbelievable and I was unable to restrain a groan, but she was already on me, dragging me back against the saddle.

I said, "You have nothing to gain—everything to lose. Do you think that we could ever live together after a betrayal like this? That I could look at you and not remember?"

The great dark eyes widened and I knew that I had struck deep. She wavered, genuine pain in her eyes and I pushed my hands out towards her. "Anything later than now is no good."

It worked. Her hand went outside the blanket coat

and came out clutching a knife so sharp that she was through the rope in one easy slice. As she repeated the performance on my ankles, Nachita emerged from the tent and handed me the Enfield in its shoulder holster. I struggled into the straps and said, "I'll be too late at the main gate. Is there another way?"

"The wall crumbles at the top of the village near the church, señor. Easy to climb. I could show you."

He glanced enquiringly at her as he said this and she nodded. I grabbed her hand as she turned away, pulled her round and smiled. "Believe it or not, but I intend to come back."

But she didn't believe me, not for a moment, I could tell as much from her eyes. To be honest, I wasn't too confident myself considering the way things were going.

I took the nearest horse bare-back, with nothing but a rope halter to hang on to, putting my heels into him hard and galloped into the mist, urging him on with a clenched fist.

Nachita was beside me in an instant, drawing abreast to lead the way, riding magnificently, his old rifle in one hand. We went headlong through rough broken ground that had my heart in my mouth, turned into a deep arroyo with a few inches of rain water in the bottom, scrambled up a steep bank at the other end and emerged into the open no more than twenty or thirty yards from the wall at the top end of the village.

I could see what he meant at once for in places the adobe brick had crumbled, reducing the height to about ten feet. I pushed my horse against the wall, stood on its back and Nachita crowded his horse in beside me to hold things steady for a moment. My height, as always, was the trouble. I was perhaps a foot short, but a quick

jump took care of that and the gaps between the
crumbling brick made excellent footholds.

I gave Nachita a quick wave and dropped straight
over the other side into a small courtyard. There was a
door in the far wall which proved to be unlocked. I
opened it and found myself in a narrow alley that emptied into the square no more than a couple of steps
away.

When I peered round the corner I found I was perhaps forty yards from the church. The cart van Horne
had mentioned was in position a couple of yards in front
of the porch and had been covered by some·kind of
brightly covered blanket or tapestry. The image of St.
Martin de Porres stood on it in solitary splendour.
There was no sign of van Horne and Janos, too, was
keeping well out of sight for I could see nothing of him
in the bell tower.

Somewhere I heard horses trampling over the cobbles
on their way up to the village and it came to me then
that this building here on the corner must be the stable
van Horne had referred to.

A flight of stone stairs led up from the street through
a wooden door. When I opened it, the loft door van
Horne had mentioned stood wide giving a clear view of
the church and a porch. I saw that he was standing inside, presumably sheltering from the rain.

I found the sacking in the corner as he had described,
the Winchester and the Mills bombs, ready primed, I
was pleased to see. I was barely in time for as I returned
to the loft door, De la Plata's men emerged from the left
in a solid bunch, wheeled and turned to face the porch
in a ragged line.

It couldn't have been more perfect. I was aware of
many things in that final moment. Tomás de la Plata
himself in the cavalry greatcoat. Van Horne moving

into the entrance of the porch in full regalia, including a superb gold cope, presumably in honour of the occasion.

I picked up a grenade, pulling the pin with my teeth and got ready to throw it, and in the same moment a rider thundered out of the street into the square, pulling in the horse so sharply between van Horne and Tomás that it slipped on the wet cobbles and slid back into its haunches.

Chela de la Plata, arriving too late, for van Horne was already bringing the Thompson round from behind his back and firing and a grenade sailed down from the bell tower to explode in exactly the right spot to take care of half-a-dozen men and their mounts in one breath.

I lobbed mine in for good measure with a similar result for the woman was dead. Had to be. I caught a glimpse of her, the face drenched in blood, her brother beside her, trying to hold her in the saddle and then they went down together, horses and all, as Janos leaned out of the bell tower and started to work the other Thompson gun from side-to-side.

It was a bad mistake for they were firing back by now and suddenly, he stopped shooting and leaned across the windowsill, head down. Very slowly, pulled by his immense weight, he simply squeezed through and followed the Thompson to the cobbles twenty feet below.

During this time I had fired continuously, choosing each target carefully and had picked off four of them with complete certainty. In spite of all this, several riders had passed below me to make good their escape through the alley to my right.

The square was heavy with smoke, the cries of the dying, the animals, and for a while, it was impossible to see clearly. There was a sudden rush, I got the Win-

chester to my shoulder and lowered it as a bunch of
riderless horses thundered out of the murk, crowding
towards the alley.

Too late, I saw the leg hooked over one in the centre,
recognised the fluttering cape of the cavalry greatcoat. I
caught one quick glimpse of Tomás de la Plata glaring
up at me, blood on his face, and then he and the horses
were into the alley and away.

A shot chipped the jamb of the door beside my head,
fired by someone still active down there. I fired back at
the flash and was rewarded by a scream. There was a
momentary silence, the roll of the Thompson, then silence again.

After a while, van Horne called, "Are you there,
Keogh? It's all over."

I reloaded the Winchester on the way down and went
to meet him, pausing to put a bullet in the head of a
horse that rolled on its side with the stomach showing.

Van Horne emerged from the smoke and mist, the
Thompson ready, still wearing his robes and that
magnificent gold cope. "Janos is dead," he said. "And
I can't see De la Plata."

"He got away," I told him. "Several of them made it
past me into a rear alley, which I can only presume
would bring them out at the bottom of the village near
the main gate. The other Thompson gun would have
done better work here."

"No sense in crying over spilt milk," he said. "I
thought we had him, but it was only his horse. His sister
was something I didn't foresee."

His voice was quite hoarse and he seemed to find difficulty in speaking for he suddenly pushed the Thompson into my hands, turned and walked away. I followed
in time to see him take off the gold cope and spread it
over the woman's body, then he went into the church.

• • •

I retrieved the other Thompson which Janos had dropped from the tower, checked that it still worked, then started down the main street, a Thompson in each hand. I found Moreno and a handful of others outside the hotel, as frightened a bunch of men as I have ever seen.

He hurried towards me. "Father van Horne, he is all right?"

I nodded. "How many rode out through the gate? Did you see?"

"Six, señor, and Don Tomás was one of them, riding like a madman, blood on his face."

"His sister tried to stop it happening," I said. "And got killed instead."

"Mother of God." He crossed himself as did several of those with him. "You put Jesus in my mouth, señor. We will all die for this day's work."

"Not if you have any guts left. Guns and ammunition aplenty on the ground outside the church if you rob the dead. In the meantime, I'd put a couple of men on the wall by the main gate if I were you. They can have the machine guns, not that I think they'll be needed, but it pays to take care. There's a Lieutenant Cordona with a cavalry detachment at the old *rancheria* at Huanca. He'll come galloping to the rescue if you get a message off to him."

He took a deep breath and nodded. "You are right, señor, panic is of no assistance in such a situation. At least two dozen people ran out into the open country in blind terror when the shooting started. You must understand we have seen some terrible things in these parts over the years. Whole villages slaughtered—women, children. One would think God had turned his back on Mexico."

I managed to cut him off at that point, showed the two men he selected how to pull the trigger on the machine guns and left them all to it.

I had the bar to myself, found a bottle of scotch and poured a large one. God, what a mess. All that killing, the girl dead and Tomás de la Plata still ran free. I was suddenly sick of the whole business, sick and angry at the world, but most of all with van Horne.

I went back up the street to the square where Moreno and his men already moved amongst the dead and entered the church. Van Horne was sitting on a bench at the front near the altar still wearing his alb. He didn't even turn his head as I went up the aisle.

I stopped beside him and he said, "Don't say it, Keogh, I know."

Standing there looking down at him, all the anger and frustration evaporated. The truth at last and facing up to it carried its own release.

"No, you don't," I said. "My fault as well as yours. Everything that's happened and we can always include the good Colonel Bonilla and Tomás de la Plata."

"Collective responsibility?" he said gravely. "Not really good enough. In the final analysis, a man must accept personal responsibility for his own actions."

"Which sounds as if it could have come straight out of the middle section of some theology lecture at that seminary of yours," I said.

"Very possibly."

He was unable to take the conversation any further for Moreno called from the doorway. "Come quickly, Father."

When we went out of the porch, I found Nachita on the ground against the wall. He looked half stunned, blood oozing from a contusion on the right of his forehead.

I dropped to one knee and he grabbed my coat. "He sent me, señor. The Evil One himself sent me."

I knew instantly what had happened, saw it all in one terrible moment of truth, yet things had to have their logical sequence.

"He has Victoria?"

He nodded. "And twenty-one other people, señor. Villagers from this place. Some only children."

The ones who had run into the open country in panic.

"What does he want?" van Horne demanded harshly.

"You, Father," Nachita said. "He just wants you. No one else. He gives you two hours."

FOURTEEN

INSIDE THE CHURCH away from the others, Nachita filled in the unpleasant facts. Tomás de la Plata had only five men left, it was true, but they were ample for his purpose. On the other side of the stream there was an abandoned *casa*, only the walls still standing and he had his hostages penned in there. The slightest sign of an attack and they died instantly.

The effect of all this on van Horne was considerable. The flesh seemed to have withered on his bones if such a thing were possible, the face itself to have sunk in so that he looked old and tired and past everything there ever was.

He turned without a word and went down to the vestry. I left Nachita and followed him. He had a whisky bottle in one hand, a glass in the other. His hand shook quite distinctly as he poured. He tossed the whisky back in one mouthful and had another.

"God dammit, Keogh, what are we going to do?"

"I don't know," I said. "It needs thinking about."

He brightened suddenly, probably the first quick effects of the alcohol. "We could have a go. You, me and the Indian. He'd come with us. We could take them, Keogh, between us. He's only got five to back him up now, remember."

"We wouldn't even get close," I said. "One shot, that's all it would take and he'd kill the lot of them."

He turned on me angrily. "How in the hell can you be certain? You haven't even been to take a look at the situation. Perfect cover in this mist and rain."

He was talking into the wind, we both knew that. I said, "Let's go down to the gate and look things over."

He pulled off his alb, found his shovel hat and we went out through the church. The surprise came when I opened the door to the porch.

Bad news spreads faster than the plague. I should think that virtually every living soul in the village stood there waiting in the heavy rain. Dark, anxious faces, not a sound, no open mourning. A despairing acceptance of the whole terrible business as a fact of life.

For a moment, they confronted each other, as it were, van Horne and the crowd and then a strange thing happened, infinitely beautiful, yet terrible in its way.

An old woman and a young girl stood together at the front, the girl clutching a bundle wrapped in a cloth, her thin blouse saturated, clinging to her breasts, outlining them perfectly. I remember this clearly and the great sorrow in her eyes as the old woman gave her a push forward.

The girl offered the bundle to van Horne who took it instinctively. She said simply, "Candles, Father, for the dead."

She went down on her knees in front of him and most of the crowd followed suit. There was a kind of tableau there, the kneeling people, the heavy rain rushing into the ground, van Horne looking down at the girl, the bundle in one hand.

He raised her up and when he spoke, his voice was calm, gentle, the most wonderful smile on his face. "Come inside, child, out of the rain. All of you, come inside."

It was as if I had ceased to exist for him for he turned and went back into the church without a word for me. I got out of the way and Nachita, who had been standing against the wall, joined me. Most of those present had probably not been inside a church for years and yet they were calm and orderly about it as they went in, the women covering their heads.

Nachita said, "What do they intend to do in there, señor, pray for a miracle?"

"I suppose so."

He shook his head. "I have no faith in such things. Neither does Tomás de la Plata."

My own sentiments exactly and I turned and we went down through the village together to the main gate.

Visibility was not much more than fifty or sixty yards, so heavy was the rain. They had closed the gates, barring them securely, so I went up on the wall to see what I could see, which was precisely nothing.

Nachita came up a little later with an old blanket poncho he had picked up from somewhere and a palm-woven sombrero. I put them on though I was wet enough already and stared out into an alien land.

I said, "Is there anything we can do?"

He shook his head. "The first sign of a move against him and they die."

I tried to think of Victoria and the rest of them out there beyond the stream in the old *casa* and found it an impossibility, even when I tried to concentrate on her alone. I was cold, chilled through to the centre of things, soaking wet under the old poncho, the straps of my shoulder holster rubbing painfully.

There was a curiously dreamlike flavour to it all. It was as if it could not really be happening. As if I might wake up at any moment, but to what, that was the thing.

"There is nothing to be done, then?" I said. "Is that what you are saying?"

"There is the priest, señor."

I moved away from the man who guarded this side of the gate with one of the Thompsons and Nachita followed me. I said, "He is not a priest. Not a real priest. You know this."

"It does not matter, señor. He is what De la Plata wants and I will not stand by and see my lady die."

"He might kill them all anyway," I said. "Have you thought of that?"

A shot sounded through the rain, out there in the mist somewhere and the guard on our side fired a burst in panic. Nachita grabbed his arm to stay him and we listened in the silence.

"Hello, the wall!" a voice called. "No shooting."

We waited and a man emerged from the mist, one of the villagers, his hands tied before him, a halter around his neck. The horseman on the other end was Raul Jurado.

"Señor Keogh," he called. "Don Tomás presents his compliments to the priest. He has till twelve-thirty. This is to show him we mean business."

He released the rope, the wretched man on the other end broke into a shambling run. Jurado shot him twice in the back and was into the cover of the mist in an instant.

I passed people coming down the street as I went up to the church. When I went inside, there were still a few sitting quietly on the benches. I paused uncertainly and Moreno came out of the side-chapel clutching his sombrero in both hands.

I said, "Where is Father van Horne?"

"In the chapel, señor, hearing confessions. For most people here it has been a very long time."

I brushed past him and went down towards the altar, pausing in the entrance of the tiny side-chapel. The image of St. Martin de Porres stood in a niche in the wall. Van Horne sat on a bench below and the woman before him was just getting on to her knees.

He'd said something to her quickly, got up and came towards me. He was wearing the alb again over his cassock, a violet stole round his shoulders and his calm was remarkable when one considered the state he'd been in earlier.

He said in a low voice, "Is it urgent, Keogh? I'm rather busy."

I took him by the arm, drew him along to the other end of the church and told him what had just happened. He listened gravely, then took out his watch. "That gives us an hour and a quarter."

"And no time to be wasting in this sort of bloody charade."

"They've had a lot to put up with, poor devils. A little comfort won't come amiss at this stage."

"A little comfort is it?" I pulled the purple stole from around his neck. "Don't you know what this stands for? Don't you realise what you are doing?"

"Whatever is wrong in this business is mine, not theirs." He smiled somberly. "I must say that for a man who does not believe in God, the fact of sin seems to weigh heavily on you."

"You go to hell," I said and tossed the stole in his face.

"I very probably will, Keogh." He laughed harshly, his old self again for a brief moment. "Does that thought give you any kind of satisfaction?"

"This kind of thing wasn't in the contract," I said. "It goes entirely too far. All right, in other circumstances it might just be acceptable. A priest, after all, is still a priest, whatever he has done. Whatever he has become."

"Exactly," he said gravely.

I stared at him, the full implication of what he was saying taking its own time to sink in. And yet it was as if I had always known from the first and at every point that followed. Sensed that he was not even the two people I had thought him, that he had alternated between. He was someone else. A different man altogether.

He put a hand on my shoulder as if to speak, but I recoiled in horror, turned and rushed out into the rain.

When I went into the bar at the hotel, Moreno was behind the bar polishing glasses in a mechanical way, his eyes staring into space. He pulled himself together quickly and produced a bottle of whisky and a glass.

"You saw the good father, señor?" he asked as he filled the glass. "A wonderful man. There can be few like him."

"True enough," I replied and drank my whisky.

"A man who can work miracles. It is no exaggeration to claim this, señor."

"A point of view," I said. "And what do you think he'll manage to pull out of his hat for the hostages?"

"Señor?" He stared at me, a puzzled frown on his face.

"Will he let them die?" I demanded. "Or will he

make the final sacrifice? It's an interesting thought, you must agree."

His eyes widened in horror. "Oh no, señor, never that. It would be inconceivable."

He turned as if I were the Devil himself and rushed out. In the silence following, van Horne said from behind me, "You would seem to have upset him."

"He believes you to be Christ walking the earth again," I said.

For a moment, the old anger rumbled in his voice. "Dammit, Keogh, but it's easy to see that the Jesuits schooled you."

I raised a hand. "All right, point taken."

"Good, then will you listen for a while? I haven't got long and for some reason I find it important to come to some understanding with you."

He produced one of his cigarillos, lit it and sat at the nearest table. "To start with, my name isn't van Horne. What it is, no longer matters either to me or anyone else. I told you I spent four years in a seminary and walked out."

"Another lie?"

"The story of my life." The old humour again. "Five years, Keogh. Five years and ordination at the end of it."

I stared down into my glass, the significance of what he had said drifting through to me. "It's funny," he said. "But looking back on it all now, I realise that I never really wanted it, that was the trouble. And when I walked out, the girl I thought I was in love with was only an excuse. A convenient peg to hang the blame on ever since."

I took the bottle and my glass and slumped down at the table opposite him. "I'm sorry," I said. "I don't know what to say except that it occurs to me that I am the last person in the world to have the right to throw stones at you."

"Have you ever thought of going home?" he asked.

"To Ireland?" I shrugged. "They'd shoot me on sight."

"Oh, I don't know. This civil war of yours is bound to finish sooner or later. They'll offer some sort of amnesty. They usually do. You could go back to the university. Finish that final year of medical training."

"A pipe-dream," I said. "It could never be now."

"You mean the girl?" He nodded. "You could have a point. You'd be asking a lot to expect her to find roots in such an alien culture."

"In the right clothes, you wouldn't be able to tell the difference between her and half the girls in Kerry," I said. "No, I mean more than that. You once told me I had death in the soul and you were right. I've walked in dark places for too long to change."

"I don't agree," he said. "A man is personally responsible for what he is, Keogh. He's what he wants to be and change is always possible and entirely in his own hands. If you never remember anything else I ever said to you, remember that."

He reached for the bottle and my glass. "One for the road," he said, filling the glass and took the whisky back in one quick swallow.

"What do you mean?"

"Once a priest, always a priest, Keogh. You know that, whatever kind of Catholic you are and so do I. I've done everything wrong that's possible, but that doesn't matter. There's no escape. Never has been."

He got to his feet and moved to the door. "You mean you're going out there?"

"I've no choice," he said calmly. "I never had and

not because I've suddenly turned holy at the end of things."

"What, then?"

"Pride, Keogh, foolish pride. I've played my part too well. These people believe in me. More than that—trust in me. I can't break the image now."

I caught him by the sleeve as he opened the door. "Not a single person has asked you to go—right?"

"The final nail in my coffin, boy."

He pulled himself free, went outside and stood at the top of the steps. The street was full of people again, a repetition of that earlier scene outside the church. The people were waiting and the people knew, could sense what was to happen. It showed on their faces.

As he went down the steps, they started to drop to their knees and he blessed them as he walked towards the gate. I followed at his heels. Moreno stood with his back to the gate, his hat in his hands.

Van Horne said, "Open it, my friend."

Moreno dropped to his knees, weeping bitterly.

Van Horne turned quietly to me and for the first and only time called me by my Christian name. "It takes two hands if you've got them, Emmet."

It was as if it had all happened before and perhaps this explains the strange inevitability I felt. I walked to the gates, lifted the bar without opening them and felt his hand on my shoulder.

"I once said I'd pray for you, back there in my play-acting days. I would ask you to do the same for me now, and mean it. You more than anyone else."

I was past speech, turned, clenching my teeth hard to hold back what was inside me and opened the gates. He moved a yard outside and peered into the rain. Nothing seemed to live out there. He turned and looked at me again.

"If I never did anything else for you, accept this now. You did not kill your brother, Keogh. It was life itself and people and that bloody little war you were having just like everyone else. Believe that and start living again. Don't waste your time on De la Plata. He's already damned. Now get that gate closed and God bless you."

He turned and walked away into the rain and mist and I did as I was told.

The hostages knocked on the gate within twenty minutes and streamed inside, many of them in considerable distress. Victoria was not amongst them. At first I could not believe it and ran through the crowd, pulling people apart as they embraced, searching everywhere.

I finally came face-to-face with Nachita and the fire in his eyes confirmed my worst fears. "She is not here, señor. He has not kept his word."

I turned and found a peon standing at my side, clutching his sombrero nervously. "Señor Keogh, I have a message from Don Tomás. He was most insistent . . ."

"Go on, damn you!" I shouted.

"He said that he was keeping what you value most to remember you by. He told me to say he hopes you rest content at night thinking of them."

I stood there, staring at him in the rain, caught by the enormity of it, and from somewhere beyond the wall, Jurado's voice floated out of the mist.

"Señor Keogh!"

I ran to the gate, Nachita at my back and peered outside.

"Don Tomás sends you your friend. He wanted to play the Christian. It seemed reasonable, therefore, to allow him to die like one."

There was a single shot and a horse galloped out of

the rain, plunging in fright, circling in confusion before the gate.

Van Horne had been strapped upright in the saddle against a crude wooden cross, arms outstretched, blood soaking through the front of the old cassock.

I grabbed for the reins to steady the horse and looked up at him. I suddenly realised that he was still alive. He tried to speak to me and no one else. Tried with everything he had and failed. The eyes rolled upwards, the head turned to one side.

As the sound of Jurado's horse faded into the distance, Nachita came out through the gate like a whirlwind, mounted on the first horse that had come to hand and went after him.

Not that it mattered. Not that anything seemed to have any reality any longer as the crowd surged out through the gate, strangely silent. They watched quietly as Moreno took a knife to the ropes binding van Horne and willing hands caught the body as it tumbled from the saddle.

Moreno turned to me, his eyes sad, no longer weeping. "He could have lived, señor, but chose to die instead. For us—for the people. Is not this a most remarkable thing? A saint walked amongst us and we did not recognise him."

FIFTEEN

ALL I COULD do now was wait for Nachita for there was certainly nothing to be gained by riding out into the rain myself. I went up to my room, stripped and rubbed myself down, then changed into dry clothes. I put a box of .45 cartridges into each pocket, went downstairs to the bar and helped myself to some more of Moreno's whisky while I stripped and cleaned the Enfield.

After a while Moreno himself appeared, removing his hat in a very respectful manner. "Señor, there are things at the church which belonged to him. We are not sure what to do. You were his friend . . ."

"All right," I said. "I'll come up to the church with you."

I put the poncho and sombrero back on for the rain was still falling heavily and we left the hotel and started up the street. A couple of carts, pulled by mules, passed us on the way down carrying the bodies of De la Plata's men.

"They lived without God, we shall bury them without God," Moreno explained. "The same hole does for all."

"And Señorita de la Plata also?"

"Señor, please." He looked genuinely shocked. "She, we will bury with all due ceremony. There is her father to consider, though God alone knows what the news of her death will do to that poor old man."

When we went into the square they were harnessing mules to the dead horses, getting ready to drag them off. Most of the blood had already been washed away by the heavy rain. Life continued.

Inside the church, there was a remarkable change. The benches had been moved to the sides, but a crude wooden coffin with the lid on had been laid across two of them near the entrance.

"Doña Chela, señor," Moreno murmured. "It was thought desirable to cover her now. She had been shot in the face. You understand?"

I did, all too well, and moved on to the other end of the church which was a blaze of candles.

When I first landed in Mexico I saw a procession of the Virgin through the streets of Veracruz. It was one of the most beautiful images I had ever seen except that it had a knife in the heart, which seemed to sum up Mexico admirably and the general preoccupation with death.

Van Horne lay on a table in full regalia, the gold cope over all, his hands folded around a crucifix, candles at his head and feet. He looked as if he might open his eyes at any moment.

"There was no coffin big enough to hold him, señor," Moreno whispered. "The village carpenter is already at work."

The stench of the candles was overpowering and there was nothing here for me. I had already said goodbye. I went into the vestry and Moreno followed me. The things he had spoken of were not really van Horne's. They were from the trunk that had belonged to the priest who had died at Huerta and yet I could not say so.

I said, "Keep these in a safe place. The new priest may have a use for them."

"The new priest, señor?"

"They'll send somebody, especially now that things have changed."

"And Don Tomás?"

"Is finished."

I couldn't face the church again and left the vestry by the other door, going straight down to the gates. Just as we reached the hotel, one of the guards fired a warning shot and called that a rider was coming.

I moved out through the gates with Moreno, a few more backing him up with rifles from the square. Nachita rode out of the mist, Jurado stumbling along behind, hands tied, a halter around his neck, just like the poor devil he had killed earlier.

"He couldn't run fast enough," Nachita said.

"What about the others?"

"Already gone, leaving this one to deliver the priest. The rain makes tracking difficult."

Jurado's face was still badly bruised, one eye half closed, but there was nothing but hate showing. "All right, Keogh, you've got me, but Don Tomás has your girl friend and by the time he and the boys have had their way with her . . ."

I gave him my hand across the jaw. "You can cut that out for a start. Where are they making for?"

He spat in my face. I wiped it away with the edge of my poncho and knocked him flat on his back.

Nachita said, "I could make him talk, señor."

"How long?" I said.

"No longer than it takes to light a fire."

"Then roast it out of the bastard. The sooner, the better."

And it worked, for there had never been much to Raul Jurado except brute strength and ignorance. He had broken in my two hands once before. He broke now.

Nachita put heels to his horse, the halter tightening, dragging Jurado over the rough ground and he cried out, fear in his voice. "No, not the Indian."

Remembering some of the things Janos had told me about the Yaqui I was not particularly surprised. I said, "I'll only ask you once. How many men has De la Plata got with him?"

"Five."

"Where have they gone?"

"Poneta."

I glanced at Nachita who nodded. "I know this place. Perhaps twenty-five miles from here on the other side of the Valley of the Angels. No one has lived there for many years now."

I nudged Jurado in the ribs with my boot. "Is he right?"

He nodded sullenly. "Don Tomás has used the place often in the past. From there, he can send into the mountains for men."

It had the ring of truth, so I dragged him to his feet and shoved him in the general direction of Moreno and his friends. "Keep him for the *federales*," I said. "Let them do it the legal way."

He turned, cursing me, but Moreno slapped his face. A couple of them grabbed hold of the end of the halter and they all moved back into the village, dragging him along behind.

Nachita dismounted and we followed them. "This

place, Poneta," I said. "What's it like?"

"A ruined church on the edge of a ravine, three or four streets. It was a government strong point in the early days of the Revolution. The scene of much heavy fighting. Most of the inhabitants were killed. The few that survived went elsewhere."

We turned into the courtyard at the rear of the hotel where I had parked the Mercedes. I found the map Bonilla had given us and unfolded it across the driver's seat out of the rain, for the canvas hood was up.

"How long would it take us to get there?"

"Five or six hours, señor. A little more, a little less, depending on the horses. The Valley of the Angels is twenty miles wide. All desert, no water. A place in which to take care."

"What start would you say they have on us?"

"An hour—an hour and a half."

"Could we catch them before they reach Poneta?"

"Perhaps, if we took spare horses, but he would kill her the moment we appeared."

I looked at the map again, particularly the wide desert area of the Valley of the Angels and the solution seemed plain. "What if we got there first? What if we were waiting for them?"

"Señor?" He frowned. "But how could such a thing be?"

I tapped the driving wheel of the Mercedes. "In this," I said, "all things are possible."

It was the first time I had seen him smile.

It was something of an emotional leave-taking. Moreno was reluctant to let us go having dispatched a rider to Cordona at Huanca and inclining to the opinion that I should await the lieutenant's arrival.

Before I got into the Mercedes, he gave me the

abrazo, the formal hug, patting me on the back, tears in his eyes, convinced, I suppose, that he would never see me alive again. Even so, it was interesting to note that not a single individual offered to accompany us, which all made Moreno's parting *Go with God* sound a little hollow as we drove away.

I was glad to put Mojada behind me for many reasons and I think I knew then that I would never see the place again, nor did I want to.

At the final end of things, whatever else he had been, Oliver van Horne had died for people who weren't even prepared to help themselves. One could find excuses in plenty of them. The wretchedness of their lives, the years of suffering which, in the end, had come to seem the natural order of things. But the end result was still that they would not help themselves. Would not move a finger to help anyone else.

I was filled with a feeling of indescribable bitterness. I was sick of them and I was sick of this festering land they called a country. The anger in me took control so that I went over the crown of the pass at a speed that was excessive under the conditions.

As we went down, the rain slackened and the mist thinned considerably and then the track petered out into a shallow slope running into the bottom of the great valley, dotted with mesquite and cactus trees. We went down past a tangle of catclaw and brush over tilted slabs and emerged to a flat plain of hard-baked sand.

I braked to a halt and Nachita got out and scouted around in wide circles. It didn't take long and he returned quickly. "They have passed this way, as I expected. The tracks are plain."

The old trail was clearly marked on the military map.

Straight across, which was naturally the shortest route, and there was Poneta half-way up a mountain. Twenty miles, perhaps a little less.

My own strategy was obvious. Nachita got back into the Mercedes and I drove eastward for about five miles, hugging the edge of the desert, then turned north and drove across the hard, sun-baked earth at what to Nachita must have seemed the considerable speed of twenty-five miles an hour.

We crossed without incident, reaching the foothills of the mountains on the other side of the valley in just one hour. I turned west and followed the rim of the desert for several miles until we came to the beginning of the track on that side, starting up through the narrow pass between two mountains exactly as indicated on the map.

I dropped into a low gear for it lifted steeply through slopes covered with mesquite and greasewood and as we climbed higher, a few scattered *piñones*, and Nachita dropped out and followed along behind, erasing the tire tracks with a branch from a thorn tree. The trail started to hug the side of the mountain, the slope dropping away steeply and then we crawled round a massive out-crop of rock and found Poneta perched on the edge of a ravine.

It was larger than I had supposed, must have once been reasonably important, which was to be judged mainly from the size of the church, a large, flat-roofed building in stone with a badly damaged bell tower, the result of shell fire from the look of it.

The rest of the buildings were crumbling adobe *casas*, most of them without a roof and everywhere the signs of the battle which had raged over the place.

I drove up the main street, Nachita ready with his old
Winchester, but it was ours alone except for the lizards
and the ravens perched on top of the crumbling bell
tower, watching as I braked to a halt in the centre of the
plaza by an empty fountain.

I found one of the canteens, washed the dust from my
throat and passed it to Nachita. Two or three ravens
lifted into the air calling hoarsely to each other. The sun
died. I shivered, the Celt in me again.

"A bad place. Too many men have died here,"
Nachita said.

I nodded. "We'll wait for them back along the trail
where we can see what's coming."

We found a *casa* on the edge of the village with one
wall missing, which made it an excellent hiding place for
the Mercedes as I was able to drive it right inside. We
left it there and walked back down the trail to the point
where it disappeared round the outcrop and climbed up
to the top.

The view of the desert was excellent. Nachita beat
amongst the bushes for snakes and we settled down to
wait. I had one of the Thompson guns and he, his Winchester, but it was going to be difficult to attack them
without harming Victoria, and her safety, after all, was
what mattered. Too much was going to have to be left to
chance and I had never cared for that in this kind of
business.

I lay back, head pillowed on my sombrero, smoked a
cigarette and narrowed my eyes into infinity, wondering
in a detached sort of way how Victoria was and what she
was thinking. Yet she must know that we would follow.
Had no choice.

And Tomás de la Plata? Impossible to judge which
way he would jump. He was a man who had endured

much and had been moulded by a hundred different things. The years in prison, the degradation, the humiliations endured for the cause he believed in. The long struggle. So much killing.

Yet others had been through as much and had survived. There was something deeper here. This man had been touched in the darkest depths of him and a man like that was to be feared.

I must have drifted into sleep and Nachita had obviously decided to let me be. When he brought me awake with a quick shake, it was late evening, the valley purple with shadow, the sun an orange ball.

The clatter of hooves was quite distinct on the quiet air and I peered cautiously through the brush and saw them coming up the trail below, coated with dust from the desert, weariness in every line of them, men and beasts.

And at the end we were still out of luck for Victoria and Tomás de la Plata shared the same horse, his arms around her as he held the reins. To start anything with the girl in such a position would be madness. We lay there quietly and watched them enter the village and start up the main street to the plaza.

I said, "If I can draw them off, it's unlikely he'd leave more than one man in charge of Victoria and you could handle that."

"And how would you accomplish this thing, señor?"

I told him briefly. He said, "You go to your death, you know this?"

"Maybe it's about time." I shrugged. "Just get Victoria out of harm's way when the time comes and I mean that. She's your only consideration. Forget about me, no matter what happens."

I went down through the brush in a strangely resigned mood. I would do what had to be done and if it meant the end of me, let it be so. A long time coming, surely.

Nachita helped me roll the Mercedes silently backwards out of the ruined *casa* where we had left it, then I climbed behind the wheel, the Thompson ready on the passenger seat beside me. The roar of that magnificent engine nearly tore the place apart as I put my foot down hard and took her up the narrow street to the plaza.

Tomás de la Plata, a hand on Victoria's arm, was crossing towards the church, his men walking behind, leading the horses. I braked to a halt, stayed that way long enough to see the shock of recognition in his face, then reversed. They had already started shooting as I took the Mercedes back into the narrow street. The windscreen shattered and I ducked instinctively, swerving enough to demolish one end of an adobe wall.

It slowed me a little, which was what I wanted anyway. The hounds were in full cry now and I kept on going, head down, bullets thudding into the bodywork of the Mercedes and then I was out of the village and into the open again.

I swung the wheel from side-to-side to make her swerve, then drove the Mercedes clear over the edge of the trail.

She went down the slope like a thunderbolt, tearing a path through the mesquite and brushwood and I grabbed the Thompson and got out while the going was good. The Mercedes bounced, turned over twice and tore into a clump of *piñon*, finally coming to rest upside down.

I lay in the brush hugging the ground and the Thompson and waited. A few moments later they appeared on the trail above, Tomás de la Plata and his men, one of them holding on to Victoria. They paused on the edge looking at the Mercedes, then De la Plata said something and started down with four of them, leaving Victoria and the man who was holding her.

Nachita appeared behind them as if out of thin air. Whatever was done, was done silently for the man went down without a cry and Nachita pulled Victoria back out of sight.

Which was all I had been waiting for. There was a crashing in the brushwood as De la Plata and his men approached and it was now or never for they were almost on me.

They emerged into a clear patch in a long straggling line and I stood up and started to fire, intending to take the five of them in one clean sweep. The first two went over like skittles and then the round drum magazine jammed.

It was De la Plata who fired in return, drawing from the shoulder holster of his with incredible speed like a snake striking, the bullet catching me just above the right breast, knocking me back into the brush.

As I hit the ground, I drew the Enfield, fired twice very fast to keep the heads down and allowed myself to slide down through the brush as fast as possible.

I fetched up in a thicket and paused long enough to examine my wound. The force of the shot had been considerable owing to the short range and the bullet had passed straight through, exiting under the right shoulder blade. The exit hole was smaller than I had anticipated which meant, in all probability, that his revolver was of .38 calibre.

I spat into my hand and produced no blood which was encouraging, but the sounds of movement in the brush above were not. I got out of the thicket quickly and started to work my way up the slope again, following a diagonal course to the right which would bring me back to the trail.

Someone caught sight of me soon enough, there was a cry and then another, three or four shots. A last mad scramble and I went over the edge of the trail, lungs bursting, to find one of them bearing down on me from the left like a steam engine.

I fired wildly twice without taking aim, for I had no choice in the matter, tripped and went headlong, crying out as the pain surged through me. The man running in did not fire, preferring to get close. It was the death of him for I shot him in the heart, the heavy bullet lifting him off his feet and back over the edge of the trail.

There was one round left in the Enfield and no time to reload. As De la Plata and his surviving companions appeared from the brush, I turned and ran for my life into the village.

They fired continuously, but thanks to that mad chase through the brush, the scramble up the slope, nobody's aim was anything to boast about. I put my head down and kept running, hoping to make it to the church, hoping that Nachita might take a hand in the game in spite of what I had said.

I had almost reached the fountain when I was hit again. The right leg this time, only a crease, but enough to bring me down.

When I rolled over, De la Plata's companion was some distance in front of him, a young man, full of his strength and running well. There was no time for fancy shooting. I simply aimed at his middle and pulled the trigger, was on my feet and scrambling for the church door as he went down.

He was like some creature in a nightmare that is impossible to shake off. I made it to the door, a bullet chipping the wall. When I glanced over my shoulder he was already past the fountain and running very fast, a pistol in each hand.

I staggered through the cool darkness inside, not daring to stop, fumbling for spare cartridges in my pocket. I managed to get two into the chamber awkwardly, dropping a few in the process because my right shoulder and arm were burning like all the fires of hell now and the fingers weren't working very well.

He was inside and shooting, uncertain in the light. Like a fool I fired back, giving myself away, turned and stumbled into the shadows as he replied.

I fell across a flight of stone steps and scrambled up them desperately. They turned a corner, the inner wall of the bell tower and light flooded down through a great jagged hole. I emerged on the roof and paused briefly to get my bearings. A bullet whined into the air through the opening. I fired down into the darkness twice in reply and the second time, the hammer clicked on nothing.

I was finished and I knew it. Little Emmet Keogh at the end of things at last, for he came up the steps without hesitation. I turned and went staggering along the roof to nowhere and when I reached the ultimate edge, there was no parapet, only a long fall down to the ravine below or the plaza on the other side.

When I turned, he was standing perhaps ten yards away, chest heaving, face very pale, a pistol in one hand only now. And in the end, he made the worst kind of mistake. Instead of shooting me out of hand, he had to talk.

"Who sent you, Keogh?"

His reply was a single shot that echoed across the roof

tops sending the ravens wheeling up in dark, frightened
circles. De la Plata cried out and spun round, the pistol
jumping from his hand into the plaza.

Nachita was standing by the fountain, the Winchester
at his shoulder, Victoria crouched beside him. She cried
my name suddenly and the echo mingled with the hoarse
calling of the ravens.

As I swung round, De la Plata flung himself at me
blindly, blood on his mouth, hands reaching out to
destroy. I simply moved to one side and he blundered
over the edge into the plaza.

He was lying face-down on the cobbles when
I looked, Nachita kneeling beside him. Nachita rose,
glanced up at me, then turned and followed Victoria,
who was running for the church door.

The ravens descended to the tower again, black
against a sky the colour of brass, and the sun died
behind the peaks. I was tired and the Enfield empty in
my left hand was still a weight to carry. A fine dramatic
gesture to toss it away once and for all, far out into
space over the ravine, but that would not have been the
sensible way. Not little Emmet Keogh of the left hand's
way. This was a bad place to be and night falling.

I sat down, spilled the handful of cartridges beside me
and slowly, and with great difficulty because of my
wounded shoulder, started to reload.

EVERYONE LOVES
HEARTBURN!

HEARTBURN IS . . .

"Painfully funny."

—*Time Magazine*

"Witty all the time."

—*Vanity Fair*

"A roller coaster of laughs and tears."

—*Liz Smith*

NORA EPHRON . . .

"She cooks up a fine, funny first novel."

—*Chicago Tribune BookWorld*

"Nora Ephron's first novel is warm, witty and wise."

—*Harper's Bazaar*

NORA EPHRON'S

HEARTBURN

Mary Ann Butler
9/6/85

HEARTBURN

Nora Ephron

PUBLISHED BY POCKET BOOKS NEW YORK

POCKET BOOKS, a division of Simon & Schuster, Inc.
1230 Avenue of the Americas, New York, N.Y. 10020

Published by arrangement with Alfred A. Knopf, Inc.
Library of Congress Catalog Card Number: 82-48999

ISBN: 0-671-62483-0

First Pocket Books printing April, 1984

17 16 15 14 13 12 11 10 9 8

POCKET and colophon are registered trademarks
of Simon & Schuster, Inc.

Printed in the U.S.A.

for Maria and Bob

I

The first day I did not think it was funny. I didn't think it was funny the third day either, but I managed to make a little joke about it. "The most unfair thing about this whole business," I said, "is that I can't even date." Well, you had to be there, as they say, because when I put it down on paper it doesn't sound funny. But what made it funny (trust me) is the word "date," which when you say it out loud at the end of a sentence has a wonderful teenage quality, and since I am not a teenager (okay, I'm thirty-eight), and since the reason I was hardly in a position to date on first learning that my second husband had taken a lover was that I was seven months pregnant, I got a laugh on it, though for all I know my group was only laughing because they were trying to cheer me up. I needed cheering up. I was in

New York, staying in my father's apartment, I was crying most of the time, and every time I stopped crying I had to look at my father's incredibly depressing walnut furniture and slate-gray lamps, which made me start crying again.

I had gotten on the shuttle to New York a few hours after discovering the affair, which I learned about from a really disgusting inscription to my husband in a book of children's songs she had given him. *Children's* songs. "Now you can sing these songs to Sam" was part of the disgusting inscription, and I can't begin to tell you how it sent me up the wall, the idea of my two-year-old child, my baby, involved in some dopey inscriptive way in this affair between my husband, a fairly short person, and Thelma Rice, a fairly tall person with a neck as long as an arm and a nose as long as a thumb and you should see her legs, never mind her feet, which are sort of splayed.

My father's apartment was empty, my father having been carted off to the loony bin only days before by my sister Eleanor, who is known as the Good Daughter in order to differentiate her from me. My father leads a complicated psychological life along with his third wife, who incidentally happens to be my former best friend Brenda's sister. My father's third wife had been wandering up Third Avenue in a towel the week before, when she was spotted by Renee Fleisher, who went to high school with Brenda and me. Renee Fleisher called my father, who was in no position to help since his crack-up was halfway there, and then she called me in Washington. "I don't believe it," she said. "I just bumped into Brenda's big sister and she says she's married to your father." I myself had found it hard to believe when it happened: to have your father marry your mortal enemy's older sister is a bit too coincidental for my taste, even though I go along with that stuff about small worlds. You have no choice if you're Jewish. "It's fine with me if you marry Brenda's sister," I had said to my father when he called to say he was about to, "but please have her sign a prenuptial agreement so that when you die, none of your fortune ends up with Brenda." So Brenda's big sister signed the agreement, that was three years ago, and now here's Renee Fleisher on the phone to say, hi ho, Brenda's sister married your father and by the way she's wandering up Third Avenue wearing a towel. I turned all this over to my sister Eleanor, who put on her goodness and went over to my father's apartment and got some clothes onto Brenda's sister and sent her to her mother in Miami Beach and took my father to a place called Seven Clouds, which is not an auspicious name for a loony bin, but you'd be amazed how little choice you have about loony bins. Off went my father to dry out and make ashtrays out of leaves, and there sat his apartment in New York, empty.

I had the keys to my father's apartment; I'd stayed there often in the past year because we were broke. When Mark and I got married we were rich and two years later we were broke. Not actually broke—we did have equity. We had a stereo system that had eaten thousands of dollars, and a country house in West Virginia that had eaten tens of thousands of dollars, and a city house in Washington that had eaten hundreds of thousands of dollars, and we had *things*—God, did we have things. We had weather vanes and quilts and carousel horses and stained-glass windows and tin boxes and pocket mirrors and Cadbury chocolate cups and postcards of San Francisco before the earthquake, so we were worth something; we just had no money. It was always a little mystifying to me how we had gone from having so much money to having so little, but now, of course, I understand it all a little better, because the other thing that ate our money was the affair with Thelma Rice. Thelma went to France in the middle of it, and you should see the phone bills.

Not that I knew about the phone bills the day I found the book of children's songs with the disgusting inscription in it. "My darling Mark," it began, "I wanted to give you something to mark what happened today, which makes our future so much clearer. Now you can sing these songs to Sam, and someday we will sing them to him together. I love you. Thelma." That was it. I could hardly believe it. Well, the truth is I didn't believe it. I looked at the signature again and tried to make it come out some other name, a name of someone I didn't know as opposed to someone I did, but there was the *T* and there was the *a* plain as day, even if the letters in the middle were a little squishy, and there's not much you can do with a name that begins with a *T* and ends in an *a* but Thelma. Thelma! She had just been to our house for lunch! She and her husband Jonathan—actually, they hadn't come for lunch, they'd stopped by afterward for dessert, a carrot cake I'd made that had too much crushed pineapple in it but was still awfully good compared to Thelma's desserts. Thelma always makes these gluey puddings. Thelma, her husband Jonathan (who knew all about the affair, it turned out), my husband Mark—all three of them sat there while I waddled around in a drip-dry maternity dress serving carrot cake to the rest of the guests and apologizing about the crushed pineapple.

It may seem odd to you that their coming to lunch bothers me as much as it does, but one of the worst things about finding out about a thing like this is that you feel stupid, and the idea that I actually invited them over and they actually accepted and all three of them actually sat there thinking I was some sort of cheese made it that much worse. The most mortifying part of it all is that the next day Thelma called to say thank you and asked for the carrot cake recipe and I sent it to her. I

removed the crushed pineapple, of course.
"Here is the carrot cake recipe," I wrote on a
postcard, "with the kinks out of it." I'm afraid
I put a little face with a smile next to the
recipe. I am not the sort of person who puts
little faces on things, but there are times
when nothing else will do. Right now, for
instance, I would like to put a little face at the
very end of this sentence, only this one would
have a frown on it.

I should point out that although I could
hardly believe Mark was having an affair with
Thelma, I knew he was having an affair with
someone. That was how I came upon the
songbook in the first place: I was poking
around in his drawers, looking for clues. But
Thelma! It made me really angry. It would
have been one thing if he'd gotten involved
with a little popsy, but he'd gone off and had
an affair with a person who was not only a
giant but a clever giant. I cannot tell you how
many parties we'd come home from while this
affair was being secretly conducted and I'd
said, while taking off my clothes, "God, Thelma said such an amusing thing tonight."
Then I would repeat it, word for word, to
Mark. Talk about being a fool! *Talk about
being a fool!* I even knew Thelma was having
an affair! Everyone did. She had taken to
talking indiscriminately and openly about the
possibility that her husband Jonathan would
be dispatched to some faraway State Depart-

ment post and she would stay behind in Washington and buy a condominium.

"She's talking about condominiums," my friend Betty Searle called up to say one day. "Obviously she's involved with someone."

"Are you sure?" I said.

"Of course I'm sure," said Betty. "The question is who." She thought for a minute. "Maybe it's Senator Campbell," she said. "He's talking about condominiums, too."

"Senators always talk about condominiums," I said.

"That's true," said Betty, "but who else could it be?"

"I'll ask Mark," I said.

"Do you think Thelma Rice is having an affair with Senator Campbell?" I said to Mark that night.

"No," he said.

"Well, she's having an affair with someone," I said.

"How do you know?" he said.

"She's talking about buying a condominium if Jonathan is sent to Bangladesh," I said.

"Jonathan's not going to be sent to Bangladesh," said Mark.

"Why not?" I said.

"Because we still care about Bangladesh," said Mark.

"Then Upper Volta," I said.

Mark shook his head, as if he couldn't believe he'd been dragged into such a hopelessly

girlish conversation, and went back to reading *House & Garden*. Shortly after that, the
talk of condominiums stopped.

"Thelma's not talking about condominiums
anymore," Betty called up to say one day.
"What do you think it means?"

"Maybe it's over," I said.

"No," said Betty. "It's not over."

"How do you know?" I said.

"She had her legs waxed," said Betty, and
then, very slowly, added, "for the first time."
And then, even more slowly: "And it's not
even summer yet."

"I see what you mean," I said.

Betty Searle really was a witch about these
things—about many things, in fact. She could
go to a dinner party in Washington and the
next day she could tell you who was about to
be fired—just on the basis of the seating plan!
She should have been a Kremlinologist in the
days when everything we knew about Russia
was based on the May Day photograph.
Twitches, winks and shrugs that seemed like
mere nervous mannerisms to ordinary mor-
tals were gale force indicators to Betty. Once,
for example, at a cocktail reception, she realized that the Secretary of Health, Education
and Welfare was about to be canned because
the Vice-President's wife kissed him hello and
then patted him on the shoulder.

"Anyone pats you on the shoulder when
you're in the cabinet, you're in big trouble,"
Betty said the next day.

"But it was only the Vice-President's wife," I said.

Betty shook her head, as if I would never ever learn. Later that day, she called the Secretary of Health, Education and Welfare and told him that his days were numbered, but he was so busy fighting with the tobacco lobby that he paid no attention. Two days later, the tobacco lobby rented the grand ballroom of the Washington Hilton to celebrate his ouster, and the Secretary of Health, Education and Welfare started preparing to go on the lecture circuit.

"So who do you think Thelma's involved with?" Betty said.

"It could be anyone," I said.

"Of course it could be anyone," said Betty, "but who is it?"

"What about Congressman Toffler?" I said.

"You think so?" said Betty.

"She's always talking about how brilliant he is," I said.

"And she seated him next to herself at her last dinner party," said Betty.

"I'll ask Mark," I said. "He was seated on her other side."

"Do you think Thelma Rice is having an affair with Congressman Toffler?" I asked Mark that night.

"No," said Mark.

"Well, whoever she's having an affair with, she's still having it," I said.

"How do you know?" said Mark.

"She had her legs waxed," I said. "And it's only May."

"The Ladies' Central is busy this week, isn't it?" said Mark. "Who'd you hear that from?"

"Betty," I said.

Mark went back to reading *Architectural Digest,* and shortly thereafter Thelma Rice went to France for a few weeks, and Betty and I moved on to the subject of the President's assistant, who was calling Betty in the middle of the night and saying, "Meet me in the Rotunda and I'll tickle your tits," and other bizarre remarks encompassing Washington and sex.

"What should I do about it?" Betty said one day at lunch.

"Tell him if he does it again you'll call the newspapers," I said.

"I did," said Betty, "and you know what he said? He said, 'You haven't lived till you've squeezed my Washington Post.' Then he cackled madly." She poked at her Chicken Salad Albert Gore. "Anyway, I can't prove it's him," she said, "although Thelma always says he's a notorious letch."

"That's what Mark always says, too," I said.

I should have figured it out, of course. By the time I did, the thing had been going on for months, for seven months—for exactly as long as my pregnancy. I should have known, should have suspected something sooner, especially since Mark spent so much time that summer at the dentist. There sat Sam and I in

West Virginia, making air holes in jars full of caterpillars, and there went Mark, in and out of Washington, to have root canals and gum treatments and instructions in flossing and an actual bridge, never once complaining about the inconvenience or the pain or the boredom of having to listen to Irwin Tannenbaum, D.D.S., drone on about his clarinet. Then it was fall, and we were all back in Washington, and every afternoon, Mark would emerge from his office over the garage and say he was going out to buy socks, and every evening he would come home empty-handed and say, you would not believe how hard it is to find a decent pair of socks in this city. Four weeks it took me to catch on! Inexcusable, especially since it was exactly the sort of thing my first husband said when he came home after spending the afternoon in bed with my best friend Brenda, who subsequently and as a result became my mortal enemy. "Where were you the last six hours?" I said to my first husband. "Out buying light bulbs," he said. Light bulbs. Socks. What am I doing married to men who come up with excuses like this? Once, when I was married to my first husband, I went off to meet a man in a hotel room at six in the morning and told my husband I was going out to be on the *Today* show; it never even crossed his mind to turn on the television set to watch. Now, that's what I call a decent job of lying! Not that it does any good to prove my ingenuity; it doesn't matter how smart you are if both your husbands manage to prove how dumb you are as easily as mine had.

Of course, my fling with the man in the hotel room happened a long time ago—before my divorce, before I met Mark, before I decided to marry him and become an incorrigible believer in fidelity. It is of course hideously ironic that the occasion for my total conversion to fidelity was my marriage to Mark, but timing has never been my strong point; and in any case, the alternative, infidelity, doesn't work. You have only a certain amount of energy, and when you spread it around, everything gets confused, and the first thing you know, you can't remember which one you've told which story to, and the next thing you know, you're moaning, "Oh, Morty, Morty, Morty," when what you mean is "Oh, Sidney, Sidney, Sidney," and the next thing you know, you think you're in love with both of them simply because you've been raised to believe that the only polite response to the words "I love you" is "I love you too," and the next thing you know, you think you're in love with only one of them, because you're too guilty to handle loving them both.

After I found the book with the disgusting inscription in it, I called Mark. I'm embarrassed to tell you where I called him—okay, I'll tell you: I called him at his shrink's. He goes to a Guatemalan shrink over in Alexandria who looks like Carmen Miranda and has a dog named Pepito. "Come home immediately," I said. "I know about you and Thelma Rice." Mark did not come home immediately. He came home two hours later because—are you ready for this?—THELMA RICE WAS ALSO AT THE SHRINK'S. They were having a double session! At the family rate!! I did not know this at the time. Not only did Thelma Rice and Mark see Dr. Valdez and her Chihuahua, Pepito, once a week, but so did Thelma's husband, Jonathan Rice, the undersecretary of state for Middle Eastern affairs. Mark and Thelma saw Chiquita Banana together, and Jonathan Rice saw her alone—and that man has something to do with making peace in the Middle East!

When Mark finally came home, I was completely prepared. I had rehearsed a speech about how I loved him and he loved me and we had to work at our marriage and we had a baby and we were about to have another—really the perfect speech for the situation except that I had misapprehended the situation. "I am in love with Thelma Rice," he said when he arrived home. That was the situation. He then told me that although he was in love with Thelma Rice, they were not having an affair. (Apparently he thought I could handle the fact that he was in love with her but not the fact that he was having sex with her.) "That is a lie," I said to him, "but if it's true"—you see, there was a part of me that wanted to think it was true even though I knew it wasn't: the man is capable of having sex with a venetian blind—"if it's true, you might as well be having an affair with her, because it's free." Some time later, after going on saying all these lovey-dovey things about Thelma, and after saying he wouldn't give her up, and after saying that I was a shrew and a bitch and a nag and a kvetch and a grouse and that I hated Washington (the last charge was undeniably true), he said that he nonetheless expected me to stay with him. At that moment, it crossed my mind that he might be crazy. I sat there on the couch with tears rolling down my face and my fat belly resting on my thighs, I screwed up my courage, and when Mark finished his sixteenth speech about how wonderful Thelma Rice was compared to me, I said to him, "You're crazy." It took every ounce of self-confidence I had.

"You're wrong," he said.

He's right, I thought. I'm wrong.

Well, we went around in circles. And then he asked me if I wanted to be alone for a while. I guess he wanted to drive over to Thelma's to tell her he had held fast to their love. It didn't matter. He drove off and I scooped up Sam and a suitcase full of Pampers, called a taxi, and left for the airport.

II

One thing I have never understood is how to work it so that when you're married, things keep happening to you. Things happen to you when you're single. You meet new men, you travel alone, you learn new tricks, you read Trollope, you try sushi, you buy nightgowns, you shave your legs. Then you get married, and the hair grows in. I love the everydayness of marriage, I love figuring out what's for dinner and where to hang the pictures and do we owe the Richardsons, but life does tend to slow to a crawl. The whole summer Mark was secretly seeing Thelma Rice while pretending to be at the dentist, I was cooking. That's what I do for a living—I write cookbooks. And while I did discover a fairly revolutionary and absolutely foolproof way to make a four-minute egg, and had gotten to the point where

I simply could not make a bad vinaigrette, this was not exactly the stuff of drama. (Even now, I cannot believe Mark would want to risk losing that vinaigrette. You just don't bump into vinaigrettes that good.) Before that, there had been a lot of time spent on swatches and couches and floor plans. It was almost as if Mark had a career as a columnist and I had a career as a food person and our marriage had a career as a fighter with contractors. First we fought with the Washington contractor, who among other atrocities managed to install our carpet on the sixth floor of a Washington department store; then we fought with the West Virginia contractor, who forgot the front door. "No one uses front doors in the country anyway," he said when we pointed it out, which was also what he said about the paper-towel rack and the medicine cabinet. Then we hired Laszlo Pump, a Hungarian trouble-shooter, to clean up the mess the other two contractors had made, and that was when the real trouble began. Laszlo ripped out the living room wall and vanished. We called him at home and got his wife. She said his father had died. A week later she said his dog had died. A week later she said his analyst had died. Finally we reached Laszlo. He said he had cancer.

"He has cancer," I said when I hung up the phone.

"Bullshit," said Mark.

"People don't lie about that," I said.

"Yes they do," said Mark. "Contractors do. They lie about everything. Look, we'll go to his house. We'll see how he looks. If he looks okay I'll kill him."

"We can't go to his house," I said.

"Why not?" said Mark.

"Because we don't know where he lives."

"We'll look it up," said Mark.

"We can't look it up," I said. "He has an unlisted address."

"What are you talking about?" said Mark.

"It's the latest thing," I said.

"What kind of person has an unlisted address?" Mark said. "I'll tell you what kind. The kind that doesn't want to be dead. The kind that people are trying to kill all the time."

"Why are you angry at me?" I said.

"I'm not angry at you," said Mark.

"Then why are you shouting at me?" I said.

"Because you're the only one who's here," said Mark.

I burst into tears. "I hate it when you get angry," I said.

"I'm not angry at you," said Mark. "I love you. I'm not angry at you."

"I know," I said, "but it scares me. It reminds me of my father."

"I'm not your father," said Mark. "Repeat after me, 'Mark Feldman is not my father.'"

"Mark Feldman is not my father," I said.

"Am I fat?" said Mark.

"No," I said.

"Am I bald?"

"No."

"Do I smell of Dr. Scholl's foot pads?"

"No," I said.

"I rest my case," said Mark.

It always ended up like that in the end—us against the world, Washington's bravest couple in combat with the entire service industry and their answering machines—but the point I want to make is this: I sat on that plane to New York in a state of total misery, yet part of me was secretly relieved to be done with swatches and couches and fights with contractors, and that part of me was thinking: Okay, Rachel Samstat, finally something is happening to you.

That's my name—Rachel Samstat. It's always been Rachel Samstat. I held on to it through both my marriages—through the first because I never liked my first husband's last name enough to change mine to it, and through the second because I was by then known in a small and modest way as Rachel Samstat. The cookbooks I write do well. They're very personal and chatty—they're cookbooks in an almost incidental way. I write chapters about friends or relatives or trips or experiences, and work in the recipes peripherally. Then, of course, the television show came along, which made the books sell even better.

How I got my own show is probably something you're wondering. I'm not exactly a conventional television personality, although I suppose I'm somewhat conventional when it comes to public television, which is what my show was on, not network. "Too New York" is what the last network that was approached about me responded, which is a cute way of being anti-Semitic, but who cares? I'd rather be too New York than too anything else. Anyway, I don't belong on a network. I have the kind of odd and interesting features that work out all right in life but not at all on the screen, so I'm far better off on public television, where the producers and cameramen are used to Julia Child and are pathetically grateful that I'm not quite as tall. Also, there's my blink. I blink. "Hi, I'm Rachel Samstat"— saying that, looking directly at the camera, I blink fifty or sixty times minimum. It's the looking at the camera that makes me do it; when I'm looking at a person, or a pork roast, my blinks go down to near normal.

After we taped the first show and discovered the blink, Richard, my producer, suggested I go see a professional television coach, who specialized in voices but was willing to undertake a little eyelid work on the side. She kept telling me she'd never had a failure, probably to encourage me, but the effect was to make me absolutely determined to be her first, which I was.

"I don't think I can fix the blink," she told Richard after several sessions, "but I can probably do a little something with the voice."

"We like the voice," said Richard, and thank God, because there wasn't much left of me by then that someone hadn't taken a swipe at, usually using the definite article. The voice. The blink. The hair. The chin. "She has a quality onscreen not unlike Howard Cosell," someone high up at the station is supposed to have said, and even though I choose to think he meant it as a compliment—he meant I'm the sort of person you feel strongly about one way or another—Howard Cosell was not exactly what I had in mind. What I had in mind was Imogene Coca or Elaine May. Anyway, the important thing is that I do happen to have a funny voice, and it makes people laugh. It works on television, although there's no way a voice coach would understand that, since her job is to teach everyone to sound like David Brinkley.

It's really because of Richard that the television show came up at all. I was on a talk show promoting *My Grandmother's Cookies* when Richard saw me. Actually, it was Phil Donahue he saw me on. Richard is hooked on Phil Donahue. He says that if Sigmund Freud had watched Phil Donahue he would never have wondered what women want. There I was, fielding questions about piecrust and doing my Jewish prince routine, when Richard got the idea it might make a series—me and my relatives and my friends and a few famous strangers, talking about food, talking about the role food plays in life, doing a little cooking, a middlebrow Julia Child crossed with a highbrow Dinah Shore. How we got away with it I don't know, except that we threw Proust and his madeleines into the opening credits, and I managed to get Isaac Bashevis Singer to make noodle kugel on the pilot. Also, the show cost next to nothing to produce, and what little it cost was underwritten by an oil company where someone I used to date is now in charge of parceling out money to public television. I dated him when he was Jewish—now that he works at the oil company you can't exactly tell. He was so Jewish when I dated him that he taught Hebrew school, and I, who at that point had had no Jewish education whatsoever, learned about Purim and good Queen Esther and the wicked Haman from him one night in a dormitory at Harvard while he stuck one and then two and then three fingers into me. This was before the discovery of the clitoris, when there was far too much sticking of fingers into things and not nearly enough playing around with the outsides; still, it was a nice enough introduction to the origins of Hamantaschen pastries, and I retain a special and absurd affection for Purim in spite of the fact that I have always hated Hamantaschen. That isn't true. Mark's Aunt Florence makes good Hamantaschen. Aunt Florence, who raised Mark, is a great cook; her triumph, which she serves on Thanksgiving along with the turkey, is a brisket cooked with sauerkraut and brown sugar, and it sounds perfectly awful, I know, but it's truly one of the most delicious things I've ever eaten.

I'd been planning to have Mark's Aunt Florence on the next thirteen-week cycle of my television show to discuss the brisket, as well as her tzimmes and gefilte fish, but I don't really see how I'm going to be able to now that all this has come about. I don't like blaming family members for what goes wrong with children, because someday when my kids are arrested for grand larceny I don't want anyone looking accusingly at me, but Mark's behavior was so obviously Florence's fault that even Florence knew it. "It must be my fault" were in fact her first words on the subject when I called to tell her I had gone to New York because her nephew had fallen in love with Thelma Rice. "Don't be silly," I said in reply, but what I was thinking was: You bet your sweet ass it is. Jewish princes are made, not born.

RACHEL SAMSTAT'S JEWISH PRINCE ROUTINE

You know what a Jewish prince is, don't you?
  (*Cocks her eyebrow*)
If you don't, there's an easy way to recognize one. A simple sentence. "Where's the butter?"

*(A long pause here, because the laugh
starts slowly and builds)*

Okay. We all know where the butter is, don't
we?

(A little smile)

The butter is in the refrigerator.

(Beat)

The butter is in the refrigerator in the little
compartment in the door marked "Butter."

(Beat)

But the Jewish prince doesn't mean "Where's
the butter?" He means "Get me the butter."
He's too clever to say "Get me" so he says
"Where's."

(Beat)

And if you say to him—

(Shouting)

"in the refrigerator"—

(Resume normal voice)

and he goes to look, an interesting thing happens, a medical phenomenon that has not
been sufficiently remarked upon.

(Beat)

The effect of the refrigerator light on the male
cornea.

(Beat)

Blindness.

(A long beat)

"I don't see it anywhere."

(Pause)

"Where's the butter" is only one of the ways
the Jewish prince reveals himself. Sometimes

he puts it a different way. He says, "Is there any butter?"

(Beat)

We all know whose fault it is if there isn't, don't we.

(Beat)

When he's being really ingenious, he puts it in a way that's meant to sound as if what he needs most of all from you is your incredible wisdom and judgment and creativity. He says, "How do you think butter would taste with this?"

(Beat)

He's usually referring to dry toast.

(Beat)

I've always believed that the concept of the Jewish princess was invented by a Jewish prince who couldn't get his wife to fetch him the butter.

I was not raised as a Jewish princess. Sometimes I'm accused of being one because I'm not exactly the outdoor type, but I grew up a scrappy little athlete with a scrappy little mother who wanted me to have a flashy career like her own. I wonder what she would have made of my work. My mother was a good recreational cook, but what she basically believed about cooking was that if you worked hard and prospered, someone else would do it for you.

My mother was an agent in Hollywood, a

lady agent, a classic forties career woman: she had short hair and bangs, she wore suits with shoulder pads, and she talked in a gravelly voice. She handled what were known in the business as specialty acts, which is to say mostly midgets. After they stopped making movies like *The Wizard of Oz*, the midget market dried up and she moved into actors with scars. In the meantime, we had a lot of midgets hanging around the house, and as a result my mother often served food that was a little too bite-sized. My sister Eleanor gets very churlish about my mother's cooking, and she always points out that my mother's fling with rumaki lasted considerably longer than it should have; but Eleanor hates to give credit where credit is due, and the fact is that my mother had enormous flair when she was paying attention, and when she didn't feel like paying attention she threw in a lot of butter. She could also Keep Help, which I was raised to believe was no small thing; indeed, I was raised to believe that almost the worst thing that could be said about you after you grew up was that you couldn't.

Every New Year's Day, my parents had a big party, and their friends came over and bet on the Rose Bowl and argued about which of the players on either team were Jewish, and my mother served her famous lox and onions and eggs, which took her the entire first half to make. It took her so long, in fact, that I really don't have time to give you the recipe,

because it takes up a lot of space to explain
how slowly and painstakingly she did everything, sautéing the onions over a tiny flame so
none of them would burn, throwing more and
more butter into the pan, cooking the eggs so
slowly that my father was always sure they
wouldn't be ready until the game was completely over and everyone had gone home. We
should have known my mother was crazy
years before we did just because of the mania-
cal passion she brought to her lox and onions
and eggs, but we didn't. Another thing my
mother was famous for serving was a big ham
along with her casserole of lima beans and
pears. A couple of years ago, I was in Los
Angeles promoting *Uncle Seymour's Beef
Borscht* and a woman said to me at a party,
"Wasn't your mother Bebe Samstat?" and
when I said yes, she said, "I have her recipe
for lima beans and pears." I like to think it
would have amused my mother to know that
there is someone in Hollywood who remem-
bers her only for her lima beans and pears,
but it probably wouldn't have. Anyway, here's
how you make it: Take 6 cups defrosted lima
beans, 6 pears peeled and cut into slices, ½
cup molasses, ½ cup chicken stock, ½ onion
chopped, put into a heavy casserole, cover
and bake 12 hours at 200°. That's the sort of
food she loved to serve, something that looked
like plain old baked beans and then turned out
to have pears up its sleeve. She also made a
bouillabaisse with Swiss chard in it. Later on,

she got too serious about food—started making egg rolls from scratch, things like that—and one night she resigned from the kitchen permanently over a lobster Cantonese that didn't work out, and that was the beginning of the end.

Shortly after that, she went into her blue-chip stamp phase. She wasn't alone, of course. It was 1963, and there were a lot of American women who were saving blue-chip stamps and green stamps and plaid stamps and whatever stamps their supermarkets were giving out; still, ladies in suits with shoulder pads were supposed to have more sense. My mother, who had spent years avoiding supermarkets, made at least one trip a day to the local Thriftimart. (The scar-face market had gone pretty dry on her at this point, and she had very little else to do.) She would get into her 1947 Studebaker and set off for a day in the aisles. She developed passionate and brief attachments to new products. One month she fell in love with instant minced onions. Another month it was Pepperidge Farm raspberry turnovers. The next it was frozen chopped chives. She would return home with her bags of groceries, leave them in the kitchen for the housekeeper to empty, and go up to her bedroom, where the card table was equipped with one of those little sponge-and-jar contraptions you use when you have a lot of stamps to stick.

I was living in New York at the time, and I

heard about most of this from my sister
Eleanor, who was perfecting her sanctimoni-
ousness under the aegis of my mother's pro-
gressive insanity, but I saw a little of it first-
hand when my mother arrived in Manhattan
one day with a ten-speed blender she had
purchased for me with twenty-six books of
blue-chip stamps. She had carried it onto the
plane and held it on her lap all the way to New
York. The next day my apartment was bur-
glarized, and they took the blender, complete
with warranty. They also took my typewriter,
the television set, and my gold bracelet. My
mother surveyed the wreckage and then, instead of just going out to buy a new blender for
sixteen dollars, went off to the nearby A & P
and spent six hundred dollars on groceries,
just for the plaid stamps. Then she returned
to my apartment and began pasting them into
stamp books. That's what she was doing when
the police finally arrived—sitting there at the
table, laughing her gravelly laugh and licking
every so often as the two policemen told us
what they thought were a lot of rollicking
stories about New Yorkers who'd been bur-
glarized of all the presents under their Christmas trees. We all had a drink, and then we all
had another, and four hours later my mother
was singing "When that midnight choochoo
leaves for Alabam'" and the policeman whose
lap she was sitting on was taking little nips at
her shoulder. Then she got up and did a tap
dance to "Puttin' On the Ritz" and passed out

in the middle of it. It was a fabulous pass-out as those things go. She was in midair when it happened—she had both her legs up to one side, and she'd just managed to click her heels together when her eyes clanged shut and she slid on one side of her leg to the floor. I put her to bed.

"Was I very bad?" she said on the way to the airport the next day.

"Not really," I said.

"Please say I was," she said.

My father was a specialty act himself, though not in any formal sense. He was a character actor—he worked under the name of Harry Stratton, the name he still uses—but he played the kind of characters who have no character: he played kindly lawyers and kindly doctors and kindly teachers, and he said kindly things to whatever leading actor was about to lose heart in his fight to discover penicillin or defeat the outlaws or rout the Nazis. He made a lot of money—so did my mother—and they invested it in Tampax stock, and one day they were rich, and a good thing they were, because my mother's medical bills were enormous. She drank and drank and drank and finally one day her stomach swelled up like a Cranshaw melon and they took her to a very fashionable hospital for rich people with cirrhosis and the doctors clucked and said there was nothing that could be done. My parents had moved to New York by this time, and my mother's hospital room had a

view of the East River. She lay there slowly
dying, with my father impatiently standing
by. "Pull the plug," he would say to the doctors, and the doctors would calmly explain
that there was no plug, there was just the
wasting away of life. A few of her former
clients came to see her—the scar faces frightened the nurses and the midgets made whoop-
ee on the electric wheelchairs—and now and
then she came into focus and made deals. "I
think we can get you a hundred thou on the
next one," she would say; she hadn't handled
a client in years, but she went rattling on
about points and box office and below the line
and above the line. The nurse would bring
lunch. "I think I'll take it in the commissary,"
she'd say. One day my father called and said,
"You'd better come. I think this is it." Of
course, he telephoned every day and said that,
but it always sounded like wishful thinking;
now, finally, I knew he must be right. I went
straight to the hospital, and when I went into
her room she was sleeping. Suddenly she
opened her eyes and looked at me. "I just
screwed Darryl Zanuck on the remake," she
said, and gave a little croak, which I didn't
know at the moment was a significant thing,
the actual croak—I thought it was just her
gravelly laugh—and died.

"Mother's gone," said the nurse. Not "Your
mother" but "Mother." I stared at the nurse,
stunned not so much by my mother's death,
which after all had been promised for months

and, as far as my father was concerned, was long overdue, but by the nurse's presumption. "You can call your mother Mother," I snapped, "but you can't call my mother Mother." The nurse gave me one of those withering looks that are meant to make you feel as if your thoroughly understandable rage is mere female hysteria. She pulled the sheet over my mother's face. "We're going to take Mother away now," she said in a tone so condescending that I became even more wild with anger. "She's not your mother," I shouted. "On top of which, she's not gone, she's dead. Do you hear me? *Dead*. And what you're going to take away is her body, so call it a body. Call it a corpse, for Christ's sake." The nurse was now looking at me with an expression of complete horror, which I thought at the time was on account of my behavior, but it wasn't really; it was complete horror at what was happening behind me, which was that my mother had chosen that moment to make a full recovery. The sheet began rising like a slow-motion poltergeist, and then, in a burst, my mother whipped off the cloth and shouted: "Ta da!" Then she fainted. "Fainted dead away" is what the nurse said, which just goes to show you another anomaly of hospital life, which is that they only use the word "dead" when it doesn't apply.

"We thought you were dead," I said a few minutes later, when my mother came to.

"I was," she said, "I was." She shook her

head slightly, as if trying to remember a fuzzy dream. "I floated away in a white organdy dress and black patent-leather Mary Janes," she said. "I looked like Baby Snooks. I tried to get something to wear that was more dignified, but the dignified clothes were being used on another set." She nodded; it was all coming back now. "I looked down, and there was your father, clicking a clapboard that read: 'Bebe's Death, Take One.' The camera started rolling. I was floating further and further away. I was definitely dead. Your father sold the Tampax stock and bought himself a Borsalino hat. 'Print,' he said. 'It's a wrap.'" She began tapping her breastbone defiantly. "*I* was the one who sat next to Bernard Baruch at a dinner party in 1944 and heard him say, 'Buy something people use once and throw away.' *I* was the one who stuck a Tampax into my twat in 1948 and came out of the bathroom and said, 'See if this is traded over the counter.' *I* was the one who made us rich, and now the bastard is going off and spending my money on bimbos while I'm stuck in goyishe heaven in an inappropriate costume. Fuck this, I said to myself, and at that moment I came back."

The next day, when I went to see her, she was sitting up in bed smoking Kools and doing the Double-Crostic. "I have experienced a miracle," she said. "You know what that means, don't you?"

"No," I said.

"It means there's a God," she said. "If you

believe in miracles you have to believe in God. One follows from the other."

"No it doesn't," I said. "It doesn't follow at all. It doesn't have to be the sort of miracle someone's in charge of. It could just have been an accident of some sort. Or a dream. Or a misdiagnosis on the part of the nurse."

My mother shook her head. "I was dead," she said. "You should have seen it up there. Fluffy white clouds, and little angels with pink cheeks playing tiny harps."

"Lyres," I said.

"Miss Smart and her college education," said my mother.

A week later, she checked out of the hospital, filed for divorce, and went to New Mexico to find God. And she did. She found God and she married him. His name was Mel, he honestly believed he was God, and as my first husband Charlie said at the time, "If there's one thing we know about God, it's that he's not named Mel." Mel took my mother for every penny she had, plus Charlie's old Swedish-modern couch and a set of flatware I was very attached to. Then she died again, this time for good.

I would like to ask her what a person who is seven months pregnant is supposed to do when her husband turns out to be in love with someone else, but the truth is she probably wouldn't have been much help. Even in the old days, my mother was a washout at hard-core mothering; what she was good at were clever remarks that made you feel immensely sophisticated and adult and, if you thought about it at all, foolish for having wanted anything so mundane as some actual nurturing. Had I been able to talk to her at this moment of crisis, she would probably have said something fabulously brittle like "Take notes." Then she would have gone into the kitchen and toasted almonds. You melt some butter in a frying pan, add whole blanched almonds, and sauté until they're golden brown with a few little burned parts. Drain lightly and salt and eat with a nice stiff drink. "Men are little boys," she would have said as she lifted her glass. "Don't stir or you'll bruise the ice cubes."

III

Maybe you think I walked out on Mark awfully fast if I was really so in love with him, but I probably wouldn't have if it wasn't for my therapist. I left that part out, and I hate to bring it up because until now you've been thinking that Mark was the one with the unconventional shrink, and now you're going to see we both were. Oh, well. I have a therapist named Vera Maxwell. She's fifty-eight years old and quite beautiful, she has creamy white skin and curly black hair and she wears bright red lipstick and caftans. She's famous, really, she goes on talk shows and has a lot of celebrity patients, and every so often she has to fly off to co-host Merv Griffin, or she has to take a phone call in the middle of a session from someone having a crisis at the Cannes Film Festival.

Vera is a wonderful therapist. She is loving, caring, giving and unrelenting. Of course, when I first went to her, I was unhappily married to Charlie, and now nine years had passed and I was unhappily married to Mark, and that might not sound like progress. But trust me. You'll have to trust me, because there's no real way to convey what she does in her office that doesn't sound like some sort of Yiddish mumbo jumbo. She tells the kreplach joke a lot, and the one about the man from Minsk meeting the man from Pinsk. I will tell you the kreplach joke, but the truth is you need an accent to tell it well; I would throw in a recipe for kreplach as well, but it's a pain in the ass to make kreplach.

THE KREPLACH JOKE

Once upon a time there was a little boy who hated kreplach. Every time he saw a piece of kreplach in the soup he screamed, "Aaaaah, kreplach!" So his mother decided to teach him not to be afraid of kreplach. She took him into the kitchen and rolled out some dough. "Just like a pancake," she said. "Just like a pancake," said the little boy. Then she took a piece of meat and rolled it into a ball. "Just like a meatball," she said. "Just like a meatball," said the little boy. Then she rolled up the meat in the dough and held it up. "Just like a

dumpling," she said. "Just like a dumpling," said the little boy. Then she dropped
it into the soup and put it in front of
the little boy, and he screamed, "Aaaaah,
kreplach!"

Anyway, the thing about Vera is that
she's very direct; she's not one of those
shrinks who sit there impassively and say
"Mmmmhmmm" every so often. After Mark
told me he was in love with Thelma Rice and
left me to be alone for a while, I called up Vera
in New York and told her what had happened,
and do you know what she said? She said,
"He's disgusting." That threw me a little,
because even though I knew that Vera was no
slouch at calling a spade a spade, it seemed
awfully strong.

"What should I do?" I said.

"What should you do?" Vera replied.

That may not look like a direct response, but
it was. She said, "What should you do?" with
her voice rising on the word "do," and it was
as if there was only one possible thing to do
and how could I possibly wonder what it was.
But I hung in there; I tried to get her to be a
little more specific.

"Yes, what should I do?" I said.

"Is this what you want?" Vera said. "Is this
what you want in a husband?"

Well, of course it wasn't what I wanted in a
husband. On the other hand, what I wanted in
a husband was Mark. At least that's what I'd

thought I wanted. Could I help it if Mark didn't measure up to Vera's ideas of a husband? Vera has a husband to match her ideas —his name is Niccolo, and he has a white beard and he wears crisp seersucker suits and straw hats that he tips, and Vera says that the sex she has with Niccolo is as good after twenty years of marriage as it was in the beginning, which is almost the most depressing thing she says since no one else can say that except Vera, but if Vera says it there must be something to it; and what's more, what's worse in a way, is that Vera says she is never bored by Niccolo and he is never bored by her because they never tell the same stories twice. She told me this one day when I was still married to Charlie.

"Never?" I said.

"Never," said Vera, but if she ever did tell a story twice, she said, she would change it around a little so that Niccolo would still find it interesting. Myself, I never change a story. I never even change an *inflection* in a story once it's working. Mark, on the other hand, changes his stories every time he tells them, by making them longer. He has a story he tells about his first day of work in the newspaper business. He went to his office his first day in the newspaper business in a brand-new white suit, and they told him he had to wash the carbon paper, and he believed them, and he went into the men's room and turned on the water and the carbon splattered all over his brand-new white suit. It's a good story. Mark told it to me the night we met. We all have stories like that, stories we rely on to establish our charm in the beginning of relationships. I tell one about wanting to play the ukulele in the school orchestra. They asked me what instrument I wanted to play, and I said the ukulele, and they said, but there's no ukulele in the school orchestra, and I said, then what can I play that's like the ukulele, and they said the viola. That story doesn't sound so charming on the page, but I tell it very well. In any case, by the time Mark fell in love with Thelma Rice, the story about his first day in the newspaper business had turned into a novella.

"Well, is it?" said Vera. "Is this what you want in a husband?"

"I guess not," I said weakly, and left for the plane.

I worry about telling you this kind of story. Psychoanalysis has done strange things to my dialogue, and when I talk about it I sound a little like one of those starlets on *The Tonight Show* who's just stumbled onto Eastern philosophy or feminism or encounter therapy or any other system of thought that explains everything in the universe in eight minutes. Pick a dream, any dream—I'll analyze it and give you a pep talk. This used to cause a lot of friction between me and Mark. When I first met him, he had a recurrent nightmare that Henry Kissinger was chasing him with a knife, and I said it was really his father and he said it was really Henry Kissinger, and I said it was really his father and he said it was really Henry Kissinger, and this went on for months until he started going to the Central American shrinkette. That's almost the only good thing I can say about Dr. Valdez: Mark's going to her at least ended our conflict over psychoanalysis. In fact, he was converted overnight. "What's really bothering you?" he would say. Or: "What does that remind you of?" Or: "That sounds hostile to me." Or: "I'm not your mother." All this happened before we got married, and I found it incredibly seductive.

So we got married and I got pregnant and I gave up my New York apartment and moved to Washington. Talk about mistakes. There I was, a regular at the Thalia, a connoisseur of the latest goat cheeses, an expert on alternate routes to Long Island—there I was, trying to hold up my end in a city where you can't even buy a decent bagel. I don't mean to make it sound as if it's all about being Jewish, but that's another thing about Washington. It makes you feel really Jewish if that's what you are. It's not just that there are so many Gentiles there; it's that the Gentiles are so Gentile. Listen, even the Jews there are sort of Gentile. Not that I complained. I can work anywhere, I said bravely. I had a new husband, and then I had a new baby, and then I had another baby coming, and meanwhile I had my friends and a kitchen stove with six burners. *Uncle Seymour's Beef Borscht* made the best-seller list and two weeks later I was in the Sunday *Times* crossword puzzle, 26 across—Uncle Seymour's niece, it said.

Every so often I would fly to New York for one thing or another, and would go by to see Vera. I had really graduated from therapy by then, but I liked to stop in for an oil check from time to time. I would tell her I was okay, really I was, I was working hard, things were good with me and Mark, the baby was wonderful, and then, after the session, I would walk into Balducci's and there would be the arugola and radicchio and fresh basil and sorrel and sugar snap peas and six kinds of sprouts, and I would think to myself: Even the vegetables in New York are better.

It's not just the vegetables, of course. I look out the window and I see the lights and the skyline and the people on the street rushing around looking for action, love, and the world's greatest chocolate chip cookie, and my heart does a little dance. The little dance my heart was doing as I looked out the window of my father's apartment was not exactly a polka, but at least I was where I wanted to be. If I couldn't have Mark, I could finally be back making sorrel soup. Take 4 cups of washed sorrel and cut off the stems carefully. (If you don't, the soup will be hairy, and no one will know it's the sorrel's hair and not the cook's.) Sauté the sorrel in 4 tablespoons butter until wilted. Add 2½ quarts chicken stock and 4 chopped peeled potatoes. Cook 45 minutes until potatoes are tender. Purée in a blender and add salt, pepper and hot red pepper flakes. Chill and add more salt and the juice of 1 lemon and 1 cup heavy cream. Serve with lemon slices.

The next morning the doorbell rang. I'd been up all night waiting for Mark to turn up to say it was all a terrible mistake, he really loved me, he must have been crazy, he didn't know what had gotten into him, and he would never see Thelma again if I would just come back to Washington immediately. I flung open the door to tell him I never wanted to see him again but I might consider coming back under certain circumstances, and who should it be but Jonathan Rice, the undersecretary of state and my partner in cuckoldom. I burst into tears and we fell into each other's arms.

"Oh, Jonathan," I said, "isn't it awful?"

"It's awful," he said. "What's happening to this country?" (Jonathan never takes anything personally; he always sees himself as a statistical reflection of a larger trend in society.)

Sam toddled into the living room and began methodically removing the books from the bookshelves, and Jonathan and I sat down and started on vodka mixed with Red Cheek apple juice. It turned out that Jonathan had been up half the night discussing the situation with Thelma and Mark, and when he realized neither of them was going to do a thing about it, he'd hopped on the shuttle and come to my father's, where Mark said I probably was.

"I had to talk to you," Jonathan said. "I love my wife." I'll skip the direct quotes, because it's too sickening—in less than twenty-four hours I'd had to listen to two grown men talking like saps about Thelma. He loved Thelma, Jonathan said, he had never loved anyone but Thelma, he had loved Thelma for nineteen years and would always love her even though Thelma didn't give a rat's ass about him and never had. She was a hysteric, Jonathan said, and a hopeless romantic; he'd been through this half a dozen times with her other men—the worst, he said, had been her affair with the undersecretary of the Nationalist Chinese embassy; she'd nearly had a nervous breakdown when Nixon recognized China and the Nationalists had to leave the country. "She got into bed and stayed there for weeks," said Jonathan. "Imagine my dilemma: there I was, on the Asia desk." He sighed. "Of course, normalization was psychologically hard on many Americans."

Still, Jonathan went on, he'd never seen Thelma quite so smitten with anyone as she was with Mark, and vice versa, and off went Jonathan on a long description of the presents Mark had given Thelma and the restaurants he'd taken her to and the meals they'd ordered

and the business trips she'd gone along with
him on and the hotels they'd stayed in and the
room service (room service! he'd even had
room service with her!) and the flowers that
had arrived the next day. Just thinking about
the flowers made me want to die, just thinking about the flowers he'd sent her while
occasionally bringing me home a bunch of
wilted zinnias. Mark is such a campaigner;
he never just *does* something, he crusades for
it. To realize, as I was suddenly beginning to
realize, that all his energy had been going into
Thelma Rice for all these months made me so
sad I could hardly breathe. Jonathan went
rattling on, pouring on detail after detail, to
the point that I accused him of bugging his
own telephone—he knew so much, he knew
actual dialogue—but he claimed that Thelma
simply told him everything. "We have an honest marriage," Jonathan said, and he glared
at me as if I were somehow responsible for
this whole mess because my marriage was so
hopelessly dishonest. For months I'd been
doing nothing but boiling eggs and teaching
my child to differentiate between the cat in
the hat and the fox in socks, and Jonathan
Rice, the undersecretary of state, was actually angry at *me!* It's stuff like this that got us
into Cambodia. Anyway, since Jonathan
knew so much, I asked him if he happened to
know exactly what it was that Mark and
Thelma had been doing four days earlier, on

the day the inscription in the children's book was dated. *I wanted to give you something to mark what happened today, which makes our future so much clearer.* . . . And of course he knew; the man knew everything. Four days earlier, my husband, Mark Feldman, had taken his paramour, Thelma Rice, to the Bloomingdale's furniture department, where they had looked at couches for his office. Bloomingdale's! The ultimate perfidy!

"But his office has a couch," I said.

"His *new* office," Jonathan said.

"What new office?" I said.

"The new office he wants to rent on Connecticut Avenue," said Jonathan. "And of course it needs a couch." He paused for emphasis. "You can't have a love nest without a couch." He paused again. "A convertible couch."

"I know I'm slow," I said, "but I did manage to figure the convertible part out."

The couch Thelma liked was green, Jonathan said, but Mark liked a brown tweed one, and they almost compromised on a pale yellow one but Thelma thought it would show the dirt, and just when I was becoming really sorry I'd asked, Jonathan came to the point— there was a point to his visit, it turned out— and said that he believed that if I came back to Mark, the two of us could wait the two of them out. He'd talked to the Guatemalan whiz-bang, he said—that's when I found out all three of them were seeing her—and he'd concluded that Mark's affair with Thelma would never last, because Mark had too much Jewish guilt and would never give up his children.

"Also," said Jonathan, "there's a lot Mark doesn't know about Thelma, and when he finds it out I'm sure he won't love her anymore."

"There's a lot Thelma doesn't know about Mark, too," I said.

"Like what?" said Jonathan.

"It doesn't matter," I said. "You know all this awful stuff about Thelma and you still love her, and I know all this awful stuff about Mark and I still love him, so what makes you think they're going to stop loving each other when they find out what we know about them?"

"Tell me some awful stuff about Mark," said Jonathan.

I couldn't think of much. Mark has to be reminded to clean his nails, and sometimes he says he's read a book when he's read only the first fifty pages of it, and he doesn't visit his Great-Aunt Minnie in the Hebrew Home as much as he should, but the truth is that the only really awful thing I knew about Mark Feldman was that he had betrayed me. That was a terrible thing, I don't mean to downplay it, but it wasn't the sort of thing Jonathan was looking for; Jonathan wanted to be told that Mark was a notorious plagiarist, or a shoplifter, or a scofflaw, and then he wanted to take the information home to Thelma like an old bone. Poor Jonathan. Poor pathetic doggie. The man actually believed he was going to argue her out of it. On top of everything else (not that I was going to tell him, although Thelma undoubtedly already had), Jonathan was up against a real piece of work in the sack, and it's hard to compete with that if you're the spouse who's been around for years; it's hard to compete with *anyone* new in the sack if you're the spouse who's been around for years. I really wanted to say something consoling to Jonathan, but every time the urge came over me to do so, he would drop one more piece of the betrayal into my lap: he was like a six-year-old boy who comes up to you with a shy smile, takes your hand and gently presses a snake into it. No wonder Thelma had fallen in love with Mark; if I'd spent nineteen years with Jonathan Rice, I would have run off with a delivery boy from the Fleet Messenger Service.

"I'm not going back to Mark," I said. "I'm not going to sit there while the two of them go on seeing each other on their convertible couch. I'm not going to wait this out."

"You're my only hope," Jonathan said.

I started crying again, and Jonathan put his arms around me and began muttering something about how the economy was in bad shape too, and there we were, hugging each other while Jonathan went on about the gross national product, when my father walked into the living room. He'd escaped from the loony bin in a jogging outfit.

"I'd like you to meet Jonathan Rice," I said.

"You're doing this in front of the kid?" said my father.

"It's not what you think," I said. "Mark is in love with Jonathan's wife."

"Who's Mark?" said my father.

"My husband," I said.

"It's the Thorazine talking," said my father. "They shoot you up with so much of it you can't even remember your son-in-law's name. Who was Charlie?"

"My first husband," I said.

"He's a fool," said my father.

"I thought you liked Charlie," I said.

"Not Charlie. Mark. Mark's a fool."

"What am I going to do?" I said. I started to sob. My father gave a little nod to Jonathan Rice, a little move-over-Buster-you're-in-the-way nod, and Jonathan untangled himself and stood up and my father sat down and tangled himself, and I shook and heaved and wheezed and snorted all over his sweatsuit. My father said a lot of terrific daddy things to me that made me cry even harder, partly because the dialogue was completely lifted from an obscure Dan Dailey movie he'd played a pediatrician in, and partly because he nevertheless delivered the lines so very well.

"What am I going to do?" I said.

"There's nothing you can do, baby," said my father.

"Of course there's something she can do," said Jonathan. "She can come back to him. If we both stick with it, we can sit this thing out."

"Jonathan is the undersecretary of state in charge of Middle Eastern affairs," I said.

My father looked at Jonathan. "I suppose they don't give that job to Jews," he said.

"That's right," said Jonathan.

"You want to make a pact with someone," said my father, "go call up the president of Egypt. Leave Rachel out of this." Then he told Jonathan to have a nice flight back and showed him to the door. Then he telephoned Lucy Mae Hopkins, the maid, and asked her to move into the apartment for a while to help take care of Sam. Then he called the Chinese restaurant down the block and ordered shrimp fried rice, which is something I love to eat when I'm feeling blue, shrimp fried rice with Chinese mustard and ketchup. Then, after Lucy Mae and the Chinese food arrived, he announced that he was going back to the loony bin because there wasn't room for all of us to sleep in the apartment.

"Men," he said as he left. "I hate them. I've always hated them. You wonder why I always hang around with women and never with men, it's because men do things like this." He waved his hand vaguely at me and my stomach, and jogged off into the night.

Of course, I knew he wasn't going back to the loony bin at all; he was going to see Frances. Frances is my father's mistress. She works at a paper company, and she has remained true to my father even though he keeps marrying other women and leaving her with nothing but commissions on his stationery orders. He orders an enormous amount of stationery, partly to keep a hand in with Frances, partly to have plenty of pieces of paper on which to write to me and my sister Eleanor about his will. Two or three times a month, my father threatens to cut me out of his will, and then he changes his mind, and each of these developments requires a letter. He also writes a lot of letters to Frances, promising that he'll end up with her eventually; I know this because once he accidentally put a letter to her into an envelope to me and vice versa. Frances got very excited when she opened the letter meant for me, because it had no salutation and she thought he was cutting *her* out of his will, which she hadn't realized she'd been written into in the first place. Why she puts up with him I don't know. Why any of us puts up with him I don't know. The truth is that if my father weren't my father, he would be one of the men he hates; he is incorrigibly faithless and thoroughly narcissistic, to such an extent that I tend to forget he's also capable of being a real peach.

(Another thing I like to eat when I'm feeling

blue is bacon hash. Cut some bacon into small pieces and start to cook it over a slow flame so that some of the fat is rendered. Then add diced cooked potatoes and cook slowly until the potatoes and bacon are completely crunchy. Eat with an egg.)

IV

The shock of catapulting from the peanut-butter-and-jellyness of my life into High Drama was so great that the first morning I woke up, I was honestly stunned to discover it wasn't all a bad dream. That's a hopelessly banal metaphor, but that's just what it felt like, one of those bad dreams in which you realize you're having a bad dream and then you wake up in the dream to the same old bad dream—the dream equivalent of the cereal box with the baby on it eating breakfast next to the cereal box with the baby on it eating breakfast, forever and ever.

By the second morning, I'd given up on that. I woke up and lay there, watching the baby inside me make waves on my belly, and wondered what would become of me. Mark would turn up eventually, of course—but what if he didn't? What would I do? Where would I live? How much money would I need? Who would sleep with me? This last question interested me deeply, because I couldn't imagine that I'd ever be my normal shape again. I will be seven months pregnant forever, I thought, as the tears started to drip slowly into my ears, and after that I will be eight months pregnant forever, and after that I will be nine months pregnant forever. The only men I'd have a shot at would have to be used to thoroughly misshapen women, and that pretty much ruled out everyone but doctors. Under other circumstances, doctors would never have crossed my mind. I went out with one when I was in college. I was suffering from a finger that got abscessed when I stuck a ballpoint pen into a hangnail. He took one look at it and said, "Abscesses. Diabetes." This terrified me, because it's always seemed to me that there's a lot of diabetes among Jews, even though it's hard to pin anyone down on the question. Once, in fact, I tried to; I met a diabetes specialist, and I said to him, "May I ask you a question?"

He replied: "You want to ask me if Jews have more diabetes than anyone else."

"Yes," I said.

"Everyone asks me that," he said. "They don't. There's a sect in India that has more diabetes than Jews."

This reminded me of those feminists who are always claiming that male domination is

not the natural state because there's one tribe
in New Guinea where the men lie around
weaving and the women hunt bears. Anyway,
I didn't have diabetes, I merely had an abscessed finger. I have never since been remotely interested in doctors. But who else
would bother with me? There I was, seven
months gone, swaybacked, awkward, bloated,
logy, with a belly button that looked like a
pumpkin stem and feet that felt like old cu-
cumbers. If pregnancy were a book, they
would cut the last two chapters. The beginning is glorious, especially if you're lucky
enough not to have morning sickness and if,
like me, you've had small breasts all your life.
Suddenly they begin to grow, and you've got
them, you've really got them, breasts, darling
breasts, and when you walk down the street
they bounce, truly they do, they bounce
bounce bounce. You find yourself staring in
the mirror for long stretches of time, playing
with them, cupping them in your hands, pushing them this way and that, making cleavage,
making cleavage vanish, standing sideways,
leaning over, sticking them out as far as
they'll go, breasts, fantastic tender apricot
breasts, then charming plucky firm tange-
rines, and then, just as you were on the verge
of peaches, oranges, grapefruit, cantaloupes,
God knows what other blue-ribbon county-fair
specimens, your stomach starts to grow, and
the other fruits are suddenly irrelevant because they're outdistanced by an honest-to-

God watermelon. You look more idiotically out of proportion than ever in your life. You feel such nostalgia for the scrawny, imperfect body you left behind; and the commonsense knowledge that you will eventually end up shaped approximately the way you began is all but obliterated by the discomfort of not being able to sleep on your stomach and of peeing ever so slightly every time you cough and of leaking droplets from your breasts onto your good silk blouses and of suddenly finding yourself expert in mysteries you hadn't expected to comprehend until middle age, mysteries like swollen feet, varicose veins, neuritis, neuralgia, acid indigestion and heartburn.

Heartburn. That, it seemed to me as I lay in bed, was what I was suffering from. That summed up the whole mess: heartburn. Compound heartburn. Double-digit heartburn. Terminal heartburn. The tears poured from my eyes as I lit on the image, and the only thing that might have made it even more satisfyingly melodramatic and masochistic would have been to be lying in the bathtub; nothing like crying in the tub for real self-pity, nothing like the moment when every last bit of you is wet, and wiping the tears from your eyes only means making your face even wetter.

I considered staying in bed all day. I considered getting out of bed and into the bathtub and staying *there* all day. I wondered if even considering these two alternatives constituted a nervous breakdown. (Probably not, I decided.) I contemplated suicide. Every so often I contemplate suicide merely to remind myself of my complete lack of interest in it as a solution to anything at all. There was a time when I worried about this, when I thought galloping neurosis was wildly romantic, when I longed to be the sort of girl who knew the names of wildflowers and fed baby birds with eyedroppers and rescued bugs from swimming pools and wanted from time to time to end it all. Now, in my golden years, I have come to accept the fact that there is not a neurasthenic drop of blood in my body, and I have become very impatient with it in others. Show me a woman who cries when the trees lose their leaves in autumn and I'll show you a real asshole.

I picked up the remote control unit and turned on the television set. There was Phil Donahue. He was interviewing five lesbians, who had chosen the occasion of their appearance on Donahue to come out of the closet. I could just imagine the five of them, waiting through the years for the right offer, turning down Merv, turning down Kup, turning down Cavett, watching contemptuously as their friends chose mundane occasions like Thanksgiving with Mom and Dad for the big revelation, waiting for the big one, Phil himself, to finally come clean. I contemplated lesbianism. Lesbianism has always seemed to me an extremely inventive response to the shortage of men, but otherwise not worth the trouble. It occurred to me that if I stayed in bed much longer, I would be forced to watch a soap opera. That seemed redundant, so I got up and went to group.

Under normal circumstances, I probably wouldn't mention my group. There's a real problem in dragging a group into a book: you have to introduce six new characters, bang bang bang, six new characters who are never going to be mentioned again in any essential way but who nonetheless have to be sketched in, simply because I can't really leave out of this story what happened to my group. Maybe you remember reading about it, I don't know. You'd probably remember if you did—because Vanessa Melhado is in my group. The advantage of having Vanessa Melhado in my group is that at least I don't have to introduce all six patients, since you've seen at least one of them in the movies. The other patients I'm going to have to describe by first name only: one of the many rules of group therapy is that you're not to know anyone's last name. With Vanessa, of course, you can't help knowing, she's too famous; and when my books started being published, everyone in the group learned mine; but until we all ended up on the front page together, we never knew anyone else's.

I hadn't been to my group in two years; when I moved to Washington, I'd graduated. The group held a special session in my honor, and it was really quite lovely. Everyone managed to say nice things to me except Diana, and I managed to say nice things to everyone except Diana, and Eve brought *grieven,* which are pieces of rendered chicken fat cooked with onions, and Ellis brought champagne, and even Dan, who never brings food and when he does it's only a tiny little container of cole slaw that doesn't go around, even Dan brought a cheesecake I'd given him the recipe for.

I got the cheesecake recipe from my father's second wife, Amelia, who was my family's housekeeper for years before she married him. Amelia, in fact, was what people were referring to when they said my mother was so gifted at Keeping Help. She was black—high yellow, to be exact—and ample (I think ample would be a polite way of describing her size) and covered with so many moles that she looked like a poppy seed cookie. And although it was clear that my father married her mostly to get even with my mother for marrying the Mel who thought he was God, it was still pretty inexcusable as these things went. What made it inexcusable, as far as I was concerned, was not that she was black and fat and looked like a poppy seed cookie, but that my father, in marrying her, got her to do for nothing exactly what she had been doing for a rather pleasant salary; this, it seemed to me, was going too far in the Keeping Help department. What made it inexcusable as far as my sister Eleanor was concerned was that she was sure Amelia was after my father's fortune. Since the Mel who thought he was God had already bankrupted my mother, Eleanor was positive the other half of the Tampax money would vanish as well and end up invested heavily in Amelia's only vice: wigs. "She's got at least forty of them now," Eleanor would say. "Imagine how many she'll have after he's gone."

Once I tried to engage Eleanor on the question of whether Amelia and my father had ever slept together, but she was in such a rage about the marriage there was really no dealing with her; she couldn't even enjoy empty speculation about it. Which was a shame, because Amelia was much too good-hearted to have been a gold digger, and she made my father happy, which is more than I can say of Eleanor and me, who were busy leading our own lives. Amelia cooked my father perfect meals and then sat down and giggled merrily at everything he said. In fact, she giggled merrily at everything everyone said. This put the burden of being amusing on whoever was with her, but my father loved it. My father occasionally says things like "A flying nun covers a multitude of sins" and then looks for a laugh, and it was a great comfort to him that Amelia was always good for one even if everyone else in the room was trying to ignore him.

What a cook she was! Everything she made was the lightest, the flakiest, the tenderest, the creamiest, the whateverest. She would stand at the kitchen counter—kneading dough for yeast rolls, making curls from carrots, rolling butter into balls—and tell me her secrets. She knew the mystery of my grandmother's cookies (sour cream), and she insisted there was only one true road to piecrust (Crisco). She had burn scars from her fingertips to her elbows, and she could tick them off: this one from a chicken fry for her mother's ninetieth birthday, this one from the first time she made potato pancakes, this one from a cast-iron pot she'd tended over a fire when she was growing up in the bayou. I owe her a huge debt—and her ending up with a big chunk of my father's money and a roomful of wigs would have been fine with me. But Amelia died after a year of marriage, and the only thing she ever got out of my father was a very nice grave somewhere in Louisiana.

Here's Amelia's cheesecake recipe; she always said she got it from the back of the Philadelphia cream cheese package. Make a nice graham cracker crust and pack it into a 9-inch pie pan. Then mix 12 ounces cream cheese with 4 well-beaten eggs, 1 cup sugar and a teaspoon vanilla. Pour into the pie shell and bake 45 minutes at 350°. Remove and cool 15 minutes. Then spread gently with 2 cups sour cream mixed with ½ cup sugar and bake 10 minutes more. Cool and refrigerate several hours before serving.

I took the subway to group. I always took the subway to and from Vera's; it cleared my head. I sat down, remembered to twist my diamond ring inward so the muggers wouldn't see it, and tried to concentrate on how I was going to tell the group what had happened to me. I felt mortified. Two years earlier, I had walked off into the sunset—cured! it's a miracle! she can walk!—and now I was back again, a hopeless cripple. I looked around the subway car. A Japanese man was taking pictures of the passengers. He was undoubtedly a tourist, but he was making everyone in the car uncomfortable. I tried not to look at him, but it was impossible. Once I saw an exhibitionist on the subway, and I tried not to look at him, too, but the funny thing about exhibitionists—and the reason I'm never really offended by them—is that you can't help sneaking a peek now and then to see if the damned thing is still sticking out. I looked at the Japanese man in a way that I hoped implied that I didn't really care if he took my picture, and that if he did take my picture I didn't really care that he was shooting my bad side, but then I decided I did care. So I smiled.

I look much better when I smile. In fact, when I don't smile, I look as if I'm frowning even though I'm not.

The Japanese man took my picture and nodded his head to me in a grateful fashion. I nodded back, and a man in a plaid shirt sitting next to me looked at me and winked. I immediately wondered whether he was single, and if so, whether he was a college graduate and straight. Then I thought of how awful it would be to be single again, how awful to be back on the market with the old New York ratio going against me, two hundred single women to every straight single man, packs of Amazons roaming the streets looking in vain for someone genuinely eligible and self-supporting who didn't mind a little cellulite. It was such a depressing thought that I almost began to cry—but then I remembered the Japanese man with the camera. I did not want anyone, even a stranger on the subway, to take a picture of me crying.

The man in the plaid shirt winked again, and I realized that even if he was single and a college graduate and straight, the odds were unlikely that I would ever get involved with an indiscriminate winker at pregnant women on subways. Anyone who winks at pregnant women on subways must have something wrong with him, it seemed to me. Of course, everyone has *something* wrong with him, that's for sure, but this guy probably had something *really* wrong. Perhaps he's a rapist, I thought, or a mugger. I figured that in my present physical condition I was fairly safe from rapists, but in case he was a mugger and knew how to recognize a diamond ring even when it was turned inward, I twisted the ring off in what I hoped was a thoroughly discreet manner, made an ambiguous gesture as if I were pulling at the skin on my throat, and cleverly dropped the ring into my bra.

The subway came to Union Square and I got out. There was Ellis. Ellis is in my group. He was buying popcorn at the nut stand in the subway station, and when he saw me he looked so pleased that he threw the entire contents of the box of popcorn over his head, and just stood there grinning as it settled onto and around him. He was like a living version of a snowman in a glass ball you shake the snow inside of. I was glad to see him, too, but I couldn't tell him that because another rule of group is that members are not allowed to have conversations of any sort outside the group room, so we walked together without saying a word all the way to Vera's office.

Vera was sitting at the low, round table, opening the containers of food the group members had brought for lunch. Vanessa was there, and Eve and Diana and Sidney and Dan—and they clucked over the photographs of Sam and asked when the new baby was due and looked truly horrified when I told them why I was there.

"My husband is in love with someone else"

is hard to say flat out. "My husband thinks he's in love with someone else" is as close as I came before bursting into tears. Even Diana looked truly horrified, which surprised me because Diana always gets a little smile on her face when something awful happens to me. Years earlier, I had come into group one day and burst into tears, and Diana had gotten that little smile on her face; she was really disappointed to discover that the reason I was crying was that I'd been assaulted by a cabdriver; no doubt she'd been hoping for a more personal tragedy, with longer-lasting effects. Well, now she had one.

Sidney handed me a box of Kleenex. Sidney never really says much in group—he just passes the Kleenex and looks solicitous. I wiped my eyes and managed to stop sobbing long enough to get most of the story out. Then I burst into tears again, and so did Diana.

"Why does everything happen to Rachel and nothing ever happens to me?" she cried.

"Stick it up your ass, Diana," said Ellis.

"You'd like to, wouldn't you?" said Diana. "That's the only way you like it, I bet."

"I like it all ways, which is more than I can say for your husband," said Ellis.

"Who brought the chopped liver?" asked Dan.

"I did," said Eve.

"Did you make it?" asked Dan.

"I bought it," said Eve. "Is that all right with you?"

"I was about to tell you it was delicious," said Dan. "Now I don't feel like telling you."

"Nothing's ever enough for you, is it?" said Eve.

"Every week you complain about the food," said Vanessa. "When's the last time *you* brought food to group? When's the last time you brought anything to group?"

"What did I do now?" said Dan.

"What did you do *now*?" said Eve.

"You know what this reminds me of?" said Vera.

"The old woman from Vladivostok and the camel," said Ellis.

"Please don't tell that one again," said Vanessa.

"I won't," said Vera. "But that isn't even the point. Why don't you want to talk about Rachel?"

"I'm too threatened to talk about Rachel," said Eve. "I believe in Rachel. I believe in Rachel and Mark. If they can't make it, who can?"

"Vera and Niccolo," said Ellis.

"They don't count," said Vanessa.

Everyone nodded glumly.

"Who's the other woman?" said Diana.

"It doesn't matter," I said.

"It matters to Diana," said Ellis. "All Diana cares about is finding out people's last names."

I told them a little about Thelma. I said she had a nose as long as a thumb and walked like a penguin; that made me feel better. I said Mark was a schmuck; that made me feel even better. And I said how unfair it was that I couldn't even date.

"She must be feeling better," said Ellis. "She's making jokes."

"She makes jokes even when she's feeling terrible," said Vera. "Don't let her fool you."

"Why do you have to make everything into a joke?" asked Diana.

"I don't have to make everything into a joke," I said. "I have to make everything into a story. Remember?"

"How do you feel?" asked Eve.

"Hurt. Angry. Stupid. Miserable." I thought for a minute. "And guilty."

"You didn't do this," said Eve. "*He* did."

"But I picked him," I said.

"Anyone would have picked Mark Feldman," said Vanessa.

"No last names in group," said Vera.

"Anyway, it's not over," said Eve. "He'll be back."

"And then what?" I said. "It's like a beautiful thing that suddenly turns out to be broken into hundreds of pieces, and even when you glue it back together it's always going to have been horribly broken."

"That's what a marriage is," said Sidney. "Pieces break off, and you glue them back on."

"Look at it this way," said Vanessa, "it's not a total loss. At least you got Sidney to say something."

Sidney looked quite pleased with himself.

"Are you done, Sidney?" asked Ellis.

"Yes," said Sidney.

"Because if you are," said Ellis, "I just want to say that I don't think that's what a marriage is."

"That *is* what a marriage is," said Dan. "After a certain point it's just patch, patch, patch."

"That's not what Vera and Niccolo's marriage is," said Eve.

Everyone nodded glumly again.

"Sometimes I wish you and Niccolo would get a divorce," I said to Vera. "Your marriage is very hard on the rest of us."

"I saw Niccolo last week," said Vanessa, "and he told me that occasionally at the end of the day he and Vera get irritable with each other."

"I would kill for merely irritable," I said.

"Under what circumstances did you see Niccolo last week?" Diana asked.

"He and Vera came to a screening of my new movie," said Vanessa.

"And when you become a movie star, Diana, I'll come to a screening of your new movie, too," said Vera.

"Thanks a lot," said Diana. Diana is a computer programmer.

"What do you want?" said Vanessa. "Mark

is going to turn up, and you have to know what you want when he does."

I thought about it.

"I want him back," I said.

"What do you want him back for?" said Dan. "You just said he was a schmuck."

"I want him back so I can yell at him and tell him he's a schmuck," I said. "Anyway, he's my schmuck." I paused. "And I want him to stop seeing her. I want him to say he never really loved her. I want him to say he must have been crazy. I want her to die. I want him to die, too."

"I thought you said you wanted him back," said Ellis.

"I do," I said, "but I want him back dead."

I smiled. It was the first time I'd smiled about the situation. I looked around the room, expecting everyone to be smiling back, but they were all looking in my direction as if something strange was going on. Ellis was the first to speak. "You haven't by any chance hired an assassin without telling us first, have you?"

I turned to look behind me. A man wearing a nylon stocking over his head was standing at the door, holding a snubnosed revolver. He grabbed me around the neck, pulled me to my feet, and pressed the gun against my temple. "On the table," he said. "Money, jewelry, anything you've got that I want. Hold anything back and I'll kill the lady just like this—" And for an instant, he aimed the gun

't say things you don't mean," I said.
tepped out into the vestibule and ran
door of the building to the street. I rode
up and walked into Vera's office. Every-
tood up, looking a little embarrassed,
era went to call the police. There was a
hugging while she was out of the room.
ing is against the rules, too, but so is
ry, so no one cared.

ney'll be here in a few minutes," Vera
when she came back. She looked around
oom. "You must all feel that I failed to
ect you."

on't blame Vera," I said. "It was my
t."

ou always think it's your fault," said Va-
a. "You're much too guilty."

Can't anything ever be Rachel's fault?"
ed Diana.

He saw me on the subway," I said. "He
me take my ring off and stick it into my
. He must have followed me here, only I
walking with Ellis so he couldn't rob me
he way."

I hope you and Ellis weren't having a
versation outside the group room," said
1.

We weren't," said Ellis, "but if we had
n, we probably would have been talking
ut what a creep you are."

here was a long silence.

This is going to get into the papers," said

at the wall, pulled the trigger and fired. Everyone jumped at the explosive crack and turned to watch a framed photograph of Theodor Reik break into shards and fall to the floor. A second later, a framed Chivas Regal ad with a caption that said "The bottle is either half empty or half full depending on how you look at it" fell off the wall, too.

"I always hated that picture," said Sidney.

"This is not the time to talk," said Vera.

She took off the strands of antique beads from around her neck, and her three lacy wedding bands, and put them into the middle of the table. Everyone started to throw money onto the pile. Vanessa unsnapped the gold necklace she'd been given after something (though not that much) had happened between her and John Wayne in Mexico. Diana made a great show of removing her plastic bracelets and throwing them ceremoniously into the taramasalata.

The man in the nylon stocking pressed the gun into my temple so hard that I almost cried out. I closed my eyes. "Your turn, lady," he said.

I could feel the diamond ring I had slipped into my bra pressing against my breast. Mark had given me the ring when Sam was born. We had gotten to the hospital when the contractions were coming only five minutes apart, and Mark sat in the labor room, next to me, holding my arm, whispering, singing, making little jokes, doing everything right. I'd

been absolutely positive that he wouldn't—
that he'd turn into the kind of hopeless father
who goes through the whole business under
the delusion that it's as much his experience
as it is yours. All this starts in Lamaze class-
es, where your husband ends up thinking he's
pregnant, and let me tell you he's not. It's not
his body, it's not his labor, it's not his pain—
it's yours, and does any man give you credit or
respect for it? No. They're too busy getting in
on the act, holding their stopwatches and
telling you when to breathe and when to push
and taking pictures of the kid coming out all
covered with goo and showing them to your
friends at dinner parties and saying what a
beautiful and moving experience it was. Not
Mark. He just sat there helping me to get
through, and he stayed completely calm when
the doctor said there was something wrong,
perhaps the umbilical cord was around the
baby's neck; and he looked so impassive when
he glanced over at the fetal monitor and saw
that the baby had stopped breathing that I
didn't even realize how serious the situation
was; he just kept on whispering and singing
and making little jokes as they rushed me into
the operating room and knocked me out for
the emergency Caesarean.

When I came to, he was standing next to
me. He was wearing a green surgical smock
and a mask, and he was crying and laughing,
and in his arms was Sam, our beautiful Sam,
our sunray, pink and gold and cooing like a

tiny dove. Mark laid him
lay down next to me on
held us both until I fell a

Two hours later, when
me the ring. He'd just gon
The diamond was in an a
rounded by tiny little diam
a delicate ice flower. The r
it back to the jeweler and
"Rachel and Mark and San

I've always wondered wl
done about the diamond ring
other circumstances. If I'd
didn't have a choice, because
nylon stocking was the man i
and he'd seen me put the ring
subway. But suppose he hadn'
handed it over? Would I have
hold on to the ring? I don't kno
that when the man in the p
nylon stocking said, "Your turn
gesturing toward my bra. So I re
bra and gave it to him. He moti
put the other things into a bag,

"Now everyone lie down on
said. He kept the gun presse
head and began backing out
holding me against him. "No
police," he said. "Otherwise I
He opened the door to the hallwa
the nylon stocking. We got int
and started down.

"I'm sorry about your ring,"

"Do
He
out th
back
one
and
lot o
Hug
robb
"]
said
the
prot
"
fau
"
nes
"
ask
"
saw
bra
wa
on

co
Da

be
ab

Vanessa. "That's going to be my fault." Everything Vanessa did ended up in the papers.

"Good," said Diana. "We're going to find out everyone's last names."

"I have something terrible to say," said Ellis. "I was attracted to him." He looked thoroughly ashamed of himself. "He had a nylon stocking over his face and I was attracted to him."

"I saw him without the nylon stocking," I said.

"And?" said Ellis.

"And I was attracted to him, too."

"But you're desperate," said Ellis.

"That's true," I said. "But don't rub it in."

V

*O*ne afternoon, some months before all this happened, I was working in the kitchen in our house in Washington trying to perfect my system for a four-minute egg. Here's how you make a four-minute egg: Put an egg into cold water and bring it to the boil. Turn off the heat immediately and put the lid on the saucepan. Let it sit. In three minutes, you will have a perfect four-minute egg. It just so happens that the world is not waiting breathlessly for a three-minute way to make a four-minute egg, but sometimes, when you are a food person, the possible irrelevance of what you are doing doesn't cross your mind until it's too late. (Once, for example, when I was just starting out in the food business, I was hired by the caper people to develop a lot of recipes using capers, and it was weeks of tossing capers into just about everything but milkshakes before I came to terms with the fact that nobody really likes capers no matter what you do with them. Some people *pretend* to like capers, but the truth is that any dish that tastes good with capers in it tastes even better with capers not in it.)

Anyway, there I was, boiling eggs at three-twenty on a Thursday afternoon. I know the exact time, because I looked at the clock as soon as I heard the shout. A man was shouting —screaming, actually. A fight, I thought. A terrible fight, I thought. A fight so terrible that someone is going to get killed, I thought. I went to the front door and opened it. The shouting stopped. I went back to the eggs. That evening, when Mark came home, I said, "If someone was murdered on this block this afternoon, it happened at three-twenty." Mark paid no attention at all. At the time I thought this was because he thought I was turning into the sort of melodramatic woman who is forced to imagine excitement and romance and intrigue because she's stuck at home all day; but I realize now that his affair with Thelma was just beginning, and his reaction was simply the one you affect when you're becoming involved with someone else and you're determined not to be remotely interested in or amused or touched by the person you're married to.

Now that I think about it, perhaps I *was* turning into a certain kind of melodramatic woman—not the kind who fantasizes because she's housebound but the kind who's simply trying to get her husband's attention because she knows that he's somewhere else, with someone else. Even then, back when the affair was starting, mustn't I have had an inkling? I can't bear that I didn't, but that's not the reason I'm telling the story about the man down the block who was murdered, so I'll get back to it.

Three days later. A Sunday. Mark and I were on our way out to lunch. The police. A half-open door to the house across the street. On the floor of the foyer, a huge brownish stain. "If there's a dead body in there," I said to the policeman outside, "it happened at three-twenty on Thursday afternoon." There was. It was Mr. Abbey, a meek little man who had had his last fling with rough trade. And I was the only witness! I don't mean to get so excited here, but I've always wanted to be a witness. I've always wanted to swear to tell the truth, the whole truth, and nothing but the truth and spar with lawyers and be sketched by courtroom artists. Now my time had come! And I knew nothing. It really was depressing, and not just for me, but for the homicide detective on the case, who kept trying to pry information out of me.

"You know more than you think," Homicide Detective Hartman kept saying, as he urged me to search my memory for the additional details he was certain were buried there.

"No I don't," I said.

A few days after Mr. Abbey's body was discovered, Homicide Detective Hartman came back to take another crack at my subconscious. He was full of interesting information. He told me that Mr. Abbey had spent the last morning of his life at a furniture auction. Afterward, a friend who was there had asked him to lunch. Mr. Abbey refused. He said he had seen a beautiful black man cruising the bus terminal the night before, and was going back to find him. And that was the last anyone saw of Mr. Abbey.

I was fascinated by the story. I couldn't believe that anyone would be so sexually driven that he might actually skip lunch—and after an auction! I think of myself as a healthy person with a strong sex drive, but it's never occurred to me to forgo meals. I said this to Mark later. I said, perhaps this is the difference between homosexuals and heterosexuals, perhaps this relentless priapism is characteristic of the obsessive, casual sex that lasts so much later in the lives of homosexuals than in heterosexuals. And Mark got this look on his face, this incredulous look, that at the time I thought meant he couldn't believe I could have such a short memory. Had I forgotten the first months of our courtship? The hours and hours of sex, the smell of it everywhere, in the air, on the sheets, on my hands, in my hair—had I managed to forget all that? (Of course I hadn't; on the other hand, we never once had less than three meals a day, so there.) Now, of course, I know about Thelma, and I realize that Mark's incredulity arose simply because I knew so little about him and *his* relentless priapism, knew so little about *men*. When will I ever learn? When will I ever understand that what's astonishing about the number of men who remain faithful is not that it's so small but that there are any of them at all?

I see that once again I've gotten off the track, that I've drifted back to Mark, to Mark and Thelma, but I can't help myself. When something like this happens, you suddenly have no sense of reality at all. You have lost a piece of your past. The infidelity itself is small potatoes compared to the low-level brain damage that results when a whole chunk of your life turns out to have been completely different from what you thought it was. It becomes impossible to look back at anything that's happened—from the simplest exchange between the two of you at a dinner party to the horrible death of Mr. Abbey—without wondering what was really going on. See the couple. See the couple with the baby. See the couple with the baby having another baby. *What's wrong with this picture*? Everything, as it happens.

But I was telling you about Mr. Abbey's death for a reason, and it has nothing to do with betrayal. I simply wanted you to understand that when my group was robbed, I was almost grateful: it gave me another shot at being a witness to a crime. And this time I knew stuff, I really knew stuff. I had actually laid eyes on the bugger. I couldn't wait to be deposed, or whatever it is they call what they do to you.

They took us to the station house in a paddy wagon. This was fairly insulting, since we were the victims, but the detective in charge of the case had so many statements to take that he wanted to do it with stenographers and typewriters and tape recorders nearby. We spent the afternoon in a small green room and each waited his turn. First the police talked to Vera, because she was in charge of the premises, as they say, and then they talked to Vanessa, because she was the most famous and beautiful (I've come to terms with the fact that Vanessa is the most famous and beautiful, but it really irritated me that day since after all I was the one who knew the most about what happened), and then they talked to Diana because she insisted she would hold them responsible if she missed her Supersaver flight to Los Angeles. Finally Detective Nolan got to me.

I told him everything. I said the robber was about six feet tall. Sandy hair. Watery blue eyes. A little squint. Pinkish complexion. A long, thin nose on a wide, shiny face. Weighed about 165—I can never be sure what men weigh. A fat neck. A red and green plaid cotton shirt, a khaki jacket, jeans and running shoes. I first noticed him when a Japanese man on the subway took my picture. My guess is that the Japanese man has a picture of the robber.

"What did the Japanese man look like?" asked Detective Nolan.

"Japanese," I said. "You know."

"I know," said Detective Nolan. "Small and Oriental and wearing a dark gray suit, with a camera around his neck."

"Yes," I said.

"What kind of camera?"

I shrugged. "I thought I was doing pretty well till we got to this part," I said.

"You are doing very well," said Detective Nolan.

"You say that to everybody," I said.

"No I don't," he said.

"Yes you do," I said. "I was a witness to something else recently, and the detective kept telling me how well I was doing, but I wasn't really."

"What else were you a witness to?" said Detective Nolan.

"A murder in Washington," I said. "I wasn't actually a witness—I just heard the shouting. Why?"

"I just wondered," said Detective Nolan.

"You just wondered if I was the kind of woman who attracts criminals the way other women attract alcoholics or sadists." (I have a friend who attracts dwarfs. Every time she turns around, a dwarf is following her. It's very disturbing.)

"No," said Detective Nolan. "What made you notice the man on the subway?"

"He winked at me," I said.

"I see," said Detective Nolan.

"It was probably my fault," I said, "because I was smiling at the Japanese man, because I'd rather have my picture taken when I'm smiling because when I'm not smiling I look as if I'm frowning, and that's when the robber winked at me, so I wondered if he was single, and then he winked again and I wondered if he was a mugger, and that's when I put my diamond ring into my bra."

"You mean you just looked at him and automatically wondered if he was single?"

"Well, he winked at me," I said.

"What made you think he might be a mugger?"

"I didn't really *believe* he was a mugger," I said. "I just realized that he might not be a suitable object for fantasy. I didn't even know if he'd gone to college."

"Are you sure there wasn't some detail you can't quite remember that alerted you in some way?"

"Like the bulge of his revolver under his jacket?" I said.

"Yes," said Detective Nolan.

"I don't think so," I said, "but it's possible that he was looking at my ring before I twisted it backwards, and I knew that. Subconsciously, I mean."

"Subconsciously," said Detective Nolan.

"I just remembered something," I said. "The Japanese man was wearing a little identification card. The kind they give you at conventions."

"Excellent," said Detective Nolan, and left the room. A few minutes later he came back and sat down.

"How long do you think it would take me?" he said.

"To find the Japanese man?" I said.

"To have therapy," he said. "How long would it take?"

"What's wrong with you?" I said.

"Nothing much," he said.

"Nine years," I said.

"How long did it take you?" he said.

"Nine years," I said. "Of course, I've had two years off for good behavior, but now I'm back. And there was nothing much wrong with me, either. That's why I graduated in the first place. The ones there's really something wrong with are in forever."

"Why did you start nine years ago?" asked Detective Nolan.

"I wanted a divorce," I said.

"From this guy who's being so terrible to you now?"

"From the first one," I said. I looked at him. "Diana told you, didn't she? I know she did. That bitch."

"I'm sorry to bring it up," said Detective Nolan. "It's not even relevant. Although it might explain why you were wondering whether the guy on the subway was single."

"That's true," I said.

"I was thinking of going into therapy because I can't decide whether to have a hair transplant," said Detective Nolan.

"You already have an awful lot of hair," I said.

"It's not mine," said Detective Nolan.

"It looks pretty good," I said.

"You think so?" he said.

"Yes," I said.

"I'm just telling you that so you know something about me, and since I know something about you, we're even."

"I don't think you need therapy," I said. "You might be the only person in America who doesn't."

I finished being interviewed by Detective Nolan, and gave him my father's telephone number and my number at home in Washington just in case. It wasn't until I was past the newspaper photographers and on the subway that I wondered whether Detective Nolan was single. He wasn't exactly my type, but look where my type had gotten me. Then I wondered if he was uncircumcised. Then I wondered if I could be happily married to a policeman. Then I wondered why I was so hopelessly bourgeois that I couldn't even have a fantasy about a man without moving

on to marriage. Then I stopped wondering.
For one thing, the subway arrived at my stop
and I got off. For another, it seemed clear to
me that it would never matter. When I got to
my father's apartment, I was sure, Mark
would be there.

And he was.

VI

I met Mark Feldman at a party in Washington at my friend Betty's. Betty Searle and I went to college together, and we always used to talk about living together afterward; but one day Betty said that I was a brunette and belonged in New York and she was a blonde and belonged in Washington, and she was right. Betty went off to Washington and became famous for her local television show, her dinner parties, and her affairs with a first-rate cross section of the American left wing. Every Christmas she had a party that everyone in Washington came to, and there, one Christmas, was Mark. I recognized him the minute he walked in because I'd seen him on *Meet the Press*, and once you see that beard you never forget it. He has a black beard, but the part of it that's on the left side of his chin has a little white stripe in it, where the skin underneath has no pigment. Just like a skunk is what you're thinking, and you're right, but it can look very odd and interesting. I've always liked odd and interesting-looking men because I'm odd and interesting-looking myself, and I always figured I had a better shot at them than at the conventionally good-looking ones. (Water seeks its own level, et cetera.) My mother would have loved Mark Feldman's beard. "A scar but not" is what she would have called it.

Mark is a syndicated columnist, that's why I'd seen him on television. He writes about Washington as if it's a city like any other (it's not), filled with rich and interesting characters (it's not). He's known for being chronically perverse about politics. For instance, some people think it's terrible that Washington doesn't work, but Mark thinks it's wonderful, because if it worked, something might actually be accomplished and then we'd really be in bad shape. This is a very clever way of being cynical, but never mind.

"Stay away from him," Betty said, when she saw me looking over at him.

"Why?" I said.

"He's trouble," she said.

"Please don't throw me in the brier patch," I said.

So Mark Feldman and I went out to dinner. He told me the story of his first day in the newspaper business. I told him the story of wanting to play the ukulele in the school orchestra. And then we went to bed. We stayed there for about three weeks. Every so often he got up to write a column, and I got up to call my answering machine in New York to see if there was any reason not to be in Washington for a while longer. There wasn't.

At some point in those three weeks, we had gotten out of bed for some reason or other, and we were taking a walk near the Pension Building. It's a huge, block-square structure with a frieze of Civil War soldiers, thousands of soldiers moving cannons and guns and wagons and horses slowly around the perimeter of the building. We went up the stairs to the entrance, and the guard let us into the inner courtyard. It was barely lit. The guard went down the hall and turned on the lights, and suddenly I could see the huge open space in the center of the building, pillars three stories high, leaded glass at the top. For many years, the inaugural balls were held in the Pension Building. We could hear the guard's radio, with an old Sinatra song coming from it. Mark held out his hands.

"I can't dance," I said. "I've never been able to."

"I believe in you, Rachel," he said.

We started to dance.

"You didn't believe me," I said.

"I'm not going to step on your foot," Mark said.

"I know that," I said.

"No you don't," he said.

He stepped back and put his right hand on the front of his waist and his left hand on the back.

"Right here," he said. "That part of you is mine for the next three minutes. After that I'll give it back. But you have to give it to me for now."

"I have to trust you," I said.

"Right."

"I have to *follow* you," I said.

"Right."

"Oh, God," I said.

"You can do it, Rachel," he said, and he put his arms out again. We started to dance. I closed my eyes. And I relaxed. People are always telling me to relax—the hairdresser tells me to relax, and the dentist, and the exercise teacher, and the dozen or so tennis pros who have attempted to do something about my backhand—but the only time I think I've ever really relaxed in my entire life was for three minutes in the Pension Building dancing with Mark Feldman.

"I'm dancing," I said.

"I love you," he said.

So we were in love. We were madly in love. We flew back and forth on the Eastern shuttle and we called each other on various WATS lines and I became best friends with his best friends and he became best friends with my best friends, and there were presents and concerts and three-pound lobsters at the

Palm, and then one day I came down to Washington and walked into his apartment and found a Virginia Slim cigarette butt in an ashtray. *Who's been eating my porridge?* Mark said it was the maid's. I pointed out that the maid smoked Newports. Then he said it was his sister's. I pointed out that his sister had stopped smoking. Then he said he had bummed it from a copy girl at the office. I said that even copy girls at the office weren't naive enough to smoke Virginia Slims. Then he got angry and said if he'd wanted to live with a detective he'd live with a detective and why didn't I trust him? Then I got angry and said if he was going to bum cigarettes he ought to bum Marlboros so I wouldn't think he was cheating on me, and why didn't he at least have the decency to empty the ashtray into the garbage disposal.

Next thing you know, we were at a party—a party for his book about Washington—and I looked across the room and saw him talking to a reporter from the *Sydney Morning Herald,* and she started laughing, and even her laugh had an Australian accent. I walked over and carefully linked my arm through his. "Oh," she said, "Mark was just telling me the most amusing story about his first day in the newspaper business."

Then off he went on his book tour.

"Hi, I'm Irv Kupcinet, and my guests to-night are Mark Feldman, syndicated colum-nist and author of the new best-seller Return

to Power; *Toby Bright, director of the Insti-*
tute of Sexual Analysis and herself the best-
selling author of Good in Bed; *former British*
Prime Minister Harold Wilson; and Graham
Kerr, the Galloping Gourmet, who is here
today to talk about Jesus Christ."

A couple of days after I saw the show on
television, I was having lunch with my friend
Marie, at the omelet place on Sixty-first
Street.

"I met Mark," Marie said.

"When?" I said.

"I was in Chicago a few days ago when he
was on his book tour."

"Where did you meet him?"

"*Playboy* had a party for some book."

"And?"

"He seemed nice," Marie said. "I couldn't
really tell that much. It was crowded and all."
She started playing with her ratatouille filling.

"Marie?"

"I keep thinking about it," Marie said. "You
know. If it were reversed, what would I want
you to do? What do you think?"

"I think it takes two people to hurt you," I
said. "The one who does it and the one who
tells you."

"I know," said Marie. "Shit."

"But I'd want you to tell me," I said. "Who
was she?"

"The one who wrote the sex book," said
Marie.

"They were together at the party," I said.

"And later," said Marie. "At the hotel."

"That bastard," I said.

"Look," said Marie, "he's got a big book, he's having a fling, it'll go away."

"Listen," I said. "I had a book. I did the Kup show. And I didn't fuck the Galloping Gourmet, and he wasn't into Jesus Christ then, either."

"I feel terrible," said Marie.

"Don't you dare steal feeling terrible from me," I said.

"This isn't fair," said Marie. "You're so much better at this than I am. You've been in group."

Of course, we could talk for days about why Marie told me. I'm glad she told me—it saved me from finding out at a later time—but still you have to wonder. Anyway, Mark and I broke up. I flew down to Washington and collected my things and had a big fight with Mark in which he accused me of the thing men think is the most insulting thing they can accuse you of—wanting to be married—and he took me to the airport and my duffel bag burst in the middle of the National Airport parking lot and all the whisks and frying pans and cookbooks fell out on the ground and then we had another big fight over whether it was his Julia Child or mine that I was taking back to New York (it was his) and that was that.

"Well, you knew he was trouble from the very beginning, didn't you?" said Vera after it was over. Which is the kind of thing Vera is always saying, and which I fundamentally agree with but nonetheless get extremely irritable about.

"Of course I knew that," I said. "I told it to you right after I met him. And you know what you said? You said, 'Everybody has a past.'"

"I never said that," said Vera.

"You certainly did say that," I said.

"What I said was that people are capable of change," said Vera. "If you don't think people can change, what are you doing here?"

"Investing my money in caftans," I said.

The telephone rang and Vera answered it. "What's the split on the paperback?" she said to whoever was calling. "What does your agent say?" She nodded. "Well, hold out for sixty-forty over two hundred fifty thousand." She hung up and looked at me.

"You think I picked Mark because I knew what was going to happen," I said.

"Did I say that?" said Vera.

"You don't have to say it, Vera."

"Well?" she said.

"No," I said. "No."

"An old man goes to buy a horse," said Vera. "Have I told you this story?"

"I can't tell yet," I said. "They all sound alike in the beginning."

"Goes to buy a horse," said Vera. "The horse trader says, 'I can sell you a very nice horse for five hundred rubles.' 'What else do you have?' says the old man. The horse trader says, 'Well, for one hundred fifty rubles I can sell you a donkey. He won't live as long, but he'll get you from Kiev to Vilna.' The old man buys the donkey, and two weeks later it drops dead. So he goes back to the horse trader and says, 'How was I to know?'"

"Is that a story about how smart you are, or how dumb I am?" I said.

"Both," said Vera.

"Well, at least this time I get to be a person in the story. The last time you told one of your Russian parables I was a bag of chickens."

There was a long pause.

"Well?" said Vera.

"It's not as simple as that, Vera," I said. "You want everything to be simple. You think I'm just standing there, and this army of men is walking by, shouting, 'Choose *me*, choose *me*,' and I always pick the turkey. Life's not like that. I can't even find a man who lives in the same city I do."

"Of course you can," said Vera.

Well, of course I couldn't. The next man I was involved with lived in Boston. He taught me to cook mushrooms. He taught me that if you heat the butter very hot and put just a very few mushrooms into the frying pan, they come out nice and brown and crispy, whereas if the butter is only moderately hot and you crowd the mushrooms, they get all mushy and wet. Every time I make mushrooms I think of him. There was another man in my life when I was younger who taught me to put sour cream into scrambled eggs, and since I never ever put sour cream into scrambled eggs I never really think of him at all.

Two months passed. I flew to Boston every other weekend. The man in Boston flew to New York every other weekend. I was deeply involved in piecrust. I was perfectly happy. And Mark turned up. Mark turned up full of repentance and bearing gifts. He sent flowers. He sent jewelry. He sent chocolates, and not those overly refined Swiss ones either—nice chewy, nutty American ones. He called up and said psychoanalytic things on the phone. He said he had made the worst mistake of his life and he wanted me back and he would love me forever and he would never hurt me again. He said he wanted to marry me. He said he was going to marry me. He said I might as well get used to the idea. He asked me to marry him on the IRT downtown local, and he asked me to marry him on the Forty-ninth Street crosstown bus. He asked me to marry him so often—and I refused so often—that when he failed to ask me for a day or so, I started to worry. He campaigned for me. He spoke of babies. Forever and ever. "Let's sing all the songs we know about marriage," he said to me one morning. Picture a little love nest, he sang, out where the roses cling. Picture the same sweet love nest, I sang back, think what a year can bring.

There were two reasons I didn't want to marry Mark. First of all, I didn't trust him.

And second of all, I'd already been married.
Mark had already been married, too, but that
didn't really count; it certainly didn't count in
the way it usually counts, which is that it
makes you never want to get married again.
Mark's first wife was named Kimberly. (As he
always said, she was the first Jewish
Kimberly.) Mark and Kimberly were married
for less than a year, but he had enough material from her to last a lifetime. "My wife, the
first Jewish Kimberly," Mark would begin,
"was so stingy that she made stew out of
leftover pancakes." Or: "My wife, the first
Jewish Kimberly, was so stingy she once tried
to sell a used nylon stocking to a mugger." In
truth, the first Jewish Kimberly really was
stingy, she recycled everything, and she once
blew up their apartment and most of what
was in it while making brandy out of old
cherry pits.

My first husband was stingy, too, but that
was the least of it. My first husband was so
neurotic that every time he had an appointment, he erased the record of it from his
datebook, so that at the end of the year his
calendar was completely blank. My first husband was so neurotic he kept hamsters. They
all had cute names, like Arnold and Shirley,
and he was very attached to them and was
always whipping up little salads for them with
his Slice-o-Matic and buying them extremely
small sweaters at a pet boutique in Rego Park.
My first husband was so neurotic he would

never eat fish because he'd once choked on a fishbone, and he would never eat onions because he claimed he was allergic to them, which he wasn't. I know, because I snuck them into everything. You can't really cook without onions. "Is this an onion?" Charlie would say, his eyes narrowing as he held up a small, translucent object he had discovered floating in the sauce that covered his boneless dinner. "No, it's a celery," I would say. It didn't really fool him; at the end of every meal he would leave a neat little pile of small, translucent objects on his plate. God, was he neat. My first husband was so neat he put hospital corners on the newspaper he lined the hamster cage with.

The reason my marriage to Charlie broke up—although by now you're probably astonished that it lasted even a minute—was not because he slept with my oldest friend Brenda or even that he got crabs from her. It was because Arnold died. I felt really sad when Arnold died, because Charlie was devoted to Arnold and had invented a fairly elaborate personality for Arnold that Arnold did his best to live up to. Hamsters don't really do that much, but Charlie had built an entire character for Arnold and made up a lot of hamster jokes he claimed Arnold had come up with, mostly having to do with chopped lettuce. Also, and I'm sorry to tell you this, Charlie often talked in a high, squeaky voice that was meant to be Arnold's, and I'm even sorrier to tell you that I often replied in a high, squeaky voice that was meant to be Shirley's. You enter into a certain amount of madness when you marry a person with pets, but I didn't care. When Charlie and I were married, I was twenty-five years and eleven months old, and I was such a ninny that I thought: Thank God I'm getting married now, before I'm twenty-six and washed up.

Anyway, when Arnold the hamster died, Charlie took him to one of those cryogenic places and had him frozen. It wasn't at all expensive, because the body was so small, on top of which there wasn't any additional charge for storage because Charlie brought Arnold home in a nice Baggie with a rubber band around it and simply stuck him into the freezer. I could just see Cora Bigelow, the maid, taking Arnold out one Thursday thinking he was a newfangled freeze-dried potato treat in a boil bag; boy, would Charlie be in for a shock the next time he went to put an eensy-weensy bouquet of flowers next to Arnold's final resting place, directly to the right of the ice cube tray. I mean, what are you supposed to do with a first husband like that? I'll tell you what: divorce him. I'll tell you something else: when you divorce a first husband like that, you never look back. You never once think: God, I wish Charlie were here, he'd know how to handle this. Charlie never handled anything if he could help it. He just made a note of it in his Mark Cross datebook and erased it when the problem had cleared up.

I left Charlie after six years, although at least two of those years were spent beating a dead horse. There have always been many things you can do short of actually ending a bad marriage—buying a house, having an affair and having a baby are the most common, I suppose—but in the early 1970s there were at least two more. You could go into consciousness raising and spend an evening a week talking over cheese to seven other women whose marriages were equally unhappy. And you could sit down with your husband and thrash everything out in a wildly irrelevant fashion by drawing up a list of household duties and dividing them up all over again. This happened in thousands of households, with identical results: thousands of husbands agreed to clear the table. They cleared the table. They cleared the table and then looked around as if they deserved a medal. They cleared the table and then hoped they would never again be asked to do another thing. They cleared the table and hoped the whole thing would go away. And it did. The women's movement went away, and so, in many cases, did their wives. Their wives went out into the world, free at last, single again, and discovered the horrible truth: that they were sellers in a buyers' market, and that the major concrete achievement of the women's movement in the 1970s was the Dutch treat.

I left Charlie everything—the cooperative apartment, the house in the country, and Shirley, Mendel, Manny and Fletcher. I took my clothes and my kitchen equipment and two couches I had brought to the marriage. I asked Charlie for a coffee table, but he wouldn't give it to me. The moving man sat there reading the section on vaginal self-examination in my spare copy of *Our Bodies, Ourselves* while Charlie and I fought about furniture. I said we had three coffee tables; the least he could do was to give me one. He said I had both couches and where was he supposed to sit anyway. I said that I'd brought both couches to the marriage, but that all three coffee tables had been accumulated *during* the marriage and I ought to get *something* that had been accumulated during the marriage. He said I could have Mendel. I said Mendel was a washout, even for a hamster. He said he'd brought furniture to the marriage, too, but that I'd given it to my mother when she'd run off with the Mel who was God and it had never been seen again. I said the furniture we'd given to my mother was Swedish modern and revolting and we owed the Mel who was God a big favor for taking it off our hands. He said he would never give me the coffee table because he'd just realized I'd packed the carrot peeler along with my kitchen equipment and now he had no way to make lunch for Shirley and the boys. On his way out to buy another carrot peeler, he said he would never forgive me for what I'd said about Mendel. At the end of the move, the mover shook my hand solemnly and said, "I had five others this week just like this one. Yours wasn't so bad."

Of course, afterward Vera said I'd set it up so it would happen that way, set it up so that there would be no way Charlie could possibly give me the coffee table and I could therefore walk away from the marriage with the happy knowledge that Charlie was as stingy as I'd always said he was. "You picked him," Vera said, "because his neuroses meshed perfectly with yours." I love Vera, truly I do, but *doesn't anything happen to you that you don't intend?* "You picked him because you knew it wouldn't work out." "You picked him because his neuroses meshed perfectly with yours." "You picked him because you knew he'd deprive you the way your mother or your father did." That's what they're always telling you, one way or another, but the truth is that no matter whom you pick, it doesn't work out; the truth is that no matter whom you pick, your neuroses mesh perfectly and horribly; the truth is that no matter whom you pick, he deprives you the way your mother or your father did. "You picked the one person on earth you could have problems with." "You picked the one person on earth you shouldn't be involved with." There's nothing brilliant about that—that's life. Every time you turn around you get involved with the one person on earth you shouldn't get involved with. Robert Browning's shrink probably said it to *him.* "So, Robert, it's very interesting, no? Of all the women in London, you pick this hopeless invalid who has a crush on her father." Let's face it: *everyone* is the one person on earth you shouldn't get involved with.

And what is all this about *picking,* anyway? Who's picking? When I was in college, I had a list of what I wanted in a husband. A long list. I wanted a registered Democrat, a bridge player, a linguist with particular fluency in French, a subscriber to *The New Republic,* a tennis player. I wanted a man who wasn't bald, who wasn't fat, who wasn't covered with too much body hair. I wanted a man with long legs and a small ass and laugh wrinkles around the eyes. Then I grew up and settled for a low-grade lunatic who kept hamsters. At first I thought he was charming and eccentric. And then I didn't. Then I wanted to kill him. Every time he got on a plane, I would imagine the plane crash, and the funeral, and what I would wear to the funeral and flirting at the funeral, and how soon I could start dating after the funeral.

Is this inevitable, this moment when everything leads to irritation, when you become furious that he smokes, or that he coughs in the morning, or that he sheds crumbs, or that he exaggerates, or that he drives like a maniac, or that he says "Between you and I"? You fall in love with someone, and part of what you love about him are the differences between you; and then you get married and the differences start to drive you crazy. You fall in love with someone and you say to yourself, oh, well, I never really cared about politics, bridge, French and tennis; and then you get married and it starts to drive you crazy that you're married to someone who doesn't even know who's running for President. This is the moment when any therapist will tell you that your problem is fear of intimacy; that you're connecting to your mother, or holding on to your father. But it seems to me that what's happening is far more basic; it seems to me that it's just about impossible to live with someone else.

And soon there's nothing left of the marriage but the moments of irritation, followed by the apologies, followed by the moments of irritation, followed by the apologies; and all this is interspersed with decisions about which chair goes in the den and whose dinner party are we going to tonight. In the end, what's left is a social arrangement. You are a couple. You go places together. And then you break up, and the moving man tells you yours wasn't so bad. But it was. Even when you end a marriage you want to end, it's awful.

I started out telling you all this because I wanted you to understand why I so resisted getting married again. It seemed to me that the desire to get married—which, I regret to say, I believe is fundamental and primal in women—is followed almost immediately by an equally fundamental and primal urge, which is to be single again. But there was Mark. With his big brown eyes and his sweetheart roses. Forever and ever, he said. Forever and ever and ever, he said. *I'll be loving you always. . . . Not for just an hour, not for just a day, not for just a year, but always.*

For a long time, I didn't believe him. And then I believed him. I believed in change. I believed in metamorphosis. I believed in redemption. I believed in Mark. My marriage to him was as willful an act as I have ever committed; I married him against all the evidence. I married him believing that marriage doesn't work, that love dies, that passion fades, and in so doing I became the kind of romantic only a cynic is truly capable of being. I see all that now. At the time, though, I saw nothing of the sort. I honestly believed that Mark had learned his lesson. Unfortunately, the lesson he learned wasn't the one I had in mind: what he learned is that he could do anything, and in the end there was a chance I'd take him back.

VII

Your husband's here," Lucy Mae Hopkins said, as she opened the door to my father's apartment for me. Then she rolled her eyes. Lucy Mae Hopkins had given up men for Jesus forty years earlier, and she couldn't understand why anyone else wouldn't, given the choice. I walked into the living room. Mark was sitting on the couch, reading a book to Sam. He looked up and gave me a nod and went on reading. I sat down in a chair and noticed a blazer Mark had draped over the back of it. A new blazer. The man had broken my heart and then gone out and bought himself a new blazer! To make matters worse, it was a nice blazer. I fingered the material.

"Britches," said Mark. Britches is a store in Washington where Mark buys his clothes. The man had broken my heart and had then gone out and bought himself a new blazer and the first word out of his mouth was Britches!

Mark finished reading to Sam and sent him off to the kitchen for a cookie. He looked at me. "I'd like you to come back," he said.

I shook my head no, not because I was refusing but because I couldn't believe that that was all he had to say. Not a word about Thelma. Not a word about how he must have been crazy. Not a word about how he was sorry. Perhaps this is Mark's way of being understated, I thought. And then again, perhaps not. In fact, probably not. I kept on shaking my head. I couldn't stop shaking my head. "I love you," he said. He said it with the animation of a tree sloth. "I want you to come home," he said. "You belong at home."

"I'm not coming home if you're going to see her anymore," I said.

"I'm not going to see her anymore," he said.

There was a long silence. I kept expecting him to reach out for my hand, or touch my face. He didn't. Rachel, I said to myself, this will not do. You cannot go anywhere, much less home, with a man whose idea of an apology does not include even a hypocritical show of affection. Say no. Tell him to drop dead. Crack one of your father's atrocious lamps over his head. Go into the kitchen and invent the instant waffle. Anything.

"I know this is difficult for you," Mark said, "but it's difficult for me, too."

And then Mark started to cry. *Mark* started

to cry. I couldn't believe it. It seemed to me that if anyone was entitled to cry in this scene, it was going to be me; but the man had run off with my part. "I'm in a lot of pain," he said.

There has been a lot written in recent years about the fact that men don't cry enough. Crying is thought to be a desirable thing, a sign of a mature male sensibility, and it is generally believed that when little boys are taught that it is unmanly to cry, they grow up unable to deal with pain and grief and disappointment and feelings in general. I would like to say two things about this. The first is that I have always believed that crying is a highly overrated activity: women do entirely too much of it, and the last thing we ought to want is for it to become a universal excess. The second thing I want to say is this: beware of men who cry. It's true that men who cry are sensitive to and in touch with feelings, but the only feelings they tend to be sensitive to and in touch with are their own.

Not that I knew this at the time. If I had, I could have stayed in New York with my pathetic dreams of Detective Nolan and six kinds of smoked salmon. What I actually did, though, is that I looked at Mark, sitting there, a picture of misery, and I crumbled. I can't stand to see a man cry, that's the truth. I can't stand to see a woman cry either, but the only woman I ever really see crying to any extent is me, and even though you may think I do an awful lot of it for someone who can't stand to see it, the fact is that I cry much less now than I used to. When I was young, a rude salesman at the hardware store could make me cry.

"All right," I said to Mark. "I'll come home."

"Good," said Mark, and he stopped crying. "You can put the ring back on now," he said.

I shook my head no.

"For God's sake, Rachel," he said. "Put the ring back on."

"I gave it away," I said.

"You what?" he said.

"I gave it away."

"To whom?" he said.

"To a celebrity auction," I said.

"Is this a joke?" he said.

"Yes," I said, "and not a bad one, all things considered."

"Put the ring back on," he said.

"Only part of it was a joke," I said.

"Which part?" said Mark. Mark used to like the fact that I make jokes in adverse circumstances, but clearly the charm of that had begun to wear thin.

"The part about the celebrity auction was a joke," I said. "The part about giving it away wasn't."

"You gave the ring away," said Mark.

"Not of my own free will," I said.

"Someone took it away from you," said Mark.

"Yes," I said.

"Do you want me to guess who it was?" he said.

"My group was robbed," I said.

"That's funny," said Mark. He started to laugh. "By an outsider, or by someone in the group?"

"By an outsider," I said, "and it's not funny. He held a gun to my head."

"Just because you don't think it's funny doesn't mean I don't think it's funny," said Mark. "Maybe I can get a column out of it." He began to nod slowly, the way he does whenever he gets an idea for a column and it's just started ticking away. Mark writes three columns a week, and while most of them are about political life, just enough of them are about domestic life that I sometimes felt as if I were living with a cannibal; things barely finished happening before Mark was chewing away at them, trying to string them out, turn them upside down, blow them up into 850 words for tomorrow's newspaper. Sometimes, when he was really worried about what to write about next, he would sit at dinnertime, his eyes darting desperately around the room. Was there a column in the salt and pepper shakers? In the paper napkins? In the Cuisinart food processor? "Have you noticed how hard it is to peel a hard-boiled egg?" he'd say. "Yes," I'd say. "You think there's anything to it?" he'd say. Or: "Have you noticed that English muffins don't taste as good as they used to?" he'd say. "Yes," I'd say. "You think there's anything to it?" he'd say. I don't mean to sound innocent and passive about all this; I loved looking for things for Mark to write columns about. I brought home anecdotes about parking lot attendants and supermarket checkers for him to munch on. In fact, it occurs to me that one of the reasons I sometimes felt that nothing had happened to me since my marriage was that every time something *did* happen, Mark got a column out of it and in essence made it all seem as if it had happened to him. You should see the column he got out of Mr. Abbey's murder. *My* murder, my very own personal murder, and he ran off with it and turned it into an essay on homosexuals and urban crime and practically got us all killed by the Gay Rights League. He even raided Sam's life. Sam was barely two years old, and the column about the time he swallowed the nail polish remover had run in 109 papers and the one about his first dead guppy was about to be anthologized by the Oxford University Press. Someday Sam was going to grow up and sit down to write about his life and there wouldn't be anything left of it to write about.

"You can't get a column out of my group's robbery," I said.

"Why not?" said Mark.

"Because it happened to *me*," I said. "On top of which, it was really awful."

"I'm sorry," said Mark. "Did he hurt you?"

"He twisted my arm," I said.

"Show Daddy where," said Mark.

"Oh, shut up," I said. Then I smiled. I couldn't help it. And so did he.

"I'll buy you another ring," said Mark.

"We don't have the money for another ring," I said.

"That's true," said Mark. "We didn't even have the money to insure this one."

We sat and looked at each other for a moment.

"It's sort of fitting," I said.

"Meaning what?" said Mark.

"Meaning it was a symbol of how good things were, and now that things aren't, it's just as well it's not here to remind me."

"I hate it when you say things like that," said Mark.

"I know," I said. "Do you still love her?"

"I don't want to talk about it," he said.

"But you're not going to see her anymore," I said.

"I already said that," he said.

"And the two of you aren't going to see that Guatemalan frittata together anymore, either."

"Rachel."

"Just say yes or no."

"I told you I wasn't going to see Thelma anymore, so obviously we're not going to see Dr. Valdez together anymore, either."

"Good," I said.

"Thelma doesn't really believe in that stuff anyway," he said.

"Rachel."

"Yes."

"If we leave now we can make the last plane."

The last Eastern Airlines shuttle between New York and Washington leaves at nine o'clock at night. When Mark and I were single and he lived in Washington and I lived in New York, we could never have a serious fight late at night, because there was no way to slam out the door and go home. There was something I liked about the fact that our lives and temperaments were controlled by an airline schedule, but the truth is that there were many things I liked about the Eastern shuttle. Not the comfort, and not the courtesy of the flight attendants, both of which were negligible. But the things you were supposed to like. The fact that it tended to leave when it said it was going to and to get there on schedule an hour later. The fact that you didn't need a reservation and always got a seat. The fact that there was something so utterly no-nonsense about it, just like its passengers. No one ever seemed to be going from one end of the Eastern shuttle to the other for fun. No one ever seemed to be *traveling*. They were all simply going to meetings that were in offices that happened to be in another city. Everyone carried a briefcase. Everyone was dressed for success. Everyone was serious. Indeed, it seems to me that the Eastern shuttle was almost a perfect reflection of the Puritan tradition in its attempt to make a virtue out of suffering, abstinence and plainness; and it always seemed fitting that one Eastern shuttle flies New York to Boston, where the Puritan tradition began, and the other flies New York to Washington, where those produced by that tradition are rewarded with the power to force the rest of the country to heel to its values. I loved that it took such an austere conveyance to get me to Mark; there was something wonderfully romantic about it. I looked like everyone else on the shuttle, I dressed like everyone else, I carried the *New York Times* and the *Washington Post* and the *Wall Street Journal* like everyone else. But everyone else was on their way to work, and I was on my way to Mark.

Then, one day, Mark and I were on the Eastern shuttle and he asked me to marry him. This was when he was asking me to marry him a couple of times a week, but he had never asked me on the Eastern shuttle.

"This is your chance to say yes on the Eastern shuttle," he said.

"No," I said.

"This is your chance at a really bad metaphor," he said.

"No," I said.

"This is your last chance," he said. "I'll ask

you to marry me again and again, but I'll never again ask you on the Eastern shuttle."

So I said yes.

Our friends the Siegels gave us ten shares of Eastern Airlines stock for a wedding present. Ha ha. The fare on the shuttle went to fifty dollars. And to fifty-four dollars. And to fifty-eight dollars. Arthur Siegel said: "It's a good thing you two met before the fare went up, because no fuck is worth $116 round trip." Ha ha. I moved to Washington and Sam was born and Arthur said that the money I saved not taking the Eastern shuttle almost paid for the baby's diapers. Ha ha. Eastern shuttle jokes. Not particularly funny jokes, but what do you expect?

Anyway, just try flying the Eastern shuttle with a baby. Try flying any plane with a baby if you want a sense of what it must have been like to be a leper in the fourteenth century, but try the shuttle for the ultimate in shunning. All those men in suits, looking at you as if your baby is going to throw up over their speech drafts; all those men in suits who used to look at me with respect when I pulled out my American Express gold card, now barely able to conceal their contempt for me and my portable Wet Ones.

And just try flying the Eastern shuttle with a baby *and* with a husband who is barely speaking to you. Mark deserted me the minute we got to the terminal at La Guardia and went off to buy magazines and newspapers and to call the office to make sure something important hadn't happened while he was off in New York on a trivial personal errand. I got on line for the plane. Sam was cranky and tired, and I was holding him and the duffel bag and the shopping bag full of Pampers and trying to write out my boarding pass with a pencil stub and my glasses fell off my nose and when I leaned over to pick them up, a stack pack of Ritz crackers fell out of my pocket onto the floor. The man next to me in line picked them up and asked me if he could help. I almost cried; I wanted to cry, but I was afraid crying would make my glasses fall off my nose again. He was a dark-skinned man with a rather thrilling foreign accent I couldn't place. Gratefully I handed him the shopping bag, and he carried the duffel bag to the baggage conveyor belt. When he came back, he smiled, and I noticed he had three subcutaneous cysts on his face—those little lumps that save Robert Redford from being too handsome. I wondered if he'd consider having his subcutaneous cysts removed if we got married. I wondered if I could live with someone with a foreign accent. I wondered where he was from, and how his family would feel about his marrying a Jew. I wondered if wherever he was from was the kind of place where they refer to Jewish women as Jewesses.

"Where are you from?" I said.

"From?" he said.

"What country are you from?" I said.

"My cauntry," he said with a smile, "ees bery beautiful."

I nodded. He nodded. I nodded. He nodded. So much for marrying foreigners, I thought. So much for my vow not to have marital fantasies about strangers.

I took an aisle seat on the plane, put Sam in the middle, and saved the window for Mark. He turned up a few minutes later and handed me the early edition of the *Daily News*. There was Vanessa, on page one, coming out of the police precinct; she looked wonderful. Inside was a riveting story about the glamorous group and the robbery. The story identified me as a "cookbook author," which always irritates me a little bit since they aren't merely cookbooks, but at least it didn't say that I was a distraught, rejected, pregnant cookbook author whose husband was in love with a giantess. According to the article, Sidney and Dan not only discovered each other's last names at the police precinct but also discovered that they were distant cousins. I wasn't sure what the readers of the *Daily News* were going to make of that detail, but I was positive my group would waste hours discussing its possible relevance. In fact, it seemed to me it might make sense to disband the group entirely, since we were bound to be spending so much time in the next year talking about the robbery and its effect that we would never again have time to discuss anyone's actual life. I wondered whether Mark had read the story, but I knew that if I asked him what he thought of it he would simply use it as yet another occasion to insult my adventures in psychoanalysis in order to punish me for insulting his. I looked over at him. He was immersed in *Casa Vogue*. It was as if he were pretending he wasn't with me, that I was just some hopeless woman who didn't even bother to space her pregnancies, much less respond properly to sitting in the same row with important Washington journalists who are trying to concentrate on home-decorating tips. And I'll tell you the capper. The stewardess came down the aisle to collect the fares. Now, Mark and I always split things up. I paid my way; I always paid my way. We both earned money, and the money we earned went to pay for what we did. But wouldn't you think that on this night of all nights he ought to have put my shuttle fare on his credit card? Well, he didn't.

I looked at him and was about to say something, when Meg Roberts poked her head over the back of the seat in front of us.

"I thought I was going to see you at Betty's the other night," she said.

"Fare, please," said the stewardess.

I fished in my bag for my credit card and handed it to her.

"At Betty's?" I said.

"At her birthday party," Meg said.

"Omigod," I said. I looked at Mark. He

shook his head; he had forgotten, too. I was off in New York crying my eyes out, and he was in Washington fucking his brains out, and we had both forgotten Betty's thirty-ninth birthday party. The only way Betty would ever forgive me would be for me to tell her why, and if I told her why she'd tell everyone in Washington, and then everyone in town would know something about our marriage that I didn't want them to know. I know all about Meg Roberts' marriage, for example, because Meg confides in her friend Ann, who confides in Betty, who confides in me. What I know is that Meg Roberts sleeps with presidential candidates, and her husband sleeps with presidential candidates' press secretaries' secretaries. They seem very happy.

"How was the party?" said Mark.

"Wonderful," said Meg, and popped back down.

Actually, there is no possible way a seated dinner party in Washington can ever be wonderful. After only half an hour of drinks, you are seated, seated forever, trapped between two immensely powerful men who think it's your function as their dinner partner to draw them out. You draw them out. You ask them about the Salt talks. You ask them about the firearms lobby. You ask them about their constituencies. You ask them about the next election. Dinner ends and everyone goes home. It always amazes me that women like Meg Roberts ever manage to get anything sexual going in Washington, although obviously she knows something about drawing men out that I don't.

Sam threw up on Mark's new blazer.

"Shit," said Mark.

"I'm sorry," I said. Sam started to cry. There was a kind of odd murmur in the seats around us, as the smell began to penetrate to the adjoining rows. At any moment the murmur would probably build to a hiss, and then to a chorus of boos, and ultimately Sam and I would be stoned to death with Bic pens.

"What am I apologizing for?" I said. "It's not my fault."

"I know it's not," said Mark. "I'm sorry."

"It's not your fault either," I said.

"This whole thing is my fault," he said.

"If you really believed that, you would have paid my shuttle fare," I said.

I picked up Sam and stood up to go to the bathroom with him. Mark began to wipe off his blazer with his handkerchief.

"You bought that blazer with Thelma Rice, didn't you?" I said, and started for the back. I didn't even have to hear the answer. Mark's impulse to fall in love is always accompanied by his impulse to purchase clothes with the loved one looking on. Sometimes it seemed to me that I had spent half my marriage in the men's department watching small white-haired tailors on their knees making chalk marks on Mark's trouser cuffs.

I went back to the bathroom and laid Sam

on the top of the toilet seat to change his clothes. Toilet seats in airplane bathrooms are not even big enough to change baby piglets on. Sam's head kept flopping off the cliff sides of the toilet seat as I changed his overalls and T-shirt and diaper. When I finished, I checked out the mirror to see if I looked older, or sadder, or wiser. I didn't; I just looked tired. Well, I was going home. I was going home with my husband. I loved my husband. The city of New York was a wonderful place, but it seemed terribly unimportant next to my marriage. So much for sorrel soup. I had never thought my marriage could survive an infidelity, but it would. It had been unrealistic of me to expect that the situation would never come up. They say all marriages go through something like this. I became dizzy as the clichés raced through my head. I put Sam on the bathroom floor and threw up. In the main cabin, the pilot was announcing our descent to the Washington area. Yes indeed, I thought. I wiped myself off and went back to my seat.

VIII

I see that I haven't managed to work in any recipes for a while. It's hard to work in recipes when you're moving the plot forward. Not that this book has an enormous amount of plot, but it has more plot than I've ever dealt with before. My other books just meandered from one person to the next, whereas this one has a story with a beginning and an end. That's one of the things that makes it different from most of what has happened to me in my life: I know when it began and when it ended. When my first marriage collapsed, I made a lot of notes about the hamsters and the fight over the coffee table, but I could never be sure whether the end of my marriage to Charlie was the beginning of a story or the end of one. But the story I'm telling here began the day I discovered the affair between Mark and Thelma, and it ended exactly six weeks later. It has a happy ending, but that's because I insist on happy endings; I would insist on happy beginnings, too, but that's not necessary because all beginnings are intrinsically happy, in my opinion. What about middles, you may ask. Middles are a problem. Middles are perhaps the major problem of contemporary life.

In any case, all I meant to say was that because this book tells a story, there aren't as many recipes in it as there are in my other books, so if you bought it because you thought there were going to be lots of recipes in every chapter, I'm sorry.

On the other hand, I've gotten to the point in the story where I return to Washington, and that brings me to the Siegels, finally to the Siegels; and therefore it brings me to the linguine alla cecca recipe. The four of us went to Italy a few years ago, and Julie Siegel and I managed to wangle the recipe from the proprietor of a restaurant in Rome. We also spent quite a lot of time after that trip working in pesto, because we went to Italy in 1977, and in 1977 everyone was eating pesto. As Arthur Siegel said one day: "Pesto is the quiche of the seventies." Arthur had a way of saying things like that—of summing up the situation so perfectly that you never wanted another spoonful of pesto again—and whenever he said something like that, Mark always ran off with it and turned it into a column. Arthur used to complain bitterly about having his best remarks stolen, but the truth is he rather liked it; he was a running character in Mark's columns, and he enjoyed a certain notoriety at Georgetown Law School, where he taught criminal law while waiting for the Kennedys to return to power. As for the linguine alla cecca, it's a hot pasta with a cold tomato and basil sauce, and it's so light and delicate that it's almost like eating a salad. It has to be made in the summer, when tomatoes are fresh. Drop 5 large tomatoes into boiling water for one full minute. Peel and seed and chop. Put into a large bowl with ½ cup olive oil, a garlic clove sliced in two, 1 cup chopped fresh basil leaves, salt and hot red pepper flakes. Let sit for a couple of hours, then remove the garlic. Boil one pound of linguine, drain and toss with the cold tomato mixture. Serve immediately.

Arthur and Julie and Mark and Rachel. The Siegels and the Feldmans. It's not just that we were best friends—we dated each other. We went steady. That's one of the things that happens when you become a couple: you date other couples. We saw each other every Saturday night and every Sunday night, and we had a standing engagement for New Year's Eve. Our marriages were tied together. We went to Italy, we went to Ireland, we went to Williamsburg, we went to Montreal, we went to St. Martin, and Mark drove and I navigated and Julie suggested wrong turns and Arthur fell asleep. Then, when we got to wherever we were going, Mark wanted to eat and I wanted to see the market and Julie wanted to go to the museum and Arthur wanted to take a crap. We had flat tires together and we ran out of gas together; in some fundamental sense, we were always on the road, merrily on our way to nowhere in particular. Two of us liked dark meat and two of us liked light meat and together we made a chicken.

I suppose that I honestly believed that if I couldn't save our marriage, the Siegels could. Which is why I called them from New York the night I discovered Mark's affair. They were shocked. They were astonished. There was consternation in every syllable they uttered. All of this was a relief to me—suppose they'd known! Suppose they'd known and hadn't told me! Suppose they'd known and told me!

"With Thelma Rice?" Julie said on the phone. "Omigod."

"Julie, what am I going to do?" I said.

"Pick up the phone, Arthur," said Julie. "It's Rachel."

"Hello," said Arthur.

"I'm sorry to call so late," I said.

"That's okay," said Arthur. "Obviously you've finally figured out who Thelma Rice is having the affair with and you're calling to tell us, and I appreciate it even if it is one in the morning."

"It's Mark," I said.

"Did something happen to Mark?" said Arthur. "Jesus Christ, Rachel. What is it?"

"Arthur," said Julie, "Thelma Rice is having the affair with Mark."

"He says he's in love with her," I said.

"He told you this?" said Arthur.

"Yes," I said.

"Why did he tell you this?" said Arthur.

"I found a book she'd given him with an inscription in it, and when I confronted him, he said he was in love with her."

"He said he was in love with her or he said he was fucking her?" said Arthur.

"He said he was in love with her but he said he wasn't fucking her," I said.

"Where are you?" said Julie.

"In New York," I said. "At my father's."

"Where's Sam?" said Julie.

"With me," I said.

"Does he know what's happening?" said Arthur.

"I don't think so," I said. "I've been crying for eight hours now, and he hasn't even noticed."

"I know," said Julie. "When Alexandra was two I cried for eight *months* and she never noticed."

"Does Mark know you're there?" said Arthur.

"I don't know," I said.

"That fuckhead," said Arthur. "He's gone crazy."

"That's what I said to him," I said. "But he denied it."

"Of course he denied it," said Arthur. "That's the truest sign of insanity—insane people are always sure they're just fine. It's only the sane people who are willing to admit they're crazy."

"Did you know about this, Arthur?" said Julie.

"Of course I didn't know about it," said Arthur. "How could you think I would know about it and not tell you?"

"I told him he had to stop seeing her," I said.

"And what did he say?" said Arthur.

"He said he wouldn't. And he said I should stay with him anyway and have the baby. He said, 'I am in love with Thelma Rice. I still have feelings about you, of course, and we are going to have another baby, so I suggest we just get from day to day.'"

"Oh, shit," said Julie.

"Listen, Rachel, sit tight," said Arthur. "I'm going to talk to him."

Arthur and Julie will go over there and beat some sense into Mark, I thought when I hung up the phone. Arthur and Julie will glare at him until he withers under the moral opprobrium of their gaze. Arthur and Julie will take the power of our friendship and club him into submission. This was not exactly the romantic scenario I had had in mind—I would have preferred Mark to have a more voluntary kind

of blinding vision—but it would have to do.
After all, Mark might be willing to give me
up, and my vinaigrette, but he would never
give up the four of us. And Thelma would
never fit in. For one thing, she was too tall.
Arthur and Julie and Mark and I were all
approximately the same size, which is one
reason we traveled so well together. It's hard
to walk in lockstep with people a lot taller
than you are, because they take longer strides,
and you always feel like a little puppy scamp-
ering to keep up. For another thing, Thelma
Rice really didn't care about food—that was
clear from her gluey puddings—while the four
of us had a friendship that was a shrine to
food. We had driven miles to find the world's
creamiest cheesecake and the world's largest
pistachio nut and the world's sweetest corn on
the cob. We had spent hours in blind taste
testings of kosher hot dogs and double chocolate chip ice cream. When Julie went home to
Fort Worth, she flew back with spare ribs from
Angelo's Beef Bar-B-Q, and when I went to
New York, I flew back with smoked butterfish
from Russ and Daughters. Once, in New Or-
leans, we all went to Mosca's for dinner, and
we ate marinated crab, baked oysters, barbecued shrimp, spaghetti bordelaise, chicken
with garlic, sausage with potatoes, and on the
way back to town, a dozen oysters each at the
Acme and beignets and coffee with chicory on
the wharf. Then Arthur said, "Let's go to

Chez Helene for the bread pudding," and we did, and we each had two. The owner of Chez Helene gave us the recipe when we left, and I'm going to throw it in because it's the best bread pudding I've ever eaten. It tastes like caramelized mush. Cream 2 cups sugar with 2 sticks butter. Add six beaten eggs, then add 2½ cups milk, one 13–ounce can evaporated milk, 2 tablespoons nutmeg, 2 tablespoons vanilla, a loaf of wet bread in chunks and pieces (any bread will do, the worse the better) and 1 cup raisins. Stir to mix. Pour into a deep greased casserole and bake at 350° for 2 hours, stirring after the first hour. Serve warm with hard sauce.

For the most part, Arthur Siegel is remarkably content. Once when we played Do You Have Any Regrets, the only thing he could come up with was that we hadn't ordered some fried onion rings at Chez Helene along with the bread pudding. When we played What Do You Wish You Were Named, I wanted to be named Veronica because it's luscious and I'm not, Julie wanted to be named Anthea because it's thin and she's not, Mark wanted to be named Sasha because it's dashing and he's not, and Arthur thought it over and said it seemed to him his name suited him just fine. It does. Arthur is chunky but solid, as an Arthur should be, and he has a red handlebar mustache that almost compensates for the fact that he is almost completely bald. I'll tell you how sensible Arthur is: he doesn't even mind being bald.

Arthur and Mark had grown up together in Brooklyn. They went to Columbia, and then Mark went to journalism school there and Arthur went off to law school at Yale. They both ended up in Washington. Julie was a legislative assistant on Capitol Hill when Arthur met her. She has curly blond hair and goo-goo-googly eyes and big pearly teeth like the girl in the Coca-Cola ad, and every so often Arthur stares across the room at her as if he cannot believe she's his. All of this is mystifying to Julie, who believes she's just a fairly average plump girl from Texas who snagged a nice Jewish husband solely due to what she calls shiksa madness.

The Siegels got married and moved into a two-bedroom apartment on Connecticut Avenue, and Mark would bring his girl friends to breakfast on Sundays. The first Jewish Kimberly passed through their lives. Then more girl friends. Then Mark turned up with me, and suddenly there we were, the four of us. Together. We would sit around, doing nothing, nothing at all, lazy Sundays with clouds in the coffee and papers all over the living room and dusty Sunday light coming through the color-coordinated Levolor blinds. Arthur would say that the trouble with Washington was that there wasn't a decent delicatessen. Julie would say that the trouble with Washington was that there weren't any late movies on television. I would say that the trouble with Washington was that it was so goyish. Mark would say that the trouble with Washington was that too many people there spent too much time figuring out what the trouble with it was. We would all say these things as if we had never said them before, and argue over them as if we had never argued over them before. Then we would all decide whether we wanted to be buried or cremated. Then we would move on to the important matters. Should they paint their living room peach? Should they strip down their dining table? Should they buy a videotape recorder? Should they re-cover the couch?

"I don't see what was wrong with it before," said Arthur after they re-covered the couch.

"Nothing was wrong with it before," said Julie.

"What color is this anyway?" said Arthur.

"Taupe," said Julie.

Arthur shook his head. "I've always been terrible at colors," he said. "It comes from having grown up with the single-row box of crayons instead of the big box. If I'd had the big box I would now know taupe and cerise and ecru. Instead, all I know is burnt sienna. And what good does it do me? Never once have I heard anything described as burnt sienna. Never once have I heard anyone say, 'Follow that burnt sienna car.'"

"I think there's a column in this," said Mark.

"Goddammit, Feldman," said Arthur.

"You can have it if you want it," said Mark.

"What do you mean, I can have it if I want it?" said Arthur. "It's *mine*. I'm the one who gets to say, 'You can have it if you want it.' Not you."

"What are you going to do with it?" said Mark. "Write it up for the *Yale Law Review?*"

"He doesn't have to do *anything* with it," I said. "He can simply add it to his repertoire."

"Thanks, Rachel," said Arthur. He looked at Mark. "Don't break up with her, okay?" he said. "Promise me you won't."

"Jesus Christ," said Mark. "You'd think *you* were going with her."

"We are," said Arthur. "The two of us are going with the two of you."

"You used to like me when I was unattached," said Mark.

"Not as much as I like you as a couple," said Arthur, and he gave Mark a playful punch on the arm.

"You're punching me because you want me to think you're kidding, but you're not," said Mark.

"You'll never know, will you?" said Arthur. "The truth is, I wish you two would get married."

"Arthur, for God's sake," said Julie.

"I can't help it," said Arthur. "I like being married. I want everyone I care about to be married. That's the kind of guy I am. Warm. Generous. Expansive. Charming."

"You just want everyone to be in the same pot you're in," said Mark.

"I like the pot I'm in," said Arthur. "I like how it goes along. What's for dinner and which movie should we see and where are my socks."

"Where are your socks?" said Mark. "Where are my socks? Where are all the missing socks?"

"They're in heaven," said Arthur. "You die, you go to heaven, and they bring you a big box, and it's got all your lost socks in it, and your mufflers and your gloves, and you get to spend eternity sorting them all out."

"I think there's a column in this," said Mark.

"Goddammit, Feldman," said Arthur.

Mark and I got married. You should have seen Arthur at the wedding. He stood with his head cocked at a jaunty angle, winking wildly and uncontrollably at the judge. He had done it. He had talked Mark into it. By the simple example of his own contentment, he had persuaded his best friend to give up bachelorhood. At the end of the ceremony, he whipped a glass from his pocket and placed it on the ground, and when Mark smashed it into the judge's Oriental rug, Arthur whooped around the room and danced the kazatsky. Three months later, I was walking up Connecticut Avenue, through the park at Dupont Circle, and there were Arthur and an unidentified female in a mad clinch on the park bench.

"I saw Arthur this afternoon," I said when I got home. "Kissing a . . ." I gestured absently with my hand and shook my head.

"Woman," said Mark.

"How long have you known about it?" I said.

"I don't know anything about it," said Mark. "I was just finishing the sentence. With Arthur, he's kissing a woman or a bagel. I took a guess." He looked at me. "Who was she?"

"I don't know."

"What did she look like?"

"Thin. Pretty. Big tits. Your basic nightmare."

We looked at each other.

"Should we do anything?" I said.

"He's my friend," said Mark. "We don't meddle in each other's lives."

"Of course we do," I said, "we meddle constantly. That's what true friendship is about."

"What did you have in mind?" said Mark.

"I don't know," I said.

"Maybe it's just a fling," said Mark. "He's almost forty, he probably feels nothing's happening to him—"

"It's just a passage," I said angrily.

"Yeah," said Mark.

"Shit," I said.

"Look, I hated the book as much as you did," said Mark.

"I know," I said. "I just feel betrayed. Never

mind Julie—he's cheating on us, you know what I mean?"

"I know what you mean," said Mark.

"One of the things I love about you is that you know what I mean even when I don't," I said.

"Actually, I don't," said Mark. "I just say I do."

"Maybe it's not serious," I said.

"Maybe it's just a fuck," said Mark.

"Yeah," I said.

"And I'm a ballerina," said Mark.

Two nights later, Arthur rang the bell in the middle of the night and announced that he was in love.

"A stewardess?" said Mark.

"A flight attendant," said Arthur.

"You must really be in love," said Mark.

"I am," said Arthur.

"Is this a midlife crisis or something?" said Mark.

"Don't reduce my life to some dime-store philosophy so it's easier for you to handle," said Arthur. "For twenty years I've watched you fuck around and fuck up and cheat on this one and cheat on that one. Did I ever judge you? Did I ever purse my lips? Did I ever say tch tch tch? Did you ever hear those words from me?"

"Tch tch tch?" said Mark. "Those words? I never heard those words because your tongue was so busy hanging out of your mouth you couldn't get them out. Listen to me. You're married. You've been married eight years. You've got a kid. Don't throw it away for a fuck."

"I suppose you're going to tell me things are going to be the same in bed with you and Rachel after eight years," said Arthur.

"No," said Mark, "but it'll still be good."

"It just won't be as often," said Arthur. "Instead of a couple of times a week it'll be a couple of times a year."

"I'll be almost fifty in ten years," said Mark.

"You know how old you have to be before you stop wanting to fuck strangers?" said Arthur. "Dead, that's how old. It doesn't stop. It doesn't go away. You put all this energy into suppressing it and telling yourself it's worth it because of what you get in exchange, and then one day someone brushes up against you and you're fourteen years old again and all you want to do is go to a drive-in movie and fuck her brains out in the back seat. But you don't do it because you're not going to be that kind of person, so you go home, and there's your wife, and she wears socks to bed."

"Socks again," said Mark.

On and on they went. It was late. Two in the morning. Three in the morning. We sat around the kitchen table in the yellow glow of the high-crime lights on the street, and I listened to Mark. Marriage was a trust, he said. Betray that trust and you have nothing, he said. I felt so smug. My husband the convert. My husband the true believer. My husband the husband. See a marriage counselor, he said. Do something.

And they did. The Siegels went to see a very nice marriage counselor named Gwendolyn. Gwendolyn left her husband three months later, but the Siegels survived. The four of us resumed normal activities. We went to Ohio for the shoofly pie and we went to Virginia for the ham. We were able to discuss other friends' marital difficulties without Julie's looking hurt and Arthur's looking guilty. Last summer they came to visit us in West Virginia, and Julie and I spent a week perfecting the peach pie. We made ordinary peach pie, and deep-dish peach pie, and blueberry and peach pie, but here is the best peach pie we made: Put 1¼ cups flour, ½ teaspoon salt, ½ cup butter and 2 tablespoons sour cream into a Cuisinart and blend until they form a ball. Pat out into a buttered pie tin, and bake 10 minutes at 425°. Beat 3 egg yolks slightly and combine with 1 cup sugar, 2 tablespoons flour and ⅓ cup sour cream. Pour over 3 peeled, sliced peaches arranged in the crust. Cover with foil. Reduce the oven to 350° and bake 35 minutes. Remove the foil and bake 10 minutes more, or until the filling is set.

I keep thinking about that week in West Virginia. It was a perfect week. We swam in the river and barbecued ribs and made Bellinis with crushed peaches and cheap champagne. We lay out on the lawn, the sunlight dappling through the copper beech, and Alexandra got her kite into the air and Sam applauded madly and scampered behind her, screaming with joy. Is it hot enough for you, we said, and the water isn't cold once you get in. We methodically rubbed sun block onto the arms of our children and poured another pitcherful into our glasses. So we were grownups. So what? Arthur lifted his glass. "I love you," he said. "I love us." The phone rang. Mark ran to get it and then called me into the house. We stood with the phone between us and listened to the lady in the hospital say that she had the results of the amniocentesis. The baby was normal. It was a boy. We ran back to the Siegels and drank to the baby. "You're going to have a brother," we told Sam. He started to cry. "Nathaniel," I said. "Can you say Nathaniel?" "No," said Sam. "Tummy hurts." Mark took him then, and walked him down to the river. They found a frog. Sam held it cupped in his hands, and giggled. I remember thinking: Lucky me, lucky us, lucky Sam, lucky Nathaniel. *What's wrong with this picture?*

IX

Arthur and Julie lived just a few blocks from our house. The morning after Mark and I got back to Washington, I slid out of bed and went over to see them. Arthur opened the door and gave me the kind of look you give someone who's just had a death in the family and hugged me in a long, speechless, what-can-I-say sort of way.

"How are you?" he said.

"I'm back," I said. "How am I?"

"You're back," he said.

"Mark came to New York yesterday," I said. "He said he would stop seeing Thelma, so I came back."

Arthur nodded.

"What do you think?" I said.

"I don't know," said Arthur.

Julie came out from the bedroom. She put her arms around me and patted me quite a lot, and I cried on the shoulder of her terry-cloth bathrobe.

"Did you see him?" I said.

They nodded.

"I even saw her for a few minutes," said Arthur.

"Look," I said, "I'm putting you in an awkward position here."

"No, no," said Julie.

"What did he say?" I said.

"It doesn't matter," said Arthur.

"Why doesn't it matter?" I said.

"Because he's crazy," said Arthur.

We went into the kitchen and sat down with some of Arthur's fetishistically brewed coffee. Arthur makes coffee by putting eggshells and cinnamon sticks and an old nylon stocking into the coffeepot. His coffee tastes like a very spicy old foot.

"The week you came to West Virginia two months ago," I said.

"What about it?" said Arthur.

"Did we have a good time that week?"

"Terrific," said Julie.

"Did Mark and I seem happy?"

"Yes," said Julie.

"I was wondering about it," I said, "because Mark told me that our marriage had been terrible for a long time, and now I can't remember whether or not it was."

"He told us that, too," said Arthur.

"What else did he tell you?" I said.

"He said you were mean to him," said Arthur.

"I probably am," I said.

"Don't be ridiculous," said Julie.

"I am," I said. "All summer long I was snapping at him because he was never there."

"Of course you were snapping at him," said Julie. "He was having an affair."

"But I didn't know," I said.

"You must have known," said Arthur. "I knew."

"I thought you said you didn't know," said Julie.

"I didn't know about Thelma," said Arthur, "and I didn't know for sure, but I thought he was up to something. All those trips to the dentist."

"What was the matter with me?" I said. "If you could see it, why couldn't I?"

"Stop beating up on yourself," said Julie. "You trusted him. You have to trust someone you're married to, otherwise you'd spend your entire life going through the phone bills and American Express receipts."

"It's going to be all right," said Arthur.

"You're only saying that because you have to leave to teach a class and it's a good exit line," I said.

"I'm saying it because I have to leave and teach a class," said Arthur, "but it's true. He'll come to his senses. Jesus Christ, Rachel. Sam's still a baby and you're pregnant."

Arthur kissed us both goodbye and went out the door. Julie waited until she was sure he'd taken the elevator.

"I didn't know Mark was having an affair," said Julie. "I want you to know that. I don't know what I would have done if I'd known, but I didn't know."

"I know," I said. "What should I do, Julie?"

"Go home. Go on working. Take care of Sam. Have the baby. Wait the thing out. Eventually he'll get tired of her. Eventually she'll turn into as big a nag as he thinks you are. Eventually he'll get just as bored in bed with her as he is with you. And when that happens, he'll decide that it's less trouble to stay with you."

"But Mark isn't going to see Thelma anymore," I said. "So how is he going to get tired of her?"

"He will," said Julie.

"He will what?" I said.

"He'll see her again, and he'll get tired of her."

"And I'm supposed to sit there like a lox in the meantime?"

"Yes," said Julie. "If you want to stay married."

"That's a terrible thing to say," I said.

"I know," said Julie, "but it works. I did it. Sometimes I don't know why I did it, because it's so horrible and painful and humiliating, waiting the damned thing out. Sometimes I think I'd have been better off if I'd just left."

"Aren't you glad you're still with Arthur?"

"Oh, sure," said Julie.

"Then what is it?"

"I don't know," said Julie. "Sometimes the idea of being single interests me. For example, I woke up this morning and realized I'm never going to have bondage. It's just never going to come up with me and Arthur. I don't want to have it particularly, but it's never going to come up."

"I've never done it either," I said, "though I guess if I wanted to I could always ask."

"Arthur would just laugh at me," said Julie.

"Although I'm not sure what Mark would tie me to," I said, "since we don't have a headboard. You pretty much need a headboard, don't you think?"

"I don't know," said Julie. "That's the whole point."

"I guess you could always check into a hotel," I said. "Hotel beds have headboards."

"You could call room service for the rope," said Julie.

"It's really bad, isn't it?" I said.

"It's always bad when it happens," said Julie. "And then it gets better. You'll see. In a while, you'll be able to spend entire fifteen-minute periods without thinking about what they did together."

"And in the meantime," I said, "I can think about all the things in my future if it doesn't work out."

"What besides bondage?" said Julie.

"Amyl nitrates," I said. "Threesomes. Japanese movies. Roller disco. Thai food."

"I thought you hated Thai food," said Julie.

"I do," I said, "and if my marriage breaks up, I'll never have to have it again. It may be worth it."

Julie looked at me. "I think something happens to them," she said.

"You mean men," I said.

"I'm not saying they're worse," said Julie. "I'm saying they're different."

"You are too saying they're worse," I said.

"I know," said Julie.

"So what do we do?" I said.

"We hang on," she said, "and if it doesn't work, we try again with the next one."

When I got home, Mark was out in his office writing a jolly column about the Eastern shuttle. I walked into the kitchen and found Sam with Juanita, the maid. She was teaching him to say "Lie down with dogs, get up with fleas" in Spanish, which in some ways is the motto for Juanita's life. Juanita had lain down for twelve years with her husband, Hernando, and when he finally crawled out of her life, taking her Sears, Roebuck charge card with him, he left behind a rash of bad debts and old girl friends and faulty automobile parts that seemed destined to dominate Juanita's life forever. At least once a week she would turn up late for work, and explain through sobs that the Sears credit department was about to seize a stereo component she knew nothing about, or that her husband had stolen the spare tire from her car trunk, or that someone named Theresa had turned up at the front door asking for Hernando's stopwatch. "I tol' her he takes two minutes, drunk or sober," said Juanita. "What she need to time it for?" Juanita was a very brave woman, really—she was single-handedly supporting her three children—and I always tried very hard to love her, but she made it difficult because she was so disaster-prone. One morning, for example, on her way to work, she was stuck in a traffic jam on the Beltway, and when she got out of her car to see what was holding things up, in that split second, someone crept in through the passenger door of her car and stole her purse. Another time, she was standing in line in the Georgetown Safeway when a woman in front of her collapsed, and after Juanita revived her with mouth-to-mouth resuscitation, the woman tried to have her arrested for making improper advances.

Juanita looked up from Sam when I came in and burst into tears.

"Juanita," I said, "I'm not up for this. Whatever it is, I'm not up for it."

"Oh, Missee Felman, I feel so bad for ju," said Juanita. Even Juanita knew about it! The day after I'd left for New York she'd turned up to discover Mark and Thelma having a heart-to-heart talk on the living room couch.

"I know that lady," said Juanita. "She no good."

"I know," I said.

"*I* know," said Juanita. "I work for her ten years ago."

"What's wrong with her?" I said.

"She very messy," said Juanita.

Juanita gave me a big hug, which was awkward since she was only about four feet six inches tall, and a hug from her felt like the Heimlich maneuver. Then she pulled back and managed a huge smile that was meant to cheer me up—but instead revealed her mouthful of gold teeth, which only served to remind me of the time I had spent two days on the telephone with her dentist, negotiating a long-term payment for Hernando's root canal work.

"Everything be okay," she said. "You see."

I went up to the little room on the third floor that I used for an office. In the typewriter was an article I'd been writing about potatoes. I took it out of the typewriter and put in a fresh sheet of paper. I must write all this down, I thought. Someday I may write something that's not a cookbook, and this will all be grist for it. But I couldn't. To write it down was to give it permanence, to admit that something real had happened. I walked around the room trying to pretend that nothing had happened. I thought about potatoes. The first time I made dinner for Mark I made potatoes. The first time I made dinner for just about anyone I ever cared for I made potatoes. Very very crisp potatoes. I must make some potatoes tonight, I thought; mashed potatoes. Nothing like mashed potatoes when you're feeling blue. I could hear Mark's typewriter from the office over the garage; I kept hoping he would leave, go out for more socks, so I could dash into his sanctuary and go through the phone bills and the American Express receipts, but he was still there, tapping away. Maybe *he's* making notes for a novel, I thought. Worse, maybe he's making notes for a *column*. That would really do it. There would be my entire marital disaster, reduced to an 850-word column in 109 newspapers. I knew just how he'd write it, too. He'd write it in that dumb Hemingway style he always reserved for his slice-of-life columns. *The old man had told him it would happen. The old man had said to him, Sasha, it will happen someday. You will be on the river. You will be going downstream. You will hit a log.*

The phone rang.

I picked it up.

"Rachel, it's Betty."

"Oh, God," I said. "I'm so sorry."

"I know, I know," said Betty.

"You know?" I said.

"It must have been awful," said Betty.

"How do you know?" I said.

"It's in the paper," said Betty.

"In the paper?" I said.

"Why didn't you tell me that Vanessa Melhado was in your group?" said Betty.

"The robbery's in the paper?" I said.

"In the Style section," said Betty.

"We're not allowed to tell anyone who's in the group," I said.

"What's she like?"

"We're not allowed to tell that either," I said. "Listen, I feel terrible about missing your party."

"I understand," said Betty. "I knew something awful must have happened to you if you weren't there, and now I see that it did."

"Yes," I said. "It was awful."

"Anyway, it doesn't matter," said Betty, "because I found out who Thelma Rice is having the affair with."

"Who?" I said.

"You're not going to like it," said Betty.

"Who is it?" I said.

"Arthur," said Betty.

"Arthur Siegel?" I said.

"Yes," said Betty. "They were having drinks in the Washington Hilton yesterday afternoon. Nobody has drinks in the Washington Hilton unless something secret's going on."

"Arthur isn't having an affair with Thelma Rice," I said. "Nobody is having an affair with Thelma Rice."

"How do you know?" said Betty.

"I just know," I said.

"Tell me," said Betty.

"Okay," I said, "but you can't tell this to anyone."

"I promise," said Betty.

"I saw Thelma at the gynecologist's, and that's when I found out."

"What?" said Betty.

"She has this horrible infection," I said. "You don't even want to know about it."

"Oh, God," said Betty.

"She made me promise not to tell anyone," I said, "but she almost didn't have to because it's so disgusting I almost couldn't. I'm only telling you because I want you to know it's not true about her and Arthur."

"Then why was she having a drink with him?" said Betty.

"That's part of it," I said.

"What are you talking about?" said Betty.

"She wanted some legal advice," I said. "She got the infection in a Vietnamese restaurant in Virginia, and she wants to sue them."

"She got it from something she ate, or from the toilet seat?" said Betty.

"The toilet seat, I guess," I said, "although I'm not sure. Maybe from the spring rolls."

"Oh, God," said Betty. "Poor Thelma."

"Poor Thelma?" I said.

"I feel so sorry for her," said Betty.

"Don't feel too sorry for her," I said. "It's curable. Eventually."

"Maybe I should have her and Jonathan to dinner," said Betty.

"Don't," I said.

"Why not?" said Betty. "It's not catching, is it?"

"No," I said, "it's just that she's so depressed, she's no fun to be around."

"I think we should have a dance," said Betty.

"What?" I said.

"The three of us. You, me and Thelma."

"I hate dances," I said.

"It'll be fun, Rachel," said Betty.

"I can't dance," I said.

"Come on," said Betty. "Where do you think we should do it?"

"The White House," I said.

"That's a great idea," said Betty. "They're always talking about opening it up to the public. I'll call the social secretary."

"Betty—"

"And let's have lunch, the three of us, next week. Tuesday."

"Tuesday I have to be in New York to do a cooking demonstration."

"Rachel, you really are impossible," said Betty. "Thelma and I will have lunch on Tuesday. We will plan the dance. It will make Thelma feel better about her infection, and you'll have something to take your mind off the robbery—"

"My mind isn't *on* the robbery," I said.

"Good," said Betty. "Start making your guest list."

"Thelma's going to want to invite the

Kissingers," I said. "Is that the kind of dance you want to have?"

"Goodbye," said Betty, and hung up.

POTATOES AND LOVE: SOME REFLECTIONS

The beginning

I have friends who begin with pasta, and friends who begin with rice, but whenever I fall in love, I begin with potatoes. Sometimes meat and potatoes and sometimes fish and potatoes, but always potatoes. I have made a lot of mistakes falling in love, and regretted most of them, but never the potatoes that went with them.

Not just any potato will do when it comes to love. There are people who go on about the virtues of plain potatoes—plain boiled new potatoes with a little parsley or dill, or plain baked potatoes with crackling skins—but my own feeling is that a taste for plain potatoes coincides with cultural antecedents I do not possess, and that in any case, the time for plain potatoes—if there is ever a time for plain potatoes—is never at the beginning of something. It is also, I should add, never at the end of something. Perhaps you can get away with plain potatoes in the middle, although I have never been able to.

All right, then: I am talking about crisp potatoes. Crisp potatoes require an immense amount of labor. It's not just the peeling, which is one of the few kitchen chores no electric device has been invented to alleviate; it's also that the potatoes, once peeled, must be cut into whatever shape you intend them to be, put into water to be systematically prevented from turning a loathsome shade of bluish-brownish-black, and then meticulously dried to ensure that they crisp properly. All this takes time, and time, as any fool can tell you, is what true romance is about. In fact, one of the main reasons why you must make crisp potatoes in the beginning is that if you don't make them in the beginning, you never will. I'm sorry to be so cynical about this, but that's the truth.

There are two kinds of crisp potatoes that I prefer above all others. The first are called Swiss potatoes, and they're essentially a large potato pancake of perfect hash browns; the flipping of the pancake is so wildly dramatic that the potatoes themselves are almost beside the point. The second are called potatoes Anna; they are thin circles of potato cooked in a shallow pan in the oven and then turned onto a plate in a darling mound of crunchy brownness. Potatoes Anna is a classic French recipe, but there is something so homely and old-fashioned about them that they can usually be passed off as either an ancient family recipe or something you just made up.

For Swiss potatoes: Peel 3 large (or 4 small) russet potatoes (or all-purpose if you can't get russets) and put them in cold water to cover. Start 4 tablespoons butter and 1 tablespoon cooking oil melting in a nice heavy large frying pan. Working quickly, dry the potatoes and grate them on the grating disk of the Cuisinart. Put them into a colander and squeeze out as much water as you can. Then dry them again on paper towels. You will need more paper towels to do this than you ever thought possible. Dump the potatoes into the frying pan, patting them down with a spatula, and cook over medium heat for about 15 minutes, until the bottom of the pancake is brown. Then, while someone is watching, loosen the pancake and, with one incredibly deft motion, flip it over. Salt it generously. Cook 5 minutes more. Serves two.

For potatoes Anna: Peel 3 large (or 4 small) russet potatoes (or Idahos if you can't get russets) and put them in water. Working quickly, dry each potato and slice into ⅟₁₆-inch rounds. Dry them with paper towels, round by round. Put 1 tablespoon clarified butter into a cast-iron skillet and line the skillet with overlapping potatoes. Dribble clarified butter and salt and pepper over them. Repeat twice. Put into a 425° oven for 45 minutes, pressing the potatoes down now and then. Then turn up the oven to 500° and cook 10 more minutes. Flip onto a round platter. Serves two.

The middle (I)

One day the inevitable happens. I go to the potato drawer to make potatoes and discover that the little brown buggers I bought in a large sack a few weeks earlier have gotten soft and mushy and are sprouting long and quite uninteresting vines. In addition, one of them seems to have developed an odd brown leak, and the odd brown leak appears to be the cause of a terrible odor that in only a few seconds has permeated the entire kitchen. I throw out the potatoes and look in the cupboard for a box of pasta. This is the moment when the beginning ends and the middle begins.

The middle (II)

Sometimes, when a loved one announces that he has decided to go on a low-carbohydrate, low-fat, low-salt diet (thus ruling out the possibility of potatoes, should you have been so inclined), he is signaling that the middle is ending and the end is beginning.

The end

In the end, I always want potatoes. Mashed potatoes. Nothing like mashed potatoes when you're feeling blue. Nothing like getting into bed with a bowl of hot mashed potatoes already loaded with butter, and methodically adding a thin cold slice of butter to every forkful. The problem with mashed potatoes, though, is that they require almost as much hard work as crisp potatoes, and when you're feeling blue the last thing you feel like is hard work. Of course, you can always get someone to make the mashed potatoes for you, but let's face it: the reason you're blue is that there *isn't* anyone to make them for you. As a result, most people do not have nearly enough mashed potatoes in their lives, and when they do, it's almost always at the wrong time.

(You can, of course, train children to mash potatoes, but you should know that Richard Nixon spent most of his childhood making mashed potatoes for his mother and was extremely methodical about getting the lumps out. A few lumps make mashed potatoes more authentic, if you ask me, but that's not the point. The point is that perhaps children should not be trained to mash potatoes.)

For mashed potatoes: Put 1 large (or 2 small) potatoes in a large pot of salted water and bring to a boil. Lower the heat and simmer for at least 20 minutes, until tender. Drain and place the potatoes back in the pot and shake over low heat to eliminate excess moisture. Peel. Put through a potato ricer and immediately add 1 tablespoon heavy cream and as much melted butter and salt and pepper as you feel like. Eat immediately. Serves one.

X

I don't want to string this part out. You don't really need to hear a blow-by-blow account, because it isn't all that interesting. The first night back I made shrimp curry. (The recipe's in *Uncle Seymour's Beef Borscht* if you want it.) The next night chicken stuffed with lemons. (Marcella Hazan.) The next night, takeout from Scott's Bar-B-Q. Mark and I sat at dinner and made conversation. The word desultory applies. We talked about everything except what had happened. I tried not to cry. I tried hard not to ask where he went in the afternoon. I tried hard not to go into his office and turn it upside down looking for more evidence, but finally I decided what the hell, go take a look, how much worse can it get, and it turned out Mark had locked his office door and I couldn't get in. At one point over the weekend Mark asked me how I made my vinaigrette, but I wouldn't tell him. I figured my vinaigrette was the only thing I had that Thelma didn't (besides a pregnancy), and I could just see him learning it from me and then rushing over to her house with a jar of Grey Poupon mustard (the essential ingredient) and teaching her the wrist movement and dancing off into a sunset of arugola salads. I must seem to be putting too much emphasis on this vinaigrette of mine, but war is war.

Perhaps you are wondering whether we had sex. Normally I don't like to get into this area, because it embarrasses me, but since it's probably crossed your mind I'd better deal with it. We had sex. We always had sex. That's one of the most perplexing parts of the story; that's one of the reasons why Mark's relationship with Thelma had come as such a surprise to me. Now that I look back on it, we hadn't been doing anything particularly inventive in that department of late, but I have never been big on invention in that department. Why kid around? Every so often I browse through books full of tasteful line drawings of supplementary positions—how to do it standing and in the swimming pool and on the floor—and I'm always mystified. On the floor! Why would anyone want to do it on the floor when a bed was available? I'll tell you the truth: even sex on a beach seems to me to be going too far.

On Tuesday morning I took the shuttle to New York for my food demonstration in the Macy's housewares department. I do food demonstrations from time to time, although I do more talking than actual demonstrating. Occasionally, serious food people come to observe, and I can see them sneer as they watch my hopelessly sloppy chopping. Serious food people do not take me seriously, and they're right not to. I more or less backed into the food writing business, and before anyone in the food establishment could decide what to do with me, there I was, writing articles and doing demonstrations and appearing on television and essentially taking money from their pockets.

What they say about me is I have no real training as a cook, I'm basically a performer, I clip recipes from other people's cookbooks and pass them off as my own, I don't have an original point of view, and I am a sellout. (This last accusation always makes me cross, because I would love to be a sellout if only someone would ask.) They used to say that I was wrong about nouvelle cuisine, but I turned out to be right about it, so they don't say that anymore. My position on nouvelle cuisine is that it's silly.

What I say about them is they use too many adjectives. I hate adjectives. I also hate similes and metaphors, just can't do them, never have been able to. Anyone who wants to write about food would do well to stay away from similes and metaphors, because if you're not careful, expressions like "light as a feather" make their way into your sentences, and then where are you? The problem, though, is how to do without adjectives. If you write about food, you can't really do without them; but if you do *with* them, you run the risk of writing sentences like "The fish was juicy but the sauce was lumpy," or "The sauce was creamy but the veal was stringy," or, to sum up, "The noun was (complimentary adjective) but the other noun was (uncomplimentary adjective)." This is a particular danger for food writers who review restaurants, which I have never done and never will. You have to draw the line somewhere.

Obviously I didn't start out in life wanting to be a food writer. These days there are probably people who do—just as there are now people who start out wanting to be film critics, God help us—but I started out wanting to be a journalist. Which I became. I was a reporter for the *New York World-Telegram and Sun* and I lived in a junior two-and-a-half, and whenever I was home alone at night I cooked myself a perfect little dinner. None of your containers of yogurt for me; no, sir. I would pick a recipe from Michael Field or Julia Child and shop on the way home and spend the first part of the evening painstakingly mastering whatever dish I had chosen. Then I would sit down to eat it in front of the television set. At the time I thought this was wildly civilized behavior, but the truth is it was probably somewhat Mamie Eisenhowerish. In any case, I learned to cook. Everyone did— everyone my age, that is. This was the mid-1960s, the height of the first wave of competitive cooking. I'm always interested when people talk about the sixties in the kind of hushed tone that is meant to connote the seriousness of it all, because what I remember about the sixties was that people were constantly looking up from dessert and saying things like: "Whose mousse is this?" Once, I remember, one of my friends called up to say his marriage had ended on account of veal Orloff, and I knew exactly what he meant. It was quite mad, really. I was never completely idiotic—I never once made a quiche, for example—but I held my own, and I'm afraid that I'm still known in certain circles as the originator of a game called If You Had to Have Only One Flavor Soufflé for the Rest of Your Life, Would It Be Chocolate or Grand Marnier?

Anyway, there I was at the *World-Telegram* when the food editor retired. There was a pause before the next food editor arrived, and I was asked to fill in and write the "A Visit With" column. You know the kind of column it was: I would go to interview famous people in their homes, and they'd talk about their dinner parties and their decorators and their indispensable housekeepers, and then, in the end, they'd give me a recipe. The recipes weren't much—you'd be amazed at how many legendary hostesses tried to get away with newlywed garbage like chicken Divan and grapes with sour cream and brown sugar— but the interviews were really quite fascinating. People would say the oddest things about the servant problem and the extra-man-at-the-dinner-party problem and tipping at Christmas and how you could tell the economy was getting worse because of all the chicken you were starting to see at dinner parties. "Dark-meat chicken," one woman said to me contemptuously.

It was just a mild little column in a newspaper no one read, but as a result of it, I began to have a field of expertise. That's probably putting it too strongly—it wasn't as if I had become an expert in law or economics or seventeenth-century England—but that's how it felt: having spent my life knowing nothing much about anything (which is known as being a generalist), I suddenly knew something about something. I certainly knew enough to make jokes in the food-world language. I learned that the words "monosodium glutamate" were almost automatically funny, especially aloud, as were "The R. T. French's Mustard Tastemaker Award," "The Pillsbury Bake-Off" and "The National Chicken Cooking Contest." This gave me an edge as a food writer that almost made up for the fact that I think that certain serious food-world subjects, like coulibiac of salmon (another automatically funny phrase), are not worth bothering with.

(Another argument I have with serious food people is that they're always talking about how *creative* cooking is. "Cooking is very creative" is how they put it. Now, there's no question that there are a handful of people doing genuinely creative things with food— although a lot of it, if you ask me, seems to consist of heating up goat cheese or throwing strawberry vinegar onto calves' liver or relying excessively on the kiwi. But most cooking is based on elementary, long-standing principles, and to say that cooking is creative not only misses the point of creativity—which is that it is painful and difficult and quite unrelated to whether it is possible to come up with yet another way to cook a pork chop—but also misses the whole point of cooking, which is that it is totally mindless. What I love about cooking is that after a hard day, there is something comforting about the fact that if you melt butter and add flour and then hot stock, *it will get thick!* It's a sure thing! It's a sure thing in a world where nothing is sure; it has a mathematical certainty in a world where those of us who long for some kind of certainty are forced to settle for crossword puzzles.)

Normally I enjoy doing food demonstrations —I like giving my speech, I like the way it laces in and out of the subject of food. But when I was about halfway through the demonstration at Macy's—I was right in the middle of cooking Lillian Hellman's pot roast—I realized I was in trouble. Lillian Hellman's pot roast is the sort of recipe that makes my reputation in the food world what it is, since it contains all sorts of low-rent ingredients like a package of onion soup mix and a can of cream of mushroom soup. It even has something called Kitchen Bouquet in it, although I always leave it out. You take a nice 4-pound piece of beef, the more expensive the better, and put it into a good pot with 1 can of cream of mushroom soup, an envelope of dried onion soup, 1 large chopped onion, 3 cloves chopped garlic, 2 cups red wine and 2 cups water. Add a crushed bay leaf and 1 teaspoon each thyme and basil. Cover and bake in a 350° oven until tender, 3½ hours or so.

The reason the pot roast recipe gets to me is that it's an occasion for a point I like to make about couples in America. What I say is that I think Lillian Hellman had a remarkable effect as a literary heroine, although not the effect she was always accused of having. I have no problem with her political persona, or with her insistence on making herself the centerpiece of most of the historical conflicts of the twentieth century; but it seems to me that she invented a romantic fantasy about her involvement with Dashiell Hammett that is every bit as unrealistic as the Doris Day movies feminists prefer to blame for society's unrealistic notions about romance. The Doris Day fantasy, you may recall, is that the big man and the little woman march into the sunset together and live happily ever after. The Lillian Hellman fantasy is that the big man and the *big* woman march into the sunset together, fighting and cursing and drinking and killing turtles, but they, too, live happily ever after (until, of course, one of them dies, leaving the other free to reinvent the romance). I'm not saying that Lillian Hellman was the first writer to animate this fantasy couple—and even Hammett had a hand in it, with his Nick and Nora Charles. But Hellman's version was presented as fact, not fiction, so it makes you think it's possible. And is it?

It's a small point, just an aside that gets me through measuring the liquid ingredients, but it occurred to me as I delivered it yet another time that I had always zipped through that part of the speech as if I had somehow managed to be invulnerable to the fantasy, as if I had somehow managed to escape from or rise above it simply as a result of having figured it out. I think you often have that sense when you write—that if you can spot something in yourself and set it down on paper, you're free of it. And you're not, of course; you've just managed to set it down on paper, that's all.

The truth is that I'm at least as big a sap about romance as old Lillian was, probably even bigger.

I'll give you another example. I've written about cooking and marriage dozens of times, and I'm very smart on the subject, I'm very smart about how complicated things get when food and love become hopelessly tangled. But I realized as I stood there doing my demonstration in the middle of the Macy's housewares department that I had been as dopey about food and love as any old-fashioned Jewish mother. I loved to cook, so I cooked. And then the cooking became a way of saying I love you. And then the cooking became the easy way of saying I love you. And then the cooking became the only way of saying I love you. I was so busy perfecting the peach pie that I wasn't paying attention. I had never even been able to imagine an alternative. Every so often I would look at my women friends who were happily married and didn't cook, and I would always find myself wondering how they did it. Would anyone love me if I couldn't cook? I always thought cooking was part of the package: Step right up, it's Rachel Samstat, she's bright, she's funny, *and she can cook!*

I got so depressed and angry thinking about all this that I gave the onion an enormous whack and sent it flying into the front row of spectators, right into some lady's Literary Guild tote bag. Everyone laughed, and I

tossed my head blithely as if it were the sort of
thing I do all the time—which it's not—and
that's when I saw Richard. Richard is my
producer. (I love being able to say things like
that. My producer. My doctor. My accountant.
My floor man. My agent. My maid.) Richard
Finkel, who produced my television show, is
tall and red-haired and cannot see even with
his glasses on, and he was squinting through
the crowd at Macy's while I retrieved the
onion. As if he weren't obvious enough already, he began to wave wildly at me, and I
immediately felt better. I love Richard. That I
should have spotted him at that exact moment was really quite odd: the first night
Richard and I slept together, he did an imita-
tion of his father eating an onion, and I can
almost never think of raw onions without
remembering him, lying naked in bed, taking
mad, passionate bites of an imaginary onion
and producing spectacular belches. It's a miracle I didn't fall in love with Richard on the
spot, because I'm silly enough to think that
any man who would imitate his father eating
an onion is a suitable love object; but I didn't.
I'll tell you who would have fallen in love with
Richard had she been there: Brenda, my former friend and current step-relative-once-
removed. Brenda was always falling in love
with men whose attraction utterly mystified
me, and whenever I would ask her what she
saw in them, she would say things like: "He
does a wonderful Sophie Tucker." Brenda fell

in love with her husband Harry because he did a brilliant bit about a two-thousand-year-old man, and she always said she knew the marriage was over a week after it had begun, when she discovered that Harry had lifted the entire routine from Mel Brooks.

Richard and I slept together only a few times. We had one of those affairs that you begin by saying, "We're making a big mistake," and what you mean by that is not that you're getting in over your head but that you're just killing time. Richard and I killed a little time and then went back to being friends. Then I started seeing Mark, and Richard started seeing Helen, and things got complicated. Richard never really liked Mark, and I didn't really like Helen—that was the complication. Helen is one of those people who never say anything, not because she's shy but because she's learned—in a way I always mean to—that if you don't say anything, you make people far more nervous and self-conscious and careful around you than if you do. People like me, we just rush into the vacuum of silence people like Helen float around in; we blather and dither and yak-yakyak, and people like Helen just sit there and smile into the wind.

"Does she hate me?" I said to Richard after I first met Helen.

"Of course not," said Richard.

"Then why doesn't she ever say anything?" I asked.

"She's shy, that's all," said Richard.

"I don't think so," I said.

"You always underestimate how intimidating you are," said Richard.

"Bullshit," I said.

"He's wrong about Iran," Richard said after he first met Mark.

"Tell him," I said. "Don't talk to me about Iran. I couldn't care less."

"I tried to tell him," said Richard, "but it's very hard to interrupt a monologist."

"He's not a monologist," I said. "He just likes to talk. Some people like to talk."

"Leave Helen out of this," Richard said.

"I wasn't even thinking of Helen," I said.

"Bullshit," said Richard.

Then we all got married. It's hard when you don't like someone a friend marries. First of all, it means you pretty much have to confine your friendship to lunch, and I hate lunch. Second of all, it means that even a simple flat inquiry like "How's Helen?" is taken amiss, since your friend always thinks that what you hope he's going to say is "Dead." You feel irritated because your darling friend has married beneath himself, and he feels irritated because you don't see the virtues of his beloved. Then, if your friend's marriage fails, he becomes even more irritated at you, because if you had been a real friend, you would have prevented him physically from making the mistake, you would have locked him up in a closet until the urge to get married had passed. Of course, I tried that with Brenda, and it didn't work either. Long before we learned that Harry had pilfered the two-thousand-year-old-man routine from Mel Brooks, it was clear that he wasn't good enough for Brenda, and I made the mistake of telling her so. And when I turned out to be right, when they finally broke up after eight miserable years, was she grateful to me for tipping her off in the first place? No indeed. She slept with my husband Charlie, and as an extra bonus we all ended up with Harry's crabs.

I was dreading having to tell Richard about Mark and me; I could just imagine the look of smug satisfaction that would cross his face. But that wasn't what happened. What happened was that I finished my food demonstration and Richard swept me off to a dark bar and said, "I have to talk to you," and before I could even hold up my hand to indicate that I had to talk to him, too, he began.

"I had a vision that something horrible was wrong," said Richard. "And it is."

"A vision?" I said. It's not like Richard to talk of visions. Richard doesn't even like to hear about dreams.

"I went to have my hair cut yesterday," said Richard. "I was sitting there, trying to read the paper, and Melanie, who cuts my hair, was working away, and it suddenly crossed my mind to ask her how things were with her and Ray. She's been engaged to Ray for a couple of years. So I ask her. And she rolls her eyes. And she tells me he's fallen in love with someone else. He's come to her, he's told her he's in love with someone else, but he still wants to be friends. So she says to him, I don't want to be friends with you. And he says, why not? And she says, because you're a real shithead, that's why. Melanie looks at me and says, 'Can you believe it? Can you believe his nerve? You know what he says to me after that? He says, "You mean you're not even going to cut my hair anymore?" Can you dig this? The guy falls in love with someone else while he's engaged to me and he actually thinks I'm going to go on cutting his hair. Fuck him. What do I want with him if he wants to be such an asshole?' She rolls her eyes again, and she's snipping away, and suddenly I'm looking dead ahead into the mirror, and something weird starts to happen to me. Maybe a vision is putting it too strongly, but that's what it felt like. I thought to myself: Do not ask for whom the bell tolls, Richard Finkel, it tolls for you."

"Richard," I said, "what are you talking about?"

"I *knew*," said Richard. "At that moment I *knew*."

"You knew what?" I said.

"I knew Helen was in love with someone else."

"Helen," I said.

"My wife," said Richard. "Helen. Remember? The one you hate."

"I don't hate Helen," I said. "Helen hates me."

"It was suddenly clear," Richard said. "Helen was in love with someone else, and she was going to tell me about it, and there wasn't the remotest chance that when she did I was going to be as healthy and strong about it as this girl who cuts my hair."

"And *is* Helen in love with someone else?" I said.

"Yes," said Richard. "I came home and I told her about my vision, and when I got through, do you know what she said to me? She said, 'I think we'd better have a talk.'" Richard shook his head. "'I think we'd better have a talk' are the seven worst words in the English language."

"Helen is in love with someone else," I said.

"Yes," said Richard.

"That is really weird," I said.

"You don't know the half of it," said Richard.

"Yes I do," I said. "Ask me how Mark is."

"How's Mark?" said Richard.

"He's in love with someone else," I said.

"You're just saying that to make me feel better," said Richard.

"No I'm not," I said. "Mark has fallen in love with someone else, and he's treating me like an old beanbag."

"Oh, sweetie," said Richard, and he gave me a big hug. Then he ordered two more drinks. Doubles. Then he gave me another hug. One thing I have to say about marital crises is that people certainly do hug you a lot when you're going through them.

"Is it a boy or a girl?" said Richard.

"Is what a boy or a girl?" I said.

"The person Mark's fallen in love with," said Richard.

"I know you don't like Mark," I said, "but that is truly an absurd question."

"It's a girl, right?" said Richard.

"Right," I said.

"That's what Helen's fallen in love with, too," said Richard.

"Oh, sweetie," I said.

We looked at each other. It was a tricky moment. It's always a tricky moment when a friend tells you his marriage is in trouble: you have to be very careful what you say, in case he rides it out. This moment, however, was trickier than most. It would have been a terrible mistake, for example, for me to have said "Good riddance to bad rubbish" to Richard, although that's what I thought. It would have been an even bigger mistake for me to have introduced the word "dyke" into the conversation, but I didn't have to worry about that.

"Did you know she was a dyke?" said Richard.

"There's no way to tell if someone's a dyke,"

I said. "All sorts of attractive, feminine women are dykes. In fact, if anything, I would say that Helen isn't quite attractive enough to become one."

"That's not funny," said Richard.

"Yes it is," I said. "Anyway, she's not necessarily a dyke; she's just having a thing with a woman."

"I suppose you're going to tell me that it's normal and natural, and that all women have tendencies of that sort."

"No," I said, "but it's not as much of a stretch for women as it is for men. It's not that big a deal."

"It's a big deal if it's your wife," said Richard. "And I'll tell you the worst part of it. The worst part of it is that she's fallen in love with someone that I introduced her to. She's fallen in love with her secretary, and I got her the job."

"I'm not following you," I said.

"Joyce Raskin," said Richard. "The secretary. She used to work at Channel Thirteen, and she got laid off. I'd always liked her, and Helen was looking for a secretary, so I gave Joyce Helen's number and now she's sleeping with my wife."

"Well, don't blame Joyce," I said.

When my friend Brenda slept with my first husband, Charlie, I made that mistake—I blamed Brenda. It seemed quite unsurprising that Charlie would betray me—he, after all, was a man, and men had been betraying me

since the first grade. *But she was my friend!*
She had been my friend since the day we'd
met, when we were both five years old and
standing on line for books in kindergarten;
and I have never forgotten that moment because she turned around and I looked at her
and decided she was the most beautiful thing
I'd ever seen. Her flaxen hair came to her
waist, her eyes were deep green, her skin was
white as snow, just like a stupid fairy tale. I
always hoped that Brenda would eventually
lose her looks—my theory being that I would
grow up and gain mine, she would lose hers,
and we'd end up more or less even—but she
never did. What made this worse when we
were young was that every summer we went
to camp together and performed as an act in
the camp talent show, and she always got to
be the girl and I always had to be the boy. I
had been deeply and smolderingly resentful of
Brenda for years simply because I so wanted
to be the girl and never got to be, and the truth
is that I was secretly pleased when she slept
with Charlie because I was exonerated from
the guilt of all those years of feeling jealous of
her and was plunged suddenly into a warm
bath of innocent victimization.

That's the catch about betrayal, of course:
that it feels good, that there's something immensely pleasurable about moving from a
complicated relationship which involves
minor atrocities on both sides to a nice, neat,
simple one where one person has done some-

thing so horrible and unforgivable that the
other person is immediately absolved of all
the low-grade sins of sloth, envy, gluttony,
avarice and I forget the other three.

It wasn't until years later, when the extent
of the betrayal was finally revealed to me, that
I realized how wrong I'd been to blame
Brenda. Years later, Brenda, the creep,
turned up at my father's wedding to her big
sister and came up to me, dripping with earnest, weepy sincerity.

"I really hope we can be friends again," she
said.

"I seriously doubt we're ever going to be," I
said.

"But I miss you so much," said Brenda. She
started to cry.

"Don't pull that on me," I said. "I didn't do
anything to you, you did it to me. Remember?"

"Yes," said Brenda. "And I'll never forgive
myself. Please forgive me."

Be reasonable, Rachel, I said to myself.
This woman is now a relative. Are you never
going to speak to her again because of one
afternoon's indiscretion? Because of one afternoon your husband went out to buy light
bulbs and didn't?

"Please forgive me," Brenda went on. "If I
could take back any week of my life, it would
be that week in Florida."

That week in Florida! I couldn't believe it!
Months before the afternoon of the light
bulbs, Brenda had been so forlorn about her

marriage to Harry that Charlie and I had
taken her along with us to the Pillsbury Bake-
Off. To perk her up! Can you imagine? I had
spent the week wandering through the Grand
Ballroom of the Fontainebleau Hotel, judging
the sweet 'n' creamy crescent crisps, and now
it turned out that Brenda and Charlie had
spent the week watching X-rated movies on
the pay TV upstairs and fucking like rabbits.
There I was at my father's wedding reception,
there was my father telling yet another worn-
out anecdote about how he told Howard
Hawks to stuff it, there was my new step-
mother passing the guacamole, and I was in
such a rage about that week in Florida I could
hardly see straight. I wasn't angry at Brenda,
you understand. I'd spent so many years being
angry at Brenda that I didn't have the energy
to be any angrier. It was Charlie I wanted to
kill. I'll admit it was a delayed reaction, but I
honestly wanted to call him up and tell him to
go to hell and threaten never to see him again.
Since I really hadn't seen him since our marriage ended five years earlier, this would have
been a fairly empty gesture, but I still felt like
making it. I was in a real mess with Mark, no
question of that, but at least I knew whom to
blame.

"Why shouldn't I blame Joyce?" Richard
said to me. "She was my friend."

"But Helen is your wife," I said.

"But I never trusted Helen," said Richard.
"She just used to sit there and drink her Tab,

and I could never figure out what was going through her head."

"Well, now you know," I said.

"What's that supposed to mean?" said Richard.

"I don't know," I said, "but it was meant to make you feel better, not to make you mad."

"I'm sorry," said Richard. "Tell me about you and Mark."

We went out to the street. It was a clear October day, and we started walking uptown, arm in arm. When you're pregnant, it's especially nice to walk arm in arm with someone who's tall, because your stomach fits in so neatly. I told him about me and Mark and Thelma. By the time I got through, we had walked all the way from Macy's to Central Park, and when we got to the park, Richard kissed me. Richard kisses very nicely. So does Mark, but one of the things that happen in marriage is that the kissing stops. We walked over to the zoo, watched the Delacorte clock strike five, and sat down on a bench facing the seal pond. Richard kissed me again.

"I think I cooked too much for him," I said.

"You're crazy," said Richard.

"I think I was so entranced with being a couple that I didn't even notice that the person I thought I was a couple with thought he was a couple with someone else."

Richard put his hand on my stomach. It was hard and round as a basketball. "I think you should come home with me," he said.

I shook my head no.

"I mean it, Rachel," said Richard. "It'll be terrific. I've never slept with anyone who was seven months pregnant."

"I'm sure Helen will like it, too," I said.

"Helen moved out this morning," said Richard. "So you can move in if you want to. There's even room for the kids. I'm serious, Rachel. I once did a documentary on Lamaze, so I'm prepared to go into labor with you. We can go take a refresher course."

"I'm not big on Lamaze," I said.

"Then we can go take a class in anti-Lamaze," said Richard.

"But we're not in love," I said.

"How do you know?" said Richard.

"Because I'm still in love with Mark. And you're still in love with Helen. And we would just huddle together, two little cuckolds in a storm, with nothing to hold us together but the urge to punish the two of them for breaking our hearts."

"Marry me," said Richard. He stood up and said it again, loudly. "Marry me, Rachel."

There were a dozen people sitting on benches and wandering around the seal pond, and I could see them turning to watch.

"I mean it, Rachel," said Richard, very loudly now. "I want to marry you. I should have married you in the first place."

"Marry him, Rachel," shouted a young man sitting two benches away. "Give the kid a father."

There was a cheer from a couple on another bench, and scattered laughs.

"Richard, sit down," I said. "Please."

"Do you want to bring a child into the world under these circumstances?" he shouted. He was moving toward the seal pond now, and he jumped onto the parapet surrounding it. "I want to marry you and you want to marry me—you just aren't in touch with it. Marry me, Rachel. I'm constant. I'm immutable. I'm probably drunk, but I mean every word of this. When I say forever, I mean forever. And if you want me to sit down and stop shouting at you and making a public spectacle of myself, you'll have to say yes." There was a huge cheer from the spectators. "You hear this?" said Richard. "There's a groundswell of support here." He looked at me and raised both hands in the air in a victory salute. "Marry me," he shouted, "and you will never have to set foot in the city of Washington again. Marry me and you will never have to pretend you know the difference between Iran and Iraq. Marry me and you will never again have to listen to someone tell you who he thinks the next assistant foreign editor of the *Washington Post* is going to be." He tossed his head and smiled in what I'm sure he thought was an extremely handsome gesture. Then he turned around and leapt backward into the seal pond. There was a huge flapping of flippers as the seals who were lying on the rocks dove into the water. Everyone ran to the fence and watched as Richard swam several circles around the pond in a perfect Australian crawl and then pulled himself up to dry on the rocks. "Think it over," he shouted to me, and then fell backward in a mock collapse. About a minute later, he was arrested by the park police for disturbing the peace. He was extremely good-humored about it. They wrapped him up in a horse blanket and took him to the precinct in the park and wrote out a ticket and sent him home. I made him some eggs and put him to bed.

"Stay here," he said.

"No," I said.

"Where are you going?"

"To my father's for the night. I've missed the last plane."

"Rachel," said Richard, "it had nothing to do with how much you cooked for him. It had nothing to do with how much you wanted to be a couple. It had nothing to do with you."

"It must have had something to do with me," I said.

"Why?" said Richard.

"Because if it didn't, there's nothing I can do about it."

"That's my point," said Richard.

"I know that's your point," I said, "but I can't accept it."

"Well, if you ever do," said Richard, "you ought to do what I did. I feel much, much better."

"Are you suggesting I ask someone I'm not

in love with to marry me and then jump into the seal pond?" I said.

"I'm suggesting that you make a wild and permanent gesture of size," said Richard, "and mine was to ask you to marry me and jump into the seal pond. Yours can be anything you want."

"The only wild and permanent gesture of size that has ever crossed my mind," I said, "is to have my hair cut."

"You'll think of something," said Richard. "And when you do, I'll be here." Then he smiled and fell asleep.

XI

The next morning, I flew back to Washington. I felt better; at least someone wanted to be married to me. It wasn't the person I was married to, but it was better than nothing. I took a cab home. Maybe he's missed me, I thought as we came around the corner. Maybe he's come to his senses. Maybe he's remembered he loves me. Maybe he's full of remorse. There was a police car parked in front of the house. Maybe he's dead, I thought. That wouldn't solve everything, but it would solve a few things. He wasn't, of course. They never are. When you want them to die, they never do.

Mark was sitting in the living room with two Washington policemen. The police were telling Mark how much they liked his column and drinking beer. It's always a shock to me that the police are willing to drink your beer. I spent so many years as a child watching Jack Webb turn down beer on *Dragnet* that I've come to believe it's practically insulting to offer a policeman even a cup of coffee. When I walked in, both policemen stood up, and one of them shook my hand and announced solemnly that he had come to return my diamond ring. There was a receipt, which I signed, and then he handed me a small brown envelope tied with string. I opened it. The ring was inside, wrapped in tissue, along with a letter from Detective Nolan. "Dear Ms. Samstat," it said, "I am sending this to Washington, as I understand from your therapist that you are living there again. We caught the perpetrator and he confessed, so it will not be necessary for you to appear in court. If you turn up in New York at any point, give me a call. I am bald now." There was a phone number and his name, Andrew Nolan. Andrew. Not a bad name. Andy. AndyAndyAndy. No, Andy. Please, Andy. Yes, Andy. Don't stop, Andy. I love you, Andy. I started to put the ring back on my finger, but the diamond was loose in the setting. A sign. I was sick and tired of signs. I showed it to Mark. He glared at me. Another sign.

The police left, and Sam came rushing downstairs, shouting, "Mommy, Mommy," and jumped into my lap.

"Thelma called yesterday," Mark said, "and she's very angry at you, and I am, too."

"Where were you, Mommy?" said Sam.

"New York City," I said, "but I'm back now."

"She had lunch with Betty yesterday," said Mark, "and Betty told her you said she had herpes."

"I never said herpes," I said.

"You must have said something," said Mark.

"I said she had an infection," I said.

"Well, she's furious at you," said Mark.

"*She's* furious at *me*," I said. "That's rich." All my life I had wanted to say, "That's rich." Now I finally had gotten my chance. "That's really rich," I said. "Listen, you bastard. You tell Thelma that if she keeps calling here, I'll tell Betty she has the clap."

"Clap hands," said Sam, and clapped his together.

"I'll get it into the Ear, too," I said. "'What hopelessly tall and ungainly Washington hostess has a social disease, and we don't mean her usual climbing?'"

Mark stood up and strode out of the room and slammed the door behind him. I heard the car start, and he drove off.

I read Sam a story, but I could barely concentrate. When is this going to stop hurting? I wondered. How was I ever going to get through? There was one bright spot in my life, my child, and I couldn't even focus on him. I've been shot in the heart, I thought. I've been shot in the brain, I thought, and all I can

come up with are clichés about being shot in
the heart. I knew there were women who
understood these things, who could walk
around as if they were under water until the
smoke cleared, who could keep their big
mouths shut, who could even manage the
delicate moment when they confronted their
rivals at a dinner or the supermarket or the
Saks Jandel winter clearance sale, but I clearly wasn't one of them. My mother once caught
my father kissing someone at a party, and she
never forgot it; every time she got tanked
she brought it up. A mere kiss. What would
she have done with a full-fledged love affair
during a pregnancy?

I knew it wasn't Thelma's fault that any of
this had happened. She was never my friend.
We had never even had lunch! And I had long
since ceased to believe in the existence of that
mystical sisterly loyalty women are alleged to
feel toward one another. But knowing all this,
I nonetheless hated her with every swollen
inch of my being. I hated her for turning Mark
from the man I had fallen in love with into a
cold, cruel stranger; it was almost as if he had
become her mirror image, and was treating
me the same way Thelma treated her husband Jonathan.

I could just imagine the next Washington
evening all four of us were invited to. I could
just imagine Thelma doing her gracious lady
number, holding out her hand like the Queen
of England ready to mend a fence with an

unruly colonial nation, paying me a totally hypocritical compliment about the black *schmatta* I had been stuck wearing since my fifth month of pregnancy. "Oh, Rachel," she would say, "I always find that dress so very becoming." I wanted more than anything to be a good girl under those circumstances. To button my lip. To let one go by. I wanted more than anything to be the kind of cool and confident person who could treat her as if she were no more trouble to me than an old piece of chewing gum I had accidentally stepped in. But clearly I wasn't cut out to be that kind of person.

And what would happen if everyone found out? What would happen if this tacky little mess became common knowledge; what would happen when the four of us became that year's giggle, or gossip, or simply what Walter Winchell used to call a Dontinvitem? It was hard enough putting a marriage back together without becoming known publicly as a marriage-in-trouble; a marriage-in-trouble is welcomed with about as much warmth as cancer.

I took Sam into the kitchen and handed him over to Juanita. Then I went out the back door and over to Mark's office. The door to it was open, as I'd expected; he'd left the house in such a hurry he hadn't locked it. I sat down in his desk chair and opened the drawer and pulled out the file with the phone bills in it. It was all there, as I knew it would be: local phone calls that Mark had charged to our home number; long-distance calls to France in May; calls in August to Martha's Vineyard. I pulled out the American Express bills. (What did masochistic women do before the invention of the credit card?) I went through the receipts: the Marriott Hotel in Alexandria, the Plaza Hotel in New York, the Ritz-Carlton in Boston. And the flowers—so many flowers.

I felt like a character in a trashy novel; I even knew which trashy novel I felt like a character in, which made it worse: *The Best of Everything*. At least I wasn't going through the garbage, but that was only because it hadn't turned out to be necessary. The first flowers were sent in mid-March. Mid-March. I suddenly remembered: in mid-March, when the nuclear power plant at Three Mile Island overheated, I had become so worried about its blowing contaminated air in our direction that I had taken Sam with me to a food demonstration in Atlanta. For years, Mark had been haranguing me about my total lack of interest in politics, and finally I had got interested—so interested I had actually left town—and where had it got me? It had got me and Sam to Atlanta, and my husband and Thelma to bed. That would teach me to be political.

I put the papers back into the files and shut the drawer. Then I sat there, looking out the window. There was a newspaper open on the desk. I glanced down at it and realized that I hadn't seen that day's *Post*. I stared—it *wasn't* that day's *Post*. It was the Sunday real estate section. I felt a knot in my stomach, and lost my breath for a moment. I opened it to Houses—D.C. Mark had been through the section carefully. He had marked all the houses with four bedrooms or more in decent northwest Washington locations. I closed my eyes to stop the dizziness. So they were looking at houses. Well, why was I surprised? They were looking at blazers and couches; could houses be far behind? There were little scribbled notes next to a few of the listings. Addresses. Information about maids' rooms. One of the houses appeared to have a pool.

I went back to the kitchen and sat with Sam while he had lunch. I sang "The Itsy Bitsy Spider" fourteen times. Sam went up for his nap, and I borrowed Juanita's car. I drove to Cleveland Park, where the Rices lived. I drove past their house. The shades were drawn in front; it looked as if no one was home. I was about half a block past the house, thinking about tootling over to the Marriott Hotel in Alexandria and bursting in on them with a can of Raid, when I saw our car. I stopped short and backed up. Our car, definitely. I parked and got out and stood on the curb, staring into it. There was Sam's baby seat, strapped into the back. Sam's baby seat was always strapped into the back of the car, but somehow, at this moment, it seemed the ultimate obscenity—Mark's involving even the baby seat in his affair.

I walked up to the house and looked for signs of life. The Rices lived in a large wood house bordered by rhododendron and azalea bushes. I stepped onto the lawn and tried to see through a crack below a drawn window shade, but the bushes were in the way. I was trying to move quietly, but there were crunching leaves and twigs everywhere I stepped. Suddenly I tripped and fell. I realized I'd twisted my ankle, and for a moment I thought I'd strained my stomach muscles, but the pain went away. I looked to see what I'd tripped on and saw that it was a wire that surrounded the house. I began to follow it to see where it led, turned the corner, and gasped. There was a body lying face down on the ground under a rhododendron bush. Jonathan Rice. Maybe he's dead, I thought. It crossed my mind as his leg twitched that I had had that thought twice in less than two hours about two completely different men, and I couldn't decide which of them I was more disappointed to find out I was wrong about.

Jonathan was lying there wearing a set of earphones. He turned and looked at me. He barely blinked. He took off the earphones and sat up.

"You really shouldn't have said that thing about the herpes, you know," he said. "Thelma was very fond of you."

"But now she's not," I said.

"Now she's not," said Jonathan. "Now she's very angry. And they're looking at houses. And they found something they like on Twenty-first Street, but Thelma thinks they need five bedrooms and Mark thinks they can make do with four."

I wondered who was handling the Middle East while Jonathan was out spying in the bushes, but he had put on the earphones again, and now he was shaking his head. "They're talking about buying it right away and getting it all ready, and a few months after you have the baby Mark and Thelma will move in. He thinks he can get joint custody."

I was having trouble breathing again, and I put my hand on my stomach.

"What's the matter?" said Jonathan.

"I tripped on your wire," I said, "and I think I strained my stomach muscles."

A few minutes later, as Jonathan was giving me the next bulletin—something about how Mark and Thelma were going to finance the purchase with a bank loan, which Jonathan took as an occasion to lecture me on rising interest rates—I had another pain.

"Jonathan," I said.

Jonathan put his fingers to his lips, as if something really cosmic were going on in the house.

I pulled the earphones from his head.

"Jonathan," I said. "I'm in labor."

* * *

I don't remember very much. I remember that Jonathan sprang to his feet and bounded into the house. I remember that Mark came out a few minutes later. I remember the drive to the hospital: I accused Mark of looking at houses; he accused me of snooping in places I didn't belong. I remember the labor room, and my obstetrician suddenly appearing, Marvin, my obstetrician, taking charge, being a professor, explaining my labor to a group of interns: the baby is in the transverse position and we can't risk waiting for it to turn itself, given the prematurity; another Caesarean is indicated. Are there any questions? One of the interns raised his hand. "I really enjoy your column," he said to Mark. The interns left. "Your husband can watch," Marvin said to me. "It really isn't allowed with Caesareans, but we'll sneak him into the delivery room." He was so pleased with himself, Marvin was, so pleased that he would be able to give this lovely couple he was on a first-name basis with the opportunity to share in the birth of their second child. Wrong couple, I wanted to say; that was last year's couple. This year things are different. This year my husband is a stranger. Do not let this stranger see me eviscerated.

The anesthetist put the needle into my back and I waited for the epidural to grab hold. Mark was standing next to me. One contraction. Two contractions. Three. Then the dullness, the easing off, the mermaid sensation. I watched the fetal monitor bleeping steadily as they wheeled me into the delivery room.

"Tell me about when Sam was born," I said to Mark.

He looked at me.

"Start where the doctor says there's something wrong," I said.

Mark nodded. "The doctor took me outside the labor room and said there was something wrong, they were losing the heartbeat. And we went back in and he told you the baby was in distress. And you said, 'Is our baby going to die?'"

I had heard this dozens of times.

Mark went on: "And he said, 'We're going to do an emergency Caesarean.' And they took you away. You were really brave. I was terrified. And I sat out in the waiting room, and the man sitting across from me was eating a sausage pizza. And fifteen minutes later the doctor came out, and took me into the delivery room, and there was Sam, making these funny little noises. They put him into my arms, and you woke up and you said, 'Is that our baby?' And I laid him down on you. And I lay down next to you."

I was crying.

"That was a great day," I said.

"Can you feel this?" said the doctor. The knife.

"Yes," I said. "A little."

I turned my head away from Mark. A nurse

wiped my face and said, hold on, it's going to be all right. The pediatrician, our pediatrician, came into the delivery room. "If I am going to be your pediatrician," he had said when Sam was born, "we are going to have to understand something. You are never to call me and say, 'I'm sorry to bother you.' You are never to call me and say, 'This is probably nothing.' If you think it's worth a phone call, I want to hear about it. Got it?" Mark and I had sat there with our floppy little bundle. We were so proud—so proud of ourselves, of our baby, even of our pediatrician's patter. We marched into parenthood so full of hubris. We were on our second marriages; we had got the kinks out of the machinery; we would bring up our children in a poppy field of love and financial solvency and adequate household help. There would be guns for our daughters and dolls for our sons.

After Sam was born, I remember thinking that no one had ever told me how much I would love my child; now, of course, I realized something else no one tells you: that a child is a grenade. When you have a baby, you set off an explosion in your marriage, and when the dust settles, your marriage is different from what it was. Not better, necessarily; not worse, necessarily; but different. All those idiotically lyrical articles about sharing child-rearing duties never mention that, nor do they allude to something else that happens when a baby is born, which is that all the power struggles of the marriage have a new playing field. The baby wakes up in the middle of the night, and instead of jumping out of bed, you lie there thinking: Whose turn is it? If it's your turn, you have to get up; if it's his turn, then why is he still lying there asleep while you're awake wondering whose turn it is? Now it takes *two* parents to feed the child—one to do it and one to keep the one who does it company. Now it takes two parents to take the child to the doctor—one to do it and one to keep the one who does it from becoming resentful about having to do it. Now it takes two parents to fight over who gets to be the first person to introduce solids or the last person to notice the diaper has to be changed or the one who cares most about limiting sugar snacks or the one who cares least about conventional discipline.

No one ever tells you these things—not that we would have listened had anyone tried. We were so smart. We were so old. We were so happy. We had it knocked.

"Can you feel this?" the doctor said.

"No."

He was cutting now. Far, far away. A minute passed. Then two. Let the baby be okay, please let him be okay. I opened my eyes and saw a nurse crossing the room to the pediatrician. In her arms I could see the baby's wet head and spiky black hair. I could see an arm, such a skinny arm. Long skinny legs. *Move. Please move.* A flutter kick. A noise like a tiny cough. A tiny cry.

Nathaniel.

I closed my eyes.

He was fine, I could hear them saying that. He's fine. He's going to be fine.

So. Nathaniel was early. I could hardly blame him. Something was dying inside me, and he had to get out.

XII

*I*t was a complicated Caesarean, and there were complications. Nathaniel was on the eighth floor of the hospital, with tubes and monitors stuck all over his little froggy body, and I was on the fifth, with tubes and monitors all over mine. I lay in bed in a Percodan haze; I spent hours turning my marriage over in my mind. What had happened? What had gone wrong? *He was crazy.* I kept coming back to that. It was a simple enough answer, but accepting that answer meant accepting that I would never really know what had happened, accepting the mystery. I hate mystery, and I'm not the only one who does. Nature abhors a mystery too.

Vera flew to Washington. She spent a day with me in the hospital. She rubbed my head and listened while I floated trial balloons at her. I told her I thought I had spent too much time cooking and not enough time paying attention. I told her I thought that having a baby had changed our lives together. I told her I had been impatient and mean and snappish and irritable, and that it was no wonder Mark was drawn to someone who hadn't heard all his stories before and didn't shoot him a reproving look every time he uttered an opinion he had stolen from his best friend.

"All this may be true," Vera said, "but it isn't the point. The point is to figure out what you want."

"Maybe we just ran out of things to renovate," I said. "Maybe that was the problem. Maybe if we'd just gone on buying houses and fighting with contractors and arguing over whether to bleach the floor or stain it dark, we would have lived happily ever after."

"Did you hear me?" Vera said.

"I actually believed it was possible to have a good marriage," I said.

"It is possible," said Vera.

"No it's not," I said. "And don't tell me about your marriage, I don't want to hear about it. You got the last good one. For the rest of us, it's hopeless. I know that, but I never really get it. I go right on. I think to myself: I was wrong about the last one, but I'll try harder to be right about the next one."

"That's not the worst lesson to take through life," said Vera.

"But it doesn't work," I said. "It's kreplach. Remember?"

Vera looked at me, and her eyes filled with tears. She does this sometimes, especially when I'm being hateful and difficult; she responds by having all the feelings I'm refusing to have. Now she reached over and took my hand, and we both began to cry.

Mark came to the hospital every day. Every day except for Thelma's birthday. On Thelma's birthday, he called to say he had to go to New York for an interview. I know it was Thelma's birthday because Betty called the next day to tell me all about it. It seems that Jonathan Rice had planned a surprise birthday lunch for Thelma, and everyone gathered in the restaurant, ready to pop out from under the table when she arrived, but she never turned up.

"Can you imagine?" said Betty.

"I'm afraid I can," I said.

"I wish I could figure out who she's sleeping with," Betty said.

"It's probably Mark," I said.

Betty laughed. "Rachel, wait till I tell that to Mark," she said. "It'll kill him."

"I'll tell him myself," I said. "He just turned up."

"What was that about?" Mark said.

Stifle yourself, Rachel.

"Nothing," I said. "Just the Ladies' Central."

I got out of bed and into a wheelchair. Mark wheeled me and my intravenous equipment to the elevator and we went up to see the baby. We were lucky. I kept telling myself that. Nathaniel was on a floor with newborns who had real problems—there were blue babies, babies missing kidneys, babies with holes in their hearts—and there was nothing wrong with him except that he was small. He wasn't even the smallest. Still, he was ours, and he looked like a sack of bones. They'd shaved his head for the monitors, and there were tiny Band-Aids all over his body, taping the tubes here and there. We couldn't hold him. All we could do was reach in through the holes with our hexachlorophene-scrubbed hands and feed him, awkwardly propping up his floppy body by the neck. He had weighed four pounds when he was born. He was feeding well, catching up, but he was such a tiny thing. I waved a little red clown we'd put into the Isolette in front of his face. Maybe he saw it. Mark sang him a song. *Hush-a-bye, don't you cry, go to sleep-y, little baby.* I wondered where they had gone to celebrate her birthday. *When you wake you shall have all the pretty little horses.* I wondered what he had given her for her birthday. *Blacks and bays, dapples and grays, all the pretty little horses.* I wish I'd known it was Thelma's birthday; I would have sent her a present myself. *Hush-a-bye, don't you cry, go to sleep-y, little baby*. A garrote.

Arthur and Julie came to see me. One day while I was in the hospital, they discovered that their decorator had taken the four thousand dollars they had given him for furniture and spent it all on cocaine. The next day, their daughter was suspended from school for flushing six gerbils down the lavatory toilet. The next day, a bat moved into their kitchen. They brought me all of it, every day, and Julie rustled up a hairdresser to come wash my hair, and Arthur made rice pudding the day they took the tube out of my nose and I could eat bland food. Rice pudding is the only thing Arthur cooks, but he cooks it perfectly, with exactly the right proportion of rice to raisins. There's an awful lot of nursery food in this book already, so I won't give you the recipe. My feeling about rice pudding is that if you like it, you already have a good recipe; and if you don't, there's no way anyone will ever get you to eat it, unless you fall in love with someone who likes rice pudding, which I once did, and then you learn to love it, too.

My last day in the hospital, Marvin, my obstetrician, took out the stitches. Then he swiped an apple from a big basket of fruit Betty's boyfriend had sent me, and he sat down in a leatherette chair. I suspected he was going to ask if I was having a postpartum depression, but the last thing I wanted was for my obstetrician to know that in my case a postpartum depression would be superfluous. I am very fond of Marvin, even though he once asked me to endorse his book on premenstrual tension, but I wasn't up for a heart-to-heart talk with him.

"Do you believe in love?" said my obstetrician.

This is what I get for calling him by his first name, I thought. This is the price I pay for insisting that if he's going to call me by my first name I get to call him by his. Do I ask him if he gets turned on sticking his hands into ladies' pussies? Do I ask him if he gets off feeling their breasts for lumps?

"What?" I said.

"Do you believe in love?" he said.

Sometimes I believe that love dies but hope springs eternal. Sometimes I believe that hope dies but love springs eternal. Sometimes I believe that sex plus guilt equals love, and sometimes I believe that sex plus guilt equals good sex. Sometimes I believe that love is as natural as the tides, and sometimes I believe that love is an act of will. Sometimes I believe that some people are better at love than others, and sometimes I believe that everyone is faking it. Sometimes I believe that love is essential, and sometimes I believe that the only reason love is essential is that otherwise you spend all your time looking for it.

"Yes," I said. "I do."

I went home.

Nathaniel stayed in the hospital.

Both of us got stronger.

I behaved myself.

I said very little.

I attempted to follow the budget debate.

I went to a dinner party and held up my end.

They took Nathaniel out of the Isolette and I could hold him and feed him.

I read Sam a lot of stories about baby brothers.

I did not say, how are you, how are we, do you still love her, do you love me at all, are you still thinking of buying a house with her, what did you get her for her birthday, is it over with her, is it ever going to be over.

Two weeks passed.

Betty called. She asked if we wanted to come to dinner. "We have lobsters," she said. "You bring dessert. Bring one of your Key lime pies."

XIII

*I*f I had it to do over again, I would have made a different kind of pie. The pie I threw at Mark made a terrific mess, but a blueberry pie would have been even better, since it would have permanently ruined his new blazer, the one he bought with Thelma. But Betty said bring a Key lime pie, so I did. The Key lime pie is very simple to make. First you line a 9-inch pie plate with a graham cracker crust. Then beat 6 egg yolks. Add 1 cup lime juice (even bottled lime juice will do), two 14-ounce cans sweetened condensed milk, and 1 tablespoon grated lime rind. Pour into the pie shell and freeze. Remove from freezer and spread with whipped cream. Let sit five minutes before serving.

I realize now that I should have thrown the pie (or at least done the thinking that led to the throwing of the pie) several weeks earlier than I did, but it's very hard to throw a pie at someone when you're pregnant, because you feel so vulnerable. Also, let's face it, I wasn't ready to throw the pie. I should add that the pie was hardly the first thing I'd thought of throwing at Mark, but every other time I'd wanted to throw something at him, I couldn't bring myself to do it. Once, for example, right after I found out about him and Thelma, I'd been seized by a violent impulse, but the only thing I could see to throw at the time was a signed Thonet chair, and I am far too bourgeois to throw a signed Thonet anything at anyone. Some time later, especially while I was in the hospital, I gave considerable thought to smashing Mark's head in with a very good frying pan I had bought at the Bridge kitchenware company, but I always knew I would never do anything of the sort, and in any case, smashing your husband's head in with a frying pan seems slightly too fraught with feminist content, if you know what I mean.

(Even now, I wonder if I would have thrown the pie had we been eating in Betty's dining room. Probably not. On the floor in Betty's dining room is a beautiful Oriental rug, and I would have been far too concerned about staining it. Fortunately, though, we were eating in the kitchen, and the kitchen has a linoleum floor. That's how bourgeois I am: at the split second I picked up the pie to throw it at Mark, at the split second I was about to do the bravest—albeit the most derivative—thing I had ever done in my life, I thought to myself: Thank God the floor is linoleum and can be wiped up.)

On Saturday afternoon, after Betty called, I went out for a walk to buy the pie ingredients. I took Sam with me. We had a long talk about how Nathaniel would be coming home from the hospital on Monday, and how much Sam was going to love him, and how he was going to feed him some delicious spiders. We bought the food at Neam's. It was a beautiful day, so we decided to walk down to the toy store on M Street. On the way we passed the jewelry store where Mark had bought me the diamond ring, and I remembered that I hadn't yet taken it in to have it fixed. It was in a little envelope in my purse.

I could see Leo Rothman, the owner, sitting on a stool behind the counter—Leo, the dear, white-haired man who had marched with the Abraham Lincoln Brigade in the thirties and been thrown out of the Labor Department in the forties and was now a millionaire jeweler who buzzed only white people through his electronically operated door. He buzzed me in and gave me a big kiss. When Mark was courting me, when he was pursuing me with flowers and balloons and jewels, Leo was the man Mark bought the jewels from, and as a result Leo felt almost proprietary about our marriage: he had outfitted the courtship, the wedding, the birth of the first child, the first child's silver spoon; and he didn't seem to mind that except for the diamond ring, none of Mark's purchases had amounted to more than a few hundred dollars.

I told Leo about the robbery, and he said it would take just a minute to reset the stone. Sam and I waited while he got out his instruments and went to work. We were making conversation. Chitchat. Nothing much. He said did I know the diamond in the ring was a perfect stone. I said Mark had told me that. He said it wasn't the kind of diamond I'd ever have trouble selling if I ever wanted to—he had told Mark he'd be glad to buy it back for what Mark had paid for it. I said I was glad to hear that. He asked me how I liked the necklace. The necklace, I said. Leo looked up, and the loup dropped from his eye. "I must be thinking of another customer," he said.

"No you're not," I said. "I knew Mark had bought something while I was in the hospital." So he had bought her a necklace for her birthday. I was lying in the hospital with a tube up my nose and he had bought her a necklace. "That rascal," I said.

"I shouldn't have said anything," Leo said.

"I'm glad you did," I said. "Now I know what to be prepared for. There's nothing worse than opening a box with a necklace in it when you're not in the mood for a necklace." I kept talking, I couldn't stop. "Once," I said, "I was in the mood for a nightgown, and Mark kept dropping hints about what he'd gotten me for my birthday, and finally I said, 'I don't care what it is as long as it's not a suitcase,' and it was a suitcase. Was my face red." Leo was focused on the ring again; I'd bored him so thoroughly he barely grunted a response. He finished resetting the stone and handed the ring back to me. It was such a beautiful ring. The diamond caught the afternoon sun and made a rainbow on the wall of the store. Sam ran to the reflection, and I waved the ring this way and that, moving the rainbow while he giggled and leapt and tried to catch it in his hands.

"How much?" I said.

"No charge," Leo said.

"How much for the ring?" I said. "How much would you give me for the ring?"

Leo looked at me.

"You don't really want to sell it," he said.

"I really want to sell it," I said. "Do you really want to buy it?"

"Of course," he said.

"I love the ring, Leo," I said, "but it really doesn't go with my life. It would never have been stolen in the first place if I hadn't been wearing it on the subway, and if you've got a ring you can't wear on the subway, what's the point of having it? It's sort of like a mink coat. If I had a mink coat, I'd have to take cabs every time I was in New York, and the next thing you know we'd be even broker than we are now. Mark's so romantic, he probably spent every penny of his savings on the neck-lace."

Leo nodded. "For the down payment," he said.

"For the down payment," I said.

"It's a beautiful necklace," said Leo.

"Now I'll have a necklace I won't be able to wear on the subway either," I said. "How much for the ring?"

"Fifteen thousand," Leo said.

"Fifteen thousand," I said.

"That's what Mark paid for it," Leo said.

Right after my mother left my father and ran off to New Mexico with Mel, my father gave me some money. It was quite unexpect-ed. I had gone over to visit him—I was mar-ried to Charlie at the time—and in the middle of a long and rather sentimental conversation about how termites had once eaten the entire garage door of our house in Beverly Hills one Sunday when we weren't looking, my father whipped out his checkbook and wrote me a check for three thousand dollars. "But why?" I said, hoping he wouldn't notice I had snatched it from his hands and stuffed it into my back pocket. "Because you're a good girl," said my father. I put my hand over the pocket, as if the check were going to fly right out and back into the checkbook and erase itself. I could feel the paper through the cloth; I kept running my finger over the outside of the pocket and feeling the check crinkle inside. My heart started to pound: I realized I had just been given the means to walk out of my marriage.

"Fifteen thousand it is," I said to Leo. Ten years had passed; the cost of walking out of a marriage had gone up.

I went home with Leo's check and made the pie. I was in a trance. Well, perhaps it wasn't a trance, but it was as close to a trance as I'll ever get: I was speechless. I said nothing—nothing at all—for several hours. At eight, Mark and I took the pie to Betty's. It was just us—me, Mark, Betty and Dmitri, whom Betty lives with. Dmitri used to be the Yugoslavian ambassador to the United States. When his tour ended, he went back to Belgrade and opened a chain of laundromats. Then he moved back to Washington and went into high-priced sherbet. Mark always used to throw Dmitri in my face as an example of someone who managed to be interested in food and politics simultaneously, but the truth is that what Dmitri was really interested in was money; to the extent that he was at all political, it lay in his understanding that in a socialist country you can get rich by providing necessities, while in a capitalist country you can get rich by providing luxuries. Dmitri is the most good-natured man I have ever known, which infuriates Betty, which makes Dmitri laugh, which makes Betty laugh. They seem very happy together. Not that you can tell. Look at all the people who thought Mark and I were happy. Me included.

When we got to Betty's, Mark and Dmitri went into the kitchen to boil the lobsters, and Betty and I sat in the living room while Betty talked about the dance she and Thelma and I were apparently giving. Apparently we were giving it at the Sulgrave Club. Apparently the crepe man had already been booked. Apparently all that was lacking was my guest list: Thelma and Betty had already drawn up theirs. Apparently the Kissingers were on Thelma's list, just as I'd predicted. I sat and listened and drank an entire bottle of white wine as Betty went on and on, and by the time I got to dinner, I was tipsy. We ate the lobsters. I don't remember the conversation. I do remember realizing that no one seemed to be noticing that I hadn't said anything the entire evening, and that no one seemed to mind. I must try this again, I thought; I must try again someday to sit still and not say a word. Maybe when I'm dead.

After the lobsters, I took the Key lime pie out of the freezer and put the whipped cream on it and sat it in front of me. I was going to give it five minutes to thaw slightly (see recipe). And that's when Betty turned to me and said, "Rachel, you didn't tell me about Richard and Helen!"

"What about Richard and Helen?" said Mark.

"They're getting a divorce," said Betty. "I bumped into him this week in New York."

"I always hated that woman," said Mark.

"I sort of liked her," said Dmitri.

"When did you meet her?" said Betty.

"Here," said Dmitri. "Rachel and Mark brought them over one night. No one else would talk to her, so I did. She wasn't so bad."

"You're the only person on this earth who's ever found anything even halfway nice to say about her," said Betty.

"I did think she was a dyke," said Dmitri.

"That makes me so furious!" Betty screamed. "Why didn't you tell me?"

"I did tell you," said Dmitri, "and you said, 'Don't be ridiculous.'"

"Goddammit," said Betty.

"Why are you angry at Dmitri?" said Mark.

"Because she *is* a dyke," said Betty.

"No shit," said Mark.

"And if Dmitri wasn't so good-natured about everything, he would have put it more forcefully, and I might have believed him, and then none of this would have come as a surprise to me." She glared at Dmitri. "I hate surprises," she said.

Dmitri stood up to go make the coffee and on his way he kissed Betty on the neck. "Don't try to make up to me," said Betty. She was smiling.

"Helen's a dyke?" said Mark.

"She left Richard for her secretary," said Betty.

"Did you know this, Rachel?" said Mark.

I nodded.

"I couldn't get over it," said Betty. "I kept

thinking about it on the shuttle on the way home. How could you know someone for that long . . . how long have they been together?"

"As long as Rachel and I have," said Mark.

"Exactly," said Betty. "How could you be with someone that long, be *married* to them, and not know?"

"He has to have known," said Dmitri. "*I* knew."

"He says he didn't know," said Betty. "But how could he not? How could you be married to someone and not know something like that?"

"Maybe it wasn't true when he first met her," said Dmitri.

"Of course it was true," said Betty. "You don't just become a dyke, bang, like that."

"Sure you do," said Dmitri. "It's like being allergic to strawberries. You eat strawberries all your life and then one day, bang, you get hives."

"Don't be ridiculous," said Betty.

"The last time you said 'Don't be ridiculous' to me, I was trying to tell you that Richard's wife was a dyke," said Dmitri.

"And now you're trying to tell me she was merely an incipient dyke," said Betty. "Which is it?"

"I have no idea," said Dmitri. "I'm just trying to drive you crazy." He kissed her again.

"I don't believe people change that much," said Betty. "And don't tell me they do, Rachel.

Don't give me that New York psychological
bullshit about how people are capable of it.
They aren't. Which brings me back to my
question: how is it possible to be married to
someone and not know something so fundamental?"

I was starting to get dizzy.

Perhaps I ought to say something, I
thought. Either that or I'm going to fall into
the pie. Perhaps I ought to say that it *is*
possible. I could hear Mark changing the subject. He was saying something about Zbig-
niew Brzezinski. Perhaps I ought to say that
you can love someone—or want to love
someone—so much that you don't see anything at all. You decide to love him, you decide
to trust him, you're in the marriage, in the
day-to-dayness of the marriage, and you kind
of notice that things aren't what they were,
but it's a distant bell, it's through a filter. And
then when something does turn out to be
wrong, it isn't that you knew all along, it's
that you were somewhere else.

"He must have been living in a dream,"
said Betty. She stood up to get the coffee cups.
Mark and Dmitri were discussing détente.

In a dream. I suppose so. And then the
dream breaks into a million tiny pieces. The
dream dies. Which leaves you with a choice:
you can settle for reality, or you can go off, like
a fool, and dream another dream.

I looked across the table at Mark. I still love
you, I thought. I still look at that dopey face of

yours, with that silly striped beard, and think you are the handsomest man I've ever known. I still find you interesting, even if right now you are being more boring than the Martin Agronsky show. But someday I won't anymore. And in the meantime, I'm getting out. I am no beauty, and I'm getting on in years, and I have just about enough money to last me sixty days, and I am terrified of being alone, and I can't bear the idea of divorce, but I would rather die than sit here and pretend it's okay, I would rather die than sit here figuring out how to get you to love me again, I would rather die than spend five more minutes going through your drawers and wondering where you are and anticipating the next betrayal and worrying about whether my poor, beat-up, middle-aged body with its Caesarean scars will ever turn you on again. I can't stand feeling sorry for myself. I can't stand feeling like a victim. I can't stand hoping against hope. I can't stand sitting here with all this rage turning to hurt and then to tears. I CAN'T STAND NOT TALKING!

I looked at the pie sitting right there in front of me and suddenly it began to throb. They were talking about the State Department now. If I throw this pie at him, I thought to myself, he will never love me. And then it hit me: he *doesn't* love me. It hit me with a shimmering clarity: that was all there was to it. It didn't matter if he was crazy. It didn't matter if I was innocent or guilty. Nothing mattered except that he didn't love me. *If I throw this pie at him, he will never love me. But he doesn't love me anyway. So I can throw the pie if I want to.* I picked up the pie, thanked God for the linoleum floor, and threw it. It landed mostly on the right side of Mark's face, but that was good enough. The cream and the lime filling clung to his beard and his nose and his eyelashes, and pieces of crust dropped onto his blazer. I started to laugh. Mark started to laugh, too; I must say he handled it very well. He laughed as if all this were part of a running joke we'd forgotten to let Betty and Dmitri in on. He wiped himself off. He said, "I think it's time for us to go home." He stood up. So did I. I turned to Betty, who was staring wide-eyed at the two of us. "By the way," I said, "I'm not coming to the dance." And we went home.

Of course I'm writing this later, much much later, and it worries me that I've done what I usually do—hidden the anger, covered the pain, pretended it wasn't there for the sake of the story. "Why do you feel you have to turn everything into a story?" Vera once asked me. I remember when she asked me, in fact. It was right after my marriage to Charlie broke up, and I was living in an apartment where everything made into something else—the couch made into a bed, the coffee table made into a dining table, the end table made into a stool. "How are you?" people would ask me, in that intimate way people asked the question in those days. How *are* you. I couldn't bear it. So I told them about my apartment where everything made into something else. Then a friend called and said, "I have one piece of advice for you. I give it to all my friends whose marriages break up: Don't buy anything at Azuma." I added that to my repertoire.

Vera said: "Why do you feel you have to turn everything into a story?"

So I told her why:

Because if I tell the story, I control the version.

Because if I tell the story, I can make you laugh, and I would rather have you laugh at me than feel sorry for me.

Because if I tell the story, it doesn't hurt as much.

Because if I tell the story, I can get on with it.

My last day in Washington I read the Sunday papers. I made French toast for Sam. I went to the hospital to see Nathaniel. I asked the pediatrician if Nathaniel could go to New York when he got out of the hospital the next day. The pediatrician said he could if he took the train. I called Nathaniel's baby nurse and told her we would be going to New York on the train the next day. I called Richard in New York and told him we would be moving in for a few weeks, until I found an apartment. I came home and started dinner. I made a bouillabaisse, and crème brulée, and in between there was a salad. I taught Mark to make the vinaigrette. Mix 2 tablespoons Grey Poupon mustard with 2 tablespoons good red wine vinegar. Then, whisking constantly with a fork, slowly add 6 tablespoons olive oil, until the vinaigrette is thick and creamy; this makes a very strong vinaigrette that's perfect for salad greens like arugola and watercress and endive.

We got into bed and Mark put his arms around me. "That was a lovely evening," he said. He fell asleep. I lay there. Two years earlier, when I had been pregnant with Sam, Mark would sing me a song every night and every morning. We called it the Petunia song. It was a dumb song, really dumb. Mark would make up a different tune and lyrics each time, but it never rhymed, and it was never remotely melodious. *I sing to you, Petunia, I sing a song of love, I sing to you even though you are bigger than the last time I sang the Petunia song to you.* Something like that. Or: *Oh, Petunia, I sing to thee, even though it's much too early and I have a hangover.* You get the idea. Really dumb, but every time Mark sang it, I felt secure and loved in a way I had never dreamed possible. I had always meant to write down some of the words, because they were so silly and funny and made me feel so happy; but I never did. And now I couldn't remember them. I could remember the feeling, but I couldn't really remember the words.

Which was not the worst way to begin to forget.

RECIPE INDEX

almonds, toasted	40
beans, lima, with pears	32
bread pudding, Chez Helene's	133
cheesecake	66
eggs, four-minute	80
hash, bacon	57
Key lime pie	208
linguine alla cecca	128
peach pie	141
pot roast, Lillian Hellman's	168
potatoes	
Anna	157
mashed	159
Swiss	157
sorrel soup	47
vinaigrette	222